Also by Lawrence Verigin

DARK SEED

Winner of the
2014 Chanticleer Clue Thriller Award
for
International Intrigue and World Events

Finalist for the
2015 Eric Hoffer Award Montaigne Medal
for
Thought-Provoking Books That Illuminate,
Progress, and Redirect Thought

For my mother, Kathy Verigin,
and her mother, Nora Kabatoff,
for showing me the enjoyment
reading good stories can bring.

PROLOGUE

October 15, 2001

The location was hidden in plain view. The grand copper-roofed structure dwarfed the surrounding buildings of the old city.

The elegant chateau offered the discretion and privacy the attendees required. As each man arrived, he was tactfully escorted to the upper east wing of the historically dedicated hotel. If any of the guests or tourists noticed, they would think the man was just another wealthy patron or dignitary, thus severely underestimating the true scope of his wealth and power.

After making her way to the edge of the main corridor, Summer Perkins peered around the corner. Behind her, people wandered and mingled around the stores and restaurants. In front of her was a short hallway with an elevator at the end. A large man in a black suit stood on each side of the stamped gold doors.

Summer placed her cheek against the cool rock, wishing she could melt into the granite wall to not be seen. Noticing she was perspiring, she held on tighter to the small digital camera in her left hand.

Three men came into view from the side entrance and stopped in front of the elevator. All wore dark, knee-length coats.

The man in the middle was the one she'd hoped to see. His coat was open, showing the black tailored suit underneath. A discoloration the size and shade of a penny, between his chin and right cheek, was his most distinguishing mark.

The oversized guard on the right pressed the button pointing upward.

Summer held her breath, brought the camera to her side, and pressed the button. The click was barely audible to her ears, but all three waiting men turned her way. It felt like the temperature of the room rose twenty degrees in an instant. Her heart raced.

The one Summer wanted to digitally capture looked directly at her. Even from a distance of forty yards, his dark eyes bored into her.

That may not have been my best thought-out plan. With three determined, slow steps she backed around the corner.

Summer jumped and swallowed a scream when a hand touched her shoulder.

"There you are." His grip tightened. "You okay?"

"Fine, Mike." She twisted off his hand and started walking.

He followed. "Let's skip the Citadel. There's only an hour left of daylight and we're leaving in the morning. Let's go get a drink at L'Oncle Antoine instead."

"All right." Summer quickened her pace. "As long as it's somewhere other than the Chateau." She was determined to keep the reason she had just put them in jeopardy to herself.

The opulence was befitting the status of the evening's occupants. Two large chandeliers of strung crystals glistened as they expanded across the ceiling. Fir-paneled walls displayed portraits of the railroad in its infancy and the St. Lawrence Basin's pioneering days. A large rectangular table made of maple stood at the center of the room, atop the polished granite floor.

Each man sat in an oxblood leather chair and held a monogrammed crystal snifter or tumbler containing his drink of choice. Each would make business magazines' lists of the top fifty of the world's wealthiest people, if he chose to publicize his financial holdings. Only a few had that desire. These men directed those who the rest of the world *thought* were the most powerful people.

Davis Lovemark rose and called the meeting to order.

"My last duty as chairman," he whispered to himself as he stood at the head of the table. He was well aware that his aura of confidence and control had often been interpreted as arrogance. He was dressed for the part in his hand-tailored gloss black suit of the finest cloth. Even though he'd recently celebrated his sixtieth birthday, he kept his six-foot-tall frame fit and trim.

Davis began the meeting in the same tradition performed for generations. "Gentlemen, let us begin with a toast to our success." He'd never been able to shake the last hint of a British accent in his voice.

Even though the group possessed a variety of native languages, it was customary to speak English during their meetings.

The members all raised their glasses and tapped the table with their free hands.

After the room settled, Davis said, "Let us take a moment to recognize each brother who has passed on since we last met." Because the families had worked together for so long, many did feel like brothers. He scanned the room, raising his hand to give the penny-size coppery discoloration between his chin and right cheek an absent light scratch.

The men acknowledged the sentiment with nods and lowered eyes.

The majority of the men at the meeting were entrepreneurs. The group worked independently, yet cooperated for common goals. Davis had been the leader for the last seven years. He often wondered whether the others recognized what a monumental task it was, given the times they were living in.

"Now, let's get down to the business at hand. We will begin with the most current events." Davis raised the top page in the stack of papers laid in front of him. "You all have the latest information on the events that occurred on September eleventh in the United States. An addendum has been added about the subsequent American attack on Afghanistan that has just begun."

Most men nodded and a few leafed through papers in front of them.

Davis noticed an olive-skinned man who he knew well, staring at him. The man's eyes were brimming with emotion, his expression full of pain. He opened his mouth as if to speak, but Davis gently shook his head. The man closed his lips. Davis knew that his estranged son had died in Two World Trade Center. He'd been at the wrong place at the wrong time; an unfortunate casualty.

Davis continued, "The central banks have everything in place to funnel funds to all parties involved. Margins have been set."

Wry smiles registered on the faces of a few of the men.

"Mr. Carter." Davis looked at the man seated three down to his left. Malcolm had remained loyal to the group, unlike his traitorous older brother Jack. "Do you have any new information about the reorganization of the tracing system at the US Federal Reserve?"

Malcolm Carter rose to his feet, answering in his pronounced Texan drawl, "Yes, Davis." Tall and slender, he had a thick gray buzz-cut, hazel eyes, and thin lips. "The recurring layering problem has been solved. It's been detected in all other central banks. Going forward a third layer of protection will be applied for all transactions."

Davis reached for the snifter of cognac beside his stack of papers. "Do you think that will finally solve the problem?"

"You can bet on it." Malcolm spoke for approximately ten

minutes about banking system security.

After he finished and took his seat, Davis stood again. "Our next order of business is an update on the controlled pharmaceutical testing and genetic engineering. Dr. Schmidt."

A portly man two seats to Davis' right rose to his feet. Gray hair surrounded shiny white skin on the top of his head. He wore a charcoal suit, accentuated by a royal-blue-and-purple-patterned tie and a matching handkerchief tucked into his left breast pocket. Dr. Hendrick Schmidt spoke with authority in a heavy German accent. "A few months previous our facility in Bolivia was dismantled."

Davis noticed how Hendrick had aged in the last few years. He had to place his hand on the edge of the table for support. Regardless of all of his manipulation of food, the environment, and pharmaceuticals, stress would get him in the end.

"Just hours ago, I completed the procurement of an ideal location in Colombia," Hendrick said. "Human testing will resume within eight months. We are still on schedule for full implementation of our goal by 2020."

A number of hands went up around the large table. This project was the largest the consortium had ever undertaken, and it was a contentious issue. Only a select few knew all the details; the others wanted further discussion. It had caused a rift within the group, with the opposition accusing the insiders of *playing God* with the world's population.

Davis wondered why this particular project had generated such a strong, negative reaction. It was no different from previous ones that manipulated the direction of the world, just more aggressive. And this project had been set in motion over fifty years ago and would come to fruition within the next twenty. It was too late to stop it even if they wanted to.

After trying to answer many questions, Hendrick shot a quick glance of agitation at Davis and took his seat.

"Dr. Schmidt will continue to give updates in the future," Davis said. "In time, we hope everyone will be comfortable with our goal."

There were still murmurs within the room, but Davis chose to move forward. "Global Mark Communications controls the majority of the media. However, as always, we need to be vigilant about recruiting new sources, especially with the burgeoning Internet. Without individuals within each area of the media, no matter how small, we cannot communicate to the masses, implement our strategies, and drive our future forward. With your people's help we can continue to develop those relationships."

The change of subject seemed to settle the attendees down.

Davis turned over another page. "Now, can the next chairman update everyone on the new information gathering resource?" He gestured to the man next to him. "Mr. Da Silva."

The man who stood was the same height as Davis Lovemark. He, too, had papers in front of him, but he didn't distribute any around the table. His black suit wrapped around his barrel-chested frame. Wavy, salt-and-pepper hair framed a strong-featured face with thick lips, a pronounced nose, and a dimpled cleft chin.

Davis watched Carlo Da Silva's almost black eyes survey the room. His speech was acute, with a Spanish accent and detectible lisp. "We are making grand progress with our personal information gathering and Internet filtering programs. Although there is still much work to be done, we have our foundation set. In a short period of time our database will contain the vital information needed."

Carlo went on about details that only the few who knew physics and engineering could understand. After he finished, there were more confused looks than nods of agreement.

"Mr. Paden was not able to attend." Davis reached for a small stack of papers and handed them to the young man behind him for distribution. "Hydraulic fracturing is becoming more prevalent. Stronger regulations are being called for after the most recent earthquake and watershed contamination in Texas. For those of you who have any concerns after reading Mr. Paden's report, you can contact him directly."

Another page was turned. "Mr. Svetlov." Davis gave the floor over to the man farther on his right.

Ivgeni Svetlov was a sturdy man who spoke with a terse Russian accent. "Everyone has a copy of the latest gold sheet. Note the new list of stocks that are scheduled to rise, and the best currencies. Also, the roll programs are working well again. The future continues to look very profitable. Remember: alone we are vulnerable; together we are invincible."

The meeting continued with another two hours of reporting, strategizing, voting, and planning.

Finally, the departing chairman turned over his final piece of paper. "There is much work to be done. We have the necessary tools to lead the world in this new age of progress." Davis paused and made eye contact with every man in front of him in the lavish room. "The next phase is in place. We will assist the people and, in turn, profit in kind."

Applause erupted.

Davis raised his hand, happy his term was over. "Communication between us will continue as always. When it is time to gather again, the new chairman will contact you or your successor. I wish you all a good evening and rich, fulfilling lives."

Davis Lovemark stood next to the new chairman, Carlo Da Silva, drinks in their hands, in front of the window of his suite. They looked out at the twinkling lights of the old city, toward the blackness that was the St. Lawrence River.

Davis turned to the man beside him. "The decisions made tonight will irreversibly impact the world for generations to come."

A sardonic smile crossed Carlo's thick lips.

CHAPTER 1

February 17, 2002

My eyes had to adjust after I closed the scratched and dented door behind me. None of the outside sunlight permeated the windowless room; the artificial light was hazy. The stench of stale beer and something putrid I couldn't identify assaulted my nostrils. The grime on the walls could be felt without touching them.

A long, chipped wooden bar ran up the right side of the room. Five patrons sat on stools in front of it, but there was no bartender present. All of the men had looked in my direction as I entered, but after the door was closed and the natural light was gone, they'd resumed talking or staring into the drinks sitting in front of them.

A pool table stood in the middle of the room, a foot-long tear in its faded green felt.

"The Old Man Down the Road" by John Fogerty played on the jukebox just loud enough to hear.

Along the left wall was a bank of six burgundy vinyl booths. The first one had a top-to-bottom rip in its back.

I was supposed to find her in one of the booths. This wasn't the kind of place I would've chosen to meet. From what little I remembered about Summer, this wasn't a typical spot for her to hang out in, either.

The booth backs were high, so I couldn't see the top of any occupant's head. I had to walk down the row and check each one for her.

A woman came out from a back room carrying a large bottle of pickled eggs under her right arm and holding a big bag of beef jerky in her left hand. She looked well seasoned, with over-managed shoulder-length blonde hair and pouty bright red lips. She wore high black pumps, black fishnet stockings, a short, tight black skirt, and a sheer black blouse. Her black bra had ample bosom to push up.

I realized that I'd stopped and was staring. She didn't even notice me as she proceeded behind the bar.

I continued past each booth toward the back of the room. They were all empty until, in the last one, I recognized her profile.

"Hi, Summer."

She didn't acknowledge me as I slid in across from her. Her pretty face was pale and expressionless, her green eyes vacant. She didn't blink. She didn't move. She looked past me as if I wasn't there. "Summer, it's Nick."

I reached across the table, past her folded eyeglasses, and touched her shoulder. Her upper body slowly, then with momentum, fell over. Her head hit the wall with a dull thud.

Shit, shit. Shit!

I swung around to her side. Grabbing her small, limp wrist, I felt for a pulse. Nothing. I placed two fingers on the artery of her neck. Nothing! Her skin was still warm.

Holy fuck, she's dead. What the hell was going on? I stared at her. This was awful. *Poor girl.*

I took a deep breath. I had to compose myself.

An older guy in loose jeans and a white T-shirt walked by me,

10

looking straight ahead. Even though he was ten feet away when he passed, I could tell by the acrid smell following him that he'd just smoked a cigarette. I turned to peer around the booth and saw him perch on the farthest stool at the bar. None of the barflies could see Summer from that angle.

I tried to find a pulse on her wrist again, just in case I did it wrong the first time. Nothing. *This is crazy. How can she be dead?*

With one finger, I opened up her brown leather jacket to see if there was blood or any visible markings on her. Nothing. Her white blouse and brown pants looked clean.

There was a slight bulge in her inside jacket pocket. A closer look revealed sunglasses.

The thing to do was to check all her pockets. Maybe there was a clue as to why she wanted to meet or something that would tell me what had just happened to her. I had to force myself to look, because I felt like I was violating her. All I found was a set of keys.

A brown leather purse sat next to her. I placed it on the table and opened it. The wallet still had money in it, so she hadn't been robbed. There were business cards in a little plastic case, some makeup, gum, and two pens. No clues. I returned the purse to her side.

I looked at her face and was about to close her eyes when I noticed it. There was the small smear of blood on her neck. I gently pulled away her blonde hair and discovered a tiny pinprick where blood had coagulated. I must've smeared it when I felt for a pulse.

Had someone stuck her with a needle?

Fighting an urge to just run out the back, I took another deep breath.

"Don't Stop" by Fleetwood Mac began playing in the background. I usually found the song motivational. At that moment, it was annoying and out of place.

After a few more calming breaths, I got up and walked over to the bar. "Excuse me."

"Yeah, hon?" The bartender's voice had a rasp with a breathy lilt to it. "What'll it be?"

"Does anyone know what happened in the back booth there?" I pointed in Summer's direction. "The woman is dead." Past experience had taught me the illusion of sounding calm, even though I was freaking out on the inside.

"Really?" The bartender pushed the tap handle away from her to stop the flow and slid the mug of beer to one of the patrons. "Wouldn't be the first time."

"We need to call 911." My voice had risen an octave; I hoped no one had heard the tremor in it. I placed my hand on the edge of the bar, which was sticky, so I pulled it back.

There was a phone beside the cash register. When I looked back at the people, all seven were staring at me. One man slid off his stool, standing.

"You sure she's dead?" the bartender asked. "Maybe she's just wasted."

"It's eleven in the morning on a workday …" I realized that made no difference to these people. "Yeah, I'm sure."

"You know why?" asked the guy sitting closest to me.

"No, I don't." No one seemed to be particularly disturbed that there was a dead woman in the back corner booth.

"We don't like to make that call unless we absolutely have to," the bartender said.

"You have to." These people were definitely not the type I was used to dealing with. "Go check her for yourself."

The bartender's eyes narrowed. Then she took the three steps needed to get to the phone, her heels clicking on the hard floor. "What's your name, handsome?"

"Nick Barnes." After watching her pick up the receiver and press three digits, I turned to the patrons. "You guys see anything?"

The guy who'd stood up said, "I don't need no trouble." He

swayed and held onto the bar for support. He was around sixty and bony, but with a gut. Gray stubble framed his ruddy face.

The man right next to me said, "I don't see nothin' unless I get paid." I could smell the alcohol on his breath. His eyes were pale, with red around the edges, his skin doughy and glistening with perspiration. "I can see anything you want, if you pay me."

The guy next over glanced at me, but kept his mouth shut. He looked younger and less seasoned than the others.

The bartender was giving the address to the operator on the other end of the line.

"Sure none of you guys noticed anything?" I asked.

"I remember seeing a guy leaving," said the oldest-looking one of the bunch. He was the one who'd been out back having a smoke. Guessing by his yellowed, wrinkly skin and dark circles around his eyes, he'd been smoking his whole life.

"They're on their way, Nick," the bartender said, coming back to stand behind the beer taps.

"I'm out of here," said the man who was standing. "I don't need this."

"Don't—"

The bartender cut me off. "He didn't do anything, Nick. Let him go."

He shuffled with a right lean to the door.

"I'm sure I know who did it," the bartender said.

Everyone looked at her.

"You guys probably didn't notice. They never notice anything." She looked directly at me. "I'm not a waitress, Nick, you know. People need to come up to the bar to get a drink. He didn't get a drink from me. Neither did the cute little girl. I wouldn't have seen either of them if he wasn't leaving when I went to the back room for supplies."

"I noticed him," the smoker protested.

"Who?" I asked.

She tilted her head to her left. "He was a little darker than you. Thicker brown hair but cut closer. Bit taller than you. Better shape than you, by the looks of it."

"Uh-huh." I wasn't in bad shape. And she wasn't taking this situation seriously enough.

"He had broader shoulders and a thinner waist, that's all." She surveyed me for another second. "I'd bet a couple years younger than you. Maybe not as good looking; something about his face."

"Faggy," noted one of the barflies.

A sly smile crossed her lips. "I wouldn't kick either of you out of bed, Nick."

The way she said my name made me shudder. She was a cougar that hunted fresh meat, preferably marinated by alcohol. Come to think of it, she'd make a good character for my book.

"I saw him too," said the youngest barfly, his speech slow. "He left just before you came in. You probably saw him outside."

That triggered a faint memory. There'd been the guy walking up Market Street, right near the front door of the bar. I didn't get a good look at his face, but he seemed out of place in the neighborhood at that time of day. He was too Caucasian and too well dressed, like he was going to a club. Too GQ.

The smoker said, as if to himself, "Fancy shoes … didn't make a sound when he walked."

I looked down at the scratched, dirt-ingrained linoleum. I scraped my running shoes across the floor. Even with rubber soles, he would've made *some* noise when he walked.

The burst of natural light distracted us as the door opened. Everyone turned to see a dark silhouette entering. Two more figures appeared, and the door closed behind them.

In front of us were two police officers in uniform, and one in plain clothes. It was Detective What's-His-Name … Cortes.

CHAPTER 2

I had a 1994 Nissan Pathfinder. I could afford something newer with less mileage, but when I moved here six months ago it didn't feel permanent. I didn't need to drive the truck much, because I was living in the Russian Hill area, in the heart of San Francisco. With me added to the nearly million other people, it was just easier to take the bus most times. I'd never been like that before. I'd driven everywhere when I lived in Seattle and grew up in Tacoma.

Due to the usual afternoon traffic, the bus wasn't moving anywhere in a hurry. That didn't bother me. I needed time to absorb what had happened.

There were two pieces of paper in my pocket. I rubbed them together with my right hand. One was a small napkin, the kind they put cold drinks on to absorb moisture. When I had left, the bartender had told me her name was Lacy and shoved it into my hand. It had her number on it and "call me" written in red. There was a slight smudge to the right on a couple of the numbers indicating she wrote left-handed. I always got an ink stain on my middle finger when I wrote as well. I'd keep the napkin in case I needed to talk to her about what happened to Summer, not for the reason she was hoping. I was feeling lonely at times these days, but not *that* lonely.

The other was a business card from Detective Cortes. I'd recognized him as soon as he entered the bar. It'd been a year and a half ago, and I'd only met him once: the day I'd found Dr. Elles dead in his office. Cortes remembered me, too.

The two deaths were eerily similar in that the only mark was a pinprick on the neck. I pointed it out this time. It couldn't have been the same killer, because I'd seen Dr. Elles' murderer die from a bullet between his eyes in Maui a year ago.

Cortes had asked me questions, and I'd responded with what little I knew. He'd wondered why the people I was supposed to meet died just before I arrived. In Dr. Elles' case, he'd been killed because he knew too much, and they hadn't wanted him to give me his research. This time, I had no clue.

Cortes had told me he was sure I didn't commit the murder and that if I could figure out why Summer wanted to meet me, it could really help him.

I closed my eyes, took a few deep breaths, and tried to clear my mind. Maybe I could meditate for a few minutes. The practice helped ground me, but I was having trouble with it lately. I couldn't get rid of all the chatter between my ears; I lacked focus. Today was no different. With the bouncing of the bus and conversing passengers, it didn't work.

I pulled the cable above my head, so the bus would pull over at the next stop.

It was only a two-block walk to my place, but uphill. The fog that had rolled in off the bay was dense and contained a misty drizzle.

I rented a nice one-bedroom in an old building that had character. There was a plaque embedded in a cornerstone beside the front entrance that said it was built in 1922. It had white stucco, blue trim, and extended picture windows. The building was still standing, so it must've been safe against earthquakes. However, the hallways had a faint smell of mold, which couldn't be good.

I walked in and threw my keys in an old wooden bowl near the door. My grandfather had carved it as gift for me. It was the only memento I had of him.

Walking over to the window in the corner, I bent over my desk and opened the blinds. The outside mist hid the view, but at least naturally brightened the room. That would help me find the phone that was hidden under something. I retraced my steps. When Summer had called I was preoccupied with going through last week's newspapers for subplot ideas. I looked toward the counter at the edge of the kitchen and saw the empty charger plugged into the wall socket. The cordless phone's battery was probably dead. Other than yesterday's short call, it'd been over a week since it was last used. The phone had never held a charge long.

I pulled off my hoodie and tossed it over my desk chair.

Sitting down on the edge of the couch, I leaned forward to look under the pile of newspapers and magazines that had fallen over and scattered. My place wasn't messy, just needed tidying. I wasn't a slob or a clean freak, but somewhere in the middle.

There it was, under yesterday's *San Francisco News* and a *Golf Digest*. I pressed the talk button and brought it to my ear. Just as I suspected—no dial tone.

I didn't want to make a long distance call on my cell; too expensive. I went to the charger and plopped the phone onto it. I'd give it fifteen minutes.

Back on the couch, the cushion sagged in the spot where my butt always landed. I moved over the blue throw blanket my mother gave me thirteen years ago when I first left for Washington State University.

I leaned back and closed my eyes. It took effort to keep them shut and concentrate. I had to block out the image of Summer's dead eyes staring at me.

My journalist training allowed me to compartmentalize what

facts I knew. The bartender and her patrons had given me some information, and listening to Detective Cortes ask them questions had added a bit more. Summer had arrived about ten minutes early. No one had noticed if the guy was with her or came in just after. Neither ordered a drink. There hadn't been a struggle. She had died between five and ten minutes after sitting down. I had a basic description of the guy, but I wished I'd paid more attention when I'd seen him just outside the bar.

I tried to picture different scenarios. Did she know the tall, quiet murderer? Had she been scared or had it happened too fast? Why would anyone want to extinguish the life of the generous, likable woman in her mid-twenties?

I racked my brain. What the hell could she have wanted to talk to me about? What was so serious that someone would kill to prevent her from telling me?

Should I be worried that I was in danger … again?

I was jerked from my thoughts when the phone started ringing. I looked up at the clock on the wall. I'd been thinking for almost thirty minutes.

Great, the phone was working. I got up to get it.

"Hello."

"Finally!" Sue's voice sounded anxious.

"I was just about to call you."

"Where have you been, Nick? I've been calling you since yesterday."

"Oh, the phone needed to be charged. Why have you been trying to reach me? I really need to talk to you."

"You and your stupid phone. Bill—"

I cut her off. "I need to talk to you about what happened. Do you remember—"

"It's about—"

We were speaking over each other and said the names at the exact same time.

"Summer Perkins."

"Bill's dead."

We both stopped talking, stunned.

"Dr. Bill Clancy is dead," Sue repeated.

I sank down on the couch. "What happened?"

"Two days ago, Bill and Ivan were on their way back from meeting someone who had new information." There was a hitch in Sue's voice. "They were crossing a canal bridge on foot in Amsterdam, and an elderly woman's car jumped the curb after being rear-ended by a delivery truck and hit him. He was thrown over the bridge. His skull was cracked against the stone wall of the canal and he drowned. A cyclist was killed too, because the car went through a bike lane before it ended up in the pedestrian lane."

"That's awful." I first met Dr. Bill Clancy at Dr. Carl Elles' funeral. He was a colleague of Dr. Elles and Dr. Ivan Popov at Naintosa, the genetic engineering seed conglomerate. He was a very kind and gregarious Englishman. "I hope he didn't suffer."

Sue sniffled. "Ivan said he would've been knocked out when he hit the wall."

"Shit. How is Ivan?"

"He said the car missed him by an inch."

Dr. Ivan Popov had helped us make sense of Dr. Elles' notes. Ivan and Bill were the ones who had convinced the Northern European Council for Ethical Farming in Norway to help us. The two had stayed to work with them to fight against genetic engineering and the pending lawsuit against the release of the book I'd written, based on Dr. Elles' research. "Was it an innocent accident?"

"Doubtful." Sue's voice went into her factual reporter mode. "Ivan said the old lady driving the car was innocent. It was like her car had been pushed at them. She's in the hospital with serious whiplash. The driver of the delivery van that caused the whole thing is suspect. Ivan dropped the envelope with the information when he went to try save Bill. When it was over, the envelope and the driver were gone."

"Yeah, that's suspect. Do you know what was in the envelope?"

"Something new. Ivan said he never had the chance to read the document."

Had the premeditated attack been intended to take out both scientists? Last fall, the media director for the Council for Ethical Farming had been killed by a car while he was riding his bicycle. They'd never found that hit-and-run driver, either.

"Should we be worried?" Sue's voice rose. "It seems to be starting again."

"Yeah, I'm getting that feeling." I moved the phone from my left ear to my right. "When is the funeral?"

"Ivan said he's flying his body back to England and that Bill hadn't wanted a funeral."

"Yeah, but Ivan can't take care of everything alone."

"I told him the same thing. He said he has others to help and that the Council now has its own security force. He'll have bodyguards with him, just in case."

"Where were the security people when Bill was run down?"

"I don't know."

I shook my head. "The Council's grown into quite the organization."

"Like they said when we were there, they have the backing of some deep-pocketed people who want to fight against genetically modified organisms." Sue took an audible breath that was magnified by the phone. "Dr. Elles' exposé has given them the facts they needed to rally."

"Too bad Naintosa's application for the injunction against publication on the exposé still needs to be sorted out."

"We were still able to get some information to the European independent media, and there's attention on the suit. It bites, but we have to wait until it's all over."

Frustration rose inside me. "Remember they said it could take years."

We were both silent for a couple of seconds, before I said, "So we don't go to England?"

"I don't see any point."

I felt sad for Bill. He had been a man with the strength of conviction to do what was right. He'd felt guilty about not helping Dr. Elles more when he'd been gathering information against Naintosa. Bill had retired and distanced himself from the trouble. But after Dr. Elles' death, he'd promised to redeem himself. Along with Ivan, the two had done what they could to help get the exposé written and follow through with the Council for Ethical Farming.

Sue cut off my thoughts. "Did you say something about Summer Perkins?"

"More bad news. She was killed today."

"What! What happened?"

"She called me out of the blue yesterday and wanted to meet me this morning. When I got to the seedy bar where she wanted to meet, she was dead."

I gave her a rundown of what happened.

"That's terrible." Sue's voice shook. "Summer called me at the magazine first thing yesterday morning. She was looking for you. Felix had told her where I was working."

"Who's Felix?"

"Our co-reporter at the *Seattle News*, remember?"

"Sort of." I didn't remember a Felix at all.

"She kept in touch with Felix after she moved to work at the *San Francisco News*. I bumped into him a while back and had mentioned I was at the magazine. When Summer called she sounded quite anxious to talk to you. She needed your opinion on something you had experience with. Then I heard about Bill and forgot about it."

"Okay, that explains how she found me. Did she say what exactly she needed my opinion on?"

"No." Sue sniffled. "What a horrible thing. She was so sweet. Why would anyone want to kill her?"

"I have no idea."

I could hear her wipe her nose with something. "What else did the detective say?"

"He asked if it could have been somehow related to Dr. Elles' death." In September 2000, I had been approached by Dr. Carl Elles to help him write his memoir on his pioneering research on genetic food engineering. When I had gone to meet him to start the project, I had found him dead at his office. The coroner had determined it was a heart attack, but later we'd found out he had been murdered by Naintosa's security force.

"Do you think it could be related?"

"The Lieutenant's dead, so it obviously wasn't the same killer. Maybe ... maybe she found out something else Dr. Schmidt was doing and wanted to tell me about it?" Dr. Hendrick Schmidt was the owner and chairman of Naintosa, an agrochemical corporation, and Pharmalin, a pharmaceutical company. Both were huge conglomerates. Dr. Schmidt was extremely powerful and connected. He, through Naintosa, was suing the Council for Ethical Farming to prevent the release of the exposé I had written from Dr. Elles' notes.

"How would she even know about Dr. Schmidt?" Sue said. "It didn't even make the news here in the States, just in Europe. And he's so private, not exactly a well-known public figure."

"Not sure. That's the only connection I can think of."

"But why kill her? Why wouldn't he just have *you* killed? I'm sure he still wants to."

"You're right and thanks for reminding me," I said. "It's not like he wouldn't want to do you in either. Remember, you were almost the first to go in Maui."

"I don't remember; I was unconscious."

I always admired how Sue could make light of bad things that happened in the past. It was like a pressure release, so she wouldn't dwell on them. "That is true."

"Sure, I've been cautious ever since we got back from Oslo," she said. "But after I heard about Bill's death yesterday, I feel like they'll be coming after us next. Now Summer …"

"If that were the case, I would've died at the bar today. We're not even sure they're related." I thought for a second. "Now that we're talking it through, Summer must've wanted to see me about something else."

"Hmm. I guess."

"And remember what the Council's lawyer said about us? That killing any of us would immediately implicate Dr. Schmidt, so we were too hot to eliminate. That's why they let us come back to the United States. Besides, I'm higher on Schmidt's list than you."

"Something may have changed. We need to be extra careful. *Accidents* happen, you know."

I got up and walked over to the big window. The mist had lifted some, and I could see more than a few blocks now. "You got to know Summer better after I left the *News*. Can you think of anything she was doing that could provide a clue?"

"That was like a year ago. We went out for drinks a few times after you'd taken off with Morgan to British Columbia. The last time was just before you came back to Seattle. That's when Summer told me she got a job at the *San Francisco News*. It was a full-time reporter position. She was excited at the advancement from junior trainee. That's it."

"And you never mentioned to her what Morgan and I were doing?" Morgan Elles had a second copy of her father's notes and had convinced me to write the exposé.

"Excuse me? You think I'd ever do that?"

"Sorry, just making sure." I rested my free hand on the back of the black leather office chair I'd bought at a secondhand store.

"You still haven't heard from Morgan?" Sue sounded tentative.

"Nope." That was still a sore spot for me, and I didn't want to talk to Sue about it anymore.

She must've sensed it, because she changed the subject back. "What are you going to do about Summer's death?"

"What's there to do? I'll just wait and see if Detective Cortes contacts me."

Sue paused and then said, "Summer's family is in Seattle, so the funeral will be here. I'll go and see if anyone says anything."

"Good idea."

"Can you please give me your cell number so I can still reach you if your phone isn't charged?"

"You don't have it?"

"You never gave it to me."

"Oh, sorry." I gave her the number.

"Make sure you're extra careful."

"I will. You too."

I walked over to the kitchen and placed the phone on the charger as soon as I hung up.

My stomach growled. I didn't feel hungry, but I hadn't eaten since breakfast. I pulled on the old fridge door. Inside were various condiments, all organic, some not easy to acquire. I had enough beer for a few days, some cheese, and a few eggs, two leftover chicken drumsticks, but that was it. A half loaf of bread sat on the counter, along with two thirds of a bottle of Aberlour Scotch, remnants of some by now stale chips in a bag, a tomato, and a banana. I needed to buy groceries.

Ever since I'd learned about what genetic engineering was doing to the world's food supply, I'd become really conscious of what I put into my mouth. I bought organic or European whenever possible, even alcohol. I'd never been like that before, but now I was strict, even almost paranoid about it.

I closed the fridge door and stared at its blank white surface. My mind went from seeing Summer's lifeless eyes to imagining the scene of Bill dying, his head smashed against the canal rock.

I had a sudden urge to run and hide. But where, I didn't know. *Snap out of it and buck up.* I needed to be strong if things were heating up again.

I'd feel better if I ate something. I'd go for a good food shop tomorrow. Today, I'd get some take-out from the Japanese place in the next block.

When I put my jacket on I zipped it right up and pulled the hood around my head. It was my subconscious protecting me from getting a needle stuck in my neck.

CHAPTER 3

There was a moving van outside, and now I knew why. After two months' vacancy, the apartment next to mine had been rented. Movers were negotiating a red sofa through its open door.

As I turned the key in my lock, I heard someone say, "Hi."

I jumped, as my heart skipped a beat. I looked around and saw a good looking young woman appear from behind the sofa. I exhaled.

She strode toward me and extended her right hand. "You must be my new neighbor."

Wow. Did I just say that out loud? No. Good. "Hi." The newspaper under my arm dropped to the floor as I went to shake her hand. "I'm Nick."

"Nice to meet you, Nick. I'm Angelica."

She had slim fingers with dark pink manicured nails. Her hand was warm. My eyes met her blue ones and my speech stalled.

"I said, how do you like living here, Nick?" She had a crooked seductive smile and perfect white teeth.

"Sorry, uh, long day. Yeah, it's fine here."

"Great. Maybe we can get together sometime. I'm new to San Francisco. Originally from Augusta, Georgia, and I know barely anyone here."

She did have a silky Southern accent.

I worked hard not to lower my gaze to her ample cleavage. "Yeah, sure. I'm pretty new to San Francisco too."

"See you soon, sweetie." Angelica turned away.

Her heart-shaped ass had a wiggle as she walked. She had sandy blonde straight hair, reaching down to her shoulder blades. You could tell she cared about her appearance. I bet she was in her mid-twenties and five-foot-four.

She turned back and gave a little wave before she went through her open door that no longer had a sofa stuck in it.

I picked up my newspaper and went inside my apartment.

She could be distracting, I thought, as I threw the paper on the coffee table with the others.

I settled on the couch and opened the Styrofoam container with the sushi in it. I was never a huge fan of sushi, but the restaurant next to the corner store was convenient and good quality.

With my left hand I fumbled with the chopsticks to pick up a piece of dynamite roll, and with my right, I opened the newspaper.

I wasn't really paying attention as I chewed and flipped pages. My thoughts jumped from Summer to Bill. Summer had been twenty-six and had just been gathering momentum in her career. And Bill had been making progress on providing more proof that the genetically engineered food he helped create was dangerous.

My mind was like a Ping-Pong ball bouncing around.

I'd never thought death was something to be sad about. I believed we were all infinite and our souls never died. We just moved onto our next adventure. The sadness came from the loss felt by the people left behind. Being murdered, however, as opposed to dying of natural causes or by accident, added the need for responsibility and accountability for the people still alive.

The soy sauce was making my throat parched, so I went to get something to drink.

My life had been pretty average, sometimes even boring. After growing up in Tacoma, I'd gone to Pullman to study journalism at Washington State University. That's where I'd met Sue. After unsuccessful attempts at seducing her, we'd become best of friends. After college, we each moved to Seattle and worked at the *Seattle News*. We both had done some hard-hitting investigative journalism. Then I got screwed by a senator who laundered information through me and lost my way for a while. Just as I was trying to pick myself up again, Dr. Elles had approached me to help him write his memoir. That's when my life had changed. After Dr. Elles' death I met his daughter, Morgan. Together, with the help of Sue, Ivan, Bill, and unknowingly, ex-oil tycoon Jack Carter, we had saved Dr. Elles' legacy and written the exposé about the dangers of genetically engineered food. Morgan, Sue, and I were almost killed by Naintosa's thugs at Jack's bible camp in Maui, and had ended up in Oslo under the protection of the Council for Ethical Farming.

Losing both parents had taken a toll on Morgan, and she had ended up leaving Oslo without telling me. Not discussing her plans with me stung.

I felt I needed new scenery, so I moved to San Francisco. The amount I'd been paid for writing the exposé was enough to live on for a couple of years, so I'd decided to write my first novel and launch my new career as an author. If that didn't work out, I could always go back to journalism. Life had become normal again, even uneventful. Until today.

I'd been holding the fridge door open. The cold air brought me back to the present, and I reached for a beer.

I sat down again on the couch and finished the last bites of sushi. Placing the container to the side of the coffee table, I vowed to throw it out next time I got up and not leave it there for days.

I closed the newspaper and saw the remote control under it.

Picking the remote up, I clicked the TV on. GMNN, the abbreviation for Global Mark News Network, was the last channel I'd watched. I stared at the world-shaped bull's-eye logo with a red arrow through the middle, displayed at the bottom right of the screen next to the scrolling news feed. It reminded me of the enormity of the parent company, Global Mark Communications, GM Comm, the largest news company in the world. The conglomerate owned tons of TV stations, half the major daily papers, including the *San Francisco News* and *Seattle News*, and a bunch of radio stations. Their latest endeavor was investing heavily into the expanding frontier of the Internet.

The anchors were talking about the war in Afghanistan. I didn't want any more bad news tonight; I was sad and paranoid enough as it was.

I changed the channel and then went to the kitchen for some Scotch.

CHAPTER 4

It was early morning and quiet, the air thick with vapor. Not a hint of breeze, yet fresh.

I'd come down to this spot between my apartment building and the steep slope behind it over a dozen times since I'd moved here. There was a walkway through the grass to an old rickety bench with a black wrought iron frame. Shrubs on each side and an arbutus tree provided privacy.

A long towel laid over the wooden slats kept the damp from penetrating my track pants. I felt cozy wrapped in the thick cotton jacket with the hood over my head.

Ships' fog horns sounded rhythmically in the distance.

I closed my eyes and focused on Summer, wondering again what had happened, then let the thought go.

Breaths in and out faded away to nothingness.

After twenty minutes I opened my eyes. The sights, sounds, and smells of the world around me came back. Birds chirped. The air tasted like water. I'd gone into the gap, but hadn't seen anything.

Transcendental meditation had been introduced to me in my last year of university. I would go through periods of practicing it every day, to not doing it for months. It helped calm me, clear the chatter from my mind, and sometimes provide me with answers. On occasion, I'd even get visions or premonitions. The gap was best described as the space between notes of sound, a nothingness that could only be achieved when in a deep meditative state.

Today had been good, and relaxing, but I had no answers to my questions about Summer.

I grabbed my towel and went back to my apartment.

I'd turned on the coffeemaker before I'd gone outside. The fresh-brewed aroma welcomed me when I opened the door. Pouring a cup, I saw the lonely, spotted banana in the bowl on the counter. It wouldn't last another day, so it would be part of my breakfast. I placed it on a plate before preparing my fried eggs and toast.

Food and mug in hand, I sat down at the computer.

I always checked my e-mail first. Other than a golf-related joke from my buddy Mike, there was nothing.

I clicked on the program that contained the manuscript for my novel and let it load. There were 256 pages so far.

The way-too-ripe banana was mush inside and I almost gagged when I put it in my mouth and choked it down.

I read the last four pages I'd written two days ago. Not bad, but I was losing track of the plot. My protagonist was a cool customer. He won every fight and was smooth with the ladies. He was a private detective, hired to investigate the slow poisoning of a prominent family. They were being killed off without a trace by a demented scientist who was using them as unknowing guinea pigs in his experiments. The detective hadn't figured it out yet.

I needed to flesh out the villain more. What if it wasn't just a family, but a whole town or county? What would the mad scientist's motivation then be?

It wasn't too far-fetched compared to what Naintosa was doing in reality. They were knowingly making people sick. Their motivations were power and greed. Since I was writing fiction, I could take it to the next level. I had originally decided against it, but maybe using genetically engineered food in the story was a good idea.

I'd kept a copy of Dr. Elles' notes and the final draft of the exposé. I'd start skimming them later for ideas. In the meantime, I'd let my theories percolate.

⫘⫘⫘

I used my vehicle when I went grocery shopping, because I didn't want to carry so many bags on the bus. I'd go for a big shop every three weeks and then supplement from a little market that sold organics in the neighborhood.

Eating the healthier diet meant that I'd had to learn how to cook and had discovered that I was pretty good at it. No more processed food or prepackaged meals—they were the worst. When I didn't want to cook, I'd found a few good restaurants close by that used safe ingredients.

I pulled out eight bags from the back of the Pathfinder, four in each hand, and headed upstairs.

Angelica was turning the corner in the hallway away from her apartment as I was coming to mine. Her hair bounced behind her in a ponytail. "You're productive in the morning." The pink sweat suit she wore clung to every curve.

"Needed food." I felt my skin warm. "Where are you off to?"

"Taking media studies classes at USF," she said as she passed. "Maybe you can cook me dinner sometime."

I hesitated, caught off guard. She was at the stairwell door before I managed to answer. "Sure."

She could be trouble, I reminded myself. Then again, maybe I needed some trouble.

After the groceries were put away, I went to the couch and turned on the TV.

On GMNN, a man in a gray suit pointed to a rising graph

displayed beside him. The vertical axis read billions, numbered one to nine. The horizontal axis had years 1900 to 2020.

"The estimated current world population is 6.2 billion." He pointed. "By 2011, it will reach seven billion. By 2020 it's projected to be 7.5 billion."

Hmm, that's a lot of people, a lot of mouths to feed.

I needed to be productive, so I clicked off the TV and went to my desk.

All morning I'd felt a lingering melancholy about Summer and Bill. But mostly, I'd concentrated on my novel.

I brought up my vague original outline, which I'd strayed from, and looked for clues. What would be the motivation for a demented scientist to slowly kill off a person or a family or a county or a state or the country? Or 6.2 billion people? No, he wouldn't want to kill everyone. And how was my studly private investigator going to uncover the plan and get the scientist? Or should I just rethink the whole frigging story again?

I went to the file containing Dr. Elles' exposé. I'd kept putting it off, but skimming it could give me ideas.

The phone rang. As I went to pick it up, I knew it was Sue.

"Should I be trying harder to convince Ivan to come home?" Sue said on the other end of the line.

I shrugged. "Has something else happened?"

"I just keep worrying that he could be next."

Ivan and Sue had really warmed to each other during our time in Norway. They'd developed a special bond and respect. I'd thought Ivan had developed a crush on Sue, even though he was thirty years her senior. She could talk him into anything, except leaving the Council for Ethical Farming. "But he's the only one left of us at the Council."

"He can work with them by e-mail from Nelson."

Ivan had a home in Nelson, British Columbia. "You know it

wouldn't be the same. Even though it's not safe at the Council, it would be even more dangerous to be by himself in Nelson. Either way, he should have a full-time bodyguard."

"Yeah, you're right. I'd just feel better having him closer."

"He'd still be a country away from us."

"I know that, jackass." Sue paused for a moment, then asked, "How's the writing going?"

Hmm, why did she change the subject? "Uh, well … slow. Being a journalist was much easier, because you report on what happened. Writing fiction, you have to make shit up from scratch."

"Why don't you go through Dr. Elles' exposé for ideas?"

"I just started doing that." Sue and I frequently thought along the same lines.

"Take some of the facts and sensationalize them to make the story more suspenseful. You know, spread the truth, dressed up as a story."

"I'm pondering going that way."

"You can add chase scenes and abductions that happened to you in real life. Write what you know."

"Already have some of that."

"Was there anything in the *San Francisco News* today about Summer's death?" Sue asked. "There was nothing in the *Seattle News*."

"No, nothing in her hometown paper or the paper she worked at." Reports on Summer's death wouldn't have been on the TV or radio news, but one would've thought that the papers would mention it.

"Interesting. I even did an Internet search and nothing came up." Sue cleared her throat. "The funeral will be on Saturday. I'll make sure to go."

CHAPTER 5

After hours of reading and no inspirational new story ideas, it was time for a break.

Maybe clean the place up a bit.

I placed the container that had held last night's sushi and the grocery bags in the garbage under the sink. Why don't they make these things recyclable? What a waste that all the plastics and Styrofoam end up in landfills.

Opening the fridge, I saw two neat rows of Full Sail Pale Ale. I figured it was late enough in the day to have a few. Sue was the one who had gotten me liking the brand. It was an inconvenience that they didn't use twist-off caps, but a tenant way before me had installed a bottle opener on the wall right beside the fridge.

At the same instant the bottle made the hiss of being opened, there was a knock at the door. In the six months I'd lived there, no one had ever knocked on the door.

I took a swig and went to see who it was. There were another two quick hard raps, not delicate in any way. I didn't have a peephole, so I had to open the door and take the chance that whoever was on the other side wasn't intending to cause me harm.

A Latino man about five-foot-eight in height, with thick, short, black hair and a moustache stood in the hall. He had on the same style of black jacket and black pants as yesterday, but wore a pale-blue dress shirt instead of white.

"Detective Cortes."

"Hello, Mr. Barnes. I thought we'd have a chat to make sure my facts are straight. You know, while everything's still fresh." He was probably born in Mexico, but moved to the States when he was young. Now that he was somewhere in his forties, his accent was barely detectible.

"Sure, come on in."

I motioned to the armchair next to the couch. "Do you want a beer?"

He walked with a slight limp. "No thanks, still on duty." He unzipped his jacket. The tightness of the shirt around his midsection revealed the likelihood that he'd consumed his fair share of barley and hops.

"I don't know what else I can tell you." I sat down in my usual sagging spot on the couch.

"How about we go through it again from the beginning?" He sat down in the chair and pulled a pad from inside his jacket pocket. "Have you figured out why Ms. Perkins wanted to meet you?"

"No, I haven't." I had decided I was going to be totally up-front with him. I had nothing to hide, and I wanted him to find Summer's killer.

He looked at his notes. "When she called you to set up the meeting, did she sound panicked?"

"More urgent than panicked." I drank from my bottle.

"How many of those have you had?" He pointed at the beer with his pen.

"Oh, it's my first one."

He nodded. "She wanted to meet you at noon yesterday and suggested the location."

I made space by separating some magazines and newspapers and placed the bottle down where I could see the wood of the coffee table. "It was eleven, and yes, she told me where she wanted to meet. I'd never been to that bar before."

I went through the events with as much detail as I could remember, even adding a few things I'd forgotten to mention before.

He listened without showing emotion, interrupted a few times, and took more notes.

When I was finished, I asked, "Do you have any idea who the guy with her was?"

"No, not yet." He looked up from his pad. "Can you give me some particulars about yourself? How old are you?"

"Thirty-one."

"You're around six feet?"

"Yes, exactly."

"About a hundred and ninety pounds?"

"One eighty-five."

He almost smiled and wrote as he spoke. "Brown hair, green eyes, no priors, left-handed."

"Uh-huh." Why did he need all that?

"Okay. Can we take a moment to talk about the last few years?"

"Sure, what do you want to know?" He had said at the bar that he was curious about what happened to me between the first time we'd met and now. "You think there's a connection?"

"Not sure. You have to admit that going to meet two people in the span of a year and a half and finding them both dead isn't something that happens to most people."

"Believe me, the thought's crossed my mind."

He smiled. "Not sure I'd want to meet up with you with that record."

His comment and smile lightened my mood. I hadn't realized I was tense.

"So what happened after Dr. Carl Elles died?"

"I'm sure you know most of it through police records, and I gave a full accounting of what happened to Interpol."

"I've done some checking and read your statement, but let's touch on a few key points anyway."

"Okay." I leaned back, settling in. "I decided to write Dr. Elles' memoir with his daughter, Morgan Elles. We had tons of notes about genetic food engineering and all the experiments he did."

Cortes looked up from his pad. "Is genetically engineered food really that bad?"

"Yes. Worse than everyone thinks."

"Then why are they doing it?"

"To make piles of money. We discovered that Naintosa's wheat and soy cause cancer and Pharmalin's working on a drug for it. They make a profit on both ends."

Cortes raised an eyebrow and sat up straight. "Really? That's unethical and illegal. They can't do that."

"And yet, they are."

He was shaking his head and I could see Cortes was a regular person, probably with a family, concerned with their well-being. "Then why isn't anyone telling the public?"

"We aren't able to tell anyone. The mainstream US media won't report on it, and Naintosa is suing the European Council for Ethical Farming."

"Who are they?"

"They're the group in Europe that was helping us get the memoir—the one that turned into an exposé—published."

"Are you named in the lawsuit?"

"Yes, but I have no money or power."

Cortes nodded in understanding. "So what happened when you were writing the memoir?"

"They caught us a few times and beat us up pretty good. I have no doubt that they would've killed us if we hadn't escaped."

"Who are *they* and how'd you escape?"

"Sigmund Thompson, who'd first introduced himself to me as a police lieutenant and we later found out worked for Naintosa's security; he admitted to killing Dr. Elles. Then there was his partner Matt Koffman and the head of security, Peter Bail. They were being directed by the owner of Naintosa, Dr. Hendrick Schmidt."

He nodded his head in recognition. "Do you know where these men are now?"

He would've known all that if he'd read the Interpol statement. Was he testing me? I went along with it. "Thompson and Koffman were killed in Maui. Bail escaped. Dr. Schmidt is still under investigation and suing the Council."

"At least he's under investigation." Cortes wasn't taking any notes, so he *was* testing me. He already knew what had happened in Maui and since then.

I tested him back. "Do you know if anyone's found Bail?"

"Not that I'm aware of. How did you escape from those professionals?"

"At first Morgan and I thought it was because we were smart and lucky, but we found out later that we were being helped by Jack Carter."

Cortes nodded. "Where is Morgan Elles now?"

"She's with family in South Africa. She needs time to grieve and regroup after losing her parents."

"Have you heard from her lately?" Cortes was writing on his pad again.

"No." I tried not to sound hurt.

"Jack Carter. Why would an oil billionaire like Jack Carter help you?"

"He said what Dr. Schmidt and his companies were doing was wrong and he didn't want them getting away with it."

"How did he have access to the information you had?"

"Good point." I'd never thought about asking Jack that. How did he know? "I'm not sure." I thought about it for a second and added, "He does know Dr. Schmidt well. Their families have known each other for generations."

Detective Cortes looked straight at me. "And he chose to help you over a friend?"

"Jack Carter is a good and fair man. He believes in doing the right thing and has the means of taking action against wrong … things." Where was he going with his questioning? It's not like Jack was under suspicion.

"Okay." Cortes looked down at his notes. "So in the end, nothing's happened with the completed exposé?"

"There's nothing we can do at the moment. Hopefully the lawsuit won't last forever and the exposé will be published in the end. In the meantime, more and more genetically engineered food is being grown and eaten."

There was a slight shake of Cortes' head.

All at once the direction of my book solidified in my mind. "I'm hoping that the thriller I'm writing will be able to get some of the information out. Even though it'll be labeled fiction, hopefully it'll get people thinking."

"Did Summer Perkins know you were writing the book?"

"Only if my friend Sue told her, which I doubt."

"Sue Clark?"

"Yes." His knowing who Sue was further proved he already knew most of the information I'd told him.

"How long before you finish it?"

"A while."

He raised his eyebrows as if prodding for a more specific time frame.

"Maybe a year."

He nodded. "I think that's good for now. I may need to speak with you again. Are you planning on going anywhere in the next few weeks?"

"No, no plans."

He got up and placed the pad back in his pocket. "Thank you for your time, Mr. Barnes."

"No problem." I followed him to the door. "I want to help in your investigation in any way I can."

He turned. "If anyone else wants you to meet with them, similar to the situation with Ms. Perkins or Dr. Elles, contact me before you see them. Maybe we can prevent this from happening again."

Was he joking? I opened the door for him. "I will."

CHAPTER 6

I'd switched from beer to Scotch on the rocks. Each sip tasted better than the last. However, the buzz wasn't slowing my mind—just blurring it.

The cursor blinked at the end of the last word I'd written. That was a while ago.

I looked out the window into the soupy darkness that only a lamp across the street could penetrate.

My thoughts skipped from Summer, to Bill, to Detective Cortes' visit, then to my book and back again. Then missing Morgan would enter. There were way too many things going on upstairs.

I should meditate. No, it never worked when I'd been drinking.

I heard a faint scrape of metal on metal. My eyes were drawn to my door. I put my glass down and watched the dead bolt latch turn a couple of degrees. Another scraping sound and the latch moved a little more.

What the fuck?

Shocked at what I saw for only a second, instinct took over. I lunged the twenty feet to the door and grabbed the latch. My shoulder hit the wall beside the door hard. Something was jamming the latch and it wouldn't turn. As I put all of my effort into it, there was a click and it snapped back shut. When it had turned back to the locked position my hand slipped, I lost my balance and fell onto the throw rug.

There was a clank of something metal falling onto the floor on the other side of the door and a scrape of a shoe.

BANG. BANG. BANG.

I was lying face up and saw splinters of door flying. I turned my head. There were three holes in the far wall plaster, about chest level.

My heart pounded. I rolled to the side, away from the door.

As the wood and plaster dust in the air settled, it was quiet. I was expecting another attempt to get into my apartment.

A door in the distance opened with voices accompanying it. I could hear it was my neighbor from around the corner and down the hall, with some of his buddies. They usually headed out to a club around this time of night. They'd have to go past my place to get to the stairs.

I got to my feet. Should I yell and warn them someone was there with a gun?

I could hear them approaching and opened my mouth. It was too late. By the volume of their voices, they were already too close.

No shots rang out.

When they got to my door their footsteps stopped. "What the hell went on here?"

It was obvious the shooter was gone.

I exhaled the breath I was holding and unlocked the door.

All three of the guys stepped back. They looked at me, eyes wide. I must've looked the same way back at them.

"What happened, buddy?" asked my neighbor. I didn't know his name, but he'd always been friendly. He was an aspiring professional who wore a suit in the day, went to the gym right after work, and then partied at night.

"Someone tried to pick my lock and shot up my door." I noticed some wood splinters on my T-shirt and brushed them off.

"You okay?" asked the most muscular of the three.

"Yeah, fine." I looked down the curve of the hall. "Did you guys see anyone?"

All three were looking at me with caution.

"You messed up in something, bud?" asked the neighbor.

"Huh? No … I have no clue why this happened."

"People don't just shoot up people's doors in Russian Hill for no reason," said the tallest one, who was probably six-foot-four.

All I could do was shrug.

"Do you need help?" the neighbor asked. "Do you want us to call the police or an ambulance or something?"

"Yeah, the police … no … I mean, I can call them." I had to call Cortes.

"You sure you're okay?" the neighbor asked again. "You seem a little out of it."

"Of course he's out of it. He just got shot at," said Most Muscular. "You want us to hang out in case the dude comes back?" The guy could've been a bouncer, easy.

"No. You guys go ahead." I turned to my door. The lock looked fine and the holes on the exterior were small compared to the interior of the door.

I went back inside and turned the latch of the deadbolt.

Maybe I should've asked them to hang around. What if the shooter was hiding out of sight until the three guys left?

Where the hell did I put Detective Cortes' card? It was in the jacket I'd worn when I went to meet Summer. I'd put it in the closet when I had cleaned up earlier. I found it and reached into a pocket. There was a piece of paper and I pulled it out. That was the bartender's number. I reached in the pocket again and found the card.

Skirting around to avoid passing directly in front of the door, I went to the kitchen and grabbed the phone.

He answered on the second ring. "Cortes."

"It's Nick Barnes. Would you be able to come over or send an officer? Someone just tried to break into my apartment and has put three bullets through my door. And I'm not sure, but they might be still around." I had slunk back deeper into the kitchen, beside the fridge, the farthest spot from the front door.

"Someone will be right there and I'll be about fifteen minutes. Can the door lock?"

"Yes. I locked it."

"Good, stay away from the door."

"Way ahead of you."

When I put the phone on the counter, I heard a creak. That was the sound a specific floorboard in the hall made. It was about ten feet from my door. *They're out there again.*

I peered around the corner of the kitchen, held my breath, and listened.

There was another faint sound. Was that from the squeaky hinge on the door leading to the stairwell? How could I hear that from here?

I kept listening and only taking breaths when I couldn't hold them anymore.

Why had this happened? For sure this wasn't a random break-and-enter. However, it seemed a bit amateur. Naintosa security would've caught me off guard and gotten in. They wouldn't have just started shooting, hoping I was standing in front of the door. This had to be someone else and about something different.

I needed to learn how to protect myself. The only way I'd done it in the past was with sheer will and some speed. That wasn't good enough anymore. I wasn't the kind of guy who liked to fight, but I was beginning to think I had no choice.

I noticed the glass of Scotch on my desk. I felt stone cold sober. It was best not to have any more right now.

The rapping sound knocked me back against the wall. "Mr. Barnes? SFPD."

CHAPTER 7

The two officers that were first at the scene had done a quick search on their way up to my apartment. Detective Cortes was minutes behind them and brought along a female officer. Cortes was dressed the same as earlier. "This is getting serious, Nick."

He went from calling me Mr. Barnes to Nick. I wasn't sure whether he felt more comfortable with me, wanted me to feel more comfortable with him, or had another tactic in mind.

I sat on the couch and he sat in the chair like earlier in the afternoon. One of the officers in uniform was standing in the hall; the other wasn't visible. The lady that came with Cortes began picking at one of the holes in the wall with a small metal tool.

"Do you have any idea why anyone would do this?" Cortes pulled out his pen and pad.

I shrugged.

"You sure you've told me everything?"

"Yes." I had my hands clasped together and lightened the grip. "It either has to do with Dr. Elles' exposé or Summer's death. It couldn't have been a random B and E."

"Why do you think it couldn't be random?"

"They were trying to pick the lock. When I rushed the door and twisted the latch closed they started shooting, thinking I was standing in front of the door."

Cortes nodded.

"Their goal was to kill me." Saying that out loud hit me hard.

"Looks like." Cortes was staring at me. "It doesn't seem to have been well thought-out."

"That's what I was thinking … amateurish."

"Nick, are you okay?"

I looked up and saw Angelica standing in the doorway. Her pink coat and high-heeled black pumps indicated she was just getting home, so there was no point in asking if she'd seen anything.

"Yeah, I'm fine." I tried to smile, but it was a feeble attempt. Sudden exhaustion weighed down on me. "I'll talk to you later."

Cortes had asked me to reenact what had happened three times. Then he suggested I get some rest.

After a couple of hours trying to sleep, I got up. I kept seeing the bullets that were meant for me go through the door and into the wall.

I made coffee, sat on the couch, and watched the police finish up their forensics.

It seemed overly bright with all of the lights turned on compared to the darkness outside.

Except for the first uniformed officer on the scene, who was still standing in the hallway, Cortes and the others were gone. They'd been replaced by three guys in civilian clothes—police, detectives, or forensics; I wasn't sure which.

The slugs had been removed from the wall and the door taken off its hinges.

Archie, the building manager, was surveying the situation. He was scratching his almost bald head and scowling in my direction, indicating that he wasn't too impressed with having a shooting in his building.

In less than half an hour, the plainclothes cops had left. Archie had hung a new door and given me the keys to a new deadbolt.

───※───

I waited until I knew Sue would be up before I called to tell her what happened. She was freaked out and wanted me back in Seattle.

Now I was sitting by myself, finishing my third cup of coffee, but not feeling wired. So now what?

Cortes had told me that the chances of the shooter coming back to my place were slim, judging by the way they had handled the attempt to get at me and with the attention from the police. However, to be safe I should go stay with a friend or in a hotel for a while. But he added, "Be extra careful wherever you go. Stay in areas with other people around. Don't get caught alone somewhere in case they are following you." Cortes also suggested I get a home security system, which Archie agreed to.

After further contemplation, I decided not to leave my place or sit around being traumatized.

I went to my computer, brought up Dr. Elles' exposé, and started reading where I'd left off.

There was a *ping* indicating a new e-mail in my Inbox. It was from Ivan to Sue and me. He gave us the good news that the Pharmalin and Naintosa lab in Bolivia was being permanently dismantled. We'd scored a win there by bringing attention to it. There would be no more illegal human testing for their genetic engineering and drugs.

Ivan also wrote that he was unable to locate the man he and Bill had met with in Amsterdam, just before Bill died. He hoped nothing bad had happened to him.

At the end he said that the Council was providing him with more protection and not to worry. He didn't expand on what that protection was, but I assumed bodyguards.

I didn't leave my place for the next three days. Even though that's where the attempt on my life had happened, I felt safest there. I had enough food … and liquor.

I'd been able to get an alarm system put in within two days.

"What are you doing?" Sue said on the other end of the line.

"Writing my novel."

"Really?"

I hesitated. "Trying to, at least. Sue, how come you never believe me when I say I'm writing?"

"Because I think you have writer's block."

"Actually I've made progress in the last couple days." I wasn't totally lying; it wasn't great progress, but progress nonetheless.

"Well, then you could use a break. Why don't you come up to Seattle for a few days? You could come with me to Summer's funeral tomorrow. Afterward we can go to McMynn's for a few drinks and something to eat. Also, it wouldn't hurt you to go to Tacoma and see your parents."

I only thought about it for a second. "No. I don't feel like it."

"Nick, I'd be nervous too if I were shot at a few days ago. That's even more reason to get out of there for a while. It'd be safer in Seattle."

"I don't know. I feel better right here."

"Are you getting depressed?" Sue's tone turned even more concerned.

"Not sure; somewhat skittish maybe."

"You're in one of your *inertia* modes. You know the best way of curing that?"

"What?"

"Move! Do something."

I knew she had my best interests at heart. "I've been thinking that I need to learn how to defend myself. Maybe take some martial arts classes or get a gun and learn how to shoot it."

"Morg— ... I mean, I've been telling you that for a while. Not getting a gun, that's too dangerous, but learning a martial art would be good. You've been involved in some scary shit and who knows how long they're going to be coming after you. Besides, it's good exercise. You need more of that."

"What about you? You're part of this too."

"Did I tell you I've been taking self-defense classes?"

Good for her. "No."

"For a couple months now, and I've learned some pretty cool moves."

"Okay, I'll look into Karate or Tae Kwon Do or something."

"Great. I want you around."

There was a moment of silence before I said, "I think being shot at in my own home has gotten to me. Sue, do you think my life is going to be in danger until they finally get me?"

"To be honest, I think the latest incident is tied to what happened to Summer. That's my gut feeling."

"Likely." I pondered for the hundredth time the ramifications of how I was being tracked for something I didn't even know I was involved in.

"Be careful and I'll call you after the funeral."

I looked at the front door. I hadn't told her that I'd propped a chair up against the doorknob and tied a string to the deadbolt latch with a small bell at the end. I'd built a barricade. What a metaphor for how I was feeling.

CHAPTER 8

I had no choice but to go out. I went three blocks away to get groceries and booze at eleven in the morning to make sure there were people around. I was vigilant, but didn't see anyone that looked suspicious or I suspected of following me.

Once at home and unpacked, I turned on my computer.

The patter of rain on the window made me look up. It'd been gray but dry while I was out.

My attention turned to the door. I hadn't propped the chair against the knob and had a sudden urge to do it. I wasn't going out again today.

After putting the barricade back up, I felt safer.

I loaded the exposé and scrolled to the place where I'd left off yesterday. It was the part about the lab and compound in Bolivia where Naintosa and Pharmalin had been conducting human experiments. *After prolonged consumption of genetically engineered wheat and soy, the villagers developed tumors and colon cancer. A drug was being developed to manage the cancer, but a cure had yet to be found.*

Something like that had to go into my novel. Could the demented scientist hold people in a compound while he performed his experiments on them? What about a cult?

I had a sudden feeling that we'd originally missed something.

I went to my hiding place in the kitchen, where I stored my important files and documents. I opened the bottom cupboard, removed the pots and pans, and slid the particleboard bottom out. Rummaging through the folders, I found the scanned documents that Jack's team had taken out of the compound.

I had only gone through the pages twice. We'd been on the run and I had been in a hurry when I included the parts I thought were important.

I sat on the floor and read slowly, paying attention to every word.

I came to an internal memo to a man named Manny. The instructions were for him to find more people to live at the camp. The birth rate had continued to slow, even with the encouragement to procreate. *The sterility factor of the food consumption was having an effect much faster than anticipated.*

How could I have missed such an important part? They knew their genetically engineered food made people sterile. They just hadn't anticipated how fast it would happen.

I went to the desk and read it a second time.

I composed an e-mail to Ivan and Sue, typing out the part that talked about sterility word for word and then apologized for having missed it before. I added that we somehow needed to get more proof.

Naintosa actually knew they were making people sterile. Was it an unexpected side effect or part of the plan? Why would they want to prevent people from reproducing? Wouldn't they want more people in the world to eat their crap food and get cancer, so they'd have to take their drugs?

The ring of the phone startled me. I looked at the time display on the bottom right corner of my computer screen. It was just after five, so it had to be Sue calling.

"How was it?" I asked.

"Very sad," Sue said. "She was too young. There was a big

turnout, and people were frustrated and angry. Her brother spoke at the service and said the police had no leads on finding the killer or a motive."

"Was there anyone there from the *Seattle News*?"

"Yeah, like six of them. I talked to Grant, who said he wrote an article about Summer's death, but the new editor wouldn't run it."

Grant was one of the really good reporters and nice guys we used to work with, a real straight shooter. "Why not?"

"He was told it wasn't a big enough story to run." Sue sighed. "The new editor, the one who replaced *dishonest Dan,* is supposed to be a corporate GM Comm guy. He cares more about the advertisers than good journalism."

"Dan was a turncoat sack of shit who'd helped Naintosa, but at least he had cared about reporting. How could the new guy not think that a journalist who grew up in Seattle, worked for the *News* in the past, and then got murdered wasn't a good story?"

"Fuck if I know," Sue said. "Mike Couple was there. I didn't know he knew Summer? Didn't you mention Mike lives in San Francisco now?"

"Yeah, I've golfed with him a bunch of times. I never knew Mike had known Summer either. Did you get to talk to him?" We'd known Mike since our university days.

"I said hi, but got sidetracked by Grant. Mike seemed kind of nervous."

That's weird. "I haven't seen Mike in a while. I'll get in touch with him and ask."

"Another thing—at the burial there was a tall good-looking guy standing at a distance from everyone else. When I made eye contact with him, he turned and walked away."

"What did you make of that?"

"Not sure. Grant saw him too and didn't recognize him either. Could be nothing, but I thought it was worth mentioning."

"Okay," I said. "Were there any police there?"

"Yeah, two who looked like detectives."

"Was one of them Latino?"

"Yeah, shorter with a gut."

"That must've been Cortes. That means they're taking her death seriously."

"I sure hope they find who killed her and who's after you."

"Me too." I checked my Outbox to make sure my message had left. "I just sent you an e-mail about genetically engineered wheat and soy making people sterile as well as giving them cancer."

"It just arrived. Wait a second while I read it."

It took her less than a minute. "I can't believe you missed something that important."

I felt a need to get up and pace the room. "It was like six sentences, with nothing to back it up. We need to find more proof."

"Let's wait to hear if Ivan knows anything about it," Sue said. "Have you left your apartment today?"

"I went to pick up a few things."

"That's a step forward. Did you notice anyone suspicious?"

"Not that I could see."

"Okay, I need to get out of these fancy clothes and have a glass of wine."

I was done for the day, too. I clicked on the TV before going to the kitchen to get something to eat and drink. The wine Sue mentioned sounded good for a change. I had a few bottles kicking around.

I'd let the missed information muddle around in my head for a while.

Returning to the couch with a sandwich in one hand and a glass of local Syrah in the other, I had to use my left foot to clear a spot on the coffee table.

The TV was on GMNN as usual. I went for the remote to change the channel, but stopped. There was the green, block-letter logo of Naintosa on the screen. The picture changed to a huge field of corn that looked ready to be harvested. The camera panned back showing the dark-haired, dark-skinned man that was usually the anchor of the news at that hour. He always had a confident look. "The EPA announced today that it has approved Naintosa's new varieties of genetically engineered corn and wheat."

Oh shit. I wondered if it was the same strain of wheat they had been testing in Bolivia.

The screen behind the anchor turned to a rolling wheat field under a clear blue sky. "The new strain will be resistant to the company's insecticide and herbicide, allowing for less of a need to use the chemicals."

That was bullshit. I couldn't believe they expected people to fall for that song and dance. Why would a chemical company like Naintosa make something that would need less use of the product they make the most money from?

There was a knock at the door.

I nearly flipped over the back of the couch. *Are they back to get me? What do I do? Where do I hide?* Then it occurred to me that they, whoever *they* might be, wouldn't knock.

There were three more knocks.

I went to the door, but to the side of it, not directly in front. "Who is it?"

"It's Angelica, sweetie. Just checking in on you."

"Wait a second." I pulled the chair from under the knob. It slipped and thudded to the floor. I pushed it to the side. When I turned the deadbolt, the little bell rang. I tried to pull off the string as I opened the door, but it was fastened tight.

"Everything okay?" Angelica was in a skin-hugging, pink, low-cut top and jeans, holding a plate of cookies.

"Yeah, fine, why?" I tried to sound casual. "What's up?"

"I just wanted to see how you were doing. It's scary what happened to you. I talked to a few other neighbors and everyone's nervous."

I leaned on the door's edge, causing it to open halfway. The bell tinkled. "I'm okay."

She looked around me and could most likely see the chair lying on its side. Then she focused on my eyes, as if searching for any sign that I had lost it. "I baked you some chocolate-chip-and-walnut cookies. Fresh-baked cookies always comfort me."

"That's very kind of you." I tried to close the door a bit when I reached for the plate, causing the bell to ring again.

"Just let me know if you need anything." She waved.

I looked down at myself after I closed the door. She must've thought I was losing my mind. I was wearing pajama bottoms and an old T-shirt with holes in it. I hadn't showered today or shaved in four days. I was quite the sight.

I placed the plate of cookies on the coffee table and went to flip the chair upright and put it in its proper place. It took a minute to untie the tight knot around the deadbolt, then I put the bell in my desk drawer.

CHAPTER 9

When I looked at the morning paper, all I could find was a small article about what I'd seen on TV the day before. When I checked the Internet, it was the same song and dance. Should I have expected anything different?

Each article proclaimed that the new and improved second generation genetically engineered corn and wheat increased yields, and decreased insecticide and herbicide use. It was all good; safe and ready to roll. No mention of the wheat causing sterility. Who knew what the new corn really did to people.

There was no mention that the first generation had poisoned people and wreaked havoc on the environment. Naintosa had just recalled what was left of those seeds. You couldn't recall what had already been planted. Seeds from those plants were released into the environment forever. The same would happen with the next generation and the next, as they used the Earth as their giant test lab. Each failed generation would mix with the others, altering plants as a legacy for all time.

Very few people really understood what Naintosa was doing. Most, including the governments, bought into their spin of "helping feed the world and making it a better place" crap.

I shouldn't have looked at this first thing in the morning. It just angered me and made my stomach churn.

A big part of the problem was that Global Mark Communications controlled most of the media. I hadn't worried about that when I had worked for them, but now that I'd distanced myself, it was concerning. The news people consumed was very much one-sided.

I wondered if Davis Lovemark, the owner of GM Comm, and Dr. Hendrick Schmidt knew each other. Most likely.

There was a *ping* of a new e-mail arriving. It was a response from Ivan. He knew nothing about the sterility issue. No one at the Council did, either. He agreed we needed to get proof somehow, because if it was true it would have huge ramifications.

It was time to look into protecting myself.

A gun was probably a good idea, but I wasn't keen on getting one. I wasn't an anti-gun advocate and it seemed like everyone in the United States had one except for me. My biggest worry was that I'd shoot myself by accident. Of course, learning how to properly use and store a gun would diminish the chances of me killing myself.

I looked over at the holes in the wall that hadn't been filled in yet.

Then there was the question of whether I could actually pull the trigger on someone. I thought about that for a while. *Yeah, if it were life or death, them or me, I could ... I would.*

I needed help buying one. I didn't know anyone who knew about guns. Okay, so everyone in America had a gun except the people I knew.

I wrote on my *To Do* list: *Find out how to get a gun permit and to locate the nearest shooting range.* That would be Step One.

Now Step Two—self-defense. There'd been times in the past that I'd needed to defend myself and that hadn't involved having to shoot the person. I'd gotten into a couple of fights when I'd been a kid and liked boxing, but flailing my fists around wasn't effective against someone who knew what they were doing. More recently, when we'd been caught by the Naintosa security thugs, escaping and running was all we'd been able to do.

A martial art would be best. Maybe I could learn how to immobilize an attacker with pressure points. I looked down at my expanding belly. Some exercise would be good. Which martial art though? The problem was, I didn't have years to learn and practice.

After over an hour of research I couldn't decide between Aikido and Karate. There were classes being offered close by for both, so I'd take a look. Maybe there was some kind of crash course for one of them.

I hadn't had things on my *To Do* list for a while; now I had two.

Flipping through the channels, I stopped on GMNN when I saw the logo behind the anchor. There was a gene graphic next to *PHARMALIN* in blue serif letters.

Now what are they doing? They'd been quiet in the media for quite a while.

The familiar anchor wore a navy blue jacket over a shiny ivory blouse. I'd always thought that her ancestry was Egyptian, because of her strong features and olive skin. The bangs of her black hair were always cut straight, just above her eyebrows. She was attractive in an exotic way.

"Pharmalin Pharmaceuticals has just applied to the FDA for approval of their as yet unnamed colon cancer drug," the anchor said. "This drug is touted to be revolutionary in the fight against cancer and is slated to be fast-tracked through the process."

The background picture turned to a man and woman in white lab coats, wearing protective goggles, looking at a Petri dish.

"The scientific community had been kept in the dark regarding

Pharmalin's new drug until recently," the anchor continued. "Details released for peer review three months ago have unanimous approval of the credibility of their results."

What? That had to be the same drug they'd been developing in Bolivia. It was meant to control cancer, not cure it.

The anchor turned her head to the right and the camera panned to a man sitting beside her in a charcoal suit and purple patterned tie. "Looks like a great day for our fight against cancer, Steve."

Pharmalin was just rolling along, jumping through the well greased hoops of the FDA to get their drug to market. They paid off the right scientists and doctors to get the results they wanted and were now beginning their media spin campaign. Crap.

The phone rang. I looked to where it was supposed to be, but it wasn't there. I'd forgotten to put it back on the charger. Looking around and listening to the rings, I spotted it on my desk.

"Howdy, Nick, it's Jack Carter," he said in his true Texan drawl. "How you been?"

Hearing from him was unexpected. "Good and you?"

"Just fine. Say, Nick, are you a golfer?"

"Uh, yes I am, sir."

"Would you be interested in going on a little golf getaway? We could catch up." He paused for a second and then continued. "Seems like things are stirrin' up and I'd like to talk to you about it … if you're not too busy."

"Of course." It took me less than a second to decide. "There are some things I'd like to discuss with you too. Your opinion would be appreciated."

"We can help each other."

"When and where?"

"I've asked Sue to come along as well."

Sue too? "Great, I haven't seen her in a while."

My phone beeped, indicating another incoming call. I ignored it.

"Ever been to Bandon Dunes?"

"No, but I've wanted to go since it opened."

"Perfect. Is tomorrow too soon?"

That would be a great way to cure my inactivity and get back out into the world. "Yeah, sure. I could make it work."

He gave me directions to a secondary terminal at the airport. "Just give them your name and they'll take care of you."

"Looking forward to seeing you again, Jack."

"Me too, Nick."

As I placed the phone on its charger, I thought back to when Jack helped save us. He'd been dressed all in black, even his face painted, with an assault rifle in his hands. He looked younger than his sixty-nine years, and virile. He knew what to do and acted on it. But that didn't affect the big heart he had. Before that night we'd grown accustomed to him being in shorts and sandals—really laid-back. I had tremendous respect for Jack Carter.

Jack had been an oil and cattle tycoon, but sold off the businesses a few years back. He had plenty of money and wanted to do good things in the world, to compensate for all the bad he and his companies had done in the past.

Before I'd met Jack I'd heard that the reason he dismantled his empire was because he was in distress after his wife died from cancer, and neither of his two children wanted to take over the family businesses. I still didn't know whether it was true.

The little red light on the phone cradle was lit. Oh yeah, someone had called while I'd been talking to Jack.

The message was from Sue, of course. She was excited and wanted me to call right away.

"I was talking to Jack Carter when you left the message."

"What do you think?" Her pitch was high.

"Let's go and find out what's happening. He has access to information we don't, or can get it easier than we can."

"I agree, but what specifically are we talking about?"

"I bet it's about what's been on the news the last two days regarding Naintosa and Pharmalin," I said. "I don't have a set schedule, but can you get away from the magazine for the week?"

"As long as I meet the deadline, which isn't for ten days, they don't care. I can always do some writing there."

"Great," I said. "What time are you leaving tomorrow?"

"I'm supposed to be at the airport at eight-thirty a.m. I think it's going to be a private plane. And you?"

"Nine o'clock. Don't you think a private plane for each of us is a little over the top?"

"Let's just go with it."

"Okay, looks like we'll be flying in at about the same time. It'll be good to see you." In case this turned out to be another adventure I'd want her along.

"Yeah, it's been six months since I've seen your mug."

I took one step toward the bedroom and then hesitated. What if the person who tried to break in discovered I was gone for a while? If they wanted something specific, not just me, they might try again. Before I started packing, I copied everything of importance I could think of onto a disk that I'd take with me. Then I made sure what little I had of value was secured in my secret hiding place.

CHAPTER 10

"Where are you off to?"

I took a sharp breath as my keys fell to the floor.

"Oh sorry sweetie, did I startle you?" Angelica was standing to my right.

How the hell did she get there without me seeing her? "I didn't hear you walk up." I bent down to get my keys. "Where're you going so early?"

"I need to get to school to do some stuff before class." She was in jeans, an open white jacket over a pink top and pink pumps. "Going on a trip?"

I looked at my suitcase and golf club travel bag. "Yeah, I'm going to play golf for a few days."

"That's good you're going to get away after what happened. Where?"

"Bandon Dunes, in Oregon."

She looked at me for a second. "Why don't you go someplace warm?"

"Someone invited me and the courses are supposed to be great."

"Oh, who?"

I was realizing she could be quite nosy. "You wouldn't know him."

"That's true. How long are you gone for?"

"Not positive, maybe a week."

"Okay, I'll keep an eye on your place for you. Do you want to give me a spare set of keys?"

"I don't have a spare set yet. You know, with the new lock. If you see that someone broke in, just call the police."

"What about your cat?"

"Huh? I don't have a cat."

"Oh. When I came over to give you the cookies, I kept hearing a bell tinkle." She shrugged. "Just like the one I had on my cat's collar at home, so the birds would hear Clementine coming."

I felt my face warm and I didn't know what to say. "Uh, yeah, that was something else."

She looked at me as if waiting for an explanation.

"Well, I'd better get to the airport."

I did what Jack had told me to do and ended up in a part of the airport I'd never been to. It was a small terminal away from the main one.

At a counter I gave my name to a pleasant young brunette. She looked at my driver's license and then a computer screen. After a moment she pointed me in the right direction.

I held onto my black suitcase handle with my right hand and my silver molded golf travel case with my left as they rolled behind me.

There weren't many people around. The few who were there walked with purpose, needing to get somewhere.

Security was tight. I wondered if the rich had to go through a metal detector and have their luggage x-rayed before September 11 just to get to their own planes. Probably not.

A shuttle bus drove me to a hangar where a small jet waited outside on the tarmac. By the name on the tail, I knew it was a rental jet. I'd only ever been on bigger commercial flights and felt excited.

The interior of the plane had a long couch along the right side. On the left there were two sets of thick tan leather seats facing each other with polished dark wooden tables set in the middle. I sat down in a chair facing forward. I was the only person there.

It was the first time since the planes hit the World Trade Center and Pentagon five months ago that I was going to fly. Even though it was a private flight, the thought gave me a twinge of anxiety.

A screen opened in the front and two pilots and a flight attendant came out of the cockpit. The pilots were both tall and had to bend over slightly so as not to hit their heads on the cabin ceiling. Their matching white shirts with gold logos over their left breast pockets and gold epaulettes on their shoulders made them look official. The flight attendant was petite and pretty. She wore a white shirt like the pilots, minus the epaulettes, but formfitting. She had long black hair, flawless brown skin, and brilliant white teeth. I guessed her origin was Filipino.

I don't know why, but I stood up.

"Welcome aboard, Mr. Barnes," said one of the men. "We'll be your crew on our short flight to North Bend. I'm Don." He pointed to the man on the left. "This here's my co-pilot, Steve." He moved his finger forward a few inches. "And lovely Susie here will make sure you're comfortable."

"Am I the only passenger?"

"Yes, sir." He looked at his wristwatch. "It's about time we head off. The flight will only take ninety minutes, which puts us in North Bend around ten forty-five." He gave me a mock salute. "See you there."

The pilots went back to the cockpit, closing the accordion type screen behind them.

"Have a seat, Mr. Barnes," said Susie. Her accent sounded more Midwestern than Southeast Asian.

I returned to the chair I'd chosen. It was comfortable with just the right soft-to-firm ratio, and it swiveled.

"Do you need anything before we take off?" She flashed her almost too-white teeth.

"No, I'm fine."

Within minutes we were moving and didn't have to wait long to take off.

The jet shuddered and shook as it thrust through the dark clouds. Then we burst out into the bright sunshine, and all was calm.

Susie offered me a mimosa, but I didn't want to meet Jack with a buzz, because I probably wouldn't stop at one. I settled for a coffee and blueberry scone.

I wondered what Jack wanted to discuss. He wasn't the type to just "catch up." Most likely it was more detail on the latest news about Naintosa and Pharmalin, but it could be something else. I wanted to ask him if he knew more about the wheat and soy causing sterility, and tell him about Summer and the attempted break-in.

The cloud cover was thick below, so there was nothing to look at and I didn't feel like watching a movie. *I should meditate.*

I closed my eyes, inhaled deep, and slowly exhaled.

We hit some turbulence, which jostled me in my seat.

Okay, try again. Relax.

"Can I get you anything else, Mr. Barnes?"

I opened one eye. "No thanks, Susie."

"How long do you plan on being in Oregon?"

"Maybe a week. Not quite sure."

"It must be nice to just go with the flow and not be on a set schedule."

I hoped to never go back to a regular job working for someone else. "It is, actually."

Meditation wasn't going to happen right now. Maybe Susie's original recommendation of a mimosa wasn't such a bad idea.

We landed right on schedule, pulling up next to a row of six parked private jets.

The pilot came out of the cockpit and unlocked the door. As it lowered, he turned to me and raised his hand to his forehead. That mock salute would get annoying if he did it all the time.

As soon as I stepped off the plane I was hit by a gust of cool, moist wind with a hint of brine in it. I was surprised that the plane had landed so smoothly, what with the air being that turbulent.

A tall man in a black suit got out of a black Suburban parked fifty feet away. His close-cropped wheat-colored hair and straight posture made me think of the military or secret service. When he got close, he spoke in an authoritative voice. "I'll take you to the resort, Mr. Barnes."

He picked up my luggage, which had been taken out of the storage hatch by a man in an orange vest, and I followed him to the large SUV.

As we approached, the back door opened. "Hello, stranger."

"Sue!"

She came out and gave me a big hug, standing on her tiptoes. "Good to see you in the flesh."

"And you." I pulled back and looked her up and down. "You look great as usual—all fit and beautiful."

Sue's perky curves were partially covered by an unzipped gray hoody. Her auburn, shoulder-length hair was tied in a ponytail. Sue's blue eyes glistened, yet the scar under her right eyebrow was still visible.

"You've been drinking already?" she said as more of a statement than a question.

"I just had two mimosas."

Sue smiled. "I had one too." She reached out and patted my belly beneath my jacket. "At least you're eating well. Or is that all booze?"

"I haven't made it to the gym lately. Besides, last time you told me I was getting too skinny."

"No, you looked good … still look good." She poked me. "You need a happy medium."

Our chauffeur was holding the open vehicle door, a blank look on his face.

"We should get in," I said.

Sue went first, sliding all the way over to make room for me.

"So what are you going to do while we're playing golf?" I asked.

"Take lessons. I told Jack I don't play but would like to learn."

"I've been bugging you for years to take it up. You'll be good at it, like every sport you try, Miss Coordinated Ex-Gymnast."

"We'll see. I brought my laptop, so I can always get some work done."

We pulled onto the highway and headed south out of North Bend. The black leather bench seat was cushy and we swayed as the big SUV navigated the windy road.

"At this time of year if you want to play golf, wouldn't you want to go to Arizona or Florida or Maui?" Sue asked. "It's a little cool here."

"You could, but the courses at Bandon are supposed to be awesome. It's more like playing in Scotland, especially at this time of year. The place is turning into a Mecca for golfers in North America."

"I suppose I'd have to be a golfer to understand. I'd rather be in a hot place."

A corner pitched both of us right in our seats. The driver could've slowed down a bit.

"You seem to be taking golf more seriously now," Sue said.

"You know, I've golfed on and off since I was a teenager. Since I've moved to San Francisco, I've been playing a couple times a week."

Sue looked out the window and my eyes followed. There were no more houses. The road wound through a forest of shore pines with cypresses dispersed among them. Open areas of dark sand were bare blotches on the landscape.

Sue turned back to me. "We do trust Jack, right?"

I noticed the driver take a quick glance back at us through the rearview mirror.

I shifted my eyes toward the chauffeur so Sue could see. "Of course. Look at how he went out of his way to help us … save us before."

Sue gave me a subtle nod of understanding. "I agree, but had to ask."

Chances were that the man behind the wheel could be trusted, but best to keep the conversation superficial.

I was distracted by large dunes out the right window. "That's a lot of sand."

"Maybe you could rent a dirt bike one afternoon while you're here?"

"That'd be fun." I'd raced motocross when I was a teenager, and every once in a while, like now, I got an itch to ride.

In a few minutes the Suburban slowed and signaled to the right. Just before the turn, a long log lay on its side with the inscription, "Welcome to Bandon Dunes."

The flat, narrow road wound through the trees for over a mile. There were what looked like patches of thick gorse and open pockets of sand in the underbrush.

We emerged from the trees and saw a large building across a ravine. The road wound down and around, then up the other side. A sign pointing to the right read "Practice Area" and "Pacific Dunes." A second sign pointing straight ahead read "Bandon Dunes" and "Lodge." We went straight.

At the top stood a two-story, wooden-shingled structure with a circular driveway in front of it. To the right were a few other buildings stained brown like the lodge, but only one story, with a half-empty parking lot behind them.

A gray shuttle bus was leaving as we entered the driveway and another was right behind us. We pulled up directly in front of the entrance.

The driver got out and we followed.

After pulling out our luggage from the back, he said, "Go to the front desk and tell them who you are. They'll give you keys for the Lodge Suite. Jack will meet you there."

"Thanks for the ride." *Should I tip him?*

CHAPTER 11

At the center of the lobby were four rock pillars, varying in height from five to eight feet. Above them the ceiling opened up to the second floor. At the far end was an entrance to a restaurant, and to the right, a comfortable-looking lounge.

The vertical-wood-paneled front desk had accent lighting shining down from a wooden trellis. There was a smiling young woman waiting for us, and when we gave her our names, she produced two keys.

"Head on up to the Lodge Suite." She pointed to the staircase with wrought iron railing that rose up through the opening in the ceiling. "Hang a right at the top and then a left down the hall."

As we lugged our suitcases and my club bag up the stairs, we saw the square opening went right to a vaulted ceiling supported by dark wooden beams.

As we reached the second floor I saw the two silver doors. "Why didn't we take the elevator?"

Sue smiled. "This place is nice, in a masculine sort of way."

The suite was at the end of the hall. We used my key to open the door.

"Should we've knocked?" Sue asked from behind.

I was already one step inside. "Probably."

The room looked smaller than it was, because of the overstuffed caramel leather couch and four chairs with big ottomans. The focal point was a wood-framed gas fireplace with a TV mounted above it. On the opposite side was a bar with various types of glasses and mugs aligned in neat rows on the counter alongside a black coffeemaker.

"This *really* is a guys' retreat," Sue said.

I could see her point. The gray walls and carpet, wood-beamed ceiling, golf pictures, and wrought iron fixtures, were definitely masculine. I liked it. There were no flowery colors or accents anywhere. It would be fine for Sue, because even though she didn't look like a guy, she acted like one at times.

Jack walked into the room from the hallway on the left. "Hey, there y'all are." The lively drawl was strong as ever.

"Hi, Jack." Sue let go of her suitcase and walked over to give him a hug.

"Good to see you." I was right behind her and shook his hand. "Thanks for inviting us."

"Glad you could make it on such short notice." He was dressed for golf in a black shirt with thin white vertical stripes and solid black pants. His weathered skin was tanned, and the wrinkles around his mouth and hazel eyes deepened when he smiled. His gray hair was thick, close-cropped, and flat on the top. I'd seen an old picture at his place in Maui of him in the marines, his hair cut the same but brown. "Looking gorgeous, Miss Sue. I see you're not starving, Nick."

"I haven't been able to get to the gym lately."

Sue snickered.

"Just jokin', son." He patted my shoulder. "We have a tee time in less than an hour. Sue, I booked a lesson for you and rented some clubs."

"Thank you," Sue said.

"Your rooms are that-a-way." He pointed to a hallway on the right. "Go ahead and change. We'll go to the driving range with you, Sue. I want to hit a few balls and loosen up before we play."

The man who drove us from the airport came through the door.

"Y'all know Lee," Jack said.

Lucky I hadn't tried to tip him. "We haven't been formally introduced."

"Lee's, uh, like my personal assistant. You may not recognize him without the camouflage on his face, but he was with us at the camp the night we got the Naintosa thugs."

Lee stood straight as an arrow, hands at his sides. That was probably as relaxed as he'd get. The two men helping Jack rescue us that night in Maui had been outfitted in all black; it had been dark, and there was a lot going on, so I hadn't recognized him.

"Sorry, that night's still a blur to me," Sue said.

"Best it stay that way," Jack said.

"Hey, how's Moose?" I remembered the young Rottweiler who'd distracted the thugs long enough for Jack and his men to get into position.

"Bigger, friendlier, and full-a-drool," Jack said.

Sue and I smiled. We'd all been really fond of that dog.

"Lee, get out of that monkey suit and ready to play," Jack ordered.

Lee blinked, then strode down the hallway on the left.

Jack smiled. "He's the strong silent type, but I trust him with my life. He's gotten me out of plenty of binds. And wait until you see him pound the ball."

Sue took the first room down the right hall. I took the farthest one.

It was a decent size bedroom with light beige walls and dark beige carpet. The furniture was made of pine. The brown duvet on the bed looked comfortable and warm. There was no need for a bedspread at the man's retreat.

Looking through my suitcase, I decided on a periwinkle-blue shirt and gray pants with a thin white stripe. It was appropriate to dress sharper when playing a good course.

I went to the window to see if I could predict the weather for the afternoon. The view was of multiple fairways cut through grass-covered dunes and ocean in the distance. Thick white clouds lurked on the horizon, but the sky above was still blue. It looked fine now, but that could change.

Going back to my suitcase, I rummaged around to find a charcoal sweater, black rain pullover, and golf cap. Then I pulled out my club bag and stuffed the clothes into the long pocket.

I was about to leave when I remembered the backup disk. Looking around the room I decided to tape it to the back of the dresser with the duct tape I'd brought with me, just as a precaution.

CHAPTER 12

J ack had set Sue up for her lesson at the driving range, then joined Lee and me to warm up.

I'd discovered that taking a big divot on the fescue grass with hard packed sand underneath was not a good strategy after I jarred my wrists. I watched Lee and Jack clip the grass as they swung; both were good players. From then on I focused on a sweeping swing, picking the ball more.

"Time to go," Jack said after fifteen minutes.

Walking to the shuttle that came for us, I could see Sue talking to a tall, preppy-looking guy near a small building at the edge of the range. She had her head tilted and was giving him her full attention.

Is she flirting with him? Why does that still get to me? I shouted, "You gonna be okay?"

She raised her hand. "Yeah, sure. See you back at the lodge after."

Jack patted my shoulder when I sat down next to him in the shuttle. "We're gonna have fun."

"Can't wait." I was looking forward to a relaxing round of golf on a great course with my worries set aside.

From where the shuttle dropped us off, to reach the first tee of the Bandon Dunes Golf Course, we only had to walk a few yards between the lodge and clubhouse.

A breeze had come up. It was cool, with a hint of freshly cut grass and ocean saltiness.

Four men in golf attire milled around the first tee box. One elderly gentleman holding a clipboard stood off to the right, next to a podium. Four of seven young men in white coveralls stood next to the bags of the men on the tee and three next to the starter. A couple of the caddies had black stocking caps on with *Looper* embroidered in white.

Lee came up and positioned himself between Jack and me, easing me to the left with his shoulder.

"What the …" *Why's he pushing me over?*

"Jack Carter," exclaimed one of the four waiting to start playing, stepping toward us. He was sixty-ish, around my height, and well groomed.

"Davis, fancy seeing you here," Jack replied. "Are you taking the game more seriously? Thought you'd be in more southern climes this time of year."

As the man walked up I noticed a discoloration between his chin and right cheek the size and color of a copper penny.

"It's been years since we've played," said the man Jack called Davis. "I'm much better now. I've been spending more time at my San Francisco office and thought I'd come up for a couple rounds."

The other three men he was with came up behind him.

"How long are you here for?" His smile looked more like a sneer. "We should play. I might be able to make some of the money back from our past wagers." He had a New York accent, but with a British stiffness.

The man looked familiar, but I couldn't place him.

"I've got some business to attend to while I'm here," Jack said.

"What've you been doing these days?" Davis asked. "You've dropped off the radar completely."

"I like it that way."

"You're not the same old Jack, my friend."

Polite conversation aside, Davis and Jack were sizing each other up. There was tension in the air.

"Times and priorities have changed," Jack said.

"Priorities are not usually good to change," Davis replied.

"It sure is in my case. You should try it."

"Not in a million years." Davis' face went serious and he nodded. "Lee."

Lee nodded back, but didn't say anything.

I suddenly realized who he was. That was Davis Lovemark, the chairman of Global Mark Communications, the world's largest media baron. I should've recognized him right away.

Lovemark turned and waved one of the others forward. "Jack, have you met my second-in-command, Russell Norman?"

"Yeah, we met once, briefly." Norman had an Australian accent, was taller, around six-foot-three, and in his fifties.

"Yes." Jack extended his hand as a courteous gesture.

The sneering grin returned to Lovemark's face as he looked to me. "Davis Lovemark. And you are?"

"Nick Barnes."

His right eyebrow rose and the smile left his face. "Oh … nice to meet you."

It was like he knew who I was. I'd never met Lovemark or his right-hand man, Norman, even though I'd worked for one of their papers.

"The tee is yours, Mr. Lovemark," said the starter with the clipboard in hand.

"Maybe we'll catch up later." Lovemark was looking at Jack, but gave me a quick glance.

"Maybe," Jack said.

We watched them tee off.

Lovemark sliced his ball into the dunes on the right. If that was an improvement, I wondered what his swing had been like before.

Norman did the exact opposite and hooked his ball into the left dunes, but got a fortuitous bounce and the ball kicked closer to the fairway.

The two big burly guys in the group who hadn't been introduced must've been assistants-slash-bodyguards. They had good swings, and knew what they were doing.

"He's improved." Jack was watching the foursome walk down the first fairway, caddies in tow.

"He was worse?" I asked.

Jack smiled and patted my shoulder.

"Do you know Mr. Lovemark well?" I asked.

"All my life." Jack turned serious. "Didn't expect to see him here."

I'd read that Lovemark came from old money. His family had been wealthy ever since the printing press was invented.

Jack bent over to take a ball out of his bag. "Let's enjoy our round."

The three young men in white coveralls, who'd been waiting off to the side, approached us.

"We'll be your caddies today, gentlemen," the tallest one said as he went straight to Jack. "Ian. Pleasure to meet you, Mr. Carter."

"Hi, I'm, John," said the caddie that approached me. "Can I carry your bag today, sir?" He was in his early twenties, light-haired, and looked like a plain old good guy.

"Sure, I'm Nick."

John had a broad, easygoing smile. "Let's have some fun."

Fun sounded good.

It had taken a good fifteen minutes for the group ahead of us to hit their second shots and progress out of our range. That was the time it should've taken to play the entire hole.

"You first, Nick," Jack said.

I looked at the long, wide, and straight fairway that had a gradual uphill rise. I put the tee in the ground and a brand new ball on top of it. As I took a practice swing the nerves kicked in. That happened on the first tee every time I played with anyone I wanted to impress. *Don't screw it up. Aim down the middle and swing easy.* I visualized the ball flight I wanted. "Play well."

"Play well," Jack and Lee said at the same time.

I hit the ball off the toe of the driver, so I didn't get all the distance I could've and it faded to the right, but still in the fairway.

"Good shot," Jack said. He motioned for Lee to go next.

Lee went up to the tee, took two languid practice swings with lots of flexibility, and then piped his drive three hundred yards right down the middle.

"Shit," said John.

"Great shot," Lee's caddie said with a Spanish accent. He was almost as tall as Lee, but not as broad and half his age.

Jack was next. With an aggressive swing he hit it as far as mine, but straight. "And we're off."

The fescue on the fairway was cut short and the ground underneath was hard and undulating. Rolling dunes on each side had long wispy grass that moved with the breeze. Sunshine made bits of moisture in the grass sparkle.

I made John stop, so I could pull my sweater from my bag.

Lovemark's group was still on the green when we got to where our first shots ended up, so we had to wait a few minutes.

My second shot looked somewhat daunting. The green was raised about ten feet and I could only see the first part of it because of a hump in the middle. There were pot bunkers on the left side that looked hungry for my ball.

Once Lovemark's group had cleared, we proceeded.

Jack's ball landed on the green, but took a hard bounce over to the right. My ball landed just short and rolled down between the bunkers. Lee hit a towering shot that bounced once and then rolled over the hump toward the pin.

As we walked I admired the layout. "What a great hole this is."

Jack smiled. "There're seventeen more of these beauties."

I didn't get the club underneath the ball with my third shot and it raced past the hole to the end of the green. A long putt, followed by a short putt that just caught enough of the hole to go in and I had managed a one over par—five.

Jack bogeyed the hole as well and Lee had a par.

As we went along we had to wait for the group in front of us on almost every shot. If they didn't hurry up, it was going to take us forever to finish.

I noticed Jack frown as he watched Lovemark, who was looking back at us with his sneer. That wasn't relaxing and fun.

The breeze was getting stronger and to the west a wall of gray cloud had neared.

Standing on the fourth tee the fairway looked like a chute with a dead end. There were large dunes on each side and straight ahead about two hundred yards out was a bunker.

"What do we do here?" I asked John.

"This is a dogleg right." He pulled a club out of my bag and handed it to me. "An easy five wood."

For the first time Lee was having a conversation with his caddie. "I'll just aim it at the right edge of the dunes and fade it."

The caddie put his hand on the top of the driver in the bag. "The wind is going to hold the ball up and it's going to go straight. Then you're going to be long and in the junk."

The look Lee gave his caddie made him pull his hand off the club and step back.

Note to self: never mess with Lee.

Lee was up first. I'd parred the last hole, but he'd parred all of the first three. Jack had bogeyed all of them so far.

The shot went exactly as the caddie predicted and disappeared into the far dunes.

Lee was stone-faced and stepped aside to watch Jack and I hit.

Both of us followed our caddies' instructions and put our shots in the middle of the fairway.

When we reached our balls, which were only a couple of yards apart, Jack said, "Isn't that something?"

I looked up and followed his gaze to the right. It looked like the green in the distance was perched right on the edge of the Pacific.

Ocean air filled my nostrils as the wind came up the chute. A mile or so out was a wall of steel-gray cloud. "Stunning."

As usual the group ahead was still playing the hole. We had to watch Lovemark chip his ball across the green before taking three putts to put it in the hole.

"Are they playing that bad on purpose just to slow us up?" I wondered out loud.

Jack attempted a smile, but I could see the underlying frustration. "If they're trying to annoy us, it's working."

Finally, the group sauntered off with no demonstrable sense of urgency to speed up the pace.

It was a long iron shot for both of us to reach the green. Jack put his ball smack in the middle. I pulled my shot and ended up in the front left bunker.

As Jack, our caddies, and I were walking, we saw Lee's ball fly out from the mounds. It was coming in too hot and skipped over the back of the green, disappearing into what looked like the ocean.

When I stepped down into the heavy burnt orange brown sand of the bunker, I could only see the surface of the green if I went up on my tiptoes. I had to hit the ball straight up in the air to clear the wall of sand only a few feet in front of me.

I swung too hard and my club didn't get underneath the ball enough. The ball clipped the top of the bunker and disappeared. "Crap."

"It went over the green," said John, holding a rake.

Jack was walking in the direction of where my ball had flown to help me find it.

As I strode to the edge I discovered that we weren't as close to the ocean as it appeared before. Past the green was about twenty feet of long grass before a cliff.

I paused for a second to take in the scenery. Forty feet below was a beach that stretched either way as far as the eye could see. The tan-colored sand looked flawless. The only sound was of waves breaking. Nothing could be seen out at sea but white caps over rolling water. The gray cloud in the distance was progressing closer.

Lee flopped his ball out of the rough to about three feet from the hole.

My ball had nestled into the taller grass. I managed to chop it onto the green and then two-putt. It had taken me six shots to complete the hole.

Jack two-putted for par.

Lee rimmed his first putt and settled for a bogey—five.

That was a great hole. I wished I hadn't screwed it up.

The next two holes followed the ocean, heading north. Each time I glanced to the west the wall of cloud was closer and darker.

As we exited the sixth green, a glint of light caught my eye. I looked over at a dune in the distance and saw a person facing in our direction holding binoculars.

Jack had come up next to me. "What's wrong?"

"There's someone over there watching us." I pointed.

"I don't see anyone," he said.

The dune was now empty. "He was there a second ago."

Jack looked at Lee, who'd stopped as well, but they didn't say anything.

We followed our caddies inland.

CHAPTER 13

"How do you like the course so far?" Jack asked after we finished playing the first nine holes.

"Best I've ever played." I motioned to where Lovemark had just sent another shot off-course. "Too bad it's so slow."

"Yeah, I hear ya." Jack shook his head. "I'll make sure they're not in front of us when we play Pacific Dunes tomorrow."

I could see that there was a temper beneath Jack's laid-back attitude.

I added up my score as we waited on the tenth tee box. Forty-two—respectable.

Each hole on this course was a masterpiece. The fairways rolled and pitched with collection areas and bunkers that challenged every player. It rewarded good shot-making and penalized poor decisions and miss-hits. The greens were undulating, hard, and true.

Behind the fourteenth hole was the largest of the fescue-covered dunes. It wasn't in play because it was fifty yards past the green. The only reason it got my attention was that I swore I saw some movement. Was there someone lying on top watching us?

Lee and Jack were observing the top of the dune as well.

It dawned on me that we hadn't seen the Lovemark group in

LAWRENCE VERIGIN

front of us for two holes.

Just as I was about to swing, I heard someone hit a ball.

I turned around and saw that Lee had shot out of turn and was walking quickly toward the dune.

Jack raised his arm. "Sorry, go ahead, Nick."

Jack and I watched the top of the dune as we approached the green, but couldn't see anything. We were fast to putt out and picked up Lee's ball, conceding him a birdie.

As we came around the big dune, Lee's caddie was standing on the path, looking nervous. Lee was descending down through the wispy grass and shrugged to us.

The caddies fell back behind us, seeming to not want to lead anymore.

"Is it common to have people watching you when you play?" I decided to ask Jack.

"Nope."

"So who do you think it was?"

"I'd say someone who doesn't want us to know they're there."

The fifteenth hole was a short uphill par three, with a big dune on the left and a large, steep faced bunker short right. The wall of now-menacing charcoal cloud was the backdrop. A shot hit too long looked like it would disappear into the abyss.

"Rain's coming," Jack said.

The dark veil was almost over us and a steady wind blew right into us.

Lee stood facing the dune that separated the last green and our tee box.

Jack took a practice swing. "When it's breezy, swing easy." He hit a hybrid club straight. It bounced once that we could see and disappeared up on or over the green.

I did the opposite of Jack's advice and pulled it left. The ball hit the side of the dune. "Kick off of there." It bounced toward the

84

green, but was stopped by some high fescue.

Lee looked rushed and swung hard. The ball ballooned and the wind knocked it down into the big sand trap. "Fuck." That was the first word he'd said out loud in hours.

We each proceeded to where our balls ended up.

Lee's bunker shot popped high into the air. I could see it spinning backward as if in slow motion. Another great shot onto the green.

My ball had settled behind a clump of wispy grass. It was steep and downhill to the pin.

"You're going to have to hack it out," said John. "But not too far or it'll roll into the bunker Mr. Donald just came out of."

"Who? You mean Lee?" That was the first time I'd heard his last name.

I took a stab at the ball and it worked. It popped out and had enough momentum to roll down near the hole.

The wind was howling now and the cumulonimbus began to dump its contents at a sharp angle.

"Better get our rain gear on," Jack shouted.

As we went to our golf bags, something hit mine so hard it broke the stand in half, dropping the bag to the ground.

Something then hit Lee's caddie, sending him backward into a heap.

There was a *whoosh* an inch from my face. I dove.

Everyone else hit terra firma too.

"Fuck!" John got hit right in the ass.

Lee was crawling on all fours when he was hit in the side. He only flinched. "That's all you got?" He got up and ran full tilt toward the dune.

There was a golf ball lying where Lee had been hit. *We're being attacked with golf balls? Really?* They weren't errant shots; these were coming in so hard and fast it was as if they were being shot out of a gun.

One struck my thigh. "Fuck." Did it break my bone? I rolled over, clutching my leg. Closing my eyes, I saw stars.

I forced myself to push back the pain and pay attention to the surroundings. I didn't know where to go. We were caught in the open, pinned down.

Where's Jack? I looked over and saw him lying behind his bag. Three balls hit the bag in succession, but missed him. He'd chosen his cover wisely.

Another ball just missed my face. I had to make a run for it. I jumped up. As soon as I put weight on my leg I stumbled from the pain. That saved me, because I'd gone down on one knee as a ball grazed my cap and sent it flying. Then I was hit in the same leg again. That put me face first onto the green.

"Nick, stay down!" Jack yelled.

It hurt like hell. All I could do was lie there and protect my face with my hands.

The rain came down in forty-five degree sheets, stinging every part of exposed skin and drenching us.

The pounding of balls stopped.

Lee came out from the dune holding what looked like an old elephant gun. "It's okay, you can all get up."

Jack yelled, "Is that the weapon?"

It was a rifle with a barrel big enough to shoot a golf ball. Underneath was a tray that held a row of maybe a dozen balls and a small compressed air tank. It looked heavy and cumbersome.

"It was mounted on a tripod. There were two guys who got away on an ATV." Lee was heading straight for Jack. "You okay?"

"Unscathed." Jack came up to me. "Nick got hit a couple times. How are you, son?"

I felt my thigh over my pants. I had two golf ball size bumps an inch apart that hurt even more when I touched them.

"Lucky they hit the meaty part." Jack was standing over me and helped me get to my feet.

I could stand okay, but was shaky to walk, so Jack aided me to my bag so I could sit down on top of it.

John was holding his butt cheek. Jack's caddie wasn't hit, but Lee's was lying facedown on the green and not moving.

Lee went up to his caddie and rolled him over. His ear was bleeding. Lee felt for a pulse on his neck.

"Is he breathing?" Jack asked.

"He's alive, but out cold. We'd better get him some help." Lee pulled a cell phone from his pant pocket and called the lodge.

I had to yell to be heard, because the wind and rain weren't letting up. "We need to get him some shelter."

Lee placed his arms under the unconscious man's armpits and picked his torso up. Each of the other caddies took a leg and they carried him behind the big dune my ball had landed on.

Jack placed my arm over his shoulder and I limped in that direction.

I was able to sit down on a raised mound covered in wet grass.

The wind was less severe there, but the rain still pelted us, making it hard to see.

Within minutes four six-wheeled Gators raced up. Sue was in one of them.

"I was getting back to the lodge after my lesson when these men were heading off," she shouted, as soon as they stopped beside us. "I just knew it was you three who were in trouble."

One Gator had a stretcher strapped to the back of it. Two men pulled it off and went straight to the unconscious caddie. A third man followed with a red first aid kit that looked like a small toolbox.

"There'll be an ambulance waiting at the lodge," a man holding a walkie-talkie stated. "Anyone else hurt?"

"Nick there got hit a couple times," Jack said. "John there got hit in the rump. And Lee … you okay, Lee?"

Lee waved the man off.

Sue was looking me up and down. "What happened?"

"Someone was shooting golf balls at us."

She raised her eyebrows, but before she could say anything the man with the walkie-talkie was beside us.

"Where were you hit?" he asked.

I pointed to my thigh. "Twice."

"Can I take a look?"

"I guess." With slight hesitation I undid my wet pants and pulled them down to my knees. There were goose bumps on my legs around dark red welts. Lucky I had clean boxers on.

"It's like someone hit a driver from ten feet away and the golf balls got imbedded under your skin." He touched my thigh.

I almost fell over. "Ouch!"

CHAPTER 14

The rotating lights of the ambulance flashed as they took away the still unconscious caddie.

"Sue, can you help Nick up to the room?" Jack asked. "Lee and I need to talk to someone in the office. We'll be up in a bit."

My leg had stiffened on the bumpy ride back to the lodge. I placed my arm around Sue to help take some of the weight off and then concentrated on each step.

Once in the suite Sue deposited me on the edge of my bed.

"Do you want me to help you change?" she asked.

"No, I can manage."

"Good." She smiled. "Seeing you in your underwear once is enough for the day."

"Ha, ha."

"I'm going to go put on some dry clothes. Call if you need me."

The two bruises on my thigh had turned into one blue and black welt the size of a grapefruit. Every movement felt like my skin over the wound was stretching to the point of tearing. I had to lie down to pull off my sopping wet pants, real slow.

Lucky my suitcase was near the bed.

Putting on dry underwear and sweatpants felt good. I used a sweatshirt to rub dry my hair before I put it on; it was too far to get a towel from the bathroom.

There was a knock at the door. "Are you ready?"

Sue helped me to the couch in the living room.

"Hard to believe," she said, after I told her what happened in full detail. "Being shot at by golf balls … that's a first."

"You saw the gun."

"I didn't get a good look."

"Well, it did happen."

"I know. It's just odd that someone would go to all that trouble. Why didn't they just use an actual gun?"

"I'm really happy they didn't use a gun with bullets."

"They must've wanted to scare you, not kill you."

"Sick fucks."

You could hear pelting on the glass of the patio door. Rain came in angled bursts and gusts.

Jack and Lee came in carrying their soaked golf bags.

"We left your bag at the shop, Nick," Jack said. "They'll have your stand fixed by morning."

Jack was already heading down the hall behind Lee, but stopped. He turned and took a closer look at me. "You might want to wear something less casual for dinner."

I had my leg propped up on the coffee table. "I don't think I can put anything tighter over the bruise."

"Okay, we'll go to McKee's Pub. It's a more relaxed atmosphere. Be right back."

Sue got up and went to the bar cabinet. There was a silver ice bucket on top of it beside the variety of glasses. "Good service, it's full."

She walked out of the room before returning a moment later holding a washcloth. She took a handful of ice and wrapped the towel around it. "Here, put this against your bruise."

The cold eased the hot sensation of my skin.

"Let's see what there is to drink." Sue opened the cabinet's dark wood doors. On the left was a small fridge; on the right were three shelves of snacks, bottled water, and little red wines. "What'll it be?"

"Scotch."

She looked at the rows inside the mini-fridge. "Is Chivas okay?"

"If there isn't any single malt."

"That's right, I forgot." She pulled out a mini bottle of Glenlivet. "It's not your Aberlour, but it should do." In her other hand she had a pale ale for herself.

Aberlour wasn't a better Scotch, it was just the one I liked the taste of best for the price.

"Any Wild Turkey in there?" Jack asked, as he came into the room.

"Wow, you change fast," Sue said.

"One set off, one set on. No muss, no fuss." He ran his hand through his one-inch gray brush cut. "There, even combed my hair."

Sue smiled and looked back into the fridge. "Here's some Turkey."

"I never did acquire a taste for finer Scotches. Good old bourbon is fine by me. Plus I know the people who make Wild Turkey and they only use locally sourced, non-genetically-modified corn."

"Good to know," I said. "I'd thought about that too. The Scotches from Scotland are fine, because they don't have any genetically engineered crops there."

Jack nodded. "Yup."

"I'll have to check what my beer is made with," Sue said, bent over and still facing away from us.

I found myself looking at Sue's round, hard butt and looked away, feeling like I'd just done something bad. I'd always admired her looks.

Lee walked up beside Jack.

Everyone wore jeans and button-down shirts, except for me.

"What'll you have, Lee?" Sue looked up at him.

I thought I saw Lee take a quick look at Sue's behind.

"Beer, please; any kind will do."

Sue came to the couch. Lee and Jack sat down in armchairs facing us from the opposite sides of the coffee table.

Lee winced when he sat down, indicating that he did have pain from being hit in the side.

"So you talked to the resort manager about the attack?" I asked.

"He, the police, and the security manager were as stunned about it as us," Jack said. "Whoever heard of getting golf balls shot at them? Why didn't they just throw spears or blow poison darts? Can't figure out what the objective of that was."

"Could someone just want to scare you?" Sue said, repeating the theory she'd suggested to me.

"That's what the police said. Seems almost juvenile though."

"It likely had something to do with me," I blurted out.

Everyone turned to me.

"What do you mean, son?" Jack asked.

"The attempted break-in at your place." Sue nodded at me.

"Yeah. A week ago, someone tried to break into my place while I was home." I looked from Jack to Lee. "When I grabbed the door to stop them, they shot right through it."

"They shot at you through your door?" Jack sounded surprised.

"Then what?" Lee asked.

"They took off."

"Any idea who it could be or why?" Jack asked. "It doesn't sound like the Naintosa security force."

"Exactly," I said. "They would've been much quieter and gotten in, not just taken off."

"Random break-in?" Lee asked.

"Maybe …" I wasn't sure how to say it. "It's hard to explain, but it didn't feel random."

Jack nodded. "Did you tell the police?"

"Yes. The same detective showed up who was at the scene when

I found Dr. Elles."

Jack tilted his head. "Interesting coincidence. What did he say?"

"Nick," Sue said, "you need to start at the beginning."

"You're right, otherwise it's confusing," I said. "First, I saw the detective again after I found Summer Perkins."

"She was a journalist for the *San Francisco News*," Sue added. "Before that, we used to work together at the *Seattle News*."

"Summer had called Sue to get my number and then contacted me wanting to meet about something. When I got to our meeting spot, she was dead. I found a tiny droplet of blood on her neck that looked to be caused by a needle."

Jack raised an eyebrow. "Really."

"Sound familiar?" Sue asked.

"Yep." Jack nodded.

"The people in the bar saw a guy with her, and I think I saw him out on the street."

"Any idea why she wanted to meet?" Jack asked.

"Not at all," I said.

"Wonder what she had that got her killed?" Jack said. "Did the detective have any theories?"

"Afterward Detective Cortes came to my place to interview me, and then I'd called him when my place was shot up. He asked a lot of questions about what'd happened to me—us—in the last two years. No conclusions, just lots of questions."

"Do you trust him?" Jack asked.

"I don't have a reason not to."

Lee reached for a pad of paper and a pen on the coffee table. "Know his first name?"

"Hector."

"I'll check him out."

"Do you think the detective had something to do with it?" Sue asked.

Lee shrugged. "Good to know about all the players."

"Well, let's see if the detective comes up with anything." I could tell Jack was thinking. He swirled what was left of his drink. "Something's going on."

"That's why I think the golf-ball attack was meant for me," I said. "The first ball hit my bag, and I was the closest to it. What if they wanted it to look like I was hit by an errant shot? An accident. But maybe the gun was hard to aim and after missing me a couple times they just went crazy and tried to hit anyone they could."

"Hmm, could be," Jack said. "That adds more urgency to what we're going to do."

Sue shrugged. "Maybe someone thinks you know something you don't?"

"I'd sure like to *know* who I'm up against." I stretched my leg.

"It could have something to do with the increase in activity lately," Jack said.

Sue and I looked at Jack. I waited for him to expand on what he'd just said.

Jack downed his drink in one swallow, leaving the barely melted ice cubes. "Let's go have dinner. We can talk more there. Hope everyone's hungry?"

Sue and I followed Jack's lead. We'd find out what he'd intended to discuss soon enough.

Lee walked next to me in case I needed support, while Jack and Sue followed. I set a slow pace.

"I couldn't help but notice you have a scar above your right eye," Jack said. "That was from the beating at my camp?"

Sue replied, "Yeah, I think it's permanent."

Jack shook his head. "Peter Bail is still out there, and Hendrick isn't any closer to being brought to justice."

"Do you think Dr. Schmidt will ever be stopped?" I felt winded after saying one sentence. Limping, thinking, and talking took a lot of effort.

"It's sad to say, but a man with that much power and resources is above the law for the most part."

It made my blood boil to think we'd almost lost our lives exposing him, and he was still free to do his damaging work.

McKee's Pub had a long walnut-stained bar stretching across one end of the room, with an array of liquor bottles aligned on glass shelves behind. The left wall of the rectangular room had a lit fireplace with a copper hearth. There was a row of wooden tables and chairs down the middle, and another along the windows. The dark wood, brass accents, and golf knickknacks gave it a Scottish pub feel.

The place was only half full. The resort didn't seem busy, but then again, it was midweek in February.

We chose an open table next to the fireplace.

Just as we sat down, Lovemark and Norman walked into the pub. They paused and nodded our way before proceeding to a table at the other end of the room.

"That's Davis Lovemark and Russell Norman," Sue said. "Do you know them?"

"I know Davis well enough," Jack said.

"Is Mr. Lovemark a member of your *club*?" I asked.

"Yes, he is … but I'm pretty much kicked out."

"Can you be kicked out of that club and live?" I asked.

"So far, so good," Jack said.

Sue and I looked at him, wanting him to explain more, but he didn't.

"They were ahead of us on the course today," I told Sue. Then I turned to Jack. "Do you think they could've had something to do with today's event?"

"That's what I was thinking," Jack said. "Davis would find it amusing."

"He's not a very good man is he?" Sue asked. "I've heard that

Mr. Norman is a slimeball as well."

Jack took a few seconds to choose his words. "Davis is a successful entrepreneur. He's taken his family's business to new heights. However, he's left a lot of carnage in his wake. Manipulation is his main tactic. You can see it throughout his entire organization, and in how the news is reported with his agenda in mind. And Russell is his puppet."

Sue and I glanced at each other. We used to unknowingly contribute to his manipulation.

A cute waitress with red hair and a gentle smile came up to our table.

Jack suggested a bottle of a Shiraz he'd had before. That was for the three of us; Lee stuck with beer.

I'd never pictured Jack as much of a drinker, but when it came down to it, I really didn't know him very well.

Jack put his finger on the menu. "You can't go wrong with the meatloaf here."

"Do they have anything without meat?" Sue asked.

"That's right, you're a vegetarian," Jack said.

The waitress suggested a great-sounding mushroom dish that wasn't on the menu. Lee ordered a rib eye rare. Jack and I went with the meatloaf.

I noticed that Lovemark at the other end of the room was looking our way while talking. One of the men who had been golfing with them earlier was standing in an alcove next to their table. He *was* their bodyguard.

A man with thick graying hair and a pronounced nose came up to our table. "Jack, I just wanted to let you know that Cal is conscious. He has a concussion, and they're going to do a CT scan."

I hadn't caught the name of Lee's caddie when we were playing.

"I feel bad for the kid," Jack said. "The attack had nothing to do with him, he just got caught in the crossfire."

"A golf ball shooting is a first for us here at the resort."

"Which hospital is he in?" Jack asked.

"Southern Coos, in Bandon."

"Okay, shouldn't be hard to find in the metropolis of Bandon. I'll go visit him in the morning."

"You can't miss it. It's right in the center of town." The man smiled and took his leave just as the waitress was coming with our drinks.

Jack glanced to the other side of the room, then focused his attention on us. "So, what have you two been up to since you got back from Oslo?"

"I'm working for a lifestyle magazine that focuses on health and green living," Sue said. "It's not just fluff; they do some hard-hitting environmental stuff too."

"Yes, I've read some of your articles," Jack said. "Your writing has more of an edge these days, and you like to stir things up."

"I take that as a compliment."

"You should. You have a lot of passion in your writing."

"Sue's always had spunk in her words," I chimed in. "But I do agree that it's been turned up a few notches."

"I think that after what happened, you know, I have changed. I feel an even stronger need to expose wrongs now."

"It's lit a fire in you," Jack said. "Which is interesting, considering that how badly you got beaten up in Maui would've had the opposite effect on most people."

Sue shrugged. "I guess."

Jack smiled at Sue. "I admire that."

I detected a slight blush on Sue's cheeks.

Jack turned his attention to me. "And you, Nick, how do you like San Francisco?"

"It's nice … foggy."

"Why did you choose to live there?"

"Writing Dr. Elles' exposé, I think, had the opposite effect on me. I wanted to get away from everyone, have a new start and some peace. It was going fine until a couple of weeks ago."

Jack and Sue looked sympathetically toward me, which made me uncomfortable. I didn't want sympathy. "The positive side is that the experiences did help me with parts of the novel I'm writing."

"How's that coming?" Jack asked.

"Well … let's say that fiction writing is harder for me, but I'm learning."

"You'll get it," Sue said.

"What about you, Jack?" I asked. "Have you just been enjoying your retirement in Maui?"

"Oh heck no, I can't fully retire. I tried. Maui's just my little getaway in paradise. I have a house on some acreage outside of Dallas that I call home." Jack took a sip of wine. "I just started a company called Moile R & D. I know the oil and gas business inside and out. Thought I'd do some good while my feet were still above ground. I've done a lot of things that have harmed the earth in my lifetime. Now I'm doing some good to compensate. Just like Carl did by having you write his exposé."

"Except Dr. Elles hoped to be around to read it," I said.

Jack nodded. "I hope to be around to see some of the benefits of what I'm doing."

"So what's Moile going to do?" Sue asked.

"We're testing watersheds for contamination from fracking."

"What's fracking?" Was that why he wanted to meet with us? Did he need some kind of writing help with his new company?

Jack leaned forward in his chair. "Hydraulic Fracturing is a method of increasing the rate at which oil and natural gas can be recovered from subterranean reservoirs. In the industry we call it fracking. They create conductive fractures in rock and shale to increase pressure and volume from reservoir to well."

"Aren't the fluids companies are using the problem?" Sue asked.

"Precisely." Jack raised his left index finger. "They're using things like acid, diesel, methanol, radium, and arsenic, just to name a few. When they inject this stuff into the ground, seventy percent of it leaks off, eventually ending up in the surrounding water system."

"That's awful," I said. "Who in their right mind would put that stuff into the ground, knowing it was going to leak into the water people drink?"

"I'll admit that my family's oil company used to do it." Jack looked somber. "It's common practice in the industry. But that doesn't make it right. There are other, safer techniques that can be used."

Sue leaned in. "So then what're you going to do?"

"We're going to test watersheds around fracking sites and be a watchdog. Hopefully, over time we can change the practices. Clean water is much more important than oil and will soon be more expensive."

"That's going to be a big battle," I said. "Big oil has unlimited resources."

"Like Davis back there." Jack jerked his neck to the left. "He has interests in oil and is like their personal publicist."

I realized I'd leaned forward as well.

"They tell GM Comm reporters what they want the public to know, lies and all, and then it gets published as fact," Jack said.

"Information laundering," I said.

"Yes, you know all about that." Jack nodded. "They also use deflection; drawing people's attention away from the real issues."

Lee topped up our wine glasses. I'd forgotten he was even at our table. He sat so quiet, listening to us and watching the room.

"But that's for down the road, once Moile is up and running. I could use your writing skills sometime later in the year if you have time."

At that moment our waitress and another brought our food.

The three of us leaned back in our chairs.

"Do y'all like this wine?" Jack asked.

"It's very flavorful," Sue said.

"We'll have another bottle then, miss," Jack said to the waitress.

We all dug in. Everyone must've been hungrier than they let on.

The meatloaf was juicy and full of stick-to-your-ribs spices. I downed the last quarter of wine in my glass when I saw the waitress coming with a new bottle.

"So, Jack …" Sue took a bite of mushroom. "Are you going to tell us why you brought us here?"

"I didn't quite tell you two why I brought you here, did I? Sorry, I tend to move ahead without helping people catch up."

"So catch us up," Sue said.

"I like the way y'all think and are willing to put your necks on the line for what's right."

"We've only done it once before," I said. "I mean, mainly me. Sue's always taking everyone on."

Sue raised her eyebrows. "You've done your fair share of *taking on* in the past as a journalist too." She turned to Jack. "So what're you asking us to do?"

"Nothing specific, yet." Jack swallowed the food in his mouth. "Naintosa and Pharmalin had been quiet ever since the exposé, the lawsuit, and most recently their lab being shut down in Bolivia. But now, in the last few weeks, there's been a pile of activity."

That's what I was hoping he wanted to talk about.

A man straddled a stool at the very edge of the bar about six feet from our table. He didn't look like he'd been out on the links earlier. He was too slick in his yellow sweater vest over a pressed white shirt and black slacks.

I watched him out of the corner of my eye and could hear his deep voice when he ordered a water from the bartender.

Lee and Jack had noticed him too.

CHAPTER 15

We'd decided to wait until we were back in the room before we continued our conversation.

The wine seemed to have helped dull the pain in my leg, but it was still tender to put weight on it.

There was a large African-American man standing at the door to our suite. He gave a gentle nod and opened the door. I recognized the stark-white scleras around his brown eyes. He had been one of the other men from the Maui camp.

"Who is he?" Sue asked, as soon as the door closed behind us.

Jack smiled. "An extra precaution. Nothing to worry about."

We each had another of the drinks we'd started the evening with, then sat in the same spots.

"You think that guy at the bar was listening to us?" I asked.

The ice cubes clinked in the glass as Jack took a sip of his bourbon. "Not sure, but why take chances?"

I couldn't tell how serious Jack thought the threat was. It was as if he didn't want us to be worried. However, if he'd called in more backup, I figured it must be serious enough.

I wanted to talk about what was on the news about Naintosa and Pharmalin. When I opened my mouth to speak, he beat me to it.

"Naintosa and Pharmalin are gearing up for something again," Jack said. "They're in the news and wanting attention."

Based on what Jack had told us earlier and my past experiences, I said, "So they're telling GM Comm what they want the public to hear?"

Jack nodded. "Nothing's ever reported that they don't want reported."

"All of us have seen the news," Sue said. "What do you think is really happening, Jack?"

"I think that Hendrick and his cronies have new confidence that your exposé and the lawsuits are contained in Europe and they can proceed with expanding Naintosa's genetic engineering. Chances are the new corn has the same cancer-causing effects that the wheat and soy do." Jack's gaze moved back and forth, from Sue to me. "My sources on Pharmalin have mixed opinions. One says they've made progress with their cancer drugs, and the other says they still haven't figured it out."

"But they say they've gone through peer reviews and it's being fast-tracked by the FDA," I said.

Jack shrugged. "Haven't figured their strategy out yet with that."

"Do you have proof for either?" Sue asked.

"No. That's what we need to get."

"While we're at it, we need to prove that their wheat and soy cause sterility," I said.

Jack eyes narrowed. "How do you mean?"

"It was mentioned in the documents your men smuggled out of the Bolivia lab. We'd missed it before. There was a note about how the villagers-slash-human guinea pigs at the camp had become sterile and they needed new people to add to the test groups."

Jack looked away in contemplation for a moment. "Hmm, come to think of it, that rings a bell. We didn't have any proof, so we couldn't add it to the exposé?"

"That's right," I said. "But it's an important side effect that we need to find out more about."

"That throws another spin into the equation," Jack said. "A big one."

Sue reached for my empty glass and got up. "I agree."

"Thanks, Sue."

"Don't expect it all the time. Watching you hobble to get yourself another drink would be painful."

Jack smiled and took a last sip of his drink.

Lee took Jack's glass and his finished beer to the bar for another.

"We need to add glyphosate to the list," Jack said.

Sue passed me my refreshed tumbler and sat down. "You mean the herbicide?"

"It's Naintosa's biggest moneymaker," I said.

Jack took his drink from Lee. "The long-term damage it's causing is turning out to be much worse than they'd anticipated."

We all seemed to exhale at the same time. Then inhale.

"So from what I gather, you two are willing to help me?" Jack leaned forward. "I want to put another round of pressure on Hendrick and his poisonous companies, hopefully stronger than the last. He needs to be stopped. Naintosa and Pharmalin are two of the biggest stumbling blocks for humanity evolving, going forward."

Sue and I looked at each other and nodded.

"Count us in," Sue said.

I felt a sudden urge to get back out there and do some good. I'd had my downtime, hiding in my apartment.

Jack looked confident. "I knew y'all would be game."

"It'll be easier with your resources," I said.

"I'm willing to bend the rules on how we get information and proof of what they're doing, if need be," Jack said. "I mean, *really* bend."

"Fine by me." I understood what he was implying. Sometimes we had to do things that were illegal, if they were for the right reasons.

With effort I stood and limped the few steps to shake Jack's hand. On impulse I shook Lee's as well.

Sue did the same.

Lee seemed to be taken off guard that we had included him.

"Sue, how much time do you have to help, what with your job and all? We know Nick has time."

"I'm busy, too. Novels don't write themselves. I have to finish the damn thing and get it published before my money runs out." I heard myself being defensive. "But, I'll make this the priority."

Everyone chuckled.

"Okay, let's say Nick is more *flexible* with his time than you, Sue. I'll pay you both, so Nick, you don't have to worry about running out of money." Jack winked. "I understand your services don't come cheap."

"I'm a freelancer," Sue said. "I just won't take on as many articles for a while."

"Okay, I'll give you ten thousand dollars each a month, plus expenses."

Sue's shoulders went back. "That's too much."

That sure would help pad my savings. "He said we don't come cheap, Sue."

Jack smiled. "There's more than enough to go around. I like you two and want to make your lives more comfortable. Plus, you really do great work."

"We appreciate it." I stayed standing, because it made my thigh feel better.

"Any chance Miss Morgan can help too?" Jack asked.

Sue looked at me as she sat back down.

There was a pang in my heart. "I don't think so. She's in South Africa staying with relatives. I don't know if she'll ever come back to the States."

"That's too bad. I know how fond you were of her. Hell, I even miss her. I'm sure it'll take some time, but I bet ya she'll be back."

"Hopefully." I wasn't sure what to say.

Jack tilted the glass back until all the liquid disappeared down his throat. "Lee and I are going to visit Caddie Cal in the morning. Then we can meet to form an initial strategy. In the afternoon, we all fly out. There's no sense in staying here to get shot at with golf balls again—or worse."

"Sounds like a plan." I sat back down on the couch. "Even though we don't get to play Pacific Dunes."

"We can come back once this is all over." Jack stood and placed his empty glass on the bar. "Good night, then."

Lee followed Jack down the hall.

"What do you think?" Sue asked me once we heard their bedroom doors close.

"You have to admit that's what we were hoping for. There's definitely something going on, and I'm happy we're going to take a harder shot at Naintosa and Pharmalin."

"Aren't you worried? You've been shot at with bullets and golf balls before we've even gotten started."

"Somehow I feel safer with Jack involved." I shrugged. "What about you? When Dr. Schmidt finds out we're poking around again, he's going to want to do to us what he wasn't able to accomplish last time."

Sue thought for a moment and then leaned closer to me. "You know how passionate I am about the world and the environment. I can't just sit back, you know? I want to get Dr. Schmidt and his fucking companies. Like Jack said, they're holding back positive evolution."

I gave her knee a gentle slap. "Me too. I can't even consider not doing this."

She placed her hand on mine. "Settled."

We weren't sure what we were going to uncover yet, but it was guaranteed to be dangerous. I was nervous, but without any doubts.

CHAPTER 16

February 26, 2002

Right after breakfast Jack and Lee left to visit Cal in the hospital. Sue had her laptop out on the coffee table. "I think we should start by doing some research. I know how much you like researching. Which do you want?"

"I'm getting better." I sat down across from her. "I'll try to find anything I can on the sterility issue, because I've already started looking into it and glyphosate."

She made notes. "I'll do the new corn and cancer drugs. Also, I want to dig further into how GM Comm operates. I know it's off-topic, but I'm curious."

"There could be a connection. Lovemark and Schmidt are in the *club* together."

"That's what I was thinking."

"We'll do the usual." I got up and stretched my leg. "It'll evolve from there."

She looked concerned. "How bad is it today?"

"Not real bad, a bit better. It tightens when I sit."

"I need to do some work on my next magazine article. What

are you going to do?"

I looked out through the patio doors. Last night's storm had passed, leaving calm blue sky behind. "I think I'll go for a walk. It'll help my thigh."

"Do you think walking around alone is a good idea?"

"I'll be careful." *What are the chances of being attacked two days in a row?*

"Stay in the resort. Jack will be back in an hour."

"Yes, dear."

Sue stuck her tongue out at me.

The same man guarding the entrance to our suite last night was there. He pulled the door all the way open for me and gave me a slight nod.

With each step it seemed like my thigh was loosening up; every movement was a good stretching sensation.

Outside the air was fresh and cool, but the ground was still damp. I headed toward the highway along the windy road through the trees. I'd go for as long as I felt it helped me.

I wasn't trying to rehash all we'd talked about yesterday, but parts of the conversation popped in and out of my head. I was curious about the "means" Jack was going to use to get the proof we needed, and if he was successful, what that would uncover.

When I reached the highway, next to the "Welcome to Bandon Dunes" sign there was a narrow road to the left. I decided to follow it.

The walk was definitely good for me. I had twice the mobility compared to when I'd started.

A hundred yards along the paved road I heard the sound of dirt bikes riding on bumpy ground. They hummed like a nest of bees, their revs pitching higher and lower over ruts.

I came to a dirt road leading toward the sound and decided to follow it. The uneven ground was harder on my injury as my leg twisted on the bumps, but I was curious, so I tried to choose the flattest spots and continued on.

The revving of the bikes stopped as I came into a clearing. Two pickup trucks sat about two hundred yards ahead at the edge of the trees. One person stood next to a truck and two others sat on its tailgate. All three were dressed in motocross gear.

Between the riders and me, a motocross track snaked through the clearing complete with jumps and berms.

As I walked closer I saw the bikes up on stands between the trucks. There were two green Kawasakis and one yellow Suzuki. All three looked a few years old and well used.

Behind me in the distance I could hear the deep throb of a four-stroke engine.

"Nick. What are you doing out here?" said the person standing next to a Dodge Ram 1500.

It was John, my caddie from yesterday. He had to be riding the Suzuki, because his pants and jersey were yellow and blue.

"Hey, John. I was just taking a walk and heard the bikes, so I thought I'd come check it out."

"How's your leg?"

"It's better. The walking is helping." I was right beside him now. "How's your butt?"

"I got a big bruise and have to stand the whole time I'm riding." John turned to the two young men in green and black riding gear sitting on the tailgate. "This is the guy I was caddying for when we were attacked by golf balls." He swiveled back to face me. "These are my two riding buddies and fellow caddies, Gary and Ryan."

"John told us what happened," said the shorter and lighter-haired of the two. "That was too crazy."

I didn't know which was Gary and which was Ryan.

"Yeah, never heard of that happening before," said the taller, darker-haired one. "I heard it took two hours this morning to repair all the divots on the green left by the shot balls."

We were distracted by the growing sound of the engine I'd noticed moments ago. All of us turned in the direction of the road. A blue four-wheel ATV had come to the edge of the clearing and stopped in the shadow of the trees.

"Did the police say anything?" John asked.

I turned back to him. "They thought it was weird too."

"Are you going to play golf today?"

"No, we're flying out this afternoon." I looked around and saw a tabletop jump on the track near us. "Looks like a nice track."

"Do you ride?" asked the sandy-haired guy.

"I used to race when I was a teenager."

There was a loud ping next to me. I looked over and saw a bullet hole with smoke seeping out of it at the edge of the pickup box. Then the tail light next to it blew out. "What the fuck!"

"They're shooting at you!" John pulled my arm as all four of us scrambled to the other side of the Dodge.

Two bullets hit the ground about ten feet in front of us. From the position of the truck and trees, the shooter couldn't get us from their angle.

We heard the ATV ride closer and stop a hundred yards away.

John looked up and then crouched back down quick. "He still can't get us from over there."

"Who are you and why is someone trying to kill you?" the lighter-haired guy asked.

"I'm nobody, really."

"You've got to get out of here," John said. "In a minute they're going to walk right up to us. Then we're all dead."

He was right. "I can't run with my bum leg."

"Take my bike," John said. "You told us you used to race."

I looked over at the Suzuki, with a full-face helmet hanging off the handlebar. Chances were good it was hidden from the shooter's view. "Okay, where do I go?"

"I'll be the lookout." The darker-haired guy snuck to the front bumper. "He's looking through the scope of his rifle."

John pointed left. "Get on the track there. Go over the jump, then over that sandy berm. Do you see the road past it?"

I could see an opening in the trees. "Yeah."

"A little ways down there's a fork in the road. Turn right. Turn right again when you hit the paved road and then right on the road to the resort. Do you know where the maintenance building is by the driving range?"

"I remember seeing it."

"Leave the bike there. I doubt he'd follow you all the way there with all the people around. And you can outrun him, cause the Suzuki goes like stink."

I took a deep breath. "Here goes nothing."

I stayed crouched as I went for the bike. The helmet was sweaty, but I didn't care. Adrenaline was flooding through me; I didn't even feel my thigh as I pulled the bike off its stand and swung my right leg over it. It only took one kick to start. I pulled in the clutch with my left hand and banged the shifter down with my left foot. It'd been five years since I'd last ridden. Muscle memory took over.

I opened the throttle with my right hand, leaned forward, and popped the clutch. I held on with everything I had, as the front tire rose and the back knobby spun, spraying the guys and trucks with sandy dirt.

Feathering the clutch twice, I raised my left foot on the shift lever at the same time. The back tire grasped for traction, sending a rooster tail twenty feet long. I shifted into fourth just before I hit the jump. That was a mistake.

The front end was too high when I launched. It was the tabletop jump and I needed to land on the downside with my front tire lower than the back. At that angle I'd wipe out when I landed, making me easy pickings for the shooter.

I pressed the back brake lever all the way down with my right foot. That instantly stopped the rear wheel from spinning and brought the front wheel down just in time for the landing.

The lip of the sand berm ahead was too steep for my speed, so I jammed on both brakes. I hit the face of the berm. The bike stopped, but I didn't. My body kept going right over the handlebars. One of the things everyone learned in racing was to not let go of the clutch, if you could help it, and stall the engine. So the bike came with me over the berm.

I landed on my back, left hand stretched out holding onto the handlebar and clutch. The engine was still running. Lucky I'd slowed down enough that the fall wasn't too bad. I jumped to my feet and pulled the bike up.

The ATV had followed me and had stopped at the top of the jump. The shooter stood up on his pegs, dressed in all black, including his open face helmet and tinted goggles. He raised his rifle.

Before he could get me in his sights I was on the bike and out of there.

The tree in front of me splintered as the bullet smashed into it. "Fuck, move!"

The road was windy and rutted. He had to follow, but his machine wasn't as nimble as mine.

I reached the fork in the road and went left. It turned into an overgrown path and I had to slow down. Shit, I was supposed to have turned right.

I took a quick look back and saw the ATV turn in my direction. He was going to have trouble with the width of this path.

I was only in second gear and had to twist and turn to avoid the underbrush. The end of a branch smacked the chin guard and the sweet smell of pine rushed into my helmet.

Through a small opening I could see the paved road about fifty yards to my right. There was no path to it, but I could make it through the forest. The trees and bushes were so close together that I had to slow down to a crawl in first gear to navigate around them.

A tree caught my handlebar and almost took me out. It stopped me instantly. I leaned to the right and twisted the bar free.

The top of a sapling blew off next to me. "Fuck!"

I shifted into second and jumped the ditch beside the paved road. Turning right this time, I pinned the throttle and went through the gears. Every time I released the clutch after a shift the front tire would rise up in the air, making me have to lean right over the front handlebars. Pavement provided perfect traction. I was in fifth gear going full out at seventy miles per hour within a couple-hundred feet.

I caught a glimpse of the blue ATV through the trees. He had to double back on the dirt path. I passed the dirt road I'd originally walked down. The two pickups had just made the turn from the track and were heading for the paved road.

I hit the brakes when I saw the Bandon Dunes entrance. Going wide and leaning hard right I just made the turn. Rolling the throttle open got me back up to full speed again. I blew by a car in front of me. Navigating the windy road at high speed was easy on the motorcycle. I had to admit, this chase was exhilarating … now that I put some distance between my pursuer and myself.

I went down and around the gully near the lodge and kept right toward the driving range. There was an SUV at the intersection and I saw it was Lee who was driving it. He must've somehow known it was me, because he followed, trying to keep up. I made the turn to the maintenance yard too fast. The bike slid across the road onto the shoulder. I let off the brakes and gave it gas to stop the slide. Once back in control I had to brake hard to avoid hitting the building.

I rode inside the large doors and leaned the bike up against a wall. "I made it." I took the helmet off and placed it on the handlebar.

Two men were standing in the doorway, mouths open, not saying anything.

"This is John the caddie's bike," I said to them, as I walked by. "He's going to pick it up."

Lee was getting out of the Suburban as I came outside. "What happened?"

"Someone on an ATV was chasing and shooting at me. I had to borrow a bike to escape."

"What? Shooting with bullets?" Without hesitation, Lee opened the passenger door. "Get in."

The silver Dodge Ram with the taillight shot out and the charcoal Ford F150 with two Kawasakis in the back turned into the maintenance yard.

"Hold on a second," I told Lee when I got next to him.

John got out of his Dodge as soon as he pulled up. "The ATV turned left before the gully and took off. I didn't want to follow it."

Lee looked around. "We'd better go. I want to get you out of the open."

"Thanks for letting me use your bike. The handlebar's a little bent from when I wiped out, but I don't think I did any real damage. You're right, it goes like stink."

John shook his head. "Man, can you ride."

Lee nudged me toward the open door to the backseat. "Let's go."

CHAPTER 17

I was shaking. Tremors. The reaction had occurred three times before, each time I'd been shot at.

"You okay?" Lee was glancing in the rearview mirror at me every few seconds as he accelerated up the road to the lodge.

"Yeah, just shook up a bit." The adrenaline had subsided and what had just happened was beginning to sink in.

The tires squealed as we blew through the stop sign and took the corner around the ravine. I grabbed hold of the door to resist being squashed into it and flung across the backseat when we straightened out.

Lee maneuvered around two shuttles and drove right up onto the sidewalk at the lodge entrance.

The second we stopped he flung his door open and raced around to the passenger side. "Get out this way."

"I think the shooter's long gone."

"Take no chances. Now move."

I slid across the seat and out the door. Lee shielded me until we were inside.

We walked at a brisk pace to the stairs and up them, taking two at a time. That's when I noticed the pain in my thigh again and slowed to a limp.

The guard outside our suite saw us coming and opened the door.

"Stay away from the windows." Lee was serious.

Sue was working at the table on her laptop and Jack was sitting on the couch. They both looked up at us.

Lee turned and went back out the door.

I collapsed on one of the padded chairs and winced. My thigh touched the armrest and stung.

"What happened?" Sue got up and came over to me.

I needed to catch my breath. "I was … shot at and chased."

"I had a feeling something was up." Jack put the pad he was writing on down. "That's why I had Lee go look for you."

"I was taking a walk, heard some motocross bikes, and went to investigate. It turned out to be John, my caddie from yesterday, and two of his buddies. Then someone came up on an ATV and shot at me. I borrowed John's bike and made a run for it. Lee saw me and picked me up."

"Holy shit," Sue said.

"Dagnabbit," Jack said. "Now we know for sure it's not safe for you to be alone."

"Are you hurt?" Sue asked.

"Couple scrapes when I wiped out, that's all." I raised my right shoulder to check whether it had full movement. It had taken the brunt of my fall. A little tight, but nothing major. "Now what do I do? I still don't know why this is happening."

Lee came back into the room, went to the patio door and looked outside. The sun was pouring in, making it hard to see out.

"I'm going to get you a bodyguard," Jack said.

That was a relief. "I wouldn't object to that." I liked my privacy and space, but right now I needed help.

"Do you really think it's okay for him to go back to his home?" Sue directed her question to Jack. "Maybe he should come back to

Seattle or go someplace where they can't find him."

"Do you want to do that, Nick?" asked Jack.

I thought about it. Running and hiding had crossed my mind several times, but it didn't feel right, not now. I wanted to know why they, whoever *they* were, were after me and I wanted to stop them. "No. I think I'll be fine with a bodyguard."

"Good." Jack turned his attention to Sue. "I think you should have one too."

"Do you think that's necessary? No one's attacked me."

"Yet," I added. "I really want you to have one."

"Don't worry. I know a woman that'd be perfect." Jack smiled. "You even have similar personalities."

"All right." Sue gave in without much of a fight.

"Lee, can you go take care of it?"

Lee turned away from the window. "Sure, right away."

"Jack, I need to learn self-defense and maybe get a gun," I said.

Now Jack looked even more concerned. "If you get a gun you have to be prepared to use it. Do you think you could ever shoot someone?"

"If it was a matter of them or me, or if they were going to hurt you or Sue, then yes."

"Okay, how about I get your bodyguard to take you to a shooting range and give you some lessons first? Then you can decide whether you want a gun."

"That'll take too long," I said.

"I'm not going to have any part in getting you a gun without you knowing how to use it."

He had a point. "Okay." I guess I had to be patient.

"Now what kind of self-defense or martial art were you thinking of?" Jack asked. "Have you heard of Krav Maga? There you could learn some effective moves quick."

The name rang a bell from when I was researching martial arts.

"What's Krag Magra?" Sue scrunched up her face. "I've never heard of it."

"*Krav Maga* was developed by the Israeli military," Jack said. "It uses elements from different martial arts, just more down to business. It's more like street fighting. It ain't pretty, but it sure gets the job done."

"That's what I need."

"Do you know it, Jack?" Sue asked.

"Some, yes."

I nodded. "Okay, I'll look into it when I get back to San Francisco."

"Now we have to agree on a strategy before we go." Sue retrieved the pad of paper she'd been using. "Nick and I have already decided what we're each going to research." She read out the notes from earlier.

"Good starting point," Jack said. "My job is to get the proof from the inside. The research you two are going to do will be valuable, but what we also need can't be obtained by traditional methods. It's not in libraries or on the Internet. We have to further infiltrate Naintosa, Pharmalin, and my ex-club."

"That sounds more interesting," I said. "Can we help you there?"

Sue perked up. "Yeah."

Jack was quiet for a moment and then shook his head. "It's too dangerous. You don't have those skills. You'd need espionage training."

I liked the sound of *espionage training*.

"We could learn if someone taught us," Sue said.

"I'll see what I can do down the road," Jack said. "In the meantime we have our starting point."

"What about what Ivan's doing?" Sue asked.

"Yeah," I said. "He's still working hard on proving the validity of the exposé, even after Bill's death."

Jack got up. "Of course, Ivan's a key component."

INTERLOGUE 1

The secure phone, which only a handful of people knew the number to, rang. It was made of wood, lacquered brown, and had gold trim. Some might have thought it was gaudy, but in the opulence of the study, within the grandeur of the estate, it fit right in.

He sat in his blood-red leather, high-back chair, reviewing a profit chart on the screen. Having a computer on top of his oversize mahogany desk wouldn't have been appropriate, so he'd had alterations made. The actual computer was hidden in a drawer. With the push of a button, a panel in the desktop moved down and a screen rose up.

The phone rang a second time. *This better be important.* He picked up the heavier-than-average receiver. "Yes?"

"Hendrick, it's Davis," said the voice on the other end of the line. "I hope I didn't catch you at a bad time?"

Dr. Hendrick Schmidt IV's body tensed. Davis Lovemark only contacted him with problems these days. "I'm just going over Pharmalin's profits." His German accent was heavy and ever-present. "Where are you?"

"I'm at Bandon Dunes."

"Where?"

"It's a golf resort in southern Oregon."

"You're on vacation again?" Hendrick could never figure out the appeal of golf, mainly because he wasn't good at it. The coordination of sports was not his forte, so he couldn't be bothered with it.

"You should be happy I'm here." Davis' British past always reflected in his accent when he was speaking to a European. "I ran into some people you know."

"Who would that be?" Hendrick knew many people who played the game, but they wouldn't be in rainy Oregon in February.

"Jack Carter, Nick Barnes, and Sue Clark. I had some fun with them on the golf course, Jack and Barnes at least."

Hendrick's lip curled and he pushed back in his chair. Those were not names he liked. They were a thorn in his side. "I've had Barnes and Jack monitored. They haven't been active or stirring up any problems in over six months."

"You should've had them permanently silenced when you had the opportunity," Davis retorted.

"Fucking incompetent, Peter Bail," Hendrick said, in a quiet tone more to himself.

"But Peter knows how these people operate. Maybe it would be a good idea to bring him back, specifically to handle them."

Hendrick tried to ignore what Davis just said. "Why do you think they're meeting together?"

"I'm not sure," said Davis. "It's always hard to know what Jack is up to. However, Nick was witness to a loose end being tied up. I fear he's been motivated again. I'm having him watched and trying to discourage him from delving further into the matter."

Hendrick had no desire to know what Davis' loose end was, but was curious about how he was discouraging Barnes.

"If you have surveillance on them as well, why don't we have our teams work together on it?" Davis said. "There's no use in doubling up."

"If it's all right with you, let's just have your people deal with them. Because they've been quiet, my operatives haven't bothered watching them too closely." That was a lie. Hendrick planned on calling the Naintosa head of security right after he got off the phone with Davis and increase the surveillance on Jack, Barnes, and now Clark. He didn't trust anybody outside his organization on matters of security.

"Suit yourself."

Hendrick swiveled his chair around to look out onto the melting snow covering his gardens. "However, I would appreciate any updates, especially if they concern me or my companies."

"Of course. I have someone going through Nick Barnes' apartment right now to see whether he's up to anything."

"Yes, good thinking."

"Hendrick, you need to take some time off—you sound tense. Get out of the snow in Germany, go to your villa on Lake Como, and relax for a while."

"Perhaps." Hendrick didn't want to tell Davis it was he and the names he just spoke of who were making him edgy.

Hendrick stared outside as he placed the receiver back on its cradle. It had begun to rain.

Are those three conspirators up to something again?

Naintosa and Pharmalin had made great strides of late and were getting much closer to achieving his goal. Hendrick didn't want anyone trying to further expose or sabotage what he and his family had worked so hard to accomplish. If the ignorant populous knew, they wouldn't understand anyway, even if it was the best thing for them.

"Father, do you have a moment to explain something to me about the Plycite gene? These numbers don't add up."

Hendrick recognized his eldest son's voice and swiveled in his chair to see Hendrick V standing at the entrance to the study. He was a younger version of himself, without the extra weight and receded hair. Not tall, but sturdy. Good German pureblood. Hendrick V was smart, cunning, and a hard worker; he was worthy of being his successor.

"It could be important to …"

"No, Junior, I have no time for your numbers now."

CHAPTER 18

There were three jets waiting for us. I thought about the pollution we were creating. Wealthy people in general created more environmental damage than poor people.

Lee said, "There will be someone waiting for each of you at your home airports."

"I'll be in touch within the next few days," Jack said. "Onward, upward, and forward."

They walked toward a nondescript white jet that was somewhat bigger than the ones for Sue and me.

I hugged her. "Let's talk tomorrow."

"You should just move back to Seattle."

"I like San Francisco, but you may be right."

The sky was clear as the plane thrust upward.

Janis, the pretty flight attendant, gave me a Scotch as soon as we reached altitude. Holding the glass, I noticed that I was still shaking and set it down in the armrest holder.

Before I drank the alcohol I wanted to meditate. I craved feeling back in balance.

Closing my eyes, I took long, deep breaths in and out. Images and my feelings toward them flooded my mind. A bullet hitting the truck, exploding the taillight; Davis Lovemark looking at me or right through me; the shooter standing up on the pegs of his ATV, pointing a rifle, and pulling the trigger; being shot at with golf balls, which made my thigh twinge; seeing Jack's caddie lying on the green, unconscious; riding the motorcycle as hard as I could, relying on my past ability; my door splintering and slugs in my wall; Summer's lifeless body. My heart pounded harder, reliving each experience.

"Can I get you anything else?" Janis asked. "Are you all right?"

I opened my eyes. "No, I'm okay."

She was just over five feet tall and curvy. "It sounded like you were having a bad dream. You were breathing hard and moving around in your seat."

"I was trying to relax, but not doing a good job of it."

"Rough day?" She flicked her blonde hair back over her shoulder.

"Couple."

"Drink your Scotch. That'll help."

"Can you get me another? This one won't last long."

When we landed, a man stood waiting at the bottom of the retractable plane stairs. As I walked down, he took off his sunglasses, put his hands behind his back, and stood straight. He wore a black suit, a white shirt, and a solid navy tie.

When I was right in front of him, he extended his right hand. "Jorge Villegas. Pleasure to meet you, Mr. Barnes." His Spanish accent sounded like his tongue was too big for his mouth, but I could understand his English.

"Hi." I shook his thick, strong, and hairy hand. I took a good look at Jorge. He was a bit shorter than me, probably five-foot-ten, but appeared to be one big muscle. He had dark brown eyes and a prominent nose with big nostrils. He must've been in his late fifties; his black hair was shot with gray, and there were pronounced wrinkles on his ashen-tinted skin.

"Jack asked me to look out for you." His voice was as strong as he looked.

"Okay." That's all I could say. If this guy was protecting me, I'd feel safe.

A man in a reflective vest brought over my luggage. Jorge took the suitcase; I took the golf club travel bag.

"Let's go," he said.

I looked at him, not registering. "Where?"

"Your car."

"Oh … of course." The two Scotches may have affected me, but I felt sober.

He stayed right next to me all the way to the vehicle. My thigh had tightened up during the flight, causing me to limp. He never asked how I became injured.

Once we climbed inside the Pathfinder I had a realization. "Can you provide any kind of ID that shows you work for Jack Carter?"

"Other than the fact that if I didn't you'd be dead already?" He sort of smiled and I knew it was supposed to be a joke, but it still sounded menacing.

He pulled out a green business card that had a graphic of a furry rodent on it; I assumed it was a mole. It read Moile R & D, Jorge Villegas, Security Advisor. I looked at his name and compared it to the way he pronounced it. The J and G in his first name were pronounced as Hs, which was typical. The LL in the last name pronounced as a J threw me off. People from Mexico that I knew said LL as a Y sound. "Can I keep it?"

"Sure." He was looking at the cards in his wallet, pulled one out, and handed it over.

It was a Texas driver's license. I was pretty good at my initial assessment of him. He was born in 1944, which made him fifty-eight, five-foot-ten, and weighed 210 pounds. He had a Dallas address.

My cell phone rang and I reached into my pocket to get it.

"This is Lee. Have you landed?"

"Hi, Lee. Yes, a few minutes ago."

"Has Jorge met you?"

"Yes, he's right beside …"

"Good. He'll take care of you." Lee hung up.

When I looked up at Jorge, he had something else to show me—a gun permit.

"We good?" he asked.

"Sure. Sorry to have asked, but …"

"No, don't be. You should've asked right away. We'll have to work on your threat detection skills. You shouldn't trust anyone until you know who they are."

Once we were on the road, I asked, "So how is this going to work? Are you going to live at my place?"

"I'll be around during the day and another person at night," he said. "You won't see us unless you need us. We'll provide surveillance from a distance. You'll have your privacy. We're like ghosts."

"I guess that would be all right." I wasn't sure whether that was enough protection.

"Don't worry, it works well," Jorge said. "Can I see your cell phone?"

We stopped at a red light and I handed my phone to him.

Jorge flipped it open and punched some numbers. "From now on when you just hit send it will automatically call me or my associate. That's your backup. I'll give you something else when we get to your home."

I took the phone back. "Do I get to meet the night shift person?"

"Only if you need them."

"How will I know you and they are out there?"

He gave me a firm look. "We will be."

I thought it was an innocent enough question; no need for the attitude. I wanted to get to know the background of my daytime protector.

A few blocks later, I asked, "Where are you originally from?"

"My home is in Dallas."

"Before that. You have a strong accent, but your English is very good."

"I'm originally from Bogota, Colombia."

That explained the difference in his accent.

"What's your security background?"

"Military and government."

"Colombian or American?"

"Both."

"What did you do?"

"That's not important. All you have to know is that I do my job very well."

"I'm sure you do."

After a moment Jorge asked, "Where are you originally from?"

"Tacoma, Washington."

He nodded.

We didn't say another word to each other for the last ten miles.

Jorge again handled my suitcase, and I carried my clubs.

When we turned the corner in the hallway to arrive at my apartment, there was a man standing in front of Angelica's open door. He was tall, slim, and wore a knee-length charcoal raincoat. He turned toward us and froze for a second. I'm sure women found his chiseled features attractive, except his nose didn't fit the rest of his face. He looked familiar. Not in a way that we'd met and talked before, but I'd seen him somewhere.

He turned back to the open door. "See you later."

The only way out was past us.

Jorge and I moved back to let him by in the narrow hall. He looked down and away as he passed. I couldn't help but stare. *Where have I seen him before?*

"That was short." Angelica stood just outside her door in a short, sleeveless, pale pink dress. The low V at the front showed off her considerable cleavage. "How was your golf trip, sweetie?"

"Huh?" I took a step forward and reached into my pocket for my keys. "All right, I guess."

She leaned against the wall and crossed her bare legs. "Who's your friend?"

"This is Jorge."

Jorge nodded, but didn't say anything.

"You here for a visit?" She pointed at my black suitcase in his hand.

"He'll be around for a while." I placed the key halfway into the lock and it jammed.

"Nice to meet you, Jorge." Her crooked smile was sultry. "See you around, Nick." She disappeared back into her apartment.

"Nice neighbor," Jorge said.

"She just moved in." I jiggled the key and it advanced a little farther, but not enough.

"Is there a problem?"

"Yeah, this is a brand new lock. It was working fine when I left, but now it's jamming." I fiddled with it some more and the key went all the way in, unlocking the door.

"Wait." Jorge put the suitcase down and moved me aside with his shoulder. He put his right hand inside his open suit jacket and opened the door with his left. A good-size gun appeared and he pointed it forward as we went inside.

Seeing Jorge's gun made me both nervous and grateful he was with me.

He moved from the main room to the kitchen, then bathroom and bedroom.

There was no one there.

"Anything out of place?" Jorge holstered his gun.

I put down the club bag and suitcase and walked over to my desk. "I had a file containing research for my book sitting on top of the keyboard. It was there to remind me to finish the work when I got back."

As I went to see whether it was under some other papers my hand brushed the mouse. The screen came alive. That stopped me. "I'm positive I turned off the computer before I'd left."

Jorge had come up beside me. "Check your computer files to see if anything's been deleted or icons on the desktop moved."

I sat down and looked. "Everything seems to be here."

"They must've just copied what they thought was important. Look around to see if anything is missing. Do you have valuables?"

"Not really, no." I got up and went to my secret compartment. Nothing there had been removed; my passport, some cash, Dr. Elles' manuscript, five disks, a couple of CDs and some important papers. "Everything is here." I slid the particleboard sheet back in place and replaced the pots and pans.

"Anything in the bedroom?"

I peered into the small box on top of my dresser where there was some jewelry I never wore. The three chains and two rings were gold, so they were worth some money. They were untouched, as was the rest of the bedroom. "It doesn't seem like a robbery."

Jorge was standing in the doorway. "They were looking for information and didn't want you to know they were here."

"You know what ..." I walked past him, back out to the main room, and went to the door. My alarm was unarmed. "I just had it put in and I'm positive I armed it before I left. How could they do that?"

He came up and examined the box on the wall. "It's not that hard."

"Piece of shit." It made me real nervous that someone got in so easy and went through my stuff.

"It's still good to have. Go check if your phone has a dial tone."

I did as he asked. I pressed the speaker button, so we could both hear the dial tone.

"Hand it over, it could be bugged." He turned the phone off and placed it in his outside pocket. "It's easiest to just get a new one."

"It doesn't hold a charge long enough anyway."

Jorge pulled a cell phone out of his inside pocket. "I should let the boss know." He turned his back to me. "Jack, it's Jorge … Nick's place was broken into while he was gone … yes … just computer and paper files. They tried to make their search undetectable but were a little sloppy." He listened for a few seconds. "Gotcha."

"What did he say?" I asked as soon as he hung up.

"Be careful."

"That's it?"

"What else can we do?"

That wasn't the answer I was looking for. "Should I call the police?"

"They can't do anything. If this has something to do with Naintosa, it's out of their sphere."

I'd heard that before and he was probably right, but I wanted to tell Detective Cortes.

"Is your computer backed up?" Jorge pointed to it.

"The important stuff." Lucky I'd had the foresight before I'd left.

"Good. Unplug it. I'm taking it with me."

"What am I supposed to do?"

"Buy a new one."

"Really?"

"They could've installed spyware. I'll have it checked out, but for now it's easier to get a new one." Jorge produced a black watch and handed it to me. There was a digital time display and buttons below it. "Wear it at all times. The gray button is an alarm and the black button is a speaker. It's only connected with me and the night-watch." He pulled back his sleeve revealing the same type of watch on his left wrist. "Got it?"

"It's kind of James Bond, but cheap looking."

CHAPTER 19

Breathe in and out, slow and steady. Eyes closed. My ass was itchy. Scratch. Breathe again. Calm. Let the mind free its thoughts and open to whatever is out there. Nothingness. Empty space.

"Nick?"

What?

"Nick, are you there?"

I opened my eyes and looked around.

"Nick, you're supposed to be wearing the watch at all times." It was Jorge's Spanish accented voice.

I looked down at my wrist. Which button was the speaker? I pressed the gray button.

"Wrong button."

I pressed the black button and said, "Hi, Jorge."

"Just checking to make sure everything was working and you're wearing the watch."

I pressed the button again. "Yes, I'm wearing the watch. I was just trying to meditate."

"You meditate?"

Is that a sarcastic edge in his voice? "Yes."

"Okay, go back to meditating."

"Where are you?"

"Around."

Why doesn't he want to tell me where he is? "I'm going grocery, phone, and computer shopping this morning."

"I'll tail you from a distance. I want to see if anyone is following you, and if so, we don't want them to know you have protection."

"Okay. Do you want me to tell you when I'm leaving?"

"You won't have to. I wouldn't be very good at my job if you did."

Okay, whatever. Do it your way.

I lowered my arm and closed my eyes. Focus on the breathing in and out. Clear the mind.

The cell rang.

"Shit." Forget meditating today.

I pushed off from the couch and went to where I'd left the phone on my desk. "Hello."

"How're your bodyguards?" Sue asked.

"They observe from a distance, not sure exactly where. I've only met one of them. He seems well qualified, but I'm not sure if he's real serious or sarcastic. I have to wear a watch speaker thing."

"Same here. It's better than having them at your side all the time. That would be awkward. Mine's a tough but nice lady from Poland."

I went back to the couch. "My place was broken into while I was away."

"Really?" Sue paused, and then said, "You kind of expected that."

"Yeah, it just proves there are people after me for a specific reason. I personally still don't think it's the Naintosa thugs, but we know it's more than one person."

"True. What did they take?"

"They took some papers and maybe copied some computer files."

"Anything important?"

"I don't have anything of much importance."

Sue cleared her throat. "I know I'm beginning to sound like a broken record, but really think about moving back to Seattle."

Without any thought behind it, I said, "You're right. I'd feel safer there."

"How about I start looking for apartments available in my neighborhood?"

She lived right downtown in a cool area. "Yeah, I'd appreciate that." Wow, I'd just decided to move back to Seattle.

"It'll be good to always have you around again." Sue was almost sounding mushy.

My watch said, "Nick?"

"I'd better go. My bodyguard is trying to get a hold of me."

I looked at the watch. Which button was it again? Why didn't they have some kind of symbol on each or "E" for emergency and "S" for speaker? I pressed the black one. "Jorge?"

"I'm having your apartment swept for any bugs or surveillance while you're out," the watch said.

I didn't see Jorge while I was grocery shopping, but I did see him from a distance when I bought the new computer and phone. Knowing he was around prevented me from wanting to crawl into my apartment, barricade myself in, and hide.

Jorge was waiting for me when I parked in my spot.

"There was no one following you," he said. "I'll help you take your stuff upstairs."

I handed him the box containing the computer.

When we arrived outside my door Jorge produced a gold key and handed it to me. "This is for your new deadbolt. I had your piece-of-shit one replaced."

I didn't know it was a cheap lock, even though Archie wouldn't have sprung for anything fancy. "I appreciate that." The key fit into the deadbolt with a smooth motion.

"I will keep a copy to use only in an emergency." He set the box down. "I should get back to my post."

My apartment looked the same as I'd left it. The people who swept it hadn't moved a thing.

I set the new black cordless phone in its place. The reason I'd chosen it was that on the package there was a burst saying, "Long-Lasting Rechargeable Battery."

Next, I began the long, tedious process of setting up the new computer. I'd chosen a laptop, so I could take it with me whenever I went away.

It was going to take over an hour, so I headed into the kitchen to grab my last cold beer. The new ones needed time to chill after I put them in the fridge along with the groceries I'd purchased.

The new computer screen was a third smaller than my old one. A blue bar moved to the right showing progress in loading a program.

The room went dim. Out the window I could see the sun setting into a wall of white that was coming in from the ocean. Fog would cover the city for the night.

Out of nowhere, Mike Couple popped into my head. It was time to catch up with him and find out how he knew Summer. The only thing we ever did together was play golf.

As I turned, I twisted funny and felt a twinge of pain shoot through my leg. The swelling had gone down, but it would take some time before the bruising was gone.

The new phone would have enough charge now. I went to get it and punched in Mike's number. After five rings, his low voice came on saying he was unavailable right now and to leave a message.

"Hi Mike, it's Nick. It's been a while. It's time we teed it up. Give me a call."

There was a gentle knock. I kept forgetting to get a peephole. I was close enough to the door to be heard on the other side. "Yes? Who's there?"

"It's Angelica."

The new deadbolt turned with ease.

There was my neighbor in a pretty pink dress with a dark pink belt around her waist, in bare feet with toenails polished pink.

"Hi there, sweetie." She leaned against the outer doorframe. A waft of floral perfume emanated from her.

"How are you?"

"Not so great. You see …" She had a coy, pouty look. "I'm making this big meal and I have no one to share it with. Would you be interested?"

I had nothing better to do and my pink neighbor sure was nice to look at. "Sure. Just give me about twenty minutes. I have to finish setting up my new computer."

"Oh, you have a new computer?" She looked past me into my apartment. "Why?"

"Uh … I wanted a laptop."

CHAPTER 20

I hadn't had dinner with a woman since Oslo when I dined with Morgan; that is, not counting Sue.

I took a quick shower, shaved for the first time in a couple of days, and put on one of my nicer blue button-down shirts and clean jeans. I checked on the computer every few minutes to make sure it was progressing.

Finally, the initial setup was done. I could add my saved files and a few programs later.

As I lifted my foot to put my shoes on, I noticed my big toe was beginning to protrude from my sock. Normally I'd wear that sock until the toe stuck right through. Tonight I thought it best to change it.

I brought a bottle of Bordeaux from my limited supply. I didn't know what we were eating, but it was a great-tasting wine.

"Come on in, sweetie," Angelica said when she answered the door.

The place smelled of braised meat, and my mouth began to water. The apartment layout was the same as mine, but she had only one window at the front. Hers was a middle unit, while mine was a corner one. The décor was tasteful and feminine. There was nothing fancy, but it was several steps up from a college student's.

A teal chair sat next to a red sofa. Teal was Morgan's favorite color. There were pink accents—a picture frame, a bowl with potpourri, and a pale-pink rug underneath the coffee table.

"Make yourself at home."

"I brought some wine—hope you like red. From the fantastic smell, I think it'll go with dinner."

"Perfect. I'll go open it." Angelica took the bottle into the kitchen.

There was a bookshelf in the corner with some textbooks and novels on it. I decided to investigate while I waited. Five framed pictures filled the empty gaps. One showed Angelica standing with an equally attractive girl in front of the Eiffel Tower; another had been taken at an outdoor café next to a canal. She must've gone on a trip to France with her friend not too long ago.

No boyfriend pictures.

I picked up a portrait of her and some people I assumed were her family, standing in front of a plantation house. She'd mentioned she was from Georgia. Angelica, her sister, and her mother all had on similar frilly white-and-pink dresses, and her father wore a charcoal suit with a pink tie. A very handsome, pink family.

"That was taken in our backyard," Angelica said, as she handed me a glass of wine. "My family's owned that property for over two hundred years, on my daddy's side."

"Impressive." I sampled the contents of the glass. "What does your family do?"

She tried the wine. "Mmm, this is really good. We grow cotton now and used to grow tobacco. My father's a lawyer, Mother is an anchorwoman for the local TV station, and my sister Becky's graduating this year."

"Good looking family, and successful."

"You think?" She brushed my fingers as she took the portrait and placed it back on the shelf. "Enough about me, I want to know more about you."

I followed her to the red sofa. She sat down in the middle, not giving me an option but to sit right next to her. When she crossed her legs, she touched my knee. "Sorry." She gave me her crooked smile. It must've been her "go to" look and I was falling for it. "Dinner needs a few more minutes to simmer." The slow way Angelica said it with her Southern accent made *simmer* sound sexy. "Now tell me about you."

"Not a lot to tell." *Is she trying to seduce me?* "What would you like to know?"

"First of all, did the police find out who attempted to break into your place and shot at you?"

"No, nothing yet. I hope you're not too nervous about that happening right next door to you."

"I'm worried about you," she said. "Is that why you have that Latino guy around that looks like a brick wall? What was his name … Jorge?"

It wasn't a good idea to expose Jorge. "He's just someone I know." A change of subject was in order. "How's school? What are you going to do when you're finished?"

She narrowed her eyes, as if not wanting to go with my subject change. From that one look, I had a sense that she was used to getting her way and could be hiding a temper behind that sultry smile.

"Are you looking for a career in the media?"

Her expression went neutral. "I want to be on the news, like my momma. After the media classes I'm going to study acting."

"That sounds like fun."

"You know, you haven't told me what you do for a living." There was something in her sweetness and mannerisms that made her look like she was acting right now. I took a close look at her blue eyes.

"What's wrong?" Her eyes narrowed again. "You're looking at me funny."

"Sorry. Nothing." I must've been overreacting. I'd become cynical over the last couple of years. Maybe she was authentically interested in me and I wasn't used to it. "What were you saying?"

"I was asking what you did for a living."

I tried to smile. "I'm a writer."

"What do you write?" She gave me a weak smile back.

I'd made us both uncomfortable. "I used to be a newspaper journalist. They seem to be a dying breed these days with the rise of the Internet, so now I'm taking a shot at becoming a fiction writer." That was true except for the real reason I stopped being a journalist.

"Yeah, all of media is changing." The tension in her face eased. "What are you writing now—a book?"

"Yeah, a thriller."

"That sounds interesting. What's it about?"

"The usual … you know, bad guy doing nasty things, and good guy chasing after him."

"Don't want to divulge the story, huh?" Her hand brushed my knee. "I'm sure it'll be great. Promise you'll give me a signed copy when it's published?"

A timer rang.

"The short ribs are ready." She got up.

"I love short ribs."

Angelica walked to the kitchen. "Have a seat at the table and I'll bring everything out."

The table was already set. Two pink candles were the centerpiece. The white plates with silver trim and silver cutlery looked formal. She must've brought them with her from home.

I took the seat facing the kitchen and placed the pale pink cloth napkin on my lap. My mother had taught me that the cook always sat in the chair closest to the kitchen. And from my seat I could watch Angelica prepare the food.

She knew her way around a kitchen. Not bad for a woman in her mid-twenties, these days. She placed green beans and potatoes onto separate platters, then put three short ribs on each of our plates and poured an *au jus* over them.

I should just relax. Why did I feel tense, on guard? She'd gone to all this trouble for me. However, there was something underneath that her mannerisms couldn't quite hide. I decided to be cautiously relaxed.

"Can you top up our glasses?" She pointed to the bottle she'd left on the table.

The green beans had slivered almonds and were mixed with a balsamic reduction. The potatoes were cut into wedges and baked with rosemary and tarragon.

"I hope you like it," Angelica said.

The short ribs covered in mushroom au jus melted in my mouth. "Everything's fantastic. Where did you learn to cook like this?"

"My mother and grandmother taught me. At one time I considered becoming a chef."

"You definitely could if you chose to." I placed a flavorful wedge of potato into my mouth and savored it. The firm exterior crunched when I bit into it, yet the centre was soft.

"I like cooking for you." She smiled. "Any … time."

I felt my face flush.

"It's all organic too, if that makes a difference." Her face went straight. "Does that make a difference to you?"

Her question was innocent enough; however, the tone and the searching look on her face made me feel there was more to it.

"Actually, it does make a difference."

"How come?"

Should I tell her anything? I wanted to explain why organic was a better choice, but the mood wasn't right for a lecture. "I like to make healthy choices."

"I can tell you take care of yourself."

Now I knew she was trying to butter me up. My shirt was big

enough to cover up my belly, but anyone could see I wasn't in the greatest shape. "Are you trying to get on my good side?"

"Maybe." The seductive smile made an appearance again. "Is that okay?"

"Of course." The image of a movie I saw a while back flashed across my mind. There was a scene with a male and a female spy sizing each other up over dinner. They'd ended up in bed afterward. As soon as she was sexually satisfied, she killed him. I gave my head a shake on the inside. *That was a movie. That didn't happen in real life ... did it? Besides, Angelica isn't a spy; she's a student. Right? Better change the subject.* "So, any plans for the weekend?" *That was lame.* I took a mouthful of food, followed by a big swallow of wine.

"Some studying. Not much. Why? What are you up to?"

"Oh, nothing. Since I don't have a regular job, weekdays and weekends are all the same to me."

"Must be nice." She slid her fork across her plate, picking up the last remnants of gravy and bits of potato. "I have brandy. Care for some?"

"Sure. That was a fantastic meal, Angelica."

She gathered my plate and hers. "Go have a seat on the couch and I'll bring it over."

As I took the few steps to the living room I looked down at my watch spy thing. I'm sure it had some sort of GPS and whoever was looking out for me this evening knew where I was.

"Do you have to be somewhere?" Angelica handed me a snifter.

"Oh ... no." I sipped the warm syrupy liquid with the alcohol aftertaste.

"You should update your watch. Or does it have special meaning to you?"

"Sort of." I sure wasn't going to tell her what the significance was.

"When's your birthday?"

"August, why?"

"No reason." She slid toward me so our knees touched. "So ... I'm guessing, because I've never seen you with anyone, that you aren't currently in a relationship?"

"Yes ... I mean no. I'm not in a relationship."

She placed her hand on my knee. It felt like we were having a role reversal. Her subtle touch stirred arousal in me.

"But you have a boyfriend, right?"

"No."

"How about the guy I saw when I was getting back from my trip?"

"He's nothing to worry about, just someone I know."

I admired the flawless skin of her face, high cheekbones, and full lips. I had a sudden intense feeling of missing being with a woman.

Angelica leaned in. Without any thought I kissed her. Her lips were soft and warm. She wrapped her hands around the back of my neck and pulled me closer. Our lips parted and my tongue felt the moist warmth of hers. The faint taste and smell of the alcohol lingered.

At the same time, we put our snifters down on the coffee table.

I wrapped my arms around her and pulled her tight against me. The feeling of her breasts against my chest and her hot tongue in my mouth gave me a full erection.

She pulled back, stood, and extended her hand. I accepted and she led me to her bedroom.

CHAPTER 21

Angelica was great—really into it. She was enthusiastic, energetic, and made sure I was fulfilled. She had two orgasms, so she must've enjoyed my skills in pleasuring her.

Then why did I feel empty and just want to get the hell out of there? I felt like the act we'd just committed was going to give me trouble.

There was just enough light coming from a streetlight through the sheer white curtains to see the outline of the room. The layout was the same as mine, but nicer furnishings arranged different.

The air had the faint smell of sex.

I looked at Angelica sleeping with her head resting on my shoulder. The blanket only covered her bottom half. She had a fantastic body. The mind, I wasn't so sure about.

I should've been happy and go with the flow of what would come, but I wasn't. Was I just thinking of myself and not caring about Angelica's feelings? She had indicated wanting more than just this evening. Could I be sabotaging a potentially good thing?

My intuition said, *Screw it, deal with the consequences later—run.*

I gave her a gentle nudge with my shoulder and it worked—she rolled over.

I pulled the blanket up over her as I slid out of bed. As quiet as I could, I crawled on the carpet to find my clothes.

I closed the bedroom door behind me and dressed in the living room.

Shit, where are my socks? I wasn't going back into the bedroom.

There were a pad and a pen on the coffee table. Writing her a note would make me feel less guilty and hopefully not make her feel bad.

Thanks for a great evening, Angela. Sorry I had to leave, but I have a busy day tomorrow.

What else do I say? Do I make her an offer? I can't just say, *See you around and leave my socks outside my door.* I settled for, *Hopefully you'll let me make you dinner in the future. Cheers, Nick.*

That should do it.

In a couple of days I might feel differently than I did at that moment and want to see her again. After all we had to live right next to each other. The urge to move back to Seattle became stronger.

I dropped the note on the dining room table and tiptoed to the door, grabbing my shoes as I went.

I couldn't lock the deadbolt; however, she had a lock on the doorknob, so I turned that. The door squeaked, no matter how slowly I closed it.

I took one step toward my apartment and froze. As my eyes adjusted to the light of the hallway, I couldn't believe who was standing in front of my door.

"Nick."

"Morgan?"

CHAPTER 22

After wondering if I'd ever see her again, there she was. Morgan looked at me, then my door, and then back at me in front of Angelica's door. "I was knocking at the wrong apartment."

"No, no, you have the right one." I walked toward her. "I was at the neighbor's having dinner and drinks." I was going to tell her the truth, but not right now. I'd wait to see how long she'd be staying.

I practically lunged the last couple of feet and embraced her. "It's so good to see you."

She hugged back. "I missed you."

I buried my face against her neck and strawberry blonde hair. Her familiar scent almost brought me to tears. "I missed you too."

She pulled back and touched my cheek with her hand. "I hope you don't mind me dropping by unexpected?"

"Not at all. I wish you'd come a few hours sooner." I felt guilty, even though I'd technically done nothing wrong.

"Oh … sorry, I've come too late in the evening."

"No, that's not what I meant."

"Why are you carrying your shoes and not wearing socks?"

I didn't know what to say. "Come on in." I opened my door

and held it for her.

Morgan had a large suitcase with her. "I came straight from the airport."

I gazed into the stunning blue eyes of the woman I'd fallen in love with.

We embraced again and our lips met.

She winced and pulled back. "Is your neighbor your girlfriend?"

"No, she isn't."

"You smell and taste like you've been with someone."

"Yes, I was with her." I let the bottled-up emotions pour out of me. "It was the first time I'd been with someone since you … tonight. I didn't know if I'd ever see you again. You left me in Oslo with no way of reaching you. You just left. It was Ivan who told me you went back to South Africa to stay with relatives." I took a deep breath. I had to pull myself together before I started whimpering like a child. "There's been a lot of stuff going on lately and I've felt alone. But, how would I have known that I just needed to be patient a few more hours? If it's any consolation I couldn't wait to get the hell out of her place."

There, I'd puked all my feelings out. It didn't help. Now I was embarrassed for sounding so wimpy.

She looked at me for a long moment, eyes misty.

"Why couldn't you have called or shot me an e-mail from time to time?"

"I know, you're right." She reached for the handle of her suitcase. "I'm going to go."

"Where? It's late. You can stay here. I'll sleep on the couch."

"No, there's a hotel I noticed a few blocks away. It's all right; I'll come see you tomorrow. I'm tired; it was a long flight."

Is she being honest? Will I see her tomorrow?

Her head was down as she went to the door.

"At least let me drive you."

"I'll be fine. I promise to come by tomorrow." She closed the door behind her.

I went to the window and watched until I saw her walk down the empty street. I exhaled in frustration.

I raised my wrist to my mouth and pressed the talk button. "Hello? Is anyone there?"

"Yes, Mr. Barnes." It was an unfamiliar male voice.

"There's a woman walking east pulling a suitcase. Can you make sure she gets to the hotel a few blocks away safe?"

"Yes, sir. I'll make sure she's unharmed."

I watched Morgan disappear in the distance and hoped she'd come back.

CHAPTER 23

O
f course I couldn't sleep. I just lay in bed, thinking.
I decided that if Morgan didn't show up by noon, I'd go
looking for her. Why did I unload my feelings all over her?
Why couldn't I have just acted casual?

Then there was Angelica. I hoped her feelings wouldn't be hurt
or that she'd cause problems. Maybe I was just a distraction for her
as well.

Muffled sounds of people talking disturbed my thoughts. On
the other side of my bedroom wall was Angelica's living room. It
was her and a male.

I sat up and placed my ear to the wall. I couldn't make out what
they were saying, but both had raised voices.

After a few moments there was quiet, then a faint squeak and
the vibration in the wall of a door closing.

I jumped out of bed and tiptoed as fast as I could to my door.
Should I open it to see who was there? What if they were right outside
and saw me? I couldn't hear any movement in the hall. Damn, I
wish I had a peephole.

I went to the window, opened the blinds halfway, and watched
to see whether anyone came out onto the street. I couldn't see the

building entrance, but if they walked away, I'd see them. The only way I wouldn't see someone was if they left from the parking area on the other side.

I watched for five minutes. No one. *Damn.*

I pressed the talk button on my watch.

"Yes, Mr. Barnes." It was the same voice from a few hours ago.

"Did you see a man exit the building within the last five minutes?"

"There was a Caucasian male, tall, late twenties, short dark hair, driving a black BMW Z3. Shall I run the plate?"

"You got the license plate number?" It sounded like the guy I'd seen leave Angelica's place before.

"Yes, sir. I was planning on running it anyway."

"Yes, I'd like to know who that was."

I'd only managed a couple of hours of sleep. It wasn't yet dawn when I got out of bed, made coffee, and started up my new computer. Might as well get some work done.

After getting the e-mail configured, I glanced out the window as my Inbox filled. It was cloudy and still outside.

I turned on the TV to the local morning news to watch for the weather report and to have background noise.

After all the messages had arrived, I scrolled down, deleting all the crap as I went. As it turned out, they were all junk.

I pondered sending Sue an e-mail about last night. I decided not to, because I felt embarrassed to have created a little soap opera. Even though Sue, and Jack for that matter, would want to know that Morgan was back, I'd wait to see what happened between us first.

I continued searching the Internet for any evidence on genetically engineered food causing sterility. I knew I wouldn't find anything incriminating, but I wanted to see whether there was even a little nugget of information I could expand upon. And I had to cover all the bases.

The phone rang. I jumped to get it, hoping it was Morgan.

"How you been, buddy? It's been a while."

"Hey, Mike. Thanks for calling back. It's been too long since we played golf. Do you have time for a round in the not-too-distant future?" Four hours on a golf course and maybe a couple of beers afterward would be more than enough time to find out how he knew Summer.

"That'd be great. Have you been playing much lately?"

"I just got back from Bandon Dunes."

"Awesome, I want to go there. Which course is better?"

"I just got to play the first course."

"Really?"

"I'll explain when we get together."

"Okay, you want to play Saturday? Us working stiffs can't just play any day of the week."

Saturday was two days away. "Sure, where?"

"How about Lincoln Park? We haven't played there for a while. It's a decent enough track and cheap."

"Sounds good. Around ten?"

"That works. See you then, buddy."

I called the course right away and booked a twosome. Then I e-mailed Mike the exact tee time.

It was almost eleven and Morgan hadn't shown up. It was time to go look for her.

As I reached for my running shoes beside the couch, the front door buzzer rang.

I sidestepped to the little box on the wall next to the door and pressed the speaker button. "Yes?"

"Can you please let me in?"

I exhaled in relief. "Sure, come on up." Thank goodness, Morgan had come back.

I ran to the bathroom to brush my teeth for a second time that morning.

Within a few minutes there was a knock on the door.

This time act normal and just be happy she's here, I said to myself as I opened the door. "Thanks for coming."

"Did you think I wouldn't?" Morgan unfastened her windbreaker, which was covered in droplets of moisture. "It's misty out there."

"That's San Francisco weather. Let me hang it over a chair to dry." As I came close to take her jacket I could smell the familiar scent of lilac from the hair product she always used. "Do you want coffee?"

"Sure." She went to the couch.

Morgan had developed a slight South African accent. Her voice was sweet to begin with, and the accent took it to a whole new level. I snuck a peek as I went to the kitchen. All five-foot-seven inches of her looked great as always.

I poured two coffees, adding sugar to mine and the right proportion of sugar and milk that she liked to hers.

"Why are you limping?" she asked.

"I hurt my thigh." I passed her the mug as I joined her on the couch.

"So ..." She seemed nervous. "How have you been?"

"Good, I guess, except for the things that have happened lately."

"What's happened?"

I brought her up to speed, telling her everything, starting with Summer's murder and ending with Jorge watching me. She only questioned the part about being shot at with golf balls, not understanding the reason for it, like everyone else.

"Wow, this is serious." She placed her mug on top of a magazine on the coffee table. "When will it end?"

"I'm not sure it will." I wanted to turn the focus to her. "Have you been in South Africa the whole time?"

She pushed her strawberry blonde hair to the side. It was shorter than before, now just reaching her shoulders. "Yes, except for the last month I was in Paris visiting an old friend." She looked right at me with her brilliant blue eyes and reached for my hand. "You know I had to deal on my own with everything that happened, right?"

Her hand was warm. Her long manicured fingers looked delicate, but she hadn't shied away from getting them dirty in the past.

"I know." Was there anything I wanted to add to what I said last night, without getting emotional? There wasn't.

"I needed to get away and be with what family I had left. I felt that if I stayed with you, I couldn't heal. I hope you understand and can forgive me."

I wanted her back in my life. I missed her. I still loved her. "I forgive you."

She squeezed my hand. "I don't know why, but I didn't want to talk to you until I was ready and knew I'd come back."

It hurt, but I was okay with her reasoning. "So what happened in South Africa?"

"I stayed with my aunt, my mother's sister, just outside of Johannesburg on their farm. Most of my relatives live around that area, so I visited them. I spent a lot of time on my own, too."

"That sounds therapeutic."

"My aunt helped me the most. She was really supportive and kept reminding me that my parents died trying to make the world a better place."

Morgan's mother, Claudia, was murdered in a car accident staged by Naintosa's security people, three years before her father was killed.

Morgan continued, "My aunt told me, when I was ready, that I could concentrate on making a difference, too. That it could be in any way I chose." A tear ran down Morgan's cheek. "I'm fortunate that I don't have to worry about money because of my parents."

I wiped the tear away, my thumb lingering on her cheek.

She took a deep breath. "I know you're also trying to make a difference …"

"Sometimes I think I don't have a choice in the matter."

She tried to smile. "I just knew you'd be in some kind of trouble."

I couldn't help but smile back. "Easy assumption."

"I want to help; work with you … if it's still possible. I want to be with you."

"I was hoping you'd say that."

I leaned in while placing my hand on the back of her neck and gently pulled her toward me until our lips met. We shared a long, lingering kiss. She felt like home.

I didn't want to spoil the mood, but we had to talk about last night. "About yesterday …"

Morgan took my hand again. "I understand. Don't worry about it. It was just unexpected."

"As long as you know that I would never have done that if I knew you were returning."

"I know." She stared into my eyes, searching as though she could see right into my soul. "Do you have feelings for her?"

"No. It was just a one-time thing, even if you hadn't come back. There was something about her that made me uncomfortable."

We kept eye contact. Morgan was the only person I'd ever known who had eyes that particular shade of deep blue. They always made me melt.

"So what would *you* like to happen with us?" she asked.

"I'd like us to be together. There's no one else I'd rather be with than you."

A fresh tear formed. "Me too."

CHAPTER 24

With Morgan back, I felt like we could take on any evil force, no matter how powerful, and prevail.

"I've kept up the meditation," Morgan said, handing me her mug for a refill.

"Does it still work well for you?"

"Meditating definitely helped to ground me and keep my head clear. I had visions of you a few times. The last one was about a week ago, and it convinced me it was time to come see you. You were in danger and needed help."

"Really? We still have our connection. Can you tell me what you saw?"

"You were in the woods walking toward something that felt dark and menacing. I was running after you to catch up, so you wouldn't have to deal with whatever was out there alone."

"That sums it up ... except for the forest part."

She shrugged. "That's what I saw."

I went to get more coffee, but stopped halfway. "Was it hard to find me?"

"No." Morgan shook her head. "Remember we talked about San Francisco being a nice place to live? In another meditative vision a few months back I saw you on a golf course with the Golden Gate Bridge in the background. So I searched the White Pages for your name and address. You can get that on the Internet now. It was easy."

"I don't like that it's so *easy* to find me." I continued to the kitchen.

"You really should be more *incognito*."

"I know. In the future, I can't leave a trail for someone to follow."

Morgan took the refilled mug from me. "Do you like San Francisco? Do you want to stay here?"

"I think it's time to go back to Seattle. Sue's been bugging me to move."

"How is Sue?"

"She's fine."

"It'd be easier to work on this project if we were all close together." Morgan took a little sip of the hot coffee. "I don't think Jack would object to my involvement."

"He told me he wanted you onboard."

"That's good to hear." Morgan leaned back on the couch. "I still have the townhouse."

"Oh, okay." Did she envision me living there with her? Was I ready for that so fast?

My black watch started talking, "Nick, are you there?"

Morgan jumped in her seat.

"It's Jack's guy I told you about who's watching over me."

Morgan surveyed the watch. "How spy-like."

I pressed the talk button. "Yes, Jorge."

"We ran the plate from last night. Can I come speak to you about it? Is this a good time for you and Morgan?"

Morgan looked startled. "He knows who I am and that I'm here?"

"That's his job." I pressed the button again. "Sure, come on up."

"Good of Jack to provide you with security."

"Yeah, nothing's happened since Jorge showed up."

There was a knock at the door.

"He was really close by," Morgan said.

When I opened the door, Jorge stood there wearing a navy blue polo shirt and holding a black leather portfolio. "Come on in."

He walked in a direct line to Morgan and shook her hand. "Jorge Villegas, pleasure to meet you."

Morgan looked him up and down. "How do you know who I am?"

"I was the person who helped Jack track you and Nick down in Christina Lake," Jorge said in his Colombian accent. "Then I followed you to Vancouver, back to Seattle, and onto Maui."

What? I hadn't known that.

"We even met briefly in Vancouver, but you didn't see me because you were blindfolded." A wry smile crossed his lips.

Morgan's eyes opened wide. "You were the one who loosened the rope around my wrists in the warehouse so I could untie myself?"

His smile grew wider.

Morgan jumped and gave him a hug. "Thank you."

Why hadn't he told me that?

Jorge blushed. He wasn't acting like a tough security agent. "You two were good, but needed a little extra help now and again."

"Thanks, Jorge," I said. "Sure would've been nice if you'd filled me in about that when we first met."

"I didn't think it would matter to you as much."

"Huh." Well, at least I knew now. "Can I get you some coffee or anything?"

"I'll only be a moment." He stood straight. "I don't want to disturb you."

"You're not disturbing us," Morgan said. "It's so nice to finally meet you."

Jorge's face turned a darker shade of blush, and he cleared his throat. Was he sweet on Morgan? Were there feelings inside that big old tough exterior?

Morgan gave Jorge a gentle smile. She was used to men acting like that around her.

Since Jorge was standing, I felt I should too.

"The BMW that left early this morning belongs to a Brad Caulder. Does that name ring a bell?"

I couldn't place the name. "No."

"He's six-foot-two, twenty-nine years old, and originally from Scottsdale. He has two priors for assault. His occupation is listed as student, but there wasn't a school on file."

"He fits the description of the man leaving my neighbor's place when we were coming from the airport."

"Yeah, my thoughts too," Jorge said.

"She said they were friends," I added.

"Well then he's her problem." Jorge gave a nod toward Morgan. "It's nice to finally meet you."

"Likewise," Morgan said.

"Jorge, what would you think if we were to move back to Seattle?" I asked.

"We can keep an eye on you two no matter where you live." He walked out of the apartment.

"Who's this Brad guy?" Morgan asked.

"He was at my neighbor's place at around two in the morning. It sounded like they were arguing."

"The neighbor you …"

"Yes." I didn't want her to finish the sentence. "From the description, it's the same guy I've seen around before."

"Why are you suspicious of him?"

"I dunno. It just seemed weird that he was there so late. But I guess it's nothing to worry about."

"Okay." Morgan reached for the coffee mug she'd placed on the table. "When do you want to move?"

"Soon. And this time, I'm not going to be listed in the White Pages." I went toward the kitchen. "I should call Sue." As I reached the phone, it rang.

Morgan smiled. "I bet you know who that is."

I placed the receiver to my ear. "I was just about to call you."

"How'd you know it was me?" Sue's voice sounded cheery.

"Intuition."

"Why were you going to call me?"

"Morgan is back, and we're both moving to Seattle."

There was silence on the other end of the line.

"Sue? Are you there?"

"Yeah … that's great. When?"

"Soon."

"Does Morgan still have her townhouse?"

"Yes."

"Are you going to live with her?"

"Not sure."

"Is she listening to your side of our conversation?"

I looked over at Morgan. "Yeah, why?"

"I'll say this once, because it needs to be said. Do what you feel is right, but be careful. Morgan's a good person … but she's kind of screwed up right now. I know it's for good reason, but she could leave again. She's hurt you once, and I don't want that happening to you another time."

"I'm tough."

"No, you're not. Not with relationship stuff."

I didn't want to consider the negative side. I'd be careful. "Why are you calling?"

"I forget." Sue paused. "I'm happy … for you that Morgan came back and that you'll be moving to Seattle. I'll talk to you later."

"Okay." I wasn't sure what to make of Sue's reaction.

"Sue's not happy I'm here and we're moving back?" Morgan said, as soon as I put the phone down.

"Of course she is."

Morgan looked as if she didn't believe me.

"Sue's been bugging me since the day I moved here." I returned to the couch. "She's also happy you've returned."

We looked at each other for a long moment. I placed my hand on her knee for reassurance. I didn't know what to do next. *Should I pick her up and take her to the bedroom? Should we just get to work? Is there more to talk through?*

"What should we do now?" Morgan asked.

CHAPTER 25

I was explaining the initial plan Jack, Sue, and I had made; Morgan was making a few notes on a pad I gave her.

The rap was abrupt and quick, like a small hand pounding. "There's more activity here today than I'm used to." I got up to answer the door.

There was another knock just before I opened the door with caution.

Angelica was standing there with her right hand raised in a fist. In her left was a piece of paper and my socks.

Why hadn't I gotten the damn peephole? "Hi, Angelica."

"Great, you remember my name today." She took a step forward as if wanting to come in.

I didn't move aside. "What do you mean?"

She held up the note I'd left and pointed to the top. It read, *Angela*.

In my rush to get out of there I'd gotten her name wrong. Crap. "Sorry about that. It was dark. Of course I know your name."

"Why did you leave last night?" Her expression softened. "I thought we had a good time. I could've made you breakfast. Can I come in? What are you doing today?"

Out of the corner of my eye I could see Morgan come up to

the open door.

"I'm sorry, this isn't a good time," I said. "Last night was nice, but things are complicated."

"Nice? Complicated?" Angelica raised her eyebrow and her face turned the same shade as her T-shirt.

"I told you I wasn't in a relationship, because the woman was gone a long time and I didn't think she'd return. Now she's back. Uh, I'm …"

"What do you mean?" Angelica looked around me. "It was just last night."

Morgan took the extra step to stand beside me. "Hi, I'm Morgan."

Angelica moved back. She looked down and then up in slow motion. A rage escalated in her eyes.

I had seriously made a bad move last night. But it was done. Angelica was justified in her anger. But the way her lips tightened, and the daggers visible in her eyes, made her downright dangerous looking. I was so grateful that Morgan had come back. If she hadn't and I had started seeing Angelica, no doubt I'd really be in a big mess of trouble.

Morgan opened her mouth to speak, but I beat her to it. "I'm so sorry, Angelica, really. It was just bad timing."

Morgan glanced at me.

I had to add, "Morgan's the one for me." It was pretty weak, but at least Morgan's face relaxed.

"Don't flatter yourself. You weren't that good." Angelica looked at Morgan. "I don't know what you see in him."

Morgan was stern. "You obviously saw something."

I swear I saw a facial tick, before Angelica said, "Nobody does that to me."

I braced for the impact of a punch or slap.

Then it was as if she'd remembered something. Although the anger didn't subside from her face, Angelica said, "But we can still

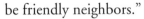

be friendly neighbors."

What?

When she turned to walk away, I saw that her fists were so tightly clenched they were red.

As soon as I closed the door, Morgan said, "That's your type? Sure she's pretty, but a psycho."

"Thank goodness it was just a one-night stand."

"She obviously hoped for more," Morgan said. "But she'll get over it."

"Have I told you I'm so happy you're back?"

We stood there looking at each other. Was Morgan deciding whether she should be angrier with me? Was she evaluating my sincerity and even the common sense of my decisions?

Nothing like this had happened before in our short relationship. How long would this upset her, and would she make me pay for it in some way? I decided to keep my mouth shut.

Morgan sighed. "Do you want to go for a walk and then get something to eat?"

❦

A wall of fog held its position west of the Golden Gate, making it clear in the city.

We ate shellfish at Fisherman's Wharf and spent the rest of the day wandering around.

It was as if we needed to get reacquainted, a first date of sorts. The conversation was light. I sensed Morgan wanted to ease back, and I was all for that.

I caught a glimpse of Jorge at one point.

The fog rolled in at dusk and contained so much moisture that it made us as wet as if we were in the rain.

"Do you want to get your stuff and check out?" I asked, as we climbed the hill that passed the hotel she was staying at.

Morgan stopped walking and turned to me. She'd been holding my hand and squeezed tighter. "Do you mind if I stay there awhile longer?"

"Why? Is there something wrong?" The afternoon and evening had gone so well that I thought we were good to move forward.

"I—I don't feel comfortable sleeping at your place … yet."

"Oh."

"It's not just that there's only a thin wall separating your bedroom from your neighbor's. I feel like we need to move a little slower right now."

She hadn't brought up Angelica since we left my place, so I'd thought maybe she was okay with the situation now. She wasn't.

We continued walking. We turned left after we crossed Pacific Avenue instead of right to my place.

"I could stay with you at the hotel."

She gave me a sympathetic smile. "How about I bring breakfast in the morning?"

"That sounds fine." I squeezed her hand.

She wasn't running away. If she wanted to go slow that was okay with me. We needed to be solid when things heated up again.

She brightened up after I didn't protest. "Make sure to give notice that you're moving to your landlord. Tomorrow's March first."

CHAPTER 26

March 1, 2002

It was daylight outside when I awoke. It wasn't until then that I'd realized I hadn't had a good night's sleep in weeks and it'd caught up to me.

I had to hurry to be ready by the time Morgan arrived. After making coffee and having a shower, I wrote out a check for the month's rent and a note giving notice. Then I ran them down to the building manager.

I was able to pour two cups of coffee before Morgan knocked on the door.

"Good morning." She gave me a soft kiss and handed me a brown paper bag. She seemed at ease.

"How are you?"

"Good." Morgan took off her navy blue water resistant jacket. "I have to get used to these cooler temperatures again, and rain."

I found her just as attractive in a sweatshirt and jeans as when she dressed up.

"Breakfast's in the bag," Morgan said.

She'd bought two breakfast croissants with bacon, egg, and

cheese. We'd both enjoyed croissants almost every day when we were in Oslo. I'd stopped eating them when I moved back to the States, because they reminded me too much of her.

"So where do we start?" Morgan took a sip of coffee. "Did you give notice?"

"Yes, I did." I sat down next to her on the couch and withdrew the wrapped sandwiches from the bag, handing one to Morgan. "I thought we'd go to the library and see if we can find anything in recent journals. It's not very likely, but we should check."

"Do you have copies of the documents taken from the Bolivia lab?" Morgan asked.

"Yes."

"I want to read them again," she said. "It'll refresh my memory."

"Now?"

"Why not?"

I went to the kitchen, opened the bottom shelf, and pulled out all the pots and pans.

Morgan had come to the kitchen to see what I was doing. "Nice hiding spot."

"It does the job." I pulled out a manila envelope and we went back to the couch.

Morgan took the documents. "The other thing we're going to research is glyphosate, right?"

"Yes, the main ingredient of Naintosa's herbicide. Your dad only mentioned glyphosate a few times in his notes. We need more details."

"I remember the weeds eventually became resistant to it and turned into super-weeds."

"Jack thinks it's an important link to what's going on."

"I remember Ivan mentioning that more unbiased research needed to be undertaken on glyphosate." She pulled all the papers from the envelope.

"Do you want me to show you where the sterility part is?"

"No, I want to read through it all. It'll get me back into it."

While Morgan read, I took what was left of my sandwich and coffee to my computer. I logged onto the San Francisco library website. The main branch on Larkin Street seemed to have the kind of journals we were looking for.

"Why hadn't we paid more attention to this?" Morgan held up a piece of paper.

"That note is the only reference to it and I think we just ran out of time. So now we can focus on proof. Sterility's a big deal, especially on the scale we're talking about."

Rain sheeted across the windshield of the Pathfinder as we drove the two miles to the library. We parked underground, so as not to have to brave the elements on the street.

"It's busy," Morgan said as we came out of the elevator onto the main floor.

I pointed through the people. "There's a directory that'll show us where the periodicals and journals are."

"You haven't been here to do research before?" Morgan asked.

"I haven't had to do any research since I moved to San Francisco." The change I brought in case we needed to make photocopies jangled in my pocket as we walked.

There was a group of people standing in front of the directory, each searching for their point of interest. We peered around them until we found ours.

Morgan nodded to the right. "Over there."

We zigzagged through the patrons to the elevators. We waited in line and managed to squeeze into the second one.

"Why is it so busy?" Morgan asked.

"No idea." I managed to maneuver my hand around an elderly gentleman's shoulder and press the button with the number four on it. "Excuse me."

When we arrived at our desired floor we were the only ones to get off.

There was no one around. Six reference computer screens sat on tables, in an alcove, in front of rows and rows of shelves containing periodicals and journals. The only sound was the faint hum of the air system circulating the musty smell of old paper.

Morgan shrugged. "Our own private floor."

The door to the stairwell opened, sounding loud in the silence. We both turned to see Jorge come into the room.

He looked around. "Don't mind me."

"I guess you can't watch us from a distance here," I said.

"No, but don't let me distract you from your work. I'm going to take a walk around to make sure it's secure. Pretend I'm not here."

Morgan went to one of the reference screens. "What do you want to research first?"

For whatever reason a fourteen-year-old memory popped into my head, and I decided to share it. "In my first year at the university, we had to manually search on index cards to find stuff."

"You're dating yourself. I'm only three years younger than you, and I always remember indexes being on the computer." Morgan began to type on the keyboard. "Let's start with genetically engineered food causing sterility."

There was nothing even close in the system.

"Yeah, I didn't think there would be anything so obvious on that." I sighed. "Let's look up glyphosate. Your father's notes contained information about what it did to the weeds, but not what it did to people after they'd consumed trace amounts for a number of years. You can't wash that stuff off before you eat the food."

"He had information on that," Morgan said. "Remember the study he obtained after he left Naintosa? In several areas of the country people unknowingly ate the genetically engineered food with that herbicide for a period of time. Their immune systems were compromised and they developed all kinds of problems. And Naintosa stated it was within their 'tolerable side effect' levels."

"Oh yeah." I remembered that particular information had really pissed Morgan off. "We need to see if there's anything more recent."

"True." As she turned to look at the screen, I caught a glimpse of agitation on her face. "Don't forget that my dad had no part in developing the herbicide or making the plants resistant to it. Naintosa did that after they took the experiments from him."

Her defensiveness was justified. "Don't worry, I remember."

There were quite a few articles. We ignored the ones from Naintosa. I jotted down all twenty-three references that could have some relevance.

Morgan and I walked into the cavernous rows reciting numbers that would point us in the direction we were searching.

"We get to do your favorite thing—research," Morgan said.

I gave her a weak smile. Yes, everyone knew I was an ex-reporter who didn't like that part of the job. That caused me trouble on a few occasions. I liked to write. I worked best when someone did the research and just gave me the results.

It took a while to find all the journals and periodicals, but we managed to get twenty-two; only one was missing.

We found a table and hunkered down. Each article would be lengthy, so it was going to take a while.

"This study states it helps farmers because there were minimal weeds," Morgan said. "However, the added cost of the herbicide offset the cost of weeding, so there were no overall savings. There's no mention of super-weeds. The genetically engineered corn in the test held up to the glyphosate." She stretched her arm as far as she could reach and placed the journal on the table. "Put the articles that don't help there."

The one I was looking at was similar, so I tossed it to the pile

Morgan had started.

The next one I read stated that glyphosate was harmless to humans and animals because of the mechanism of action it used, called the shikimate pathway, was absent in all people and animals. I made a note to find out what the shikimate pathway was.

Next, I picked up a journal I'd never heard of and looked through the index to find the pertinent article. The pages hadn't been creased and I doubted it had ever been read. The title was *Glyphosate and Modern Disease.* The hair on the back of my neck stood up.

The article was published only a month ago by Dr. Timothy Roth. The reason for the study was that Naintosa's patent on their herbicide with the main ingredient of glyphosate had just expired in 2000. Four other companies were introducing herbicides of a similar mix, therefore increasing the amount of the chemicals on the market. The sponsor was a privately funded lab I'd never heard of; I noted their name.

I skipped the part about how the research was conducted.

There was a different account of the information I'd read in the previous article: … *the shikimate pathway is absent in all mammals; however, it is present in bacteria. Bacteria in people outnumber cells ten to one and all respond to the presence of glyphosate. Glyphosate causes a disruption of the microbe's function and lifecycle.*

That was followed by detailed scientific charts and formulas that I didn't understand.

I skipped to the conclusion of *Section A*: … *glyphosate preferentially affects beneficial bacteria, allowing pathogens to overgrow. Mammals contending with toxins created by the pathogens eventually developed chronic inflammation, giving way to chronic diseases.*

At the end was a list of diseases suspected to be linked to glyphosate poisoning that needed to be studied further: *autism, gastrointestinal disease, obesity, allergies, cardiovascular disease, cancer, infertility, Alzheimer's, Parkinson's, multiple sclerosis, and ALS.*

I sat back in my chair. That was huge. How did Naintosa not know about this study and squash it?

"Are you okay?" Morgan asked. "You're sheet white."

"I've really found something here."

"I never expected to find anything," Morgan said. "Can I see?"

"Me neither. Let me finish first."

Section B was about toxicity: *Glyphosate enhances the damaging effects of chemicals and environmental toxins people are exposed to. The consequences are the diseases and conditions associated with the Western diet.*

The table of diseases from *Section A* was repeated.

What followed was about the glyphosate-autism and -Alzheimer's connections. There were certain microbes in a person's body that broke down glyphosate. However, a byproduct of that action was ammonia. Children with autism had significantly higher levels of ammonia in their blood, compared to the general population. The same with people who had Alzheimer's: ... *within these people, as they age, the excess ammonia causes encephalitis or brain inflammation.*

Section C concentrated on nutritional deficiencies: ... *glyphosate immobilizes certain nutrients and alters the nutritional composition of the treated crop.* The list of nutrients was in their scientific names and half a page long.

Glyphosate causes a disruption of the biosynthesis of essential amino acids, impairing transport and metabolism of sulfate, causing gut dysbiosis.

What's gut dysbiosis? I wrote it down.

After the reference list was a note about how the study was ongoing with further research being compiled in all areas of their findings. Genetic engineering of the crops used may have played a factor in the results and needed further study.

I remembered there were some scientific encyclopedias by the computer terminals and got up to go find one.

Morgan tossed another journal onto the far pile. "Hurry up. I'm dying to read that study."

"I just have to look something up, and then I want to make a copy of it."

When I reached the terminals, Jorge was sitting on a chair placed between the elevators and stairwell.

"Everything okay?" I asked.

"We're the only ones here."

I found what I was looking for and made note of it. Gut dysbiosis was an imbalance of gut bacteria. It caused inflammation, leaky gut, and food allergies. It sounded painful.

The photocopier was in the corner close to the restrooms. It took most of the change I'd brought to make the copy of the study.

Returning to our table I saw Morgan finishing another article.

I passed her the journal. "Here you go."

She was eager to take it.

I made notes in the margins of the photocopy before I forgot anything. That involved a second read-through before I was confident that I noted all the questions and the few answers I'd already found.

Every few minutes, I'd look up to see Morgan's facial expressions. She was reading the report with wide eyes. Several times she asked me to highlight certain parts.

"How did Naintosa let this get out?" she said after finishing. "This proves how awful glyphosate really is. The study discredits the others by digging deeper. We have to contact the head scientist."

I nodded. "Let's see if we can find him on the Internet when we get back to my place."

Morgan slumped back in her seat and looked at her watch. "It's almost six o'clock."

CHAPTER 27

I finished chewing my last piece of sushi and read the search results on the screen. "There's nothing on Dr. Timothy Roth."

Morgan sat next to me. "We'll have to look him up when we go back to the library tomorrow."

"I'm playing golf, so we'll go on Sunday."

"Golf is going to take you all day? Isn't this more important? There might be good information in the journals we haven't read yet."

"They'll still be there on Sunday. I need to get some information from my buddy Mike about Summer Perkins. That's real important too. It may involve plying him with liquor after we play, which could take all day."

"That's right, I forgot."

The front door buzzer rang.

"Who could that be?" I went to answer it.

"Nick, it's Detective Cortes," said the voice from the little white box. "Do you have a few minutes to talk?"

"Sure, come on up."

"The police?" Morgan asked.

"It's the detective who's working on Summer Perkins' case. He's the same one who was at your dad's office."

"Really? You hadn't mentioned that before." Morgan always showed a glint of sadness whenever her father was mentioned. "It's quite the coincidence."

"Sorry, I must've missed that point." It was weird that I'd forgotten to tell her that before. "It's pretty late in the evening for him to come see me."

"Do you want me to go hide in the bedroom?"

"No. Why would you do that?"

"I don't know." Morgan shrugged. "Do you trust him?"

"I think so. Lee was supposed to check him out, and I haven't heard anything negative back from him. So I guess that means Cortes is legitimate."

There was a knock at the door.

Cortes was standing there when I opened it. "I hope you don't mind me coming by unannounced at this time? It'll only take a few minutes."

There was a slight movement at the end of the hall. It was Jorge. I gave him a quick nod and blink that everything was okay.

Detective Cortes turned in the direction I had looked. "What was that?"

Jorge was gone.

"What?"

"You nodded in that direction."

"I did?" If he didn't know about Jorge, I didn't see a need to tell him.

He watched me for a couple of seconds.

"Come on in." I moved over to let him pass as I held onto the door.

"Oh, I didn't realize you had company."

She approached and held out her hand. "Morgan Elles, nice to meet you."

Cortes paused as if searching his memory bank and then extended his arm. "You're Dr. Carl Elles' daughter." He turned to me. "She came back."

I couldn't help but smile. "Yes, she did."

Morgan held onto his hand longer than needed. "You worked on my father's murder investigation, right?"

"Well, technically there was no murder investigation."

Morgan had a cold look on her face. "But you know he was murdered?"

"Yes."

"Do you want me to go in the other room while you talk?" she asked.

"No, please stay. I might want to ask you a few questions."

Cortes sat in the chair and Morgan and I on the couch.

"Have you had any progress on investigating Summer Perkins' death or who shot my door up?" I asked.

"Both are going to take a while," Cortes said. "I thought I'd stop by to see if you've thought of anything that could shed more light onto the investigation. I think the two events are connected. Has anything happened since last time we spoke?"

Should I tell him my place was broken into and that I'd been shot at with golf balls and bullets? Both Jack and Jorge had said not to tell the police and my intuition agreed, for now. "No, nothing."

Out of the corner of my eye I could see Morgan watching me.

Cortes stared at me for a moment. "Are you sure?"

Did he know something and wasn't telling me? Or can he read my expression? I shook my head.

Cortes relaxed his look. "Ms. Perkins' editor at the *News* said that she'd taken a sudden trip to Quebec City last October. She'd acted oddly ever since she got back."

"Odd in what way?" I asked.

"Not her bubbly self; more reserved and jumpy, maybe even scared. Do you have any idea why she went to Quebec City and who was the man she was with?"

"I didn't know she'd gone. Like I told you before, I didn't really know Summer."

"Okay." He turned his gaze to Morgan. "How long are you visiting for, Ms. Elles? Nick told me you now live in South Africa."

"I'm moving back to Seattle. Nick is as well."

Cortes brought out the pad from the right pocket of his raincoat. "How come?"

"Seattle's our home," I said. "There's really nothing here for me. I can write from anywhere and Morgan owns a townhouse there."

Cortes poised his pen. "Do you have an address and phone number you can give me so we can keep in touch?"

Morgan looked at me and I gave her an approving nod.

Cortes raised an eyebrow. "Is there a secret?"

"No, of course not." She gave him her address and phone number.

After Cortes finished writing, he looked up at Morgan. "Did you know Summer Perkins?"

"No, I didn't. It was sad to hear of her murder from Nick."

"Did anything happen while you were in South Africa regarding your father's book or Naintosa's security people?"

"No, nothing."

Cortes made another note and put his pad away. He produced two business cards and gave them to us. "I'll stay in touch, but make sure you contact me if you think of anything … anything."

"I already have your card." I held it out to give back to him.

"Consider it a spare." He got up and went to the door. "Be careful."

"Thanks for stopping by." I followed to close and lock the door.

"What did he mean by that?" Morgan was still on the couch.

"By what?"

"Be careful and the double '*anything.*'"

"I don't know."

"I think he knows something he didn't tell us. And he doesn't believe that nothing's happened to you since you last talked to him."

"I have that feeling too. Me not telling him everything shouldn't hinder him in finding Summer's killer anyway. And he has no reason to tell us everything he's found out."

"Hmm, you're right." Morgan got up. "I'd better go; it's getting late."

"Why don't you stay?"

"I don't think I'm ready yet. Thank you so much for being patient with me. I must be driving you nuts."

"It's okay. I guess Cortes got me nervous. I don't want you going out there alone. If you stay here we can watch out for each other, and we know Jorge has us covered."

That seemed to get her thinking. "Maybe you're right."

"How about this? We have a glass of wine and watch a movie to get our minds off everything. Then we cuddle together to sleep … only cuddle, I promise. Tomorrow after we meditate and I make you breakfast you can be a tourist while I play golf. How's that sound? Only cuddle …"

Morgan grinned.

CHAPTER 28

My left arm was numb. I opened my eyes and smiled. Morgan was facing away from me, her head resting on my extended limb.

Last night's cuddling had turned into more. It was familiar, soft and sensual. I could honestly say that with Morgan we made love, not just had sex.

My contented exhale must've been loud enough to wake her. She rolled over, revealing her full round breasts with pale rouge nipples on her ivory skin. To me they were perfect.

She covered herself with the duvet and buried her head in my sparsely haired chest. "Morning."

"Did you sleep well?"

She mumbled, because her lips were against my skin. "Best sleep I've had in ages."

"Me too." I meant it.

"What time is it?"

I raised my head and looked at my digital clock on the far nightstand. "Shoot, we'd better get up, it's eight."

She pulled away. "Where do you want to meditate, here?"

"Let me see what it looks like outside." I reached for my boxers on the floor, pulling them up as I stood.

She gave me a coy smile. "You don't have to do that."

"I don't want to give you any ideas."

I went to the window and opened the blinds. "It's sunny for a change. Put some clothes on, we can meditate outside."

I brought a thin blanket with us because the old bench in the courtyard would be damp.

"It's nice here," Morgan said. "The bushes and trees make it a little hiding spot."

"Yeah, and no one ever comes out here." I spread the blanket over the bench.

We sat next to each other, our legs touching.

"Are you going to give me instructions like you used to?" she prodded.

"You've been doing it long enough to not need any direction from me."

We closed our eyes and focused on our breathing. In and out, slow and steady. Calm. Let the mind be free of its thoughts and open to whatever was out there.

Nothingness. Empty space.

A sudden close-up of the face under the motorcycle helmet, behind the tinted goggles, came into my mind's eye. My hand reached out and pulled the helmet off. Short brown hair, a chiseled jawline with a cleft in the middle of his chin, blue eyes, all surrounded a feminine nose. The scene changed to the street. The same man walked right past me when I was on my way to meet Summer.

My eyes bolted open and I gasped. That was the same guy who had been leaving Angelica's place when I had returned from Bandon. Brad something. Could he have beaten me back from Bandon? I counted the hours. Yes, he could've.

"Are you all right?" Morgan asked. "Your body jolted so hard you almost knocked us off the bench."

"I just had a really vivid vision." I took deep breaths to try to calm down. "It's all connected."

"What's all connected? What parts?"

"The guy outside the bar where Summer died was the same one who shot at me in Bandon. And he was leaving Angelica's apartment when I got home, and he was at her place late that same night … uh … you came back."

"Really? Are you sure?"

I focused on slowing my thoughts. "It could be my brain trying to make connections and not a real vision. I can't tell."

"What I don't get is that you've seen this guy … what did Jorge say his name was?"

"Brad something. I have it written down."

"You've seen Brad a number of times and you haven't put it together until now?"

"I don't know why it's taken so long. Now I'm doubting myself. I must've been forcing an answer."

"Don't dismiss it so soon. You've had real visions before." Morgan stood up. "Let's go upstairs. I don't feel comfortable here anymore."

As we walked up the stairs, I wondered what role Angelica played. She had to be a part of it. Her job must've been to spy on me. That would explain the weird vibe I was getting off her.

"If you're right, your neighbor's a part of it, you know." Morgan stopped climbing and turned to look at me. "She seduced you to get close … for information."

Morgan could've been right. "Lucky I didn't give her any important information. I don't know any information that's important; nothing that'd be a secret, anyway."

"Why would they go to all this trouble, then? Something's going down, and you're involved somehow. We have to figure out how and why."

"Now you understand my situation. Could it be preemptive to ensure that I don't get involved?"

Morgan pondered that. "Yeah, could be."

I contacted Jorge as soon as we were in my apartment. I told him I thought the guy with the BMW was behind what was going on. He said it was a good theory, but to wait awhile before I called Detective Cortes. Jorge wanted to look deeper into who Brad was first. I also explained our day and that, if possible, I wanted someone to watch Morgan. He agreed and needed forty-five minutes to set it up.

While Morgan showered I made us some fruit salad, corned-beef hash, and toast. The whole time I thought about Brad and Angelica. All that had happened could've been planned by them. What did they have against me, or who were they working for?

By the time we finished breakfast, Jorge called and said a shadow for Morgan was in place.

I held out my arm to be next to Morgan's face and pressed the talk button.

"I want to be able to recognize her if something happens," Morgan said, toward the mic on my watch.

"Keep an eye out for a woman in her forties wearing jeans and a black shirt, with shoulder-length brown hair," Jorge said.

Morgan leaned forward. "That could be anyone."

"Hmm. She'll be wearing a silver pendant in the shape of a rose above her left breast."

"Okay, I think I could spot that."

I pulled my arm back toward my mouth. "It's time for us to go. I'll be driving, and Morgan will be walking."

"We have you both covered."

INTERLOGUE 2

All of his offices and homes had to smell like a pine forest after it rained. The oil-based air freshener was held in carafes. His secretaries and servants were in charge of replenishing them. The chemical company that produced it made sure he always had a supply on hand.

Davis took a deep breath. It calmed him. The scent permeated his navy blue suit and probably his skin for that matter.

A shadow moved across the window. The entire right wall of the room was glass. Being at the top of the American Pyramid, Global Mark Communication's US Media's head office was in the clouds or sometimes above them. Davis didn't often stop to admire the view of the city below, the harbor, or the Golden Gate Bridge in the distance.

A sultry female voice came over the intercom, "Mr. Bail is here for your ten o'clock appointment."

"Get some fresh coffee and then send him in."

Davis pondered. He'd have to get rid of his secretary. She'd worked for him for almost a year, and he'd wanted to lift her tight skirt up and see what was at the top of those long legs every time he was at this office. It finally had happened yesterday. They'd been working late and had shared a bottle of cognac.

He looked across the room at the white leather couch where the seduction had taken place. Her tall, slim body was delightful. But Davis couldn't stand for infidelity, especially in the workplace. He didn't care that she was a single mother. He'd been happily married for thirty years to Gwen, and they had two grown daughters. He never counted the first daughter he had by mistake when he was seventeen. He had no idea where she and her mother even were.

Every time he had sex with a woman other than his beloved Gwen, he couldn't stand looking at her again. The women seduced him for their own gain. This secretary had to go. He'd call his HR manager after the meeting and have it taken care of.

One of the double mahogany doors opened, being pushed by the back of his secretary. She wore high red pumps, a short red skirt, and a tight ivory-colored blouse. In her hands was a silver tray holding a carafe of coffee and what accompanied it.

Following her was a tall, strong-looking man in a black tailored suit. He had a confident stride, yet a limp in his right leg. His brown hair was cut short and beginning to gray.

Davis rose and stepped to the side of his desk. Peter looked straight at Davis as he shook his hand, his green eyes not blinking.

"Have a seat, Peter." Davis motioned to the two white leather chairs on the guest side of his glass-top desk as he went back to the business side. "Care for some coffee? It's the finest organic Colombian you can get."

"I'm sure it is." Peter smiled at the secretary.

She blushed and poured two cups. "How do you like it, sir?"

"Black, please." Peter reached out and took the bone china cup and saucer from her, making sure to brush her hand.

She flustered for a second, then added two sugars and cream to a second cup, stirred, and handed it to Davis.

"That'll be all," Davis said.

"Shall I leave the rest of the coffee?"

"Yes." He didn't smile at her or say thank you. Why bother? She'd be gone in a few hours.

Her straight blonde hair didn't move as she departed, but her hips did. Davis wondered what the next secretary would look like as he watched her leave. He'd request a younger, shorter, buxom one this time for a change.

Now, business. "I guess you're wondering why you're here?"

"Yes, sir." Peter took a sip and his eyes rose, indicating the pleasurable taste of the hot full-bodied roast. "It's not often that a man of your stature calls direct."

"I have a job for you, and I want it off the books. It's perfect for the exact experience you have. Are you able to work?"

"Sure. My leg's healed, and I'm tired of sitting under palm trees in Belize. It would be good to get back to work."

"How did you hurt your leg?"

"Caught some shrapnel."

"In Maui?" Davis knew that was the last time Peter had been employed. Not taking care of Nick Barnes, Morgan Elles, and Sue Clark was what had gotten him fired from managing the Naintosa security force.

"Yes. It kept me off my feet for a while." Peter placed a finger between his neck and the front of his white shirt collar and gave it a gentle pull for less constriction.

"But you're fine now?"

"Ready to roll."

"Good. I want you to watch and maybe take care of what you couldn't before."

Peter squinted. "What do you mean?"

Davis leaned forward. "Nick Barnes and Sue Clark met with Jack Carter recently. Now Morgan Elles is here in San Francisco with Barnes. I think they might all be up to no good and planning something."

Peter showed a glint of agitation at the names. "Why would they be a problem for you? Isn't Dr. Schmidt keeping tabs on them? Why would you need me?"

"Dr. Schmidt's main concern is Barnes. Mine is Carter. The two are connected again. I don't want my security people involved. I want this handled privately."

Peter leaned forward and placed his forearms on the desk. "So *is* Dr. Schmidt still having them watched?"

"I believe so. If anything suspicious should happen to Barnes right now, it would incriminate Dr. Schmidt."

"So what do you want me to do?"

"Find out what Carter, Barnes, and the two women are up to."

"Why don't we just go after Carter?" Peter asked. "He's the power."

"He's well protected. It would be too messy."

"Okay." Peter paused and then said, "Why don't I just go pick Barnes up and question him?"

"Do you think he'd tell you what they're doing?"

"I have my ways. It's worth a shot."

Peter's ways hadn't worked last time, but he knew how Barnes operated better than anyone else, which was why Davis was offering him the job. "Use whatever tactics you deem best."

"What if there was an accident and Barnes perished during questioning?"

"Like I said, that would cause trouble for Dr. Schmidt, so don't kill Barnes." Davis didn't bother mentioning that Peter would be taken out by Hendrick in a heartbeat, because all the heat would piss him off to no end.

Davis was enjoying this. Hendrick would find out about Peter working for him. He wouldn't hide it. And as soon as Hendrick knew, he'd call a face-to-face meeting to try to dissuade Davis from having Peter do the job. In the end, they'd decide to combine forces, and Davis would make sure Peter was in charge of the operation. He wasn't sure how much he trusted Peter's abilities, but his knowledge and personal vendetta were enough to allow him to lead. And Davis controlled Peter now, not Hendrick.

Davis reached into the bottom-left desk drawer and pulled out a black leather bag with hooped handles. He placed it on Peter's side of the desk. "This should get you started. Let me know about any expenses. There's also a bonus on performance."

Peter placed the bag on his lap and pulled the handles apart to see the contents. There were sixteen stacks of hundred dollar bills wrapped in paper sleeves that read ten thousand on each one. "Okay."

Davis pressed the red button on his desk phone. "Send in Brad Caulder." Then he looked back at Peter. "You'll have assistance. I've had two people on Barnes already but not doing a good job. They will answer to you."

The door to the office opened. In walked a younger version of Peter Bail; tall, slim, muscular, and with chiseled features, except for his small nose.

As he pressed the button that would take him down to the lobby, Peter thought about the meeting he'd just had with the arrogant asshole billionaire. He was used to dealing with his kind. He relished the opportunity of having another crack at slippery Nick Barnes, who he wouldn't let get the best of him again. Getting hold of feisty little Sue Clark and sexy Morgan Elles could be entertaining, and causing damage to Jack Carter would be a bonus. He'd spent many hours while recovering fantasizing about how to get back at all of them.

Davis didn't want him to kill Barnes because that would incriminate Dr. Schmidt. But Peter wanted to cause Dr. Schmidt pain, too. He had to figure out how to do the job required in a way that served himself best in the end.

CHAPTER 29

After turning right off Clement Street onto 34th Avenue, I wasn't far from the golf course.

Lincoln Park was a short par sixty-eight municipal course, providing the public a place to play for a reasonable price. It was as far away from a country club setting as one could get. The white ranch-style clubhouse, which sat next to the parking lot, needed restoration yet was still able to serve its purpose.

I'd arrived early enough to warm up. Mike, on the other hand, always showed up minutes before we teed off.

"Hey, buddy."

I looked up from the practice putt I was just about to make. "Hey, Mike."

"I'm early." He had a gregarious smile, which was his most endearing feature.

I looked at my walkie-talkie disguised as a watch. We had ten minutes before our tee time. "You *are* early today."

"It's the new me." He set his golf bag down and gave me a hug, slapping my back. "It's been a while. How are you, buddy?"

"Good." Today was about catching up with him, not what's been happening with me. "How about you?"

"Fine." His smile turned sad. It was always hard for Mike to hide his emotions, and that sometimes got him into trouble.

"You're looking, uh, well." I'd find out what was bothering him as our time together progressed.

He padded his pronounced belly. "It takes a lot of work and dedication to achieve this. Always gotta be fueling it."

I laughed. Every time I saw him the beer gut was just a bit bigger.

Mike was always disheveled. His red cotton golf shirt and tan khakis looked like they'd never seen an iron before. His light brown hair had an unruly curl that could never look neat.

We each practiced a few putts and then headed to the first tee.

Mike was six years my senior. He had an easygoing exterior, but a lot going on in the interior. Mike was okay at everything he did, but never great, no matter how hard he tried. And he didn't try hard very often. His heart was in the right place, and as a friend he'd always been there for me.

I pulled a windbreaker from my bag. The air was cool, the sun not yet penetrating the marine layer over the course.

There weren't many golfers out, actually none that we could see.

Mike took one practice swing. "Shall I go while you *limber up*?"

"Play well." I was twisting left and right with the club behind my neck.

Mike placed a ball on a tee and lashed at it with his driver. The ball started up the left side of the wide fairway and turned right all the way across, ending up in the rough. "Got the power fade working."

Mike called it a *power fade*. Everyone else called it a slice.

I hit my stock draw that landed in the left side of the fairway. A good start.

With our bags slung over our backs we proceeded.

"So what's new?" I asked.

"I dunno, same shit, different pile." He shrugged. "What's with the limp?"

"I hurt my leg, no big deal."

We had to separate since our balls were on opposite sides of the fairway.

I looked around while I waited for him to hit his third shot, because his second had skittered twenty yards. He just needed to swing slower.

The course was in rough shape compared to where I'd played last. Many divots weren't replaced and the grass wasn't cut short due to the time of year and soggy conditions. The Lodgepole and Monterey pines that framed each hole gave it a park-like feel.

I hit my uphill second shot fat and came up short. When my chip landed on the small green it was like it had the brakes on. The grass was furry, so I had to putt harder and settled for five shots on that hole.

Mike stickhandled for a six.

He was unusually quiet as we played along. He seemed melancholy.

"I'll never tire of this view," I said when we reached the third hole.

The par three was on a bluff overlooking the South Bay and open ocean.

I looked around. "This would be a decent track if they made a few improvements."

"It's a muni and it does its job. The views are great. If they fixed it up it wouldn't be this cheap to play."

"You're right, it has a certain charm."

Mike went quiet again, except for his labored breathing every time we went up a hill.

After a few more holes I tried to get him talking. "How's work?"

He'd pulled out a pack of cigarettes and lit one. "Good, I guess. It has its pros and cons. I prefer reporting for print than producing for TV because the pieces are longer. TV news is just little snippets. However, TV pays better and once in a while I actually get to be on camera. The station is a bit of a colon factory, though."

"Huh?"

"A place that makes shit." He looked proud of his analogy.

I couldn't help but laugh. He came up with some good ones.

"I'm not sure if being a producer is right for me." Smoke came out of his mouth as he spoke. "I'm more of a lone wolf, you know. Being in charge of others and telling them what to do is annoying. I'm doing some writing on the side for a news startup on the Internet. That's the future."

Great, he was talking and sounding like his old self.

He took another drag. "How's the book coming?"

"You should write one. You'd be good at it."

"Maybe. How's yours going?"

"It's going, just slow." I stopped walking and looked down at the ball that was half white and half covered in mud. "I seem to get distracted easily and procrastinate. I'm programmed to work on deadlines, like at the newspaper. Remember that girl Morgan I told you about?"

"Yeah, you were all bummed out about her."

"She came back."

"That's good … isn't it? Are you together, like, *together* together, like giving-her-the-business together?" He clicked his teeth twice. He still had a hint of an East Coast accent when he was excited, having grown up on Rhode Island.

I laughed. "Oh yeah."

"So write when you've worn her out and she's sleeping." Mike gave me a wink.

"Good advice. Also, remember I told you about her father and how I wrote his memoir?"

"Yeah. That's what your book should be about. You know, evil conglomerates' security thugs chasing a good guy who's trying to find the truth—all that espionage and shit."

I'd given him a PG-rated version of the events before. He'd

obviously gotten the picture. "I'm using that as inspiration. Also, one of the people involved with the memoir wants me to do some more work with them."

"Tell me the truth …" Mike gave me a questioning look. "I know that Naintosa are bastards and gave you a real hard time, but what about the science itself? Don't you think the science of genetic engineering is important? You know, to feed the growing population."

I wasn't expecting to have this conversation with Mike in the middle of a golf course. "From what I've heard and the research I've read there's enough food being produced to feed everyone. It's the distribution of it that's the problem."

"What about for the future? You're not against science and progress, are you?"

It was weird how he phrased his questions. I had to think about how to give him a proper answer. "I'm one of the last people who'd be against science and progress. What I am against is *bad* science." I'd been dealing with credible scientists against genetic engineering for almost two years and never had to explain the difference between good and bad before. It was just a given with them. "The science with genetically engineered food is for profit and control. If it were making the world a better place, I would definitely support it, but it isn't."

"*All* of it, you think?"

"All that I've seen."

"So you're not against scientific progress?"

"You know me better than that." *Where's he going with this questioning?* "If it's for the betterment and to aid in the evolution of humanity, I'm all for it. But if it actually harms people and the planet and just lines the pockets of corporations, I'm against that."

"Fair enough."

"What are you getting at?"

Mike stammered. "I was just wondering what your opinion was.

I keep hearing that we need more food and that genetic engineering is the answer."

"That's what they want you to believe. It's their marketing. You know you can't believe everything you hear in the media."

"Got that right." His mouth was still open, as if he wanted to say more, but closed it instead. He looked down at his mud ball.

"Go ahead and clean it," I said.

He handed me his half-finished cigarette. It'd been a long time since I'd had one and was tempted to take a drag, but I didn't.

He picked the ball up and rubbed it on the leg of his tan khakis, leaving a dirt strip. After returning the ball to the thick grass, he pulled his five iron from his bag. Mike swung hard, making a deep divot. The ball only traveled a hundred yards, kicking right when it landed and bounced back into the rough. "Fuck."

I bought two beers at the turn and gave Mike one. He bought two more for himself.

He wasn't playing well and seemed more fixated on his beer and smoking a cigarette per hole from then on. I gave him encouragement, but otherwise left him alone. I focused on my own game, which was going well by my standards.

By the time we reached the seventeenth hole the temperature had dropped ten degrees. Right behind us was a wall of fog moving in, the tip almost touching our noses. In front was a spectacular view of the Golden Gate Bridge, still bathed in sunlight.

"Looks like we'll finish just in time," Mike said. "Do you have a few minutes after the round for a drink or do you have to get back to your *girlfriend?*"

"I have a long leash." That would be my opportunity to ask him about Summer.

We both managed to par seventeen and eighteen. That helped Mike shoot eighty-six. I managed a respectable seventy-eight.

The fog had engulfed the course as we finished; it was the kind of mist that always made me feel like I was inhaling water.

We dumped our golf bags in front of the clubhouse restaurant and went inside.

Mike always had and always would drink Budweiser. I liked pale ale and saw that they stocked a local one I didn't mind. We decided to share some nachos as well.

We picked a beat-up table near the window, opposite the marked-up white wall hung with old pictures of the course. The chairs we sat down on were chipped, exposing bare metal tubing where green paint once was. The furniture would've been more at home on the patio outside.

"I recently saw Sue at a funeral back in Seattle, but never had a chance to talk to her." Mike drained a third of the bottle in one gulp. "How's she doing? She looked good. You guys are still tight, right?"

"Yeah, she's doing well freelancing for a progressive magazine."

"I've always wanted to *do* her, right from college, with that tight little body of hers. But I always thought you two would end up together."

I didn't want to hear Mike's fantasies about Sue. "We're just meant to be good friends."

"I don't believe men and women can be friends. The dude always has the possibility of sex in the back of his mind."

Mike had some *interesting* opinions. I wanted to focus on the information I needed. "Was it Summer Perkins' funeral you saw Sue at?"

"Yeah, I dated Summer for a while. How did *you* know her?"

He dated her? I didn't know that. "I barely knew her from when I was at the *Seattle News*. Then she called me out of the blue and wanted to meet. I was the one who found her dead."

Mike's green eyes opened as wide as they could. "Really? Fucking small world. What'd she want to talk to you about?"

"I don't know."

"No idea?"

"Unfortunately not. How long were you two together and when was that?"

"Our relationship only lasted thirty-nine days. She was too uptight. Nice rack though. We went on a trip to Quebec City and I may have gotten a little drunk on the flight back. She dumped me right after we got home."

I'd heard Mike say women broke up with him after he'd *gotten a little drunk* a couple of times before. "When was that?"

"End of last October. I even flipped for the frickin' Chateau Frontenac. Do you know how expensive that place is? She wanted to stay there. A Holiday Inn would've been just fine with me."

"I could imagine. Wasn't it hard to fly a month after September eleventh?"

He shrugged. "It wasn't so bad. Getting seats was easy, but security was tight. Maybe it was just because it's Canada."

He was answering my questions, so I kept prodding. "Why specifically Quebec City?"

"My granny lives there in the new part of the city. She's frail and I hadn't seen her in a while, you know."

"That makes sense, but what was Summer's desire to go there?" That sounded like I was pushing.

Mike looked around the room. Only the waitress stood behind the bar at the other end. Then he looked out the window. There was no one there that we could see.

"She was doing some investigative journalism on her own. Not for the paper, because it had something to do with Davis Lovemark. He's doing something shady. He's shady, you know."

I leaned in. "Do you know exactly *what* she was investigating?"

He looked down at the bottle his hands were wrapped around for a long moment.

I let him have time and drank my beer. What had Summer

discovered about Davis Lovemark and would she have wanted to tell me about it? That had to be it.

Mike took a swig and then looked right at me. "You know how there are theories about a small group of people who control everything? They pull the world's strings. You know what I'm saying? They control banking, but not just banks—federal reserves and multinational corporations, the media, governments, countries ..."

"Yeah, I know what you mean." I could tell him some stories.

He drained the contents of the bottle. "Do you believe that?"

"I'm leaning that way." I trusted Mike, but didn't want to give up everything I knew, for his own protection.

"Well, Summer had some evidence proving it was true. Something big. A real game-changer for the future."

"What?"

"Makes sense." Mike looked out the window and then back at me. "I'm guessing she wanted to talk to you because it somehow tied in with what you were doing with that memoir."

"What did she find out?"

"Davis Lovemark is the voice of the group. Through GM Comm he manipulates the media so people only hear, see, and read what *they* want everyone to believe."

"I believe that."

"The guy who owns Naintosa and Pharmalin is part of that group too. What's his name again?"

"Dr. Hendrick Schmidt the Fourth."

"That's right."

The timid middle-aged server brought out our nachos. While she was at our table, Mike took the opportunity to order another beer.

"Do you know who Carlo Da Silva is?" he asked as soon as the waitress left.

"No. Is he part of the group?"

"Yeah, he's a Spanish computer wizard dude. He's a big player

194

in the security shaping of the Internet. His family's wealth comes from shipping, wine, and banking. Very old money."

I made a mental note to ask Jack about Carlo Da Silva.

"Summer had information on four, maybe more, different guys and wanted to expose them."

I pulled a tortilla chip and cheese away from the plate. "So how was Summer going to accomplish that? She couldn't go to the mainstream media; Lovemark controls it."

Mike picked up the new beer the server just brought, pulled the bottom of his shirt up, exposing his hairy belly, and wiped the top off the bottle before taking a drink. "That, I don't know. I wish she'd been able to talk to you. It would've answered a lot of questions."

"I guess we'll never know."

"After Summer died, I went to her apartment and looked around."

"You broke in?"

"You could say that." Mike looked proud of himself. "The place had been totally ransacked. I knew where she kept her research, and the papers weren't there."

"Do you think it could've been the police?"

"The police don't leave that kind of mess."

"Neither do the thugs."

"What do you mean, thugs?"

"That's what we called the private security men who worked for Naintosa. I'm sure Lovemark and the Da Silva guy have the same type of people."

"Huh."

"I wonder who discovered Summer was gathering information on them, and how they found out?"

Mike shook his head. "I had someone I know who works at the *San Francisco News* look through her cubicle. He found a hidden file folder with a substantial amount of notes. There were also two pictures taken at the Chateau Frontenac. One was of Da Silva getting out of a limo at the entrance and one of Lovemark in front of an elevator. She had taken them."

"What were the notes on?"

"They're mainly about a seed bank. I haven't finished going through them yet, but it's some incriminating stuff."

"Really?" Maybe I could decipher her notes. "Can I see everything?"

"Sure. I was hoping you'd look at them. How about we meet tomorrow?"

"Perfect, I'm going to the library, which isn't far from your place. Why don't we meet there?"

"Okay." Mike looked as if he were holding back and then blurted out, "I've decided to continue what Summer started."

"What would be the point of that?"

"To expose the fuckers. The world has got to know. I could put it on the Internet."

"These people are really dangerous, Mike. They don't want everyone to know what they're doing. They kill people who get in their way. Remember Summer?"

Mike furrowed his brow and crossed his arms. "We'll see."

"Okay, show me her notes and we'll go from there."

"I can do it on my own, but I just need your help in figuring some of it out—kind of pointing me in the right direction."

"Let's look at the notes and go from there." That's why he'd asked me those questions while we were on the course. He was testing me. We had both come to play with ulterior motives.

We each ate a couple bites of nachos and took the last swigs from our bottles.

"Are you okay to drive?" I asked. "You've had a few."

Mike stood up. "Perfectly fine."

We collected our golf bags and walked to the parking lot.

I felt uneasy that Mike was taking up where Summer had left off. For Mike's sake, I hoped that the notes he possessed didn't amount to much, or that I could convince him I should be the one to dig deeper.

I noticed the white backup lights turn off on a dark convertible with the soft top up and then the bright red brake lights go dim. The fog made it seem like dusk, dulling the colors. Mike had parked next to my vehicle and the moving car had been right beside them. A throaty sound came from the engine as it drove away from us. As it turned to leave the parking lot I could see that it was a BMW Z3. It was the exact model Angelica's friend Brad drove. There was someone in the passenger seat too.

My chest tightened and my mind focused on being alert.

Across from our vehicles was a large dark SUV. A man came out from around it and began walking toward us. I hesitated and then realized it was Jorge.

As he approached he gave me a gentle nod and a slow blink. I took that to mean everything was okay.

"Fine spring day," Jorge said when he was close enough to us.

"For San Francisco," Mike replied.

Jorge walked right by. I didn't look back to see where he went. Mike had no clue what was going on.

CHAPTER 30

As I was pulling my golf bag out of the back of my Pathfinder, Jorge approached. There was no one else in the parking area.

"It was that Brad guy at the golf course, right?" I asked.

"Yes," Jorge said.

"Who was with him?"

"I didn't get a good look."

"What were they doing?"

"They were there when you finished your round of golf. I was watching you." Jorge knelt under my vehicle and did a visual sweep. "As far as I could tell, they were just seeing who you were with. Surveillance."

"That reinforces my theory that Brad killed Summer and shot up my place and broke in."

"He's the prime suspect."

When Morgan arrived at my place she had her suitcase with her.

"You checked out?" I asked.

She smiled. "Why waste money on a hotel room when I'm here most of the time?"

It was hard to hold back my excitement. I practically jumped her. She was equally enthusiastic and pulled my shirt off as we kissed.

We were officially together again, and I was excited mentally and physically. Gauging her response, she felt the same way.

There was a trail of clothes from the living room where we started to the bedroom where we finished.

As we lay in bed, fulfilled, I told her about my conversation with Mike.

"I wonder what the seed bank is all about." Morgan pulled the blanket up to her chin. "I'm curious to see what Summer had found."

"We'll find out tomorrow." She didn't seem as cautious and concerned as I was. I guessed it was because she hadn't met Mike yet.

CHAPTER 31

March 3, 2002

We'd decided to walk to the library.

"It's warmer this morning." I shifted the notebook I was carrying.

"The sun feels good." Morgan unzipped her blue cotton jacket halfway down.

Out of nowhere a thick hand clamped around my right arm and Morgan's left and pushed us forward.

I almost lost my balance. "What the …"

"We have to get you out of here." It was Jorge. "Run—fast!" He directed us toward an alley where a dark gray Chevy Tahoe was parked.

"Get in." Jorge went for the driver-side door.

Morgan and I got in the backseat, each from a side, slamming the doors shut at the same time.

There was a woman in the front passenger seat with shoulder-length brown hair and wearing sunglasses.

"We have to go." Jorge wasn't breathing hard at all, but his tone was urgent. "You're being followed by Peter Bail and Brad Caulder."

He started the engine.

"Peter—fucking—Bail?" That name made my temperature go up from fear to anger.

"Where did he come from?" Morgan looked and sounded tense.

At that second, Bail and Brad came rushing into the alley.

The only time we'd physically seen Bail was over a year ago when he and his thugs planned to kill us. So it *was* the Naintosa security force that was after us. Their efficiency had slipped.

Our vehicle lurched forward as Jorge punched the accelerator.

Bail and Brad jumped and rolled out of the SUV's way.

Jorge slammed on the brakes, stopping us dead.

I was able to get my hand up just in time to keep myself from hitting the headrest of the driver's seat. Morgan wasn't so lucky and her forehead bounced off the leather headrest in front of her.

There was a woman on the sidewalk pushing a stroller; an innocent person out with her baby almost got mowed over by our big vehicle. She stood motionless, staring at us wide-eyed.

"*Mierda*," Jorge growled.

I looked over at Morgan and saw Brad standing right outside her door reaching for the handle. "Morgan, look out!"

"Nick, look out!" she screamed, at the same time.

I turned to see Bail reaching for my door. I banged on the lock a millisecond before he pulled the handle. He yanked so hard the Tahoe swayed.

Morgan had also locked her door in time.

We were flung forward in our seats again and the tires squawked as Jorge put it into reverse.

Bail twisted, his back hitting the vehicle, as he didn't let go fast enough.

The lady with the stroller moved out of harm's way.

Jorge banged it into drive and hit the gas. Then again we made an abrupt stop. There were passing cars on the street.

Morgan and I turned around and saw Bail getting to his feet and racing toward us. Brad was running back to a black Suburban parked behind where Jorge's Tahoe had been.

Within a second, Bail was at my door. He pulled hard on the handle again. We made eye contact and I saw determination and anger in his glare.

Jorge jerked the SUV forward a few feet.

Bail held on with his left hand; his other reached into his jacket.

There was an opening in the traffic. Jorge turned right and accelerated, heading south.

Peter managed to hold on for thirty or forty feet before rolling away from us, across the center line toward an oncoming car. The car swerved into a parked vehicle, stopping traffic in both directions.

The black Suburban was right there. Peter was slow getting up, but once on his feet he limped to the passenger side and got in.

Jorge drove as aggressively as he could. Yellow lights were our friends, as they gave us distance from our pursuers.

I kept watching to see how close the Suburban was to us. Brad was driving erratically and they were gaining.

"Where are we going?" Morgan asked.

"To the airport," said the woman in the front passenger seat.

We entered the freeway, which was both good and bad. We were able to go faster and had more room to maneuver through the pockets of congestion, but that gave the same opportunities to the men behind us.

The lady in the passenger seat pulled out a cell phone and speed-dialed a number. "Prepare for takeoff. We'll be there in five minutes. We're being pursued."

Morgan must've noticed me watching the woman and whispered, "I think she was the one guarding me yesterday."

The lady turned to face me. "And sometimes at night, making sure nothing happened to you, Nick."

"Thanks." I didn't know what else to say at the moment.

The Suburban was two cars and two hundred yards behind us as we took the exit to the smaller terminal. We came to a stop at a security booth next to a metal arm blocking the road. A guard stepped out of the doorway.

Jorge retracted the window, produced some papers, and told him a plane number.

Bail and Brad's vehicle stopped sixty yards back in the middle of the road. There was no other traffic.

A second sentry came out of the booth. He looked at the Suburban and brushed the firearm on his belt, unsnapping the holster.

The guard dealing with us handed the papers back to Jorge and the gate went up.

I fully expected the Suburban to take a run at getting through behind us. It didn't.

"They're not going to follow us." Jorge was looking through the rearview mirror.

We drove past a parking lot and terminal building toward airplane hangars.

"Where are we going?" Morgan asked.

"You're moving to Seattle ahead of schedule," Jorge said.

"What about my stuff?" Not that I really cared about most of it.

"I'll make sure everything is packed up and sent to you," Jorge said.

"Don't forget the things under the pots in the kitchen."

We drove between two hangars and came alongside a small white jet pointing away from us. The air was wavy behind the two engines in front of the tail.

We were embarking on another quest, yet this time not as defined. However, I felt more seasoned to cope with whatever unfolded.

CHAPTER 32

The man driving us in the black Mercedes ML500 was named Sam. He'd been the one guarding our suite at Bandon Dunes. He was built like a linebacker for the Seahawks, and his voice sounded like the top string of a bass guitar.

Jorge came with us on the flight and was now in the passenger seat.

We moved along the I-5 at the speed limit from Sea-Tac Airport into the heart of Seattle. Since it was Sunday, congestion was light.

Not much had been said on the plane other than that we'd be staying in a safe place. That way we could focus on the work we were about to do and not be worried about getting abducted, tortured, or killed.

I felt anxious, so I put my head back against the seat and closed my eyes. Deep breaths, in and out.

The vision of a room filled with books came into my mind. It was a filtered gray scene of a disheveled man sitting in a chair. He had his hands cupped under his chin and was slumped over with his elbows resting on his knees. He tapped his right heel, over and over. An elevator chimed and the door opened. Out stepped someone tall with a black aura. "Mike!"

I opened my eyes. Jorge had turned his head to look at me, Sam watched me in the rearview mirror, and Morgan touched my hand.

"We forgot about Mike," I told Jorge. "He was waiting for us at the library. What if Bail knew that and got him? Can I try calling him?"

Jorge reached into the inside pocket of his black jacket and produced a cell phone. "Use this."

I took the number from my phone and punched it into the one Jorge gave me. It rang six times before Mike's voice came on, "I'm obviously busy, so leave a message or not, just do whatever the hell pleases you."

"Mike, it's Nick, so sorry we couldn't meet you today. Something's come up. Lay low, and don't work on what Summer had started. You can't reach me, but I'll try you back again soon. Like I said, lay low."

I passed the phone back to Jorge.

"What's his address?" Jorge speed-dialed a number and recited the street address that I gave him to the person on the other end of the line.

"We'll find him," Jorge said.

The traffic became heavier the closer we came to the city's center.

Jorge put out his arm. "I should take your cell phones for safekeeping. We don't want you making a call by mistake and having our location traced."

"I don't currently have one," Morgan said.

I handed him mine.

We exited the freeway, drove a few blocks, and then pulled into the oval driveway of the Hotel Nuevo.

Memories flooded my mind of when I'd met Dr. Elles at that same hotel for dinner. That evening was when I'd initially learned about genetically engineered seeds and Naintosa.

"You'll be staying here tonight," Jorge said. "We need at least another day to get your house ready."

The lobby hadn't changed. There were the two round wooden

polished tables that held colorful flower arrangements in crystal vases and framed the entry. A seating area with four couches had been arranged for guests on each side of the big square room.

A dozen people milled about.

We walked toward the front desk where four employees stood behind the long marble counter. Jorge took two faster steps and herded Morgan and me to the right, bypassing the check-in. He'd been real direct ever since he saved us on the street.

We walked past the entry to Seasons restaurant, straight to the bank of elevators.

Once on the desired floor, we went down the hall to Room 808.

The walls of the suite were avocado green. A sitting area with a couch, two upholstered chairs, and a wall unit containing a TV and small bar sat past the bathroom that was next to the entry. To the left was a bedroom behind etched-glass double doors.

I went straight to the large window and looked over and around the buildings, past the port cranes to the harbor. Even though we had arrived in a panic, it was good to be back in Seattle. It felt like we were home.

"Stay in the room. It'll be easy for Bail to trace that we've come to Seattle." The tone of Jorge's voice suggested that he knew Bail. "You must be hungry; order some room service. I'll be back soon."

After Jorge left, Morgan and I stood looking at each other.

She shrugged. "This wasn't the way I'd planned to move back."

We picked at the few appetizers we'd ordered. The TV was on, but we weren't concentrating on it.

Jorge came in carrying a rectangular cardboard box. He set it down on the square walnut-stained coffee table. "Here's your new laptop."

"How long before my things get here?" I asked.

"A few days." Jorge looked annoyed, and his accent was thicker. "They were in your place before we could get there."

"What do you mean? Again?" I stood up from the couch. "Bail and Brad were following us. How could they get back to my place so fast?"

Jorge sat down on a dark green padded armchair. "I had someone go in just after we were airborne. Your place must've been broken into just after you left in the morning. I think their plan was that you two wouldn't be coming back after they were through with you."

"I bet it was your neighbor," Morgan said.

I sat back down. "Angelica."

Jorge nodded. "Most likely."

Morgan shook her head. She didn't have to say anything; I knew what she was thinking.

"Do you know what was taken?" I asked. "Couldn't someone go into her place and take my stuff back?"

"She or they took your computer, all the papers on your desk, and some things from under the cupboard in the kitchen."

"How could she have known about my secret hiding place?"

Jorge shrugged. "You'll have to do an inventory when your belongings arrive. They went to Angelica's apartment. It looked like she left in a hurry and none of your possessions were there."

CHAPTER 33

"Have you had breakfast?" Jorge said as he entered the suite the next morning.

"Not yet," Morgan said.

"Do you mind if I join you?" he asked. "We have a few things to discuss."

After we each had a brief look at the menu, Jorge called room service.

We went over to the round table in the corner. The new laptop took up the fourth spot because my plan was to get it set up that morning.

"So what's going on?" I asked as we all took a seat.

"The house we were preparing for you has been compromised," Jorge said.

"What … already?" I said.

"Last night we discovered that the house was being watched and we found a bug."

We sounded like there was a whole team working on setting up the now-not-safe house. "How could Naintosa find it so fast?"

Jorge shrugged. "We assume it's the Naintosa security force, but we're not positive. If it is, Bail has a sizable team working with him."

"So now what?" Morgan asked.

"You'll have to stay here for a while, and you can't leave this room."

Morgan and I looked at each other. Neither of us objected. We'd been in situations like this before and knew when it was time to stay out of sight.

"Sam or I will always be outside your door. If you need something we can arrange to have it purchased."

"We're going to need clean clothes." Morgan said.

"Make a list, let's say enough for five days."

"Can I call Sue?" I hadn't talked to her in days.

"Sue has been updated and will join us when we figure out where to go."

I remembered my premonition about Mike. "Have you found Mike Couple yet?"

Jorge shook his head. "No. He hasn't shown up at his home. There are two people working on trying to find him."

I hoped the thugs hadn't gotten him.

By the end of the day, we were set up with new clothes, toiletries the hotel didn't already provide, and a printer with paper.

The computer was set up and we had plug-in cable Internet.

That night in bed we cuddled. There was comfort in knowing we were in the situation together.

It was too bad that ever since we'd known each other we'd been on the run, working under stress and she'd been grieving the deaths of her parents. I yearned for a time we could just be a regular couple. It would be great to live our lives together without having to constantly watch our backs. Would there ever be a time where we could live a safe and comfortable life?

There was enough light coming into the room from the slit in the curtains that I could see her brush her hair away from her eyes and look back at me.

"Do you think we'd still be together if we weren't in these situations and living normal, boring lives?" Morgan asked.

Would I ever get used to her thinking the same thoughts I was at the same time—our synchronistic bond? "I was just wondering what that would be like. I'd like to try it."

"Me too."

On the third day, Morgan asked for a book called *The Four Agreements* and spent the day reading.

I'd taken another stab at looking on the Internet for new information on cancer drugs and glyphosate. There was nothing we hadn't already seen.

To stay productive, I decided to use the opportunity of free time to work on my book. If my backup had been taken along with the computer, I'd have to start again from the beginning. Until I knew, I'd add new material. I wrote a motocross chase scene based on my experience in Bandon. Then I worked on a foiled abduction and escape by car like in San Francisco.

As I pondered the screen that was only half filled with words, I had a revelation that had nothing to do with my story. I'd had bits of it before, but this time the question solidified in my mind: how had our culture evolved to the point where over-farmed land, growing pesticide-laden fruits and vegetables using synthetic fertilizers, had become growing food the "conventional" way? Or what about raising animals in confined spaces; feeding them parts from their own species and grains they couldn't digest properly, injecting them with hormones, steroids, and antibiotics, on factory farms? How could that have become the norm? Now add genetically engineered food to both scenarios.

Organic was really the "conventional" way of growing food. That's how it'd been done for thousands of years. The new chemical-factory way was "unconventional."

I wrote my thoughts down. Could that be part of my book's plot?

It was one hell of a marketing scheme by the companies involved, like Naintosa. The public now believed their rhetoric, taking it as truth. Just like cattle in a feedlot.

CHAPTER 34

I was running. Where was I running from or to? There were shadows. Were they watching or chasing? Where was Morgan? Where exactly was I and who was this big dog beside me? It was Jack's Rottweiler, Moose. He was running with me, not after me. There were sounds coming from the shadows.

I was awake. The running dream had dissolved, but the sound of someone being in the shadows hadn't. I reached out and felt Morgan sleeping beside me. Dim light extended into the bedroom from the other side of the etched-glass double doors. The outline of a person appeared and the doorknob made a faint squeak.

I was out of the bed as fast as I could move and against the wall. As the door opened, I prepared to strike. I didn't have a weapon, so the force of my body would have to be my defense.

"Nick. Morgan. It's time to go."

I was about to slam the door into the assailant when I recognized Jorge's familiar accent. Lucky it was him. I wasn't going to be tortured or allow Morgan to be abducted again.

Morgan stirred. "What?"

"Nick, how did you get over here?" Jorge was staring at me.

"I didn't know it was you." I realized my hands were in a karate chop pose and lowered them. "I thought you were an intruder."

He squinted. "Uh, right."

Morgan rubbed her eyes. "Nick, honey, put some pants on."

I guess I didn't look all that threatening in my boxers.

"What time is it?" Morgan asked.

"It's two in the morning," Jorge said.

"Do I have time to take a shower?" Morgan crawled out from underneath the covers, wearing only my new long blue shirt she chose to sleep in.

"Unfortunately not," Jorge said. "We have to leave in ten minutes. I apologize for the short notice."

Morgan and I were dressed, packed, and ready to leave in six minutes.

Sam was waiting for us in the Mercedes, next to the elevator doors, in the underground parking. Morgan and I took the backseat and Jorge rode shotgun.

It was stormy and dreary, and the streets were deserted. Within minutes we were on I-5 heading south.

"Where are we going?" Morgan asked.

"To the airport." Jorge kept looking straight ahead at the rain-slicked road. "We have a safe place for you."

"Where?" I asked.

"Not far away," he said. "We have to fly there."

Sam wasn't worried about getting a ticket for speeding, and we were at Sea-Tac in a short period of time.

We drove around to where we'd arrived four days earlier, and the same jet was waiting for us. We parked next to an identical Mercedes ML 500.

"Head straight to the plane," Jorge said. "We'll stow the luggage."

The rain was coming down in cold sheets, sideways. Morgan and I ran the fifty yards, heads down to shelter our eyes. The sound of the wind and the jet engines was chaotic.

I let Morgan climb up and in first. Looking back, I could see Jorge and Sam pulling out our two satchels containing our new clothes and two other suitcases.

I hurried up the few stairs and entered the plane. It was dry and warm inside. There was a hint of stale cigar smoke being masked by air freshener.

Morgan was talking to someone directly in front of her.

Next to them was a woman who I guessed was in her forties, taller, big-boned, and fit. Her brown straight hair was tied in a ponytail and her expressionless face was attractive.

I realized who Morgan was talking to. "Sue."

Sue looked around Morgan, who was four inches taller than her. "Hi, Nick."

She came and gave me a strong hug. The powder-blue shell that I remembered helping her pick out was wet, but she felt really good in my arms.

"I was worried about you," Sue mumbled, her face buried in my jacket.

"It's gotten crazy again."

She pulled back. "I haven't been able to reach you for almost a week. Lorraine was only able to fill me in on bits of what was happening." She turned and pointed at the lady I'd noticed. "She's been my bodyguard."

"Hi, I'm Nick." I waved. "Thanks for looking after Sue."

Lorraine nodded. "My pleasure." Her Eastern European accent was heavy and didn't match her looks.

"We had to get out of San Francisco in a hurry," I said. "Peter Bail is after us again."

"What?" Sue leaned against the brown leather seat next to her. "So it is Naintosa, then."

"Looks like."

We were distracted by a set of headlights that swept across the cabin's oval windows. Morgan, Sue, and I bent over to see out. Another SUV had parked next to the two already there. Jorge and Sam rushed from the plane's luggage compartment to the vehicle. The driver and front passenger's doors opened and two big men came out into the rain. Jorge pointed in our direction and the driver opened the back passenger door. A person in a tan raincoat and black fedora jumped out and ran for the plane. He wasn't a coordinated runner. It didn't help that he was wearing dress shoes on the drenched tarmac. He almost flipped twice.

"Who's that?" Sue asked.

I looked over at Lorraine, hoping she'd answer, but her face was blank.

The man came into the cabin and removed his wet hat. He was tall and skinny. The top of his head was almost devoid of hair, and the brown and gray on the sides needed a trim. Sunken cheeks made his beak-shaped nose more pronounced. His eyes and expression exhibited caution and fear. After looking at us for a second, he took the first seat and slumped down into it.

No one said a word.

There was vibration from underneath and jolts of compartments being closed.

Jorge and Sam entered right after each other. Sam worked on closing the door, while Jorge slid the cockpit barrier open.

I caught a glimpse of two pilots.

After speaking to them for a few seconds, Jorge turned to us. "Everyone take a seat and put on your seatbelts. We have to leave now, and it's going to be a rough takeoff." He didn't make for a comforting stewardess.

The plane lurched forward faster than we could get settled, and we had to pull ourselves into the closest seats.

Jorge almost lost his footing, but managed to get to the seat across from the freaked-out skinny guy.

Sam wasn't fazed and with sure feet he took the seat behind Jorge.

The plane taxied so fast we didn't feel the usual bumps between the concrete slabs beneath us. It didn't sit and wait at the runway. As we turned, the throttle was increased and by the time we'd straightened out we were at full power.

I'd never experienced such thrust in my life. We were all sucked deep into our seats, unable to move.

We were in the air within seconds. The jet seemed to pierce the turbulence, like a bullet, at a steep angle.

Morgan was tense and her eyes wide. Sue was in danger of ripping the tops of the armrests off, she was holding them so tightly. They both stared straight ahead.

After a long ten minutes, we leveled off. That only lasted for five minutes, before we started to descend.

"Jorge, what's our destination?" I asked the back of his head, three seats in front of me.

He didn't turn around to answer. "We're almost there."

I couldn't see anything out the window. I had no idea what direction we were heading. I calculated what would be a half-hour flight at this speed in either direction from Seattle. West was ocean, south was Portland, east was Spokane, and north was Vancouver.

The plane's descent was sharper now and more turbulent than the takeoff. We bounced around in our seats.

Morgan and Sue were looking at me. I tried to give them a look of reassurance. "Exciting, huh?"

They both raised their eyebrows.

I remembered the days when they didn't particularly like each other. They still weren't really friends, but after our Maui experience, they had respect for each other. That meant ganging up on me when they felt like it.

There was static over the intercom and then a male voice, "Prepare for landing. Keep your seatbelts on, it's stormy out there."

Looking out the window, I saw glimpses of lights below as we descended out of the clouds. No indication of what city, though.

There was a sudden push and the right wing rose up about six feet.

Morgan's head hit the window next to her.

My almost-healed thigh connected with the edge of the seat, producing a sharp twinge of pain.

Sue had raised her arm fast enough to prevent her head from hitting the windowsill.

The plane dropped back down to parallel and we were jolted the other way. There were outlines of buildings and lit streets below. Water droplets streaked across the window. Gust after gust hit us, each time grabbing the wing.

"How can we land like this?" Morgan's voice cracked.

As we touched down, more wind hit the plane, lifting the right wheel from the ground. We were going to slide and flip. Then the push of air stopped and the wheel dropped. The engines wailed and the plane shuddered as we decelerated.

We'd made it. Everyone exhaled at once.

The windows were covered in rain smears and red runway lights passed by in rhythm. The plane taxied for almost five minutes before coming to a stop. A green light went on over the door and Sam got up to open it.

Jorge stood and turned to us. "Wait here."

Cold air rushed in through the open exit Jorge and Sam went through.

I couldn't see out the door. "Any idea where we are?"

"There's a helicopter over there," Sue said.

The plane vibrated as the luggage compartment was opened below us.

I'd forgotten about the tall, skinny man. He was still slumped in the front seat and hadn't said a word the whole time.

CHAPTER 35

J orge appeared in the doorway. "Let's go."

The unknown passenger stood up first. We formed a line behind him, bodyguard Lorraine at the rear.

Jorge led the way toward a good-sized passenger helicopter.

Sam was finishing stowing the gear in an outside compartment.

Everyone sheltered their faces as the rain pelted us. The saturated air had a briny undertone, indicating we were near the ocean.

As we stepped up into the helicopter, I imagined that this was what really rich people used to commute from their country estates to their office towers. I bet Schmidt and Lovemark had a few of these.

Inside, two seats faced each other with a table in the middle and two rows of five seats behind; each one a comfortable caramel leather. The seven of us had plenty of room. Two pilots sat in their positions with no partition separating us. The insulated cabin couldn't quite buffer the noise of the rotors.

I'd never been in a helicopter before. It was a weird sensation as we went straight up and forward, nose down. My stomach felt like it was in my feet.

We all hung on for another harrowing ride.

This was all happening at a fast pace, like we were being chased.

And what was with all the secrecy of where we were heading? I wondered how far behind Bail and his Naintosa thugs were.

We were flying just underneath the clouds, which wasn't very high, over the top of a city. It was pretty much all residential with no distinguishing landmarks.

The black night was turning gray. Morning was arriving.

Ahead on our left a big oval structure with a white, pillowy roof came into view. It was a stadium I recognized, but had never been in. What was it called? Oh yeah, BC Place. We were in Vancouver. I could see the downtown high-rises past the stadium now.

Gastown was ahead. That's where we'd met the lady with the plastic fruit on her head who had led us to Alice. Poor Alice. She was an odd one who hadn't made it. Alice was a night custodian at Naintosa's lab. She'd witnessed Morgan's mother's murder and, in the end, gotten killed herself. Alice had done something that I could never figure out—she'd tried to turn us in to the very people who were after her.

I looked across at Morgan, who was looking out the window.

Somewhere down there was also the warehouse where we'd been tied up and blindfolded over a year ago. But with the help of Jorge, we now knew, we'd been able to escape. The thugs had beaten me up so badly that I could barely see or walk.

Morgan must've sensed me looking at her and turned her head in my direction. I mouthed *Vancouver* and she nodded. She looked troubled and must've been remembering our time there as well.

The helicopter veered right and we crossed water, flying over a bridge.

I was trying to figure out the lay of the land. I'd never seen Vancouver from that vantage point. The distraction calmed me.

Continuing on, we flew over a wooded residential area before heading over water again. That must've been Deep Cove, an ocean inlet village, sheltered from the city. My parents had taken me there once when I was young.

It was light now; the clouds were lifting and the rain had weakened.

The helicopter slowed and descended as we approached a square wharf beside a longer rectangular dock.

We touched down on the wharf, which felt solid. They didn't cut the engine, only slowed the rotation of the rotors. Turbulent waves of noise vibrated through the cabin when the door opened. We all exited in single file, keeping our heads down to shelter our eyes from the wind the rotors created, as we moved to the longer dock. Tied up next to where we stood was a white boat about twenty feet long that had *Boston Whaler* printed on the side.

Jorge and Sam retrieved the luggage.

As soon as everything was unloaded, the helicopter lifted off. We turned around and braced our legs against the wind thrust.

Slowly the sound and sight of the helicopter diminished as it retreated into the distance.

The inlet was as calm as a lake, the only disturbance coming from rain droplets colliding with the surface. The cool water falling from the sky, mingling with the sea and the evergreens, made for an overwhelming freshness in the air. The area was sheltered by steep mountains on each side of the narrow valley. Looking up the slope, there was a wide path that ended at a cabin partially obscured by trees. Three men, all wearing the same navy blue brimmed rain hats and waterproof jackets and pants were walking down to the rocky shore.

I grabbed Morgan's and my satchels by their looped handles. I recognized Sue's suitcase and wheeled it behind me.

As we walked toward the men, Morgan was the first to recognize one of them. "Ivan." She increased her pace.

"Welcome." By the sound of his Texan accent, it had to be Jack.

When Morgan reached Ivan, she gave the five-foot-ten stocky Russian who had been a second father to her a big hug and a kiss on his bearded cheek.

"Jack, thank you for getting us." Sue went up to the man next to Ivan and gave him a hug, having to go up on her tiptoes.

Then the women switched men to embrace.

I was slower, since I had the luggage.

"So great to see you again, Miss Morgan." Jack smiled.

"Always a pleasure to be in your company, Jack." Morgan gave his shoulders a squeeze and then let go.

I didn't recognize the third man. He had a younger-looking face.

"Ivan, glad you came back," I said.

"It was not safe in Oslo anymore," he replied in his precise, thick accent.

"I told you that a month ago," Sue said.

"Yes, you did." Ivan nodded with a smile. "Over and over again."

Jack looked past us and took a step forward. "Dr. Roth, good you could join us."

We looked to see that Jack was talking to the quiet slim man behind us. His name sounded familiar.

Dr. Roth kept his head down and was shaking, making his tan coat vibrate. Was it the damp air or was he scared?

Jack extended his hand. "It's for your own safety that we brought you here."

The man left Jack's hand hanging there, not reciprocating for seconds that seemed like a minute. Then he extended his long bony fingers and shook weak-wristed.

"Well, let's get everyone out of the rain and settled in. Then we can talk." Jack patted Sam and Jorge on the backs as he stepped past them.

"You will like it here," Ivan said to Sue and Morgan.

Jack extended his hand one more time. "You must be Lorraine? Jorge had plenty of good things to say about you. Welcome to our team."

"Thank you, sir." Lorraine gave his hand a firm shake.

Sue had mentioned before that Lorraine was originally from Poland. That explained her thick speech pattern.

The man we hadn't met came over, gave me a nod, took the baggage from me, and started up the gravel path.

"Where exactly are we?" Sue asked.

"This place is called Indian Arm, just north of Vancouver," Jack said. "It's going to take a bit getting used to the damp for this Texas boy."

The vegetation was thick around us as we ascended. Green ferns and bushes with long brown leafless branches spread out above the moss, needle, and leaf-covered ground. Above, tall fir, hemlock, and cedar trees provided cover. The cabin was about seventy yards up from the water and set back in a recess. It wasn't wide at the front, giving it an illusion of being small, but when we got close I could see it was long. There was a second story on the back half. It was situated on the only flat piece of ground in sight with a retaining wall at the back to prevent the hillside from coming down. The structure had cedar shake siding and a green metal roof, helping it blend into the environment. Five wooden steps brought us up to a porch that ran along two sides.

We all filed into the cabin.

"Very nice," Sue said in front of me.

The front living room was open with a slate floor, cedar plank walls, and log beams at the corners and ceiling. There were two seating areas with comfy green-accented overstuffed couches and chairs. One focused on the granite fireplace and the other faced the front floor-to-ceiling window looking out at the water.

I turned to Jack. "Do you own this?"

"No, just renting it from a friend of a friend. It's a family's retreat, with all the comforts and conveniences we need."

"Who are the owners?" Sue asked.

"I'd rather not say," Jack said. "They're a famous couple, and they'd like to keep their hideaway secret."

By Sue's look I could tell she was curious. As a reporter she craved those details.

"Why don't y'all go stow your things in the bedrooms upstairs? There are enough for everyone," Jack said. "We can all meet back here in fifteen minutes, have some breakfast, and get familiar with what's going on."

I hadn't noticed Jack's right-hand man standing at the back of the room. "Hi, Lee," Sue and I said, at practically the same time.

There were quite a few people present—I counted eleven, five of whom were to provide us with security.

Dr. Roth was standing next to me, so I thought I should introduce myself. I extended my hand. "Hi, I'm Nick Barnes."

He was pale and looked uncomfortable. "Dr. Timothy Roth." His shake didn't have any power to it and his skin was clammy.

Sue, Morgan, and Ivan took my cue and came over to introduce themselves. The attention didn't sit well with Dr. Roth. He took a step back, his face turned red, and his eyes darted toward the floor.

"Dr. Roth has compiled research that's very important," Jack said. "We're very fortunate to have him here."

Dr. Roth looked up. "Not much choice." His voice, like his handshake, was weak.

"You're lucky we got you when we did." Jack sounded annoyed. That was the first time I'd heard him use that tone.

Was Jack trying to help him, but Dr. Roth felt he'd been brought here against his will?

"Follow me, ladies and gentlemen." Lee motioned for us to climb the sturdy, thick wooden stairs.

On the second floor there was a hall with four doors on either side. Ivan, Sue, and Dr. Roth each got their own rooms. Morgan and I shared the first one, which was the largest.

I placed our satchels on top of a dark-stained dresser. The bed was at the opposite end of a large window, so we'd have a great view of the inlet when we woke up.

Morgan sat down on the green-patterned duvet and pushed down on the mattress. "This is nice."

Someone in the owners' family must've been a photographer, because there were numerous framed pictures of the surrounding forest on the beige walls.

There was a door on either side of the king-size bed. I opened the one closest to the entry, revealing a walk-in closet. "You'll like this."

Morgan fell back on the bed and turned to look inside. "Too bad I don't have anything to put in there."

The off-white carpet was cushy as I walked around to see what was behind door number two. A master bathroom, complete with a Jacuzzi tub, separate shower stall, and dual sinks set into a granite countertop. All of the fixtures were pewter. "This place is sweet."

"I feel safe here." Morgan got up and went to her bag. "I'm going to have a shower."

I heard the sound of an engine revving and went over to the window to watch the boat that had been tied to the dock leaving.

CHAPTER 36

"Nice digs." Sue came out of her room at the same time we did.

Downstairs, Ivan, Jack, and Dr. Roth stood next to a table holding mugs of steaming liquid. Heat and the smoky smell of wood burning permeated out into the room from the fireplace.

"Grab yourselves some coffee," Jack said. "Breakfast will be ready in a minute."

"This is a beautiful cabin." Morgan took the carafe from the table, poured three cups, and handed one each to Sue and me.

"I hope it's to your liking," Jack said. "We procured this place in a rush, so we need to get more supplies."

"Is that where the boat went?" I reached for some raw cane sugar.

"Yes. Tanner, Jorge, and Sam went into Deep Cove where we have most of the stuff waiting. The rest will arrive tomorrow."

Tanner must've been the man we hadn't been introduced to.

"So we plan on being here for a while?" Ivan asked.

"As long as it's safe," Jack said.

A round-figured motherly woman walked out of a doorway near the stairs. "Y'all can adjourn to the dining room." She had a cheery smile. "Breakfast is ready."

I hung back to be the last to follow. I knew Dr. Roth would wait to be at the tail end of the procession and I wanted to try chatting with him. "Nice place, huh?"

He nodded. His look was a cross between a deer caught in headlights and someone about to jump out of their skin.

"Where are you from?"

He looked at me and then down as soon as we made eye contact. "Chicago. I, uh, I had a research lab there."

I realized why his name sounded familiar. Dr. Timothy Roth wrote the article that Morgan and I discovered in the San Francisco library. "You did a study on glyphosate, right?"

He looked even more freaked out than before. "Uh ... yes." He turned and slunk through the doorway.

Touchy guy. It was going to be tough getting to know him, but at least now I knew his credentials.

On the other side of the door was a dining room with a long oak table surrounded by twelve chairs. Plates and bowls of food sat in the center, with three place settings on either side. To the right was a large, open kitchen. A counter separated the two areas, lined with four leather-backed brown stools. The cooking area looked first-class, with stainless steel appliances, plenty of oak cupboard space, and granite countertops; hanging over the island was a rack that held clean pots and pans. The whole room smelled like bacon.

I took a seat next to Morgan, who was beside Sue. Jack, Dr. Roth, and Ivan sat on the opposite side.

"Help yourselves." Jack motioned toward the kitchen. "Rose does a fine job."

The Southern lady waved like it was no trouble.

"Rose is my chef in Dallas," Jack said. "She felt like a change of scenery and likes a little adventure."

Rose came to the table carrying a plate of toast. "This ain't anything like where I'm from. It's so green here ... and wet."

Jack smiled. "We are technically in a rainforest."

"Let us hope that there is not too much adventure here." Ivan sounded concerned.

"It seems remote and safe." I tried to sound convincing for my benefit as well as theirs.

"I'm hoping so." Jack reached for the gravy to put on his biscuits. Plates of food were passed around.

Dr. Roth looked at Jack. "Can you, uh, can you tell me what I'm doing here with all these people? You said you were going to provide me with a safe place to hide and work."

It was either Dr. Roth's shyness, introversion, fear, what now sounded like self-centeredness, or all of the above. Whatever it was, I could see everyone tiring of it soon.

Jack's eyes narrowed and he took a deep breath. "Everyone here's in the same boat and working for a common goal. Each has their strengths. You and Dr. Popov will compare notes on your findings and decipher other research I have and will obtain. Sue is a first-class journalist and researcher. Nick knows how to word what we want to say in a way everyone can understand. Morgan has natural editing ability. I provide the place, protection, connections, and fund the project."

"What should we call this *project*?" Sue said.

"Operation …" Jack looked up and to the left, scratching his chin. "Operation … exposing the truth. What I mean is the big picture of what all this genetic engineering is about—the true ramifications. I think what we each know now is just the tip of the iceberg. When we put it all together, my hope is we can figure it out."

Morgan shrugged. "What about Operation Exposing the Truth?"

"What about Operation Truth?" Sue suggested.

Everyone except Dr. Roth agreed. He just stared at his empty plate and said nothing.

"Want to see the rest of the house?" Jack stood.

We all followed Jack as he led us to a hallway.

On the right was an alcove with canned, dried, and packaged goods.

"There's the pantry." Jack pointed. "Behind the door on the left is a powder room."

Ten feet farther were two more doors.

"On the left is a nanny's room that Tanner is currently using."

"We haven't met Tanner," I said.

"He's a surveillance specialist," Jack said. "He was down at the dock when you first arrived. Sorry, I forgot to introduce him. I will when he gets back from the supply run."

Sue and Morgan exchanged a look. I wasn't sure what it meant.

"On the right is an office." Jack opened the door. "We can use it if one of us needs a quiet place to work."

We all peered inside. From behind everyone, all I could see was a floor-to-ceiling bookshelf.

There were two more doors at the end of the hall.

"That one goes outside." Jack nodded forward. "And this one goes to the basement." He opened the door to our right and flicked the light switch on the wall.

Once we reached the bottom of the stairs, Jack led us down another hallway. He pointed as he went. "There's a storage room, laundry room, movie theater, and that one there we're going to use for security."

We came into a big square open space.

"Here is where we can all work."

I could tell that furniture had been moved around from the weight depressions on the beige carpet. A pool table with a cover over it stood to one side. Next to it were two black leather recliners and a brown-patterned couch pushed against the wall. In the corner there was a large TV and a big plastic orange basketball with a hole in the top that overflowed with children's toys. In the middle of the room were four rectangular folding tables placed together to make a square. Surrounding the makeshift desk were six unfolded white metal chairs with black vinyl cushions. Two blackboards mounted on wheels stood next to the work area. Two long tan cords ran from electricity and cable outlets on the wall to a large power bar and a black modem underneath the tables.

"This is it," Jack said. "Everyone will have a new computer this afternoon and we are wired for the Internet."

"I brought my laptop," Sue said.

"Morgan and I just got a new one," I chimed in.

"I'd like us all to use clean computers while we're here, if you don't mind," Jack said. "For security reasons."

We all nodded.

"Well, there's nothing to do for a couple of hours, so y'all might as well go upstairs and relax," Jack said.

I went over to Ivan and patted him on the shoulder. "Let's go catch up."

Everyone filed back up the stairs and we made our way to the living room.

I could see Lee through the window leaning against the porch railing. Jack went outside to talk to him.

Morgan, Ivan, and Sue settled on the couch opposite the crackling fire. I chose a chair to the side of them.

Dr. Roth sat down in an overstuffed recliner that was on the opposite side of the room from us. I thought of inviting him over but I wanted to talk with Ivan before making another attempt to get to know the odd man.

"Really sorry again about Bill," I said to Ivan.

"You must miss him." Morgan slid closer to him and patted his knee.

"He was a very good man and scientist," Ivan said. "I do miss my dear friend."

Ivan had aged since we last saw him. He'd lost weight, the creases on his forehead had deepened, and his beard was now all gray.

"What made you come back?" Sue asked. "In your e-mails, you seemed set on staying in Oslo even though it wasn't safe anymore."

"Jack came to visit me," Ivan said. "I have obtained new information and the Council for Ethical Farming did not know what to do with it. Their hands are tied due to the lawsuits Dr. Schmidt and Naintosa have filed. Plus, there was an attempt on my life last week."

"What?" Morgan sat up.

"You never told us." Sue leaned toward him. "What happened?"

"It was not the best attempt, and we confirmed a long-suspected mole." Ivan crossed his arms. "I was having a late meal in the diner beside the Council headquarters. It was quiet and the restaurant was empty. I heard a foot catch a chair leg and turned just in time to see a man, who had worked for the Council ever since I had been there, trying to stick a needle in the back of my neck."

Another needle. A shiver ran through me. That was the weapon of choice for those people.

Sue placed her hand over her mouth and mumbled, "Holy shit."

"Hell." Morgan squeezed Ivan's knee.

"When his attempt failed, he ran," Ivan continued. "It was too bad he did not drop the syringe. I would have liked to know what he was going to inject me with. We have not seen him since."

"Did you tell the police?" Sue asked.

"Yes. Chief Inspector Jacques Plante at Interpol has been leading an investigation into the ongoing *incidents* involving the Council." Ivan gave an audible exhale. "It was not hard for Jack to convince me that the Council was losing their ability to protect me and my work. I think we are safest with Jack's protection."

"Agreed," I said. "What's the new information you mentioned?"

"I will show you when the new computers arrive." Ivan looked from me to Morgan. "I understand you two had a close call of your own?"

"Peter Bail tried to abduct us," Morgan said.

"That is what Jack told me." Ivan shook his head. "Dr. Schmidt does not keep failures in his employment, especially on the security team. Peter Bail failed in Maui. We find it odd that Schmidt would keep him around, especially to try to catch you."

"Bail has a sidekick named Brad who's been watching me for over a month." I hadn't thought of it before, but I agreed with Jack and Ivan's deductions about Bail.

Dr. Roth had come up to stand behind the couch.

"Why don't you tell us why you're here, Dr. Roth," I said.

Morgan, Ivan, and Sue turned to see him.

"Dr. Roth has been conducting his own experiments," Ivan said. "He was supposed to be providing Naintosa with positive results; however, that is not what the research revealed. When his benefactors found out, they tried to silence him. Am I correct?"

Dr. Roth nodded in slow motion. "Yes."

"It must've happened recently," Morgan said. "You still seem shaken up."

"Two … two days ago." Dr. Roth braced his hand on the top of the couch.

"How do you know Jack?" Sue asked.

"I don't. Or I didn't," Dr. Roth said. "He came to me and convinced me that he could protect me and my research. I'm not safe here, now that I know Naintosa is after all of you too. They have us all in one place. If they find us out here in the middle of nowhere they can take us all out at once."

"Did Jack save you?" Sue asked.

I caught on to where she was going with the question. "Yes, he saved you, right? He found you and got you out of danger."

Dr. Roth looked stubborn and less shaky. "How did Jack know

there was going to be a fire in my lab? Was his arrival there at that moment a coincidence? Him and that hulk out there." He motioned with his head to Lee who was still outside talking to Jack. "They could've had something to do with the fire!"

"No, Jack would never do that," Morgan said. "He's on our side."

"Once you get to know him, you'll see how honorable he is," Sue said.

"Why would he bother?" Dr. Roth asked. "What's in it for him to do all of this? This whole scenario costs a lot of money. I'm not going to be able to contribute to the expenses."

"Jack is a man of means, who has connections we cannot even begin to fathom," I said. "He wants to do good with the power he has and expose what's going on."

"I don't believe you." Dr. Roth looked at the floor. "I don't think there are good people anymore. Everyone's out for themselves."

"You are in a cabin filled with good people." Ivan's eyes misted up. For such a strong man, he had such a soft heart.

INTERLOGUE 3

"How much do you really trust him?" Brad asked.

"I don't trust anyone." Peter fixed his eyes on the younger man sitting in the red leather chair next to him. "Especially not you." He held his stare for intimidating effect. "But, a man has to make a living, and it's best to make that living from men who have the ability to pay well."

One of the tall double doors opened. A petite young woman came out from around the slab of mahogany on hinges.

She walked over to Peter and Brad and motioned back to where she'd come from. "Mr. Lovemark will see you now."

Both Peter and Brad gave her a good once-over. She was petite in stature in every way but her breasts, and from the looks of it, didn't mind having them as a focal point. Her tight white blouse had two too many buttons unfastened.

The men stood and went to the office they'd been summoned to. Peter made Brad open the door.

Davis was sitting behind his desk.

A second man sat facing away from the entrance on the opposite side of the desk.

Peter recognized the thick neck that held up the head with

predominantly gray hair and bald crown right away.

Davis motioned with his hand. "Brad, you can wait outside."

The corners of Brad's mouth turned down and his shoulders slumped as he turned to leave.

Peter was annoyed at the immaturity of the man he had no choice but to work with. It irritated him to the point that he considered having him purposely caught in crossfire if the opportunity presented itself.

Davis motioned for Peter to take the seat next to the other gentleman. That man rose and turned as Peter moved forward to accept the invitation.

"Dr. Schmidt." Peter didn't know his old boss would be at this meeting, but deep down he'd been prepared for an encounter. The last time they'd spoken was in December of 2000. It had been over the phone, right after Peter had had a shard of metal taken out of his leg by a private doctor. Dr. Schmidt had yelled at him for not completing his mission. He didn't care about the three members of Peter's team who were killed by Jack Carter and his men. The last words Dr. Schmidt had said early that morning were, "You're fired, and you had better fucking disappear."

"Peter." The look of controlled contempt on Dr. Schmidt's face explained his position; he didn't tolerate failures, and Peter was a failure. "I see your leg has healed."

They didn't shake hands and sat down in the matching white leather chairs.

Davis tried to mask a smile as he addressed Peter. "We're going to have a slight change in direction. Some men from Naintosa's security team will be helping you. You'll be in charge."

Peter didn't say anything, just gave a slight nod. This was inevitable. How could two separate security teams go after the same people and not collide? That meant Peter had to rethink his plan, which was to simply wipe his targets out. Now the chances of carrying that out were slim. Dr. Schmidt would make sure his men knew not to let that happen, because if it did, as Davis had said, all eyes would be on Dr. Schmidt as the person who had ordered it. Also, it was obvious that Davis had somehow gotten his way over Dr. Schmidt; how would that power play factor in?

Possible scenarios raced through Peter's mind and then stopped at one. What if the Naintosa men were the ones who pulled the triggers? That would work. Peter had to figure out a way for that to happen.

"Peter?" Dr. Schmidt said for the second time.

Hearing his name snapped Peter out of his thoughts. "Just thinking about the logistics."

"You won't have full access to Naintosa's security resources as you've had in the past." Dr. Schmidt's German accent was always thicker when he first arrived in the States and hadn't been speaking much English. "As Davis is doing with you, I want this operation to be off the books. I will lend you five men. Naintosa cannot be implicated if anything, let's say, appears to go wrong. These men will technically be working for you."

Did that make Peter's goal easier or harder?

"We will be funding the operation," Davis said. "So you still have to report to us. We make the big decisions and have the final say. Understood?"

"Understood."

"Consider this as being on probation," Dr. Schmidt said. "If you do a good job, there will be more work for you in the future."

Peter noted Dr. Schmidt's ever-present undertone of arrogance. He hadn't missed being talked down to.

"Now on to intel," Davis said. "Bring us up to speed."

Peter was sitting straight as always. "On Nick Barnes' latest computer we found searches on genetically engineered foods causing cancer, sterility, and a lot on glyphosate."

Dr. Schmidt raised an eyebrow. "Did he find anything?"

"Only one thing that stood out," Peter said. "He searched *Glyphosate and Modern Disease* and *Dr. Timothy Roth*. We found a photocopy with handwritten notes on an article by the same author. Do you know anything about this study?"

"Yes." Dr. Schmidt squirmed in his chair. "That one got through the cracks. We didn't know what was happening until it came out. Not to worry, we are discrediting the study and punishing the journal that ran it."

"Is the information true?" Peter knew that wasn't the right question to ask, but the opportunity of taking a shot at Dr. Schmidt didn't come around that often.

Dr. Schmidt's eyes grew wide and he fixed his stare on Peter. "You're not here to judge the validity and effectiveness of glyphosate. That's not what you're being paid for. Will that affect your job performance? Why does it matter to you? Glyphosate is perfectly safe."

Peter hadn't realized he would hit such a sensitive nerve. Good.

"What about this Dr. Timothy Roth?" Davis asked.

Dr. Schmidt turned his attention from Peter to Davis. "He was an independent contractor, hired to focus on the positive aspects of glyphosate for Naintosa. He obviously made mistakes in his experiments."

"What are your people going to do about him?" Davis asked.

"There is nothing to do," Dr. Schmidt said. "There was an unfortunate fire at his lab in Chicago two nights ago. Dr. Roth perished."

"That's the fire your people asked my people not to report on, right?" Davis asked.

"Possibly," Dr. Schmidt said. "I don't concern myself with every minute detail. And nor should you."

"Hmm." Davis focused back on Peter. "Okay, what next?"

"Two men I've never seen before or could identify cleaned out Barnes' apartment." Peter pulled out a photo from his inside suit jacket pocket and passed it to Dr. Schmidt. "It looked like he was moving for good."

Dr. Schmidt took a good look at the picture of two muscular men loading boxes into a cargo van and then handed it to Davis.

"I'm pretty sure they work for Jack Carter," Davis said.

"That would make sense," Peter said. "I've identified one of the two people who got Barnes and Elles to the airport, Jorge Villegas. He's definitely one of Jack Carter's men."

Dr. Schmidt shared a new fact. "Jack was seen in Oslo, Norway, one week ago with Dr. Ivan Popov."

"Who is Dr. Popov?" Davis asked.

"He was a scientist who worked for Naintosa with Dr. Carl Elles. Lately, he has been helping the Council for Ethical Farming be a thorn in my side."

Davis nodded. "Oh, that guy."

Peter had wondered what happened to Dr. Popov and whether he was still involved. Now he knew.

"Dr. Popov left with Jack," Dr. Schmidt said. "They flew to Toronto."

"Do we know where they are now?" Davis asked.

"Where do you think they are?" Dr. Schmidt looked at Peter.

"I don't know where Carter and Popov are, but my sources tell me Barnes and Elles are in Seattle," Peter said. "Which is where I'm going right after this meeting."

"Your information is outdated." Dr. Schmidt looked short-tempered. "They flew to Vancouver early this morning. Jack and Dr. Popov landed in Vancouver yesterday. They are all there, we just don't know exactly where … yet."

"That's why we need Dr. Schmidt's people." Davis watched Peter. "With only three, your group is too small to be effective."

Davis was right. Peter hated not being on top of everything. "Dr. Schmidt, have your men meet me at the Vancouver airport in eight hours."

Dr. Schmidt nodded, still looking stern.

"I guess that's it then," Davis said. "Remember, we make the final decisions. Use that phone I gave you to keep us informed."

Peter stood and walked toward the office doors. Halfway there he turned back to look at Davis. "I forgot to mention that a week ago Nick Barnes played a round of golf with a man named Mike Couple. Do you know him?"

Davis shook his head. "No."

"He's a producer for one of your local TV stations."

"Okay, so …"

"Mike Couple used to be the boyfriend of a reporter for your *San Francisco News* named Summer Perkins."

"I have thousands of employees all over the world. How would I know those two?"

"Summer Perkins was found dead in a seedy bar last month by Nick Barnes."

Dr. Schmidt swiveled in his chair to look at Peter.

"Do you think Summer Perkins' death and Mike Couple have anything to do with all this?" Peter asked.

Davis' face turned visibly red.

"Hmm, that's the same look Brad gave me when I asked him about it," Peter said. "Couple is on the run, so my bet is that it does have something to do with this."

"I can have someone else look into it," Davis said. "You have a larger task to focus on."

Without saying good-bye, Peter walked out.

Davis made a note on a monogrammed pad of paper. The minor elimination of Ms. Perkins had been a catalyst. Who knew it was Barnes she had planned to meet that day? And who the hell was

Mike Couple? Actually, Brad should've known all of that if he had done his job properly. His days were numbered.

Hendrick rose. "If only we could kill them all and make it look like Peter was the only one responsible."

That comment made Davis look up. He ran a finger across the mark he'd had since birth and sneered.

CHAPTER 37

The sun's light was still touching the top of the mountain opposite us. The weather had cleared late in the afternoon, so Morgan, Sue, Ivan, and I had decided to go down to the dock and have a look around our new hideout. The air still smelled fresh from the recent rain.

The boat had appeared small as it rounded the corner of the arm of land to the south. As it headed straight for us, it grew visibly in size. Its engine's steady rev echoed in the valley as it skimmed over the calm water.

"It's chilly." Morgan crossed her arms. "But really beautiful."

"Well, it is March and we are in Canada," Sue pointed out.

Morgan turned away from Sue, toward the water.

We'd been talking about the scenery's beauty and calmness, but there was an uneasy undertone. We weren't there on vacation; we were hiding.

What if Bail finds us here? How could we escape other than on that boat? We needed to ask Jack whether there was another way out and if he had an escape plan.

The engine slowed until it was idling, and the boat sank deeper into the water. As soon as it reached the dock, Sam reversed the engine to halt the boat's forward motion.

I pulled the fiberglass hull toward me and flipped the fender over that was tied to the railing so the boat wouldn't rub against the dock. Then I wrapped the anchored line around the forward cleat to secure it.

Jorge jumped out and tied up the stern.

The man who had to be Tanner pulled back a gray tarp as soon as Sam shut off the engine. There were about twenty boxes underneath it of all shapes and sizes, a couple of them pretty big. A dozen bags of groceries were at one side of the pile.

I noticed Sue and Morgan looking at Tanner.

He was likely in his late twenties, with light hair cut short. I guessed women would find him attractive. He was over six feet tall, medium build, and looked to be in good shape.

Tanner smiled at the two women watching him, revealing dimples and perfect white teeth.

Crap. The last thing I wanted to have to worry about right now was some pretty boy flirting with Morgan and Sue.

"Need help unloading?" Ivan stepped forward. "Hand me a big box."

Even though Ivan looked like he could easily carry one of the heavy boxes, he was almost sixty and I doubted he'd been getting much exercise in Oslo. I hoped they wouldn't take him up on his offer.

"I can do it, Ivan," I said.

"It's getting dark." Sam's voice was deep, yet soft. "You should all get back up to the house. We can handle these supplies."

Lee and Jack had come down the path.

It never ceased to amaze me how hands-on Jack was. Even though he was paying for everything and these men worked for him, he always pulled his weight.

"At least give us each one load to carry up," Morgan said.

Tanner nodded and gave her a shopping bag.

"I can take more than that."

He flashed her a smile and handed her three more.

Morgan didn't flirt back when she took the bags. That was reassuring.

Once we each had something in our hands we headed up to the cabin. The heavy box I was carrying contained a new fax machine. The path had decorative lanterns on either side providing enough light to illuminate the route.

Morgan stopped in the kitchen to give Rose the groceries while the rest of us continued on down the stairs. She joined us within a few minutes and went right to work unpacking a laptop as more supplies were brought in.

Jack appeared from the hallway. "Can everyone come here? I want to show y'all something."

Ivan, Morgan, Sue, and I followed Jack to an open door.

"This is our surveillance room," Jack said. "We've set up cameras and sensors at a 250-yard radius around the cabin. No one will get close without us knowing about them."

Seven screens were set up and working. Each displayed six individual pictures of the forest outside, except for one that showed the water's edge.

Seeing all of this made me much more comfortable.

"This here's Tanner." Jack motioned to the man who'd been on the boat and was now plugging wires into a black box.

Tanner looked up at us and nodded. "Hi."

"He set this all up," Jack said. "Someone will be in this room at all times."

"That is reassuring," Ivan said.

Jack pointed to the screens. "It's impossible to watch every camera at once, so there's a movement sensor with an alarm at each location."

On cue, a buzzer went off.

We all looked at a screen that had a pulsing red square around the picture. A large black shape was moving toward the camera, not in any hurry.

"A bear?" Morgan asked.

"Yeah, that reminds me," Jack said. "Even though we're not far from the city, we're still in the wilderness. So anytime you leave the cabin, make sure one of my boys is with you. Wilderness means wildlife."

"Shit," Sue said. "It's not bad enough that we have to worry about the thugs from Naintosa, but we also have to worry about being eaten by a frickin' bear or cougar."

"I hear Canadian raccoons would be able to take someone your size out." I couldn't resist.

Sue smiled. "Piss off."

It may have been an inappropriate time to joke, but everyone had a tension-easing chuckle.

"What happens if someone should come in the middle of the night?" Ivan asked.

"The cameras are infrared." Tanner's voice was on the high side, but I didn't detect an accent.

"That should help make all of us feel safer." Jack motioned to the doorway. "There's one other thing I want to mention."

Once in the hall, Jack pointed. "The storage room on the right has our guns and ammunition. We'll have to make some time to give y'all a crash course on how to use a gun." He placed a hand on Ivan's shoulder. "This man here's already proficient with firearms."

That reminded me again that Ivan had been in the Soviet military years ago.

As we walked back into the larger room, Morgan looked around. "Hey, where's Dr. Roth?"

"He wasn't feeling well, so he's resting," Jack said.

We spent the rest of the evening setting up the work area, only breaking for dinner. By midnight we were done and ready to begin deciphering information in the morning.

CHAPTER 38

My head throbbed. It wasn't regular headache pain or a migraine, but like a blood vessel deep in my brain that was about to pop. The headaches had started after the Naintosa thugs had beaten me up in the East Vancouver warehouse.

The noise of the hairdryer stopped, and the bathroom door opened. "Nick, you'd better get up. I know you're awake, because your forehead is all furrowed."

I opened one eye. In front of me was a white sweater that just reached the top of a pair of jeans. I followed the curves until I settled on Morgan's face. I opened my second eye. I'd never get tired of looking at her. "I have a bit of a headache."

She sat down on the edge of the bed and stroked my duvet-covered arm. "Do you still get those?"

"From time to time."

"Have you had them checked out?"

"Yeah, remember that doctor in Oslo looked at me."

"What about since then—if they're getting worse?"

"They're not getting worse. They're less frequent and not as painful. I haven't had one in months."

"Still, you need to be checked. Maybe Ivan can take a look at you?"

"I'll be fine." I sat up. "Go have breakfast. I'll get ready and meet you in fifteen minutes."

After my shower, the headache was gone. I wiped the steam off the mirror with a towel and looked at my face. I was getting more wrinkles around my eyes, or maybe the ones I already had were getting deeper. The scar on my right cheek was still visible—another reminder of getting beaten at the warehouse. Morgan said it added character. I scratched the two days' worth of stubble on my face, thinking I'd better shave. I used to go three or four days when I was alone, but since Morgan had come back, I'd tried to shave every day. She'd never said that she preferred me to be clean-shaven, but I wanted to look respectable for her.

We'd be working in the cool basement, so I threw a sweatshirt on over my T-shirt.

Everyone but Jorge was sitting around the dining table when I arrived. "Good morning."

"Sleep well?" Jack asked.

"Yeah, fine." I sat down between Morgan and Jack. "It's so quiet here."

"I missed that in Oslo," Ivan said. "The quiet reminds me of my home in Nelson. I hope to be able to go there again."

Everyone stopped eating and looked at Ivan.

"We hope you are, too," Jack said.

After we were done, most of us refilled our coffee mugs and Ivan, Dr. Roth, who was skittish as usual, Morgan, Sue, Jack, and I headed to our basement office.

Everyone had already claimed a laptop, except for Dr. Roth, who hadn't been around for the setup last night.

"That one's yours." Sue looked at Dr. Roth and pointed at a computer at the end of the table. "It's all ready to go for you."

He didn't say anything, just sat down in front of it and flipped it open.

Sue looked at me and shrugged.

"I took the liberty of loading Dr. Roth's pertinent studies onto everyone's computers this morning." Jack was the only one of us still standing. He looked like he was going outside, dressed in a thick gray shirt, loose jeans, and hiking boots. All he needed was a jacket. "They're Word documents."

Dr. Roth looked violated, but didn't say anything.

"You're not staying?" Sue asked.

"I've already read them," Jack said. "I've got a few chores to take care of."

"I have not seen your research before." Ivan nodded to Dr. Roth. "I am looking forward to reading the information."

Dr. Roth was typing and didn't acknowledge Ivan.

"Dr. Roth will explain anything in need of clarification." Jack raised his voice. "Right?"

Dr. Roth looked up. "Right … right."

Jack headed for the hallway. "See y'all in a couple hours."

I opened my computer, recovered it from sleep mode, opened Word, found the files, opened the first one, and began to read. It was the study Morgan and I had found in the library. I didn't have the copy with my notes on it, so I made new ones as I gave it another go-through.

For a good half hour, the only sounds were Dr. Roth's keystrokes.

"Brilliant." Ivan got up, walked over to the portable blackboards, and pulled one closer to us. Using white chalk, he began writing out numbers and signs. "Dr. Roth, is this the formula you used in tracing the glyphosate in the shikimate pathway?"

Dr. Roth's eyes went wide, and for the first time he smiled. "Yes, Dr. Popov, that is correct, except …" He went to stand next to Ivan, took another piece of chalk from the tray at the bottom of the blackboard, and added to the formula.

As I watched Dr. Roth, I realized the only time he felt comfortable, positive, and got out of his own way was when he was doing something scientific.

Sue and Morgan also watched the two doctors of science have their discussion in a language we didn't always understand.

They reinforced the study's findings by talking it through. The lack of a shikimate pathway in humans and animals was the approach Naintosa took to show that glyphosate was safe. Dr. Roth's findings were a game-changer. Bacteria had a shikimate pathway and we were all full of them. That was how everyone was being poisoned by glyphosate. It threw Naintosa's research out the window.

I made notes in red so I'd remember the nuances of what they were discussing.

Ivan and Dr. Roth, satisfied that they had reached the same conclusions, returned to their seats.

Next, I opened a file that contained descriptions and formulas showing how the glyphosate study was conducted. They were hard to understand, but the main formulas looked like the ones on the blackboard. I'd ask Ivan and Dr. Roth to instruct me on what they wanted put in later.

"At this rate, glyphosate use could double by 2012." Ivan pointed to one of the formulas on the board.

"That is my projection," Dr. Roth said.

"That would be disastrous, to have people ingesting that much poison, not to mention what it will do to the ecosystem," Ivan said.

I didn't want to distract the two scientists, so I made another note to have them explain the specifics of what the doubling of glyphosate use would mean.

"The glyphosate study was very thorough," Morgan said. "I don't know how Naintosa would be able to dispute it."

"I'm sure they'll find a way," Sue said.

"I'm moving onto the next part." I clicked my mouse.

That file contained notes on the next study Dr. Roth was

embarking on. It was on neonicotinoids. I spelled out the word to try to pronounce it. I'd planned on researching the insecticides before we had to leave San Francisco in a hurry.

"Dr. Roth, will your neo-n-i-c-o-t-i-noid study be similar to the glyphosate one?" Sue asked.

"Yes." Dr. Roth seemed happy with the attention he was getting. "Neonicotinoids are a class of insecticides that came onto the market for mass use three years ago. They are said to be very effective on insects, yet cause less toxicity in birds and mammals than all other insecticides. My theory is that, as with glyphosate, what the manufacturers say and what the reality is are two different things. Since neonicotinoids are so new, there is little known about them. I was just getting underway when my lab burned down. What you have is very preliminary."

I looked at the bottom left of my screen, which showed that the file was 212 pages long. *Wow, and he's just getting started.*

The first part was a history of neonicotinoids. In the 1980s an oil company began work on an insecticide derived from nicotine. Nicotine is a natural insecticide and they wanted to chemically reproduce it. The original formula was bought by DKKR in 1991.

DKKR set off alarms with me. That was the company Dr. Elles was pressured to help when their genetically engineered tryptophan killed some people and made a whole pile of others sick. They were as bad as Naintosa, but smaller.

Further in the history it stated that in 1992, Naintosa was added as a partner.

Dr. Elles was still at Naintosa in 1992, but never mentioned anything about neonicotinoids. Actually, Ivan was still there at that time too.

"Hey, Ivan," I said, across the table. "Did you know anything about the neoni-c-o-t-i-noids development while you were at Naintosa?"

Ivan looked up from his screen. "No, I did not."

Dr. Roth interrupted, "Why don't we call them *neonics*, so you don't keep stumbling over the name?"

"Good," I said. "It's hard to pronounce."

Ivan continued. "We were prohibited from the pesticide department, where they would have been working on it. We did know that after our initial engineering work on each plant was complete, the pesticide scientists would go to work on them being able to tolerate glyphosate and now, I suppose, neonics as well."

"Okay." I read on.

Next came Dr. Roth's reasoning for the study. The starting point was based on having obtained initial findings from DKKR that had never been published. Each time adverse affects had been found, that direction of research was stopped. It seemed that neonicotinoids were so effective they wiped out every living thing that moved in the fields. Right away, the insecticide began decimating higher up the food chain than expected. *Bees, whose pollination was crucial to the growing process, were being decimated.* That was not a good thing. Also, ... *birds were dying by eating the poisoned insects, or from lack of insects to eat.*

Dr. Roth's study on neonicotinoids would be the first independent study conducted. Two goals were to project what the long-term effects of the bee poisoning were and how far up the food chain would be affected by the insecticide. The second part focused on how much ingestion of the insecticide residue humans could tolerate and what were possible side effects. The third part concentrated on changes to the soil over time.

I thought about it for a second. Just like with genetically engineered food, the study Dr. Roth was planning to undertake should've been done before neonicotinoids were approved by the EPA. Not now, after they are already on the market. The EPA just relied on the results Naintosa and DKKR supplied them. Of course they would only supply favorable findings. Then again, why was I surprised?

Before we knew it, Jack came down and said it was lunchtime for anyone who was hungry. He'd told us from the beginning that there'd be structured meals, but food would always be available if someone didn't want to eat at set times.

Ivan and Dr. Roth were engrossed in another discussion and indicated they would come up later. Morgan, Sue, and I followed Jack to the kitchen.

"So, how's it going so far?" Jack passed Sue a bowl full of green salad.

"Very interesting." I scooped some chicken in what looked like a mushroom sauce onto my plate and then passed the bowl to Morgan.

Sue pulled a plate of bean fritters toward her. "It never ceases to amaze me how companies can justify using such toxic chemicals on food."

"Let's not forget that Naintosa is a chemical company first," Jack said. "Chemical profits far outweigh their genetic engineering profits. Yet, combining the two is like hitting the jackpot for them."

"What are you planning to do once the information is written in layman's terms?" Morgan asked.

Jack put his fork down. "Well, that's a bit of an evolving project at the moment. With the problems encountered trying to get your father's exposé circulated, I thought we'd expand on that route. I've had a website developed that'll debut with this report and the exposé."

"Doesn't one of the lawsuits prohibit the exposé from being published anywhere again?" Sue asked.

"Yeah, but what the hell." Jack shrugged. "It'll stay up for a while before Schmidt's people block it or get it off the Internet. That'll draw extra attention to the new report as well."

I liked Jack's stick-it-to-them attitude.

"Step Two is the media. GM Comm, as you know, controls the major media. So there isn't a hope in hell that this will get out to the mainstream public. However, there are grass roots independent media channels that will publish or talk about what we have. I've contracted a publicity company that's contacting them now. There are enough of them around the world to start the ball rolling."

"There wasn't as much impact as we wanted when the independent media ran stories about Dr. Elles' exposé in Europe," I pointed out.

"Let's just say that the people helping us now are a lot more aggressive," Jack said. "They're the kind of people Naintosa would hire, but they're working for us."

"You pay them enough and they'll be on whatever side you want?" asked Sue.

"That's the way the world turns." Jack shrugged. "Business is business. But I've used this particular company before, and they do have ethics."

"Well, that's comforting," Morgan said.

I picked up on Morgan's sarcasm. Past experience had taught me that she got feisty when we got into the mix of going after Naintosa's dirty business. I took it as passion for wanting to get the truth out.

Morgan's tone didn't faze Jack. "It should only take a week to complete the report. Then Dr. Roth and Ivan, if he wants, can start the neonicotinoid study at a safe lab I've rented locally."

"The study will take more than a year to complete," Sue said. "What are we going to do?"

"This is the safest place," Jack said. "That's, of course, if it's all right with you. There will be writing and research that'll need to be done as the study progresses. Otherwise, I suggest you work on your own projects. Like you, Nick, with your book."

"We're going to be here a long time, then," Morgan said.

It had felt temporary when we first got here, but all of a sudden I felt like a prisoner. I took a bite of chicken and then roast potato while I thought it over. We were being protected, and I was with the two people I most cared about. We were participating in work that helped the world. But somehow, deep down, I still felt this hideout was temporary.

"How about every morning we start a routine of exercise while learning self-defense?" Jack asked. "Lee's an expert at Krav Maga. When Lee and I aren't here, Jorge can teach you about firearms. Also, I'm planning on setting up a small gym by the pool table. How's seven a.m. sound?"

"How about we make it seven-thirty?" Sue said. "We should meditate first."

"Okay." Jack nodded. "That's the schedule."

CHAPTER 39

The afternoon was spent reading the rest of Dr. Roth's plans for the neonicotinoids study.

I looked up to see Tanner walk toward the surveillance room, carrying some kind of electrical part, which reminded me that I hadn't seen Jorge or Lee all day. Jack had stayed upstairs after lunch. Morgan, Sue, and Ivan were reading. Dr. Roth was writing on a pad of paper.

There were many more formulas to skim over, then eventually I reached the *Toxicity* section. After explaining how the toxicity research would be conducted, Dr. Roth had added some notes about what he hoped to prove. *Every organism has its place or job in nature. Killing off what some people may view as pests can harm the entire ecosystem.* Dr. Roth had included a list of bugs and insects and what they did. More focus was on the pollinating *bees—which are an integral part of growing food, yet are highly affected by neonicotinoids.*

The following section was about potential human side effects of neonicotinoid buildup. Some of the initial problems that may have been developing and needed investigation were: *immune system suppression, sterility …*

Wait, the insecticide made people sterile too? There was a pattern.

I noticed that I'd crossed my legs and my thighs were squeezing my groin.

The list continued with: … *kidney, liver, and stomach damage, and gastrointestinal distress.* The list of side effects was just going to grow over time.

It took me until 7:00 p.m. to finish reading.

"Dr. Roth, I wish you success with your neonics study." I stood. "I'm looking forward to seeing the results, and whether your hypotheses are proved to be correct."

He closed his computer screen onto the keyboard. "Th-thanks."

Ivan was also finishing up for the day. Morgan had gone upstairs half an hour earlier.

"I just need a few more minutes," Sue said. "Meet you upstairs."

As I walked into the kitchen and dining area, the comforting smell of stew hit my nostrils.

Rose was clearing some bowls from the table. She looked up as I approached. "Are you hungry? A few people ate already. Dinner is ready when you are."

"Give me a few minutes. Has Morgan eaten yet?"

"No, she hasn't."

Opening the door to the living room, the smell and feel of the air changed. The aroma of wood burning and the crackle that came with it escaped from the fireplace.

Jack was speaking with Lee next to the bar and looked over at me. "Your furniture and stuff have been put into storage in Seattle. All your papers, documents, some clothes, and things like your passport are up in your bedroom."

I stopped. "How did we get into Canada without our passports? Especially since security is on high alert these days?"

Lee looked at Jack and then me.

A faint smile crossed Jack's lips. "Y'all aren't terrorists."

Now was not the time where I wanted to go into detail of how

Jack was able to accomplish that, so I just nodded.

"Have a look at what's there and see if you can tell if anything other than your computer was taken."

I headed up the stairs to the bedroom.

Morgan was taking clothes out of her big suitcase, the one that had been at my apartment, and placing them in the dresser drawers.

"Glad to have your stuff?" I gave her a comforting hug.

"Yeah." Morgan gave me a kiss and then pulled back. She surveyed the open drawers filled with her belongings. Then she took her panties and tossed them back in the suitcase. "Someone's paws may have been all over my clothes. I'm going to wash everything."

There were three boxes, one duffel bag, and my black suitcase near the closet. I picked up a box, placed it on the bed, and tore the sealing tape off the top.

"Do you want me to wash your clothes too?" Morgan had closed her refilled suitcase and pulled it off the bed.

"Nah, I'm not worried about someone going through my underwear."

"Suit yourself." She gave me a kiss on the cheek as she passed, wheeling the case out of the bedroom.

My passport was sitting on top of my papers that had been in my now not-so-secret hiding spot. It didn't sit well with me that some people had so much power that they didn't need to use passports to travel from country to country, especially after September 11. Jack was a good guy, but there were bad guys with power, too.

I pulled out all of the papers and stacked them on the bed. At the bottom was the back-up disk and CD of my book—my second-to-last computer had used a disk and the last one a CD, so I had both.

Flipping through the stack, the only thing that seemed to be missing was my copy of Dr. Roth's glyphosate study.

The second box had all the papers that had been on my desk. The printouts on glyphosate weren't there. Why had they taken those? They could be found by anyone on the Internet.

The third box contained my toiletries and everything else from my bathroom. I put it to the side, because I'd already replaced pretty much everything in it.

The duffel bag had my thicker, cold-weather clothes. Since it was the middle of March, I wouldn't need them unless we were still here in November. I pushed the bag to the back of the closet.

The suitcase had my everyday clothes. I didn't feel like putting everything into the dresser or on hangers, so I just left it open in the closet. After I'd worn and washed each article I'd put them into their proper spot ... good plan.

When I opened the bedroom door to leave, Dr. Roth was walking by toward his room. I smiled, but he just proceeded, looking straight forward. *Whatever.*

As I came down the stairs, the lights in the living room turned off. The only illumination was from the fireplace.

Lee was going outside.

There was something shining out on the dark water.

"What's going on?" I'd reached the bottom step.

"Stay back." Ivan stood against the wall next to the large front window.

"There's a boat out there shining a spotlight along the shore." Sue was hunched over, heading toward Ivan.

Jack was peering around the open curtain. "I don't think they'd be able to see inside, but we shouldn't take any chances."

"Close the curtains," I said.

"Too late," Sue said.

I went to stand beside Jack. "Any idea who it is?"

"Nope," Jack said. "We saw the boat come around the inlet, but it didn't start surveying the shore until now."

The spotlight lit the room for about ten seconds. We were all still.

Once it was past, we looked out the window to watch the boat continue on. It took about five minutes before it went around the point.

Lee came inside. There were binoculars hanging from his neck.

"Did you get a look?" Jack asked.

Lee nodded. "Two men onboard that I could see. It was around a twenty-four-foot Bayliner similar to ours. I'll run the boat's numbers. Jorge's down by the dock in case a swimmer comes in."

"Okay, probably nothing." Jack's voice didn't sound convincing. "Anyone not eaten yet?"

"I could use dinner." There was nothing else we could do.

"Me, too," Sue said.

"I will take a snack to my room," Ivan said. "I am tired."

Entering the dining room, we saw Morgan at the table with a bowl of stew in front of her.

She stopped chewing. "Sorry, I couldn't wait for you."

"You missed a boat with a spotlight that came by," I said.

Morgan looked alarmed. "Do we know who they were?"

"Hopefully Lee will find out," I replied.

"Should we be worried?" Morgan asked.

"No …" Jack's voice still didn't sound convincing. "No need to worry."

Lorraine came into the dining room from the back hallway. Her brown hair was in a ponytail under a black baseball cap that had a gold emblem on it. Her gray shirt had the same logo and *Polska* written underneath it. She went straight to the kitchen and poured a cup of coffee.

"We haven't seen you since we first got here," Sue said.

Lorraine, mug in hand, walked over to us at the table. "I'm working the night shift."

"Lorraine's our eyes while we're sleeping," Jack said.

"I must go relieve Tanner." She gave us a smile and left the room.

Everyone ate delicious beef stew, except Sue who had pea soup.

Jack skipped dessert and got himself a beer from the fridge. "Anyone else want one?"

Whenever we got into the thick of things my appetite for alcohol diminished. But as soon as I saw the beer, I thought of Mike. I'd forgotten about him again. "Jack, there's a friend named Mike Couple who Jorge was trying to find for us. He was Summer Perkins' boyfriend …"

"What?" Sue looked surprised. "Boyfriend, really?"

"Only for a short time." I turned back to Jack. "Morgan and I were supposed to meet him the day we almost got abducted. He wanted to continue what Summer had been working on."

"Yeah, Jorge filled me in. We're still looking." Jack sat back down and placed the bottle on the table. "Did he tell you exactly what Summer had discovered?"

"Just that she was trying to expose something Davis Lovemark and a guy named Carlo Da Silva were doing. Something real bad."

"Something she wanted to confide to you first," Morgan added. "If you would've shown up fifteen minutes earlier you'd have suffered the same fate as her."

I shrugged. "Or saved her."

Morgan reached over and touched my hand. "Of course."

"He has all her information?" Jack intervened.

"He thinks he has most of it."

"Who is Carlo Da Silva?" Morgan asked.

"I've heard of him," Sue said.

"His family's based in Spain." Jack sounded hesitant. "He's an intelligent, wealthy, and resourceful entrepreneur. He's very involved in the shaping of the Internet."

"You must know something about what these guys are planning," I said. "They were your buddies."

"*Buddies* is an intimate word and not one I'd use to describe my relationship with them. Let's say *club members*, and Carlo is the leader at the moment. Since I've been shunned, I'm not privy to a lot of what's going on." Jack took a sip of beer and leaned in.

That made us all lean forward in anticipation of what he was going to say.

"Now, I have my theories, and the main one might have to do with what Summer found out, which ties into what we're learning. Not all of the *club* members know everything that everyone is doing all the time."

He always referred to the group as a *club*, as if trying to protect us from who they really were. We still didn't know whether they had a name they called themselves. But conspiracy theorists had a few labels.

"You have to understand that these men fancy themselves as stewards of humanity, shaping the direction of the world in the way they perceive as best. The main problem is that they tend to point in the direction that is most suited to their self-interests."

"Do they have some kind of God complex?" Sue half asked, half stated.

"Yes, most of them do," Jack said.

"No disrespect, but do you have the same complex?" Sue could ask the questions no one else had the guts to.

Morgan looked alarmed. "Sue."

"No, no, it's a good question." Jack raised his hand. "To be honest, yes, I do. It's been drummed into me by my family. But I'm trying to channel that energy for good and doing my best to be humble."

Sue exhaled. "I didn't mean to …"

"Don't worry about it, Miss Sue." Jack reached over and patted her hand. "That's why you're the best at what you do."

We seemed to have gotten sidetracked. "So what's your theory, Jack?"

"Something started way back in my grandfather's time that I've gotten wind of. I haven't had anything concrete, but I think it's the single biggest manipulation of all time. I'm hoping that what we all put together here will provide us with proof, except for a missing piece or two. Y'all started us in the right direction with Dr. Elles' exposé."

"What conclusion are you thinking we'll come to?" Morgan asked.

"I really would like y'all to figure that out without my bias. I may be wrong. I sure hope I am, but I doubt it."

"We need to find Mike," I said. "We need to know what he has."

Jack nodded. "My guess is that what Summer found tied Hendrick Schmidt to what Lovemark and Da Silva are doing. That's why she wanted to talk to you."

"That makes the most sense," I said.

"Did you give Jorge possible places Mike frequents?"

"No, just his address."

Sue pushed over the pad and pen she had with her and I wrote down the places I knew, including his mother's home in Seattle.

Jack took his last swig of beer and stood, taking the paper I'd given him. "Y'all absorbed a lot of information today, and there's a crap load of work to be done in the days ahead." He took a second to look at each of us. "I really trust you and your capabilities, and am happy we're a team."

My brain felt overloaded. I needed some rest. We all did.

Jack went downstairs and we went upstairs.

Sue was ahead and stopped at our door. "What do you two think of all of this?"

"What Jack alluded to," Morgan said without hesitation, "is a continuation of what we started with my father's work. Now we're going to get to the big picture of what it's all about. We're going to find out what my father, mother, Bill, and Ivan unknowingly contributed to with the genetic engineering."

Sue nodded. "What about you, Nick?"

"Same reason as Morgan, I guess. I want to finish what we started."

CHAPTER 40

We met in the living room at 7:00 a.m. as planned. It wasn't just Morgan, Sue, and I; Jack and Lee showed up too. Each of us wore our version of workout clothing.

"Lee and I'd like to try meditating," Jack said. "It'll do us good to have more peace in our minds."

The fireplace had already been lit, I wasn't sure by whom, so that was the coziest spot. Morgan, Sue, and I sat on the couch, facing the fire; Jack and Lee settled into the comfy chairs on either end.

I looked from Lee to Jack. "Meditation is simple in concept, sometimes difficult to achieve. All you're attempting to do is clear your mind for twenty minutes. Close your eyes and focus on your breathing. In and out. When a thought comes in, just let it pass, don't pay attention to it. It'll take practice."

"What do we do with our hands? Do we touch our thumb and two fingers together?" Jack held up his hand to show his fingers forming an O.

"I like to do that," Sue said.

"Or just leave your palms open on your lap," I said.

"Shouldn't we have a mantra or something?" Jack asked.

"Focusing on your breathing will be your mantra," I said. "Okay, close your eyes. Relaxing, breathe in and out."

Lee and Jack did as I asked. I watched them for a minute before closing my own eyes.

I wasn't relaxing. I was listening for fidgeting or altered breathing sounds from Lee or Jack. But there were none. Realizing that I wouldn't hear anything, because these men were so structured and in control of their emotions, regardless of whether they reached a meditative state, helped me finally let go of worrying about them.

In and out, deeper and deeper.

A sudden rush of positive energy enveloped me. It was as if we were sticks that had been caught up in the reeds along a riverbank. The current had worked us free and now we were in the main flow of the water.

I was the last to open my eyes. Everyone looked content.

"How was it?" I looked from Jack to Lee. "How do you feel?"

"Calm." As usual, Lee didn't use unneeded extra words.

"Yeah, relaxed," Jack said. "Pretty good for a first attempt."

I noticed that Ivan was standing behind the couch. It was distracting seeing him in a gray 1970s tracksuit with black stripes running down each side.

"I had an unusually calm and positive feeling the whole time," Morgan said.

Sue nodded. "Me too."

We had all experienced the same feeling. "I guess the five of us meditating together is a good thing. It'll help ground us while we're in this, uh, *situation.*"

"That could never be bad." Jack smiled. "I'm up for doin' this mind-bending every morning."

"I might have to start, too," Ivan said.

Jack got up. "Now for step two of our new daily routine. Let's go get some exercise and learn self-defense."

When we arrived downstairs, Lee guided us through some stretches. After we limbered up, the lesson began.

"Krav Maga is a martial art, but more brutal and efficient than all others," Lee said. "You'll be able to learn basic moves on how to defend yourselves and subdue attackers much faster than with other practices."

"This will be a crash course so y'all can get out of sticky situations should they arise," Jack said.

"Do you know this stuff?" Sue asked Ivan, who was next to her.

"I learned it long ago. This will be a good refresher."

We started with the proper fighting stance—the leg opposite our lead hand was extended forward, feet apart a little more than shoulder width, knees bent, open palms at neck level, with the lead hand out farther. Once we got that straight, we practiced moving around while staying in the stance.

Next, Lee taught us how to use the base of our hands, elbows, and knees. "Krav Maga was meant for defending yourself by using the power of the body's strongest parts, in only a few moves, to disable your attacker decisively."

It was a good workout and the moves weren't hard to learn. And it became obvious that size didn't matter when Sue, the smallest of our group, partnered with Lee, by far the biggest. He had taught us how to defend ourselves against someone trying to choke us, and Sue executed it perfectly. With Lee's hands around her neck, she raised her right arm holding it tight against her head. In a quick movement she pivoted her body right. There was no way Lee could keep his hands on her neck. Sue brought her left arm up and right arm down to trap Lee's hands. A knee to the stomach brought him down to her level, allowing for the perfect angle for an elbow to the face. A knee to the groin finished him off. We weren't supposed to actually hit each other, just stop short, but Sue got carried away. The strikes weren't with all of Sue's might and I suspected Lee was playing along, but they must've still hurt.

"I don't know what got into me." Sue tried to help him up.

"I'm so sorry."

"No, you did it just the way I taught you." Lee was a good sport about it, but by the strain in his voice you could tell the shot to the privates caused pain. "As you can see, Krav Maga is very effective."

Jack smiled. "It helps to have spunk."

Once he was back on his feet, Lee said, "Now let's practice these moves more."

"Everyone should know this," I said.

"We should've learned this a couple years ago," Morgan said.

Sue rolled her eyes at me. "You've talked about it for long enough."

"Right." I pushed her.

She assumed the stance and took a mock jab at me.

⊳⊲

After breakfast, Morgan, Sue, and I were on our way downstairs when we passed Jack and Lee in the hallway talking about something.

I interrupted them. "Did you find out who the boat from last night belonged to?"

"It was a rental from the marina in Deep Cove," Jack said. "Same place ours came from."

"That's suspicious, isn't it?" Sue asked.

"Yes, it is," Jack said. "Jorge's looking into it more."

"Do we need to move?" Morgan asked.

Jack looked distracted. "There could be all sorts of reasons that boat was searching the shoreline. It's not time to be worried yet."

But we were worried nonetheless.

⊳⊲

Ivan and Dr. Roth were already sitting in front of their computers.

"Dr. Roth's study fits well with my new information," Ivan said.

"Let's have a look at it then," I said.

Morgan, Sue, and I opened our laptops.

Ivan got up and went to the blackboard. "Before we start reading, I want to go over a theory I have."

Jack had come into the workroom and stopped to listen.

Ivan drew a seed with chalk. "This was something Bill and I were pondering. It was something that never occurred to us when we were undertaking the experiments at Naintosa." He looked at Morgan. "Your father did mention something about this in one of our last conversations. So if he were still alive, he would have figured it out."

Jack took a spare chair and sat down opposite Morgan and me, next to Sue.

"Up until now, it took generations to alter plants by crossbreeding." Ivan drew two more seeds. "And they had to be of the same species. For example, corn could only be bred with other varieties of corn to achieve the desired attributes. During the breeding, as each transition was completed, peoples' digestion became used to the new variety, as the changes were subtle over time. Now with genetic engineering, in one generation the chemical composition has changed all at once with alterations that would never occur in nature. The theory is that peoples' digestion cannot assimilate the abrupt change. That is why we are seeing such an upsurge in allergies, intolerances, and all the other problems. Peoples' bodies are treating the genetically engineered food as a foreign poison."

Sue was typing as fast as she could. That was good, because she was way better at taking notes than I was.

Dr. Roth got up, nodding his head. "In addition, when you continually add ingestion of trace amounts of glyphosate …" He took a piece of chalk and wrote some numbers and squiggles. "The poisonous reaction is tenfold."

Ivan gazed at Dr. Roth's formula. "That makes sense. Now the theory needs to be proven through research."

"That's very interesting," Jack said. "Add it to the list of studies."

"I must apologize for my fallen colleagues and myself," Ivan said. "Carl, Claudia, Bill, and I did not intend to do harm with our genetic experiments."

"Don't keep apologizing, Ivan," Jack said. "We know all of y'alls' intentions were good. Naintosa manipulated them."

Ivan would probably hold onto that guilt for the rest of his life.

Morgan's head was down and a sniffle was audible. I reached over and squeezed her hand, trying to comfort her.

Ivan sat down in front of his laptop and took a deep breath.

"Someone else would've come up with your discoveries if you hadn't," I said. "And they may've not wanted to make things right, like you."

Ivan sighed. "Perhaps."

Morgan looked up and wiped her eyes.

"My most current information has been saved into your computers under my file name," Ivan said.

"We're making good progress." Jack stood. "I've read it already, so I'll leave you to it."

I opened the first file and began to read. Everyone else did the same.

The subject was seed drift—where the genetically engineered seed was making its way from the fields where it had been planted into adjacent fields of traditional crops. This happened with the help of birds, rodents, and animals picking seeds up and either carrying them over or eating them, and the undigested seed falling on other fields in their droppings. Also, drift was caused by wind and dispersal by water.

This was something we already knew about from Dr. Elles' research, but it was occurring at a higher rate than anticipated.

I looked up. "Ivan, wouldn't Naintosa encourage seed drift? The sooner genetically engineered seeds mingle and cross-pollinate with conventional ones, the sooner all seed will have genetically engineered traits."

Ivan nodded. "Yes, of course."

"And if it's happening at a higher rate than anticipated, they are doing it on purpose," I said.

"I tend to agree," Ivan said. "But we have no proof."

"Other than catching them red-handed in the act of spreading seed in someone else's fields, how can we?" Morgan asked.

The next part was about a terminator seed Naintosa had developed that made the second generation of seed sterile. The terminator enhancement was activated when glyphosate was used. There were a bunch of scientific formulas describing how they were able accomplish it. Since I didn't understand them, as usual, I skimmed that part. In the end it meant that farmers weren't able to save their seed and had to buy new seed from Naintosa every year. That was an expense many farmers couldn't afford. Naintosa claimed that the reason for the terminator seed was to prevent seed drift. I thought about it. That part actually made sense. However, the facts showed that in reality it wasn't happening.

"Did everyone finish reading about terminator seeds?" Ivan asked.

Sue was typing on her keyboard. "I read somewhere that Dr. Schmidt was quoted as saying that the terminator technology was developed to protect Naintosa's seed patents and to make back the billions spent on research and development. But now I can't find the quote anymore. Why hadn't I saved it?"

Ivan nodded. "It was retracted."

"Terminator seeds and seed drift contradict themselves," I said. "Why would there be a problem with drift if the second generation of seed couldn't germinate?"

"Either the technology doesn't work, or they aren't activating it," Dr. Roth spoke up. "Glyphosate isn't triggering it like it's supposed to."

"My guess is they are not using the terminator technology," Ivan said.

Morgan raised her hand as if we were in class. "Since most farmers are already buying new seed from Naintosa every year, could it be a scare tactic to make farmers think they're buying terminator seeds?"

"Naintosa wants drift and they want farmers to buy their seed every year," I said. "Whatever tactic they're using is working."

"There is more to it," Ivan said. "Let us go onto the next section."

I rubbed my temples. "I need to take a short break." One of my headaches may've been coming on.

Morgan was watching me. "Let's go have lunch before we continue."

When we entered the dining room, all the fixings for sandwiches were laid out on the table.

"I made the mayonnaise myself." Rose brought over a clear glass bowl that contained the white cream. "It doesn't have all those chemicals in it that the bought junk has."

"Looks good," Morgan said.

The door from the living room opened and Jorge entered. "Guess who we found, *esconder.*"

A man stepped from behind Jorge. "Nick, Sue."

"Holy shit, Mike." I almost dropped the plate in my hands.

Mike Couple had a beard, looked like he hadn't had a shower in the week since I last saw him, and was wearing the same clothes. He held a metal black briefcase in his left hand that had a big dent in it.

Sue went over to him. "Shit, Mike."

I felt a surge of happiness mixed with almost overwhelming relief. If anything had happened to him, I'd have felt responsible.

Sue gave Mike a hug that only lasted a second before she pulled back, blinking her eyes.

When I got close enough to shake his hand I knew why. He really hadn't had a shower or changed his clothes.

Mike shrugged. "It was hard to find places to clean up while I was on the run."

"What happened?" I asked.

"Mind if I tell you while we eat? I'm starving."

Jack was standing beside the table. "Welcome, Mr. Couple, help yourself. I'm Jack."

Mike squinted. "Jack Carter, the oil guy?"

"Ex-oil guy." Jack smiled.

I introduced him to Morgan and Ivan.

Mike winked at me after taking a look at Morgan. She shook her head at me as soon as he looked away.

Mike proceeded to make a sandwich he could barely hold in his chubby hands.

I went over to the fridge in the kitchen to get Mike a Budweiser. There weren't any. Instead there were three kinds of organic beer I'd never heard of. I chose the lager for him and made a mental note to try all three later.

"We have no Bud." I handed the bottle to him.

As soon as he swallowed enough sandwich to open his mouth, he chugged half the liquid in the bottle. "Mmm." He studied the label. "Fancy."

"So tell us what happened to you." I reached over the table for lettuce and cheese.

He chewed some more and forced a swallow. "I waited the next day at the library for you and Morgan." He smiled at Morgan.

Morgan attempted a polite smile back, but I knew she didn't want any special attention from Mike.

"The guy who worked with Summer had found more papers hidden in her desk. He brought them over after I'd gotten home from our round of golf." He took another greedy drink of beer. "I read them while I waited for you. They made me all paranoid. I was the only person on the periodical floor. I waited two hours for you."

"Sorry we didn't show," I said.

"No problem; Jorge told me what happened. I think the two guys who came after you also came after me."

"Really?" Morgan looked alarmed.

"I went to take a piss and when I came out there were two guys getting off the elevator." Mike looked at Jorge standing next to the kitchen island and then back at me. "They fit the description of the men Jorge said came after you."

"They'd had time to get from the airport to the library?" I asked Jorge. "Right?"

"I would think so."

"Summer's information put me on high alert, so when I saw them I got out of there quick. Luckily the john was next to the stairwell and I'd taken the papers with me when I went to take a leak."

"What did Summer have?" Sue asked.

"I'll show you." He patted the briefcase that had never left his side. "I raced home to grab some stuff and split town. I knew I wasn't being paranoid when those same two fuckers showed up outside my apartment building and were standing beside my car."

"Really?" Ivan said.

"I grabbed what little I'd had a chance to pack and went out the back."

"Where did you go?" Sue asked.

"North." Mike had finished his sandwich and beer and could now use both hands for gesturing. "I found the nearest cash machine and withdrew what I could. Then I caught a cab to the bus depot in Oakland. From there I boarded a bus to Portland. That's where some grease-ball fucker stole my backpack and my wallet. I beat him with my briefcase, but he got away. I had to survive on the street. It was fucking awful. I nearly got rolled like five times."

"How did you find him, Jorge?" I asked.

Jorge had walked up to the table. "He phoned his mother and we tracked him from there."

"I had just decided to hitchhike or walk to Mother's house in Seattle when this big dude approached me. He told me that he'd been sent to find me and take me to where you were." Mike sighed in what sounded to be relief. "I figured he couldn't make up a story like that just to make me his love bitch, so I trusted him. He took me to the airport and put me on a smokin' private jet that flew me to Vancouver. Jorge met me and brought me here."

"It's so great they found you," I said.

Mike's eyes welled up and he looked straight at me. "Thank you, man, for having them look for me. I don't know what more would've happened to me on the mean streets of Portland or on the I-5 to Seattle if I'd been out there any longer."

"Thank Jorge and the guy who tracked you down," I said. "I just gave them what information I could. They were the ones who actually found you."

Jorge smiled. "He's thanked us enough."

"Glad you're safe." Jack stood. "Jorge, why don't you show Mike the spare room on the second floor? Mike, after you get cleaned up and rest, you can join us."

Mike wiped his eyes and nodded.

Jorge had moved over next to Jack. "All I could find out about that boat was that it was rented under a false name."

Jack's expression turned concerned. "Come down to the surveillance room after you get Mike settled."

CHAPTER 41

I felt ready to get back to work. The headache never came on, the food had helped, and I didn't have to worry about Mike anymore.

When we came back downstairs, Dr. Roth was ejecting a CD from his computer. He looked nervous as usual and fumbled with it as he slid it into his pocket.

The fax machine was chugging out paper. A small stack had already come through.

"Good." Ivan walked to the fax and pulled out the bottom page. "The information I had been waiting for has arrived."

"What's it about?" asked Morgan.

"It is a very important piece to the puzzle," Ivan said. "Something no one is supposed to know about but a colleague was able to obtain. Let me look it over first."

Even Dr. Roth, who hadn't moved from his computer since we went to have lunch, looked interested.

The fax machine beeped and stopped.

"Right now you can read the next document already in your computers," Ivan said. "It is the information we obtained the day Bill died. I was able to find and procure another copy from the geneticist who has now gone into hiding."

A solemn vibe engulfed the room.

I opened the file that our friend had lost his life over. I had to read very slowly because of the scientific wording and the fact that English was not the author's first language. Nonetheless, I was able to understand the gravity of it.

When I finished, I looked up and saw Sue and Morgan absorbed by the information. Dr. Roth was taking notes. I decided to make a summary to help me understand it.

The geneticist was part of a study commissioned by the German Agricultural Ministry on superbugs and superweeds. After the study had been completed, he'd taken it a step further on his own and had conducted an experiment on how genetically engineered food affected people. What he had found was astonishing. Over time, as bugs ingested the genetically engineered plants resistant to the insecticides sprayed on them, future generations became tolerant—hence, superbugs. The same occurred with weeds once their genes mingled with plants resistant to the herbicides; their next generations became superweeds.

However, the human-based tests showed that we were not becoming "super." Over time, as people ingested genetically engineered grain, fruit, and vegetables, their genes would alter. The same happened when humans consumed meat from animals fed genetically engineered feed, because the animals' genomes had already changed. The genetic transfer occurred when the good gut bacteria in the human digestive tract picked up the engineered genes to be compatible to them.

Proteins and enzymes from food people ate have always changed their genes and subsequently their DNA, but the genetically engineered food alters humans' genomes in ways nature had never intended. These changes would affect all generations going forward, and they were irreversible.

I thought about all the illnesses that Dr. Elles' notes had revealed, and the ones listed in this new study: various cancers, autism, dementia, heart disease, severe allergies, colitis—the list went on and on. I read over my summary, and then at the end I wrote, *it's irreversible and everyone's already doomed.*

Ivan was at the photocopier making copies of the faxed document.

"Ivan, I made a summary of this, because it was hard to understand." I pressed the print icon. "It'll come off the printer beside you. Can you please read it to make sure it's correct?"

"Yes, of course."

The printer hummed and two pages came out. Ivan took the pages and began to read.

"That explains why the diseases are going to increase," Sue said.

"Already increasing," Morgan corrected. "And it's irreversible."

Ivan walked over to me. "Yes, this is accurate."

"Let me see it." Sue extended her arm and Ivan gave her the papers.

"The only consolation is that we now know. Soon the rest of the world will know too." Ivan placed a stapled copy of the fax in front of each of us.

Jack sat down at the table next to me. Ivan had stopped him when he was coming from the surveillance room and told him he'd want to read the new information that had arrived.

The first page had two words on it: *Plycite Gene.* We all turned that page and read.

The Plycite gene created human antibodies that attacked sperm. When women ingested it in small quantities over a period of time, Plycite build-up sterilized them. It caused a condition called "immune infertility," in which antibodies were produced that attacked sperm. The antibodies were attracted to surface receptors on sperm and latched on to make each sperm so heavy it couldn't move forward.

It sounded like science fiction.

The final two pages were about what happened to the Plycite gene after it was discovered.

The company that created the gene wanted to use it for

contraception, but Naintosa had bought it last year. A Naintosa scientist had been able to isolate the genes that manufacture these antibodies and splice them into corn genes. Corn had a similar cell structure to humans. Patents were pending.

This was part of the sterility answer I'd been searching for.

Morgan looked up from reading. "But the population is growing, not receding."

"It would be too soon for Naintosa to have the Plycite gene in their corn seed on the market," Ivan said. "However, this is an indication of their future plans."

Dr. Roth sighed aloud and brought his hands to his face. "Think of the implications once you bring seed drift into the equation."

I looked around the room at the concerned faces. Jack seemed particularly upset.

With the application of the Plycite gene Dr. Schmidt, through Naintosa, could be planning on sterilizing millions, if not billions of people—on purpose.

Jack placed his hands at the edge of the table and pushed back. As he stood, the chair legs caught on the carpet and it fell away backward. His face was a mottled red with anger, his lips white. "That's the final piece of evidence I needed." He turned and left the room.

That night Morgan and I made quiet love like there was no tomorrow. That was how we felt.

CHAPTER 42

March 12, 2002

J ack, Lee, and Sue were standing in the middle of the living
room when we came downstairs.

Our new addition, Mike, walked in from the patio. As soon
as he closed the door I could smell that he'd just had a cigarette.

"We've decided to go for a hike this morning," Jack said. "Care
to join us?"

"It's real nice outside," Mike said.

I looked out the window and saw the sun was shining.

"Sure," Morgan said. "That sounds like a good change of pace."

"I wouldn't mind taking a look-see at our surroundings." Mike
must've slept sixteen hours. He had taken a shower and shaved. His
khakis were clean but, as always, shrunk short enough to get a peek
at his white socks between the pant legs and shoes.

Once we were all assembled in proper footwear and jackets, we
went out the back door.

Lee and Ivan were waiting for us outside. They each had an
assault rifle slung over their shoulders, and Lee held an additional
one that he passed to Jack.

Seeing the powerful guns made me uncomfortable. It wasn't the fact that they had to be illegal in Canada; it was that they reminded me we were hiding out from trained security people wanting to harm us. Yet the rifles provided a sense of protection.

Ivan, being a scientist, looked weird with a gun. I had to remind myself again he was ex-Soviet military.

Only twenty feet around the cabin was cleared; after that, the forest was thick. Cedar and fir added a perfume to the breeze. The ground was wet from yesterday's rain, and the underbrush of ferns and small bushes still had water droplets on them. The sun only managed to get through the trees in spots but, where it did, the rays were bright as spotlights and warm.

Jack stopped at a path. "This will take us to an area called Woodlands, about a mile and a half away. We have two vehicles parked there. Let's go take a look so you'll all know where to go in case you ever need to get out of here on foot."

Lee led the way, and we all fell behind him in single file; Jack was next, then Ivan, Sue, Mike, Morgan, and me.

I heard someone coming up behind me and froze, wishing for a split second that I had protection.

"Nice day for a hike." Jorge jogged up, carrying the same kind of military rifle the others had.

I tried not to look startled. "Do you want to go up ahead?"

"No. I will stay at the rear."

The reddish-brown ground was rocky along the narrow path. There was an abundance of slick tree roots sticking out, so we had to pay attention and watch our steps. Wherever there was a flat spot there was a puddle. The ascending and descending grades of being on the side of a mountain added to the challenge.

The inlet was always on our left and sporadically there were glimpses of it through the trees.

It didn't take long for Mike to start breathing hard. The rest of us seemed to be managing well.

There was a sudden sharp ripping sound. "Shit!"

I looked up from watching where I was stepping to see Mike on his knees.

"Fucking roots are slick as molasses and rocks sharp as knives." Mike dropped his palms in the mud to stop himself from rolling over and down the hill.

Morgan and I were closest to him and helped him up.

There was a putrid smell around him.

"You ripped your khakis," Morgan said.

There was a three-inch tear from a sharp rock at the edge of his left knee. Lucky he wasn't cut.

Mike looked down at his muddy pants. "It's a fashion statement."

Sue was laughing and waving at the air in front of her. "Good time to shit yourself. You're all brown and dirty anyway."

"It was a fart." Mike's face turned crimson. "It slipped out when I fell."

"You want us to take a break for you to catch your breath?" Jack said from twenty feet in front of us.

"I ain't no pussy." Mike wiped his hands on the front of his khakis creating a smear. "Let's go."

Morgan looked at me and gently shook her head. I knew what that meant—*you're friends with this slob?*

I had a chuckle without outwardly showing it.

We entered an area where the older trees had been cut maybe ten years ago. The underbrush was much thicker and new saplings were growing. The path became wider from then on, so I walked beside Morgan.

Sue slowed up for Mike and distracted him from his laboring by making him smile. I couldn't help noticing that she was glancing back at Morgan and me a number of times, but I didn't ask why.

The trees surrounding us were fully grown again and the slope to the water thirty feet below was steep as we came around a rocky point. Past that, the trail became a dirt road. A cabin came into view and then another. They were partially hidden in the trees and foliage.

We arrived at a one-lane, pothole-ridden, paved road. The shoulder had been widened enough for cars to turn around, with enough space left for maybe four to park. There were two white Chevy Tahoe SUVs sitting there. It had taken us forty minutes to reach Woodlands.

Lorraine was standing in front of the vehicles and waved to us as we approached. "There you are."

"I thought you were back at the house, sleeping after the nightshift," Sue said as we all walked up to her.

"We needed more supplies. How did you enjoy the hike?" Her accent was extra hard on the Hs.

"It's a beautiful country," Sue said.

Jack patted Lorraine's shoulder. "Got everything?"

"All here and ready for transport."

Jack walked around Mike, who was leaning against the nearest Tahoe, and lifted the rear hatch.

Aside from ourselves, there were no people around that I could see.

"There's water here and granola bars if anyone wants a boost before we head back," Jack said.

When I came around to the rear of the SUV, I counted eight green backpacks filled to capacity.

Jack addressed Ivan, Sue, Mike, Morgan, and me. "One of these vehicles is here at all times. If you ever need one, the spare key is right here." He reached under the rear bumper and produced a magnetized small black box. Sliding the cover back he produced a key with a Chevrolet logo on it. "Got it?"

I paid close attention to the exact spot where the key was replaced. If we reached this point and needed the vehicle, there would be no time to fumble for the key.

"Everyone ready to head back?" Jack asked.

Lee came over and handed out the backpacks.

Mine had about forty pounds of weight. "Just like carrying a set of golf clubs."

Lee had to help Mike extend the straps.

Mike finished chewing a granola bar. "What's in these packs?"

"Supplies," Jack said.

"We need a lot more food and booze now that you're here," Sue said.

Mike went to push her, but stumbled over a loose stone and almost wiped out. "Fucking rocks. They oughta' pave the whole planet."

Everyone smiled.

"What do you think?" Morgan asked me as we headed back into the forest.

"About what?"

Morgan looked concerned. "Jack's preparing us for a getaway."

"It's just precautionary." I didn't want her to be worried, but I had the same thoughts.

As soon as we reached the clearing, Lee motioned for everyone to stop.

There was something big and black on the path fifty yards in front.

Rifles came off Lee and Jorge's shoulders.

The object moved. It was a black bear.

"Don't shoot it," Sue whispered with authority.

Jorge stepped with quiet footfalls to join Lee at the front of the line. "Only if it attacks us."

The bear looked over at us.

No one moved. There was a stalemate for a minute, then as nonchalant as could be the bear moved into the bushes toward the water. We waited another minute before moving forward. By the time we reached where the bear had been, it was gone.

"It was beautiful," Sue said.

"Sure was," Jack agreed.

Everyone was more vigilant the rest of the way back. The only real noise was our footsteps and Mike's breathing.

Once we reached the cabin, we each took off a layer of clothes, had a quick breakfast, and then headed downstairs.

Dr. Roth was sitting in his usual spot when Ivan, Jack, Sue, Morgan, Mike, and I arrived.

"Mike has expressed an interest in helping." Ivan took a stack of papers that were on the printer and placed them in front of where Mike had sat down. "After you read this, we can fill in any areas that do not make sense."

"Are you sure it's a good idea to jeopardize the safety of another person with this information?" Morgan asked.

"It's a little too late for that," Mike said. "Besides, I want to help."

"Adding another writer will speed up the process," Jack said. "And Mike has been kind enough to let us poke around in his background. I'm satisfied that his assistance would be an asset."

I knew Jack would've done a background check on Mike.

"While Mike catches up, we need to move forward," Ivan said.

"Shouldn't we talk about what we've learned first?" I asked. "We never talked about the Plycite gene. It could be catastrophic."

Everyone looked at Jack. He'd had the strongest reaction yesterday by walking out of the room.

"When we put this information out to the world we need to make sure we stick to the facts," Jack said.

"Of course," I said to Jack. "But what's your opinion? I want to know what you and everyone here think. What did you mean yesterday when you said, '*that's the final piece of evidence I needed*'?"

Jack looked at all of us. "What I meant yesterday was … my father and older brother had talked on a few occasions about population control. They'd seen precursors. I've heard talk of a big undertaking by certain members of the *club* to solve overpopulation. There have been rumors about figuring out how to reduce the reproductive capacity of less desirable people and isolating the most desirable subgroups of the population. It was either that or an outright cull."

The word *cull* made me shudder.

"Slow but long-term genocide," Ivan said.

"I heard talk of how they had to do it in a way that wasn't traceable and would take a few generations." Jack sighed. "That was *talk*. There was always a lot of discussion about what I considered preposterous things. Then I heard more recently that men like Davis Lovemark, Carlo Da Silva and of course the mastermind, Dr. Schmidt, were expanding upon what was first discussed fifty years ago. Their fathers had actually come up with a plan, because there were too many people on Earth for their liking, even at that time. Now their sons are attempting to bring it to fruition."

Something didn't make sense. Jack would know better than to think it was just *talk*.

"Let me rephrase that," Jack said. "I knew they were trying to do something, but I didn't know what, if it was possible, and how far they had progressed. When I heard about what had been done at Naintosa, I got a hunch." He looked over at Ivan. "You, Carl, Bill, and Claudia weren't told the real reason Naintosa brought y'all onboard, or what designs they had for your research all along. I needed proof. The final piece fell into place for me with the Plycite gene information."

Ivan's eyes had a mist over them. "I am a major contributor to genocide."

Morgan went to Ivan's side. "None of you knew what Naintosa was going to do with what you created. You were all trying to do good things."

"That's true," Dr. Roth spoke up.

Mike looked confused, not knowing the full story of what we were talking about.

Jack took a deep, audible breath. "I have even heard that they have a goal of full implementation by 2020."

"Fuck," was all Sue said.

It was starting to make sense. Why hadn't I deduced the plan before now? Why hadn't Jack told us this sooner? To me there were still missing pieces.

"Remember, I didn't have enough proof, so I apologize for not telling you sooner," Jack said.

Twice in the last few minutes Jack seemed to have been reading my mind.

It dawned on me. "How could the people in your *club* and their families avoid being affected by the genetically engineered food, pesticides, and Plycite gene? The way they're introducing it into the population isn't being selective. How can they avoid it?"

"That's where what Summer discovered comes in," Mike said.

Everyone turned to look at Mike.

"Summer found out about a huge seed bank that's being built on an island in northern Norway. It's going to be like a vault, a big concrete bunker. She was even able to obtain a copy of the blueprints and renderings."

"How was she able to find those?" Sue asked.

"No idea," Mike said. "I don't think we'll ever know."

"The Arctic Circle is a very good location," Ivan said.

"They've also preserved tracts of farmable land in different parts of the world that they want to stay unpolluted," Mike continued. "There's a copy of a memo from Carlo Da Silva to Davis Lovemark, discussing how the properties are being protected by patrols and large enclosures. Another document by Dr. Hendrick Schmidt was about the collection of as much authentic organic seed as they could find to store in the bank. Apparently that has been going on for some time and is in an interim seed bank in Germany right now."

"Solves that problem." Being sarcastic was the only release I had preventing me from going to the corner, crawling into the fetal position, and giving up. "They have it all figured out."

The look on Dr. Roth's face indicated he wanted to go hide as well.

"Another missing link," Jack said. "It makes sense."

I had a burst of clarity. "Mike, you have to put together what Summer discovered about the seed bank. Jack, you have to write about your ex-*club* and expose them. Then at the end we have to have a section of opinions and a summary. It's the only way people will tie it all together and make sense of what's going on. We have to connect the dots for them."

"We can write it as you suggest, Nick, and see how it looks," Ivan said. "But I just do not want to tarnish the credibility of the research with opinions."

"It won't be." I was confident, as I saw a vision of how it would look in my head.

There was a shift from a feeling of defeat to determination in the air of the room.

Jack reached for a pad of paper and a pen in the middle of the table. "We all have our jobs to do. Let's get back at it."

INTERLOGUE 4

He looked out over the treetops and building roofs below, not really listening to the two men chatting in his study. The last rays of the day's light created long shadows. He leaned forward, almost touching the glass with his forehead, to follow the meandering route of the river. Water had gouged out the large gully through solid rock thousands of years ago. Men had first chosen this spot to build a castle in the year 963 AD. It was an island of sheer cliffs perched above the river. Looking to the left he could see the remnants of the rock fortifications that were built in 1340.

Buying this building had been a good idea, he thought. It was built in 1869 and renovated many times since then, the last being completed just two weeks ago. The four-story stone structure was sound and now very opulent. The designers had wanted it to have old world charm, yet with all the modern amenities. Carlo liked that, because history kept him grounded while he oversaw the future of technology and information.

Even though Carlo had many properties around the world, his main base had always been his family home outside Valencia, Spain. He'd chosen this building in Luxembourg City as a place where he could come to work and not be disturbed. In addition to the history,

Luxembourg City was a banking and political capital. The streets were almost sleepy but smelled of money. Major world decisions were made here, and men he had to associate with came here for business, so it was convenient.

Carlo turned his attention to the two men sitting at an etched-glass table in brown doe-hide chairs. The ivory button on his handmade silk jacket clinked as it hit the edge of his mahogany desk as he passed. "Thank you, Charles."

The butler nodded as he exited the room carrying an empty tray.

Davis Lovemark's British accent became more pronounced when he was in Europe. "I call the last two progress releases from your PR people 'fake-throughs.' We made them news. They distract people and you get more support from the masses. They believe what we tell them is good for them. Let us worry about what's really going on. People don't like all the boring details."

"I don't like you calling my science '*fake-throughs*,'" Dr. Hendrick Schmidt said. "Your writers could slip up and publish that."

"Don't worry, Hendrick. I only use those words around you and Carlo. The reporters think it's true. Plus, everything concerning your companies passes through my most trusted editor, George. You remember meeting him?"

Hendrick nodded but still appeared to be agitated.

"He's the best at deflecting people's attention away from the issues you don't want them to focus on," Davis continued. "And his information-laundering skills are second to none. He cut his teeth in the tobacco industry before coming to work for me five years ago."

Hendrick's eyes narrowed. "The way you use words like fake-throughs and information-laundering makes it sound like I'm a charlatan and the work my companies are doing is not true science."

"No, Hendrick. What I meant was that we're only deflecting people's attention away from what you're really doing. Your science is the most authentic of all. As you know, the populous would not believe what you—what we do …" Davis raised his hands to gesture to Carlo and Hendrick. "… is for their betterment. You know that. How many times have we been over this?"

"I know." Hendrick sat back. "These are stressful times, and I thought you had lost your focus."

Carlo sat down and interrupted, purposefully changing the subject. "I'm working on a program with a protocol controlled by algorithms that will encompass the Internet. It will not only gather personal information on everyone on the planet, but also filter what people see on the Internet. There will be layers only qualified individuals and organizations will have access to. Everyone else will only be able to search the surface. But I foresee that it will be very popular, making our information gathering that much easier."

Davis and Hendrick both gave Carlo a look of confusion.

Davis said, "As long as I have access to what information I need and my new websites are the top points of reference when people search different topics, I'm happy."

"GM Comm needs to contribute further funds," Carlo said. "But yes, your sites will be at the top of the search lists. That means GM Comm will go through yet another large period of growth and continue to dominate the media."

Davis gave a glib nod of satisfaction.

Hendrick just shrugged. They knew he didn't know much about the Internet and left Carlo in charge of figuring it out. Hopefully one or both of Hendrick's sons would soon be involved.

Carlo redirected the conversation again. "What do you think of the wine? It's from my family's vineyards. 1973 was a good year for Rioja Alavesa, and I've kept most of the harvest for my own cellars."

Davis swirled the dark liquid in his glass, smelled its contents, and took a drink. "Mmm, tasty."

Hendrick took a large gulp and then reached for a slice of bread. His prominent stomach pressed up against the table, making him strain to reach the middle, his face turning red.

"My chef makes fantastic breads." Carlo pointed at the silver platter. "The one on the left is potato-based, and on the right, corn."

Hendrick looked up. "Corn?"

Carlo smiled. "I assure you they are made with the finest ancient ingredients."

Hendrick placed cheese on top of the slice he had chosen.

"The cheese is made—and the olives grown—at my family estate. Wait until you try the boar we are having for dinner." Carlo had made sure his new business home was well stocked.

"Hendrick, you might want to take it easy on your caloric intake," Davis said. "Every time I see you, it looks like you've gained more weight. And your face gets red with the tiniest amount of exertion. Your blood pressure must be through the roof."

Hendrick sat back in his chair. "I eat and drink more when I'm under stress. My doctor assures me I'm fine. You try keeping this plan on schedule. There are nothing but problems with the natives at the Colombian lab, the gene splicing in the new corn is not reacting like we need it to, and those *fickt* are out there trying to create trouble again."

"You don't seem to handle stress as well as you used to," Davis said.

"I have barely any help from you, sitting in your glass tower, with a new secretary every week, knowing nothing of the reality happening outside of your spinning media conglomerate."

Davis made a hobby of pushing Hendrick's buttons. "You keep forgetting that you're not out there yourself actually fighting with natives, splicing genes or chasing after Jack and Barnes. You have people for all of that. You never used to worry about the minutiae before."

"Yes, but my people are idiots who move too slow, and nothing can stand in our way of being ready by 2020."

"You've trusted your people for years—most of them anyway."

Davis popped an olive into his mouth. "You just have to prod them along with a big thorny stick."

Carlo watched these two captains of the world as they bickered. He was the current chairman. It was his responsibility to keep everything progressing forward, even these conversations. "Hendrick, you're just getting caught up in the details. Let's go through the points."

Hendrick and Davis shut up, drank their wine, and listened.

Carlo's Spanish accent was not quite as strong as the pitch of his voice increased. "The use of Naintosa's herbicide and insecticide is increasing as more genetically engineered crops are planted. We have every confidence, Hendrick, that you will solve your challenges with the Plycite gene. Seed drift is increasing and will hit critical mass within the next two decades. That means Pharmalin has, let's say, ten more years to get everything sorted out with all the life-extending medications. The main seed bank will be operational by 2014, and the interim ones are in use until then. Governments are funneling more money into healthcare and are realizing they have to raise taxes further to subsidize it. In the big scheme of things, I don't see any worries. We still have eighteen years before 2020, and it seems to me that we are on schedule. Even if it takes a few extra years, what does it matter? We know it will take at least three generations before the population is at the targeted level. Then our successors will introduce the saved seed. And by the way, the list of families that will have access to the seed bank for the duration is almost complete."

Hendrick looked perturbed that he wasn't getting any sympathy for his problems staying on track, but he couldn't argue.

Davis looked smug. "We do what needs to be done and make a profit on every part of the operation."

"Precisely," Carlo said.

Hendrick's suit pocket began to vibrate. He pulled out his cell phone and looked at the incoming phone number. "I need to take this call."

A phone in Davis' pocket began to ring. He stood and flipped it open. "It's Peter." He walked to the edge of the room, next to a shelf filled with books.

"We're very close," Peter's voice came through the phone into Davis' ear. "Brad saw Jack Carter, Nick Barnes, Dr. Ivan Popov, Morgan Elles, Sue Clark, that Mike Couple guy and some muscle, just outside of Vancouver. They have to be in a boat-access cabin near where they were seen."

"Everyone together like one big happy family," Davis smiled. "How much muscle?"

"Jack's main men, Lee Donald and Jorge Villegas. There's a new member to the squad named Lorraine Badowski, ex-Polish military. She'd brought them what looked like supplies in backpacks."

"Why didn't Brad follow them? Was he afraid he'd mess up his clothes?"

"More like his hair and nails," Peter said. "We'll find out where they're holed up very shortly."

"Hurry up," Davis said. "Find out everything they know, and then make sure they're never going to get in our way again."

Peter was quiet for a few seconds and then asked, "Is that the final decision? Eliminate all of them?"

"Like I just said, I don't want any of them getting in our way ever again. I don't want details. I just want to know the mission is accomplished and soon."

Hendrick and Davis had also finally decided it was best to take out Peter and Brad when this was over, to tie up all the loose ends of people they didn't trust. That way whatever heat came back at Hendrick or even Davis could easily be deflected onto Peter. The Naintosa security leader had his own special instructions.

"It should only take a few days tops," Peter said.

"Good." Davis flipped the phone off and went back to the table.

Hendrick had finished his conversation as well and was eating another slice of bread and cheese.

"Is your little problem being dealt with?" asked Carlo.

"I assume Peter brought you up to speed?" Hendrick asked Davis.

"As I'm sure your man did."

CHAPTER 43

"It's going to be hard to meditate with everything we've learned going through our heads," Morgan said.

"It's even more important to have a clear mind now," I replied.

We all closed our eyes and focused on our breathing.

I went into my inner room and sat in the chair looking out into the cosmos. The outer world and the sound of my breathing faded away. I eased into the gap. The forest we'd hiked in yesterday came into my mind's eye. The vibrant greens and browns turned dark, as if there were a black film over them. Then the black turned to a deep red. Everything was coated in blood. The disturbing vision lingered as I came out of the gap and opened my eyes.

It hadn't been twenty minutes yet and everyone looked peaceful.

Should I tell them what I saw? Of course. My visions materialized many times in the past.

Morgan twitched and I could see movement behind her eyelids. The only one perfectly still was Sue.

Within a few minutes eyes began to open.

"It's hard not to think of things," Jack said.

"Meditation isn't as simple as I thought it would be," said Lee.

"I don't think we're safe here anymore," I blurted out.

They all looked at me.

"Did you have a premonition?" Sue asked.

I nodded. "The forest outside turned black and then blood red. It felt dangerous."

Sue turned to Jack. "We have to pay attention to his visions."

"I know," Jack said. "I have another place for us to go. We should be able to leave here in two days."

"Two days?" Morgan frowned. "How about today?"

"That's the best I can do," Jack said.

I wanted to leave now as well, but that was unrealistic. I hoped we'd be okay for a couple more days.

"Where's this other place?" Morgan asked.

"It's in Europe," Jack said. "It's for your own safety that you don't know where we're going in advance."

"We know the drill," Sue said.

Lee stood. "Krav Maga time."

As we headed downstairs, Mike rushed up behind us. "I want to learn how to kick some butt too."

Ivan was already there, stretching, in his 1970s gray sweat suit with black stripes.

Dr. Roth was at the table, reading something on his computer.

Jack, Ivan, Mike, Morgan, Sue, and I spaced ourselves about six feet apart so we wouldn't bang into one an other.

Lee stood in front. "I'm going to teach you how to disarm someone who has a knife or a gun."

That may come in handy. I found that Krav Maga and meditation complimented each other in a weird way; two extremes—relaxation and force.

Lee brought out a gun and showed us that the bullet clip was missing and nothing was in the chamber. "Nick, I'll demonstrate on you."

"Okay." I went to stand at his side.

Lee gave me the gun. "Point it at me."

I did as he asked.

"Your hands are the fastest, so they move first," Lee said. "Then, your bodyweight comes second, and your feet third, because they're the slowest. Hands, body, feet." He reached out and grabbed the barrel of the gun. His bodyweight pushed my arm to the side and against my chest. As he stepped forward, he twisted his wrist.

I wasn't resisting and was thrown off balance. When he twisted the barrel it hurt my finger on the trigger and I lost control of the gun.

"Be aware of where the gun is pointing at all times, because it's likely to go off." Lee showed that the gun in our hands was pointing away from us and to the ground.

We heard someone run down the hall and open the back door.

Tanner came from the surveillance room. "Jack, can you come look at something?"

Jack followed Tanner.

"That's basically it. Pair up and let's practice." Lee went to the covered pool table to retrieve two more firearms.

Gun in hand I went back to my original spot between Morgan and Mike.

Lee motioned to Ivan. "I'll be your attacker until Jack gets back."

With a sly squint Sue gestured to Morgan to come and get her. Morgan looked cautious.

Mike pushed me. "Come get me, you Naintosa scumbag." He bounced up and down making his stomach and man boobs jiggle.

"Lee, everyone," Jack said, in a raised voice. "Can you come here?"

The urgency in Jack's tone made everyone move quickly toward him.

Tanner ran out of the surveillance room to the back door.

Morgan, Sue, and I stood in the doorway because not everyone could fit inside.

Jack pointed at red lights blinking on the monitors. "Our lasers have been tripped in two spots. Both are in areas we don't have cameras. It could be wildlife or hikers, but I thought you should know."

"The sun's just rising," Sue said. "Don't you think it's too early for hikers?"

Jack nodded. "Jorge and Tanner have gone to take a look."

We saw Jorge pass one camera and Tanner another.

"What should we do?" Morgan asked.

"Nothing until we find out what's out there."

We waited for a half hour until we got a glimpse of Tanner and Jorge pass by another camera on their way back. When they came inside they were breathing heavy.

"Whoever it was is gone," Tanner said.

"Are you sure it was people?" Jack asked.

"Two of them," Jorge said. "We followed their tracks to Woodlands. They were just ahead of us because we heard their car leaving, but we weren't fast enough to see …"

Tanner cut Jorge off. "There wasn't any point in chasing after them. We called Lorraine to see if she could head the car off, but she wasn't in the vicinity."

Jack shrugged. "Could it have been someone coming out from one of the cabins farther up the inlet?"

Dr. Roth had moved back and was standing next to me. He was shaking.

"The footprints came in from Woodlands," Tanner said. "They came to where they tripped the laser, turned around, and went back."

"Could they see the cabin from where they were?" Jack asked.

"Yes," Jorge said.

"We need to step it up until we get out of here." Jack pointed at the monitors. "Move those lasers up farther so we have more warning. Get Lorraine to watch the Woodlands entrance all day and Sam all night."

I'd forgotten about Sam. He must've been doing stuff for us out in civilization.

"I'd like to get a few more cameras into those blind spots," Tanner said.

"We don't have any more," Jack said.

"I can patrol the area at night," Lee said.

"Then I'll do the day patrol," Jorge said.

"If Lee's outside at night, Jack, can you be in the surveillance room during the day?" Tanner asked. "I'll be here for the nightshift."

"Fine," Jack said. "I can write my part while I'm here."

"Can I do anything?" I asked.

"Your job is to assemble everything fast." Jack came up and tapped my shoulder. "You're in charge of the project."

"We won't be able to have it finished before we leave," I said. "Will the new place be setup to complete the report there?"

Jack looked at all of us. "We'll have what we need at the new location, but it'd be great if we could have everything outlined before we go. If each of you could back up your work every day, I can put the CDs into the safe. Also, e-mail me your work and I'll send it off-site."

Everyone agreed.

CHAPTER 44

I sat down on the edge of the bed. "You have a shower first. It always takes longer for you to dry your hair."

Morgan sat down next to me and took my hand. "I'm really nervous."

I looked into her bluer-than-blue eyes, seeing the fear reflected in them.

"With us figuring out that they're trying to control the population, and probably Bail and his Naintosa security knowing where we are …" Morgan shook her head. "I don't think they'll bother beating us up and interrogating us this time."

I pulled her into an embrace. "I know." I felt the same, but what could we do? I hoped we'd get out in time.

After a moment, she pulled back. "We have no other choice and have to stick to our plan."

My eyes followed her as she went to the bathroom. She'd read my mind again.

After quick showers and breakfast, we got to work.

Everyone had their assignments: Jack was writing about the masterminds of the population control plan, in the surveillance room; Dr. Roth finished glyphosate and worked on what could be preliminarily reported about neonics; Ivan, Plycite gene and seed drift; Sue, what genetically engineered foods did to people when they digested them; Mike had Summer's information on the seed bank; Morgan edited the glyphosate portion; I finished the outline.

The room was filled with the clatter of keyboards being typed on.

When the outline was done and a rough summary written, I sat back. It looked like a road map.

Maybe I should make sure I'd gotten it right? I went to the blackboard and wrote out the points: *genetically engineered food, glyphosate, neonicotinoids, and Plycite gene—pollute the environment, sterilize people, and cause multiple diseases, including cancers and eventually death. Seed drift allows for the spread of genetically engineered seed to infect regular crops.*

I still didn't know what to do with the terminator seed technology, so I put it off to the side.

Next I wrote: *Pharmalin provides drugs to extend lives of people who get diseases.*

A missing piece popped into my head and I wrote it in the corner: *Government Health Care costs rising?*

I still didn't know what to call Jack's *club*. I decided to write at the top of the board: *Group intentionally trying to control world population.*

How will they survive? *Seed Bank.*

Tanner walked down the hall to the surveillance room.

"Can I have your attention for a minute to see if I have everything right?" I pointed at the blackboard. "This is what I've got and the order I'd like to put it in."

Jack came out of the surveillance room and leaned against the wall in clear view of the blackboard.

"Is anything missing?" I asked. "What are your opinions?"

"I don't know as much as the rest of you," Mike said. "But do you realize that the people responsible for this make a fortune on every part?"

"It's sickening to think about," Morgan said.

Mike came up to the board. "Look. They make money on the genetic seed, the pesticides, and the drugs that keep people alive but don't cure them. When the unknowingly sterilized population tries to have babies but can't, they can sell them drugs for that, too. And in the end they have total control of the only good seed left."

"Do we want to add in the trading of stocks and commodities?" Jack asked.

I looked at him. "You're right. We haven't even touched on that. Could you imagine the amount of money they'd make on the stock markets with only them knowing what's happening?"

"I can write that up," Jack said.

Ivan stood. "Nick, I am now in agreement with you that we need to spell it all out in the summary of the report."

"We need to make sure people get it," Sue said. "We can't just leave it for everyone to connect the dots on their own."

"The illnesses and diseases are going to develop over time," Ivan said. "It will take years of consumption, for most, before symptoms arise. That will make it impossible to trace back to the … cartel."

Cartel. I looked at Jack and he was squinting. I wondered whether that was a more appropriate name for the *club*.

"When the diseases rise to epidemic proportions, no one will be able to determine the root causes," Ivan continued, "and all indications are that the drugs will not cure people, only extend their lives."

"All that will drain the government coffers," I said. "Aren't they going to freak out?"

Jack stepped to the blackboard. "Where does money for running the government come from? Taxes. So it's the citizens who ultimately pay. The governments will have no choice but to devote more and more money toward taking care of the sickened population. That will cause major problems in itself. Ninety-nine-point-nine percent of the politicians don't have a clue about who *really* runs their countries and what is happening here."

"Shit," Sue said.

Jack studied the blackboard. "I never saw it summarized this dramatically before. This would be by far the largest shift of wealth in history—accomplished by some of the people who already have the most wealth and power."

I saw the magnitude of what Jack had said. "The middle class will be all but wiped out. All the wealth would be with the, let's say, one percent and the other ninety-nine percent would be poor."

Jack nodded. "More like less than half of one percent of a much smaller world population. They would have *total* control."

"As Ivan pointed out, this will take generations to happen," Mike spoke up. "Why would these cartel people bother? They won't benefit from the results, and some of them may become victims as well."

"If there's one thing they are fantastic at, it's planning ahead for generations," Jack said. "Remember, these people think they're the stewards of the world, and they're convinced that this is in its best interest."

Mike threw up his arms. "And if it helps them control *all* the money and have *all* the power … why the fuck not?"

Dr. Roth's tall thin figure rose from his chair. "You … you have to admit it was a brilliant plan on their part—until it was discovered by us."

Ivan banged his fist on the table so hard all of the computers jumped. "That is why we have to get this report out."

CHAPTER 45

There was little talk and a lot of typing. The mood was solemn, yet productive.

Rose had brought down some wraps for when we got hungry.

Jack came into the workroom. "Our new place is ready ahead of schedule. We'll leave tomorrow afternoon. Two helicopters will take us to the airport."

Everyone looked relieved. The sooner we left the better.

"I suggest you pack your belongings tonight," Jack said. "There are extra backpacks in the storage room that you can use. Nick, we'll bring down your boxes in the morning."

It was 11:25 p.m. when we decided to call it a night. Sue, Morgan, and I were the last ones downstairs.

"Don't forget to back up your work," Morgan said. "One copy to the safe and e-mail to Jack."

"I think I'm going to keep a copy on me as well." Sue went to get a CD on the table beside the printer.

"Can you grab me one as well?" I asked.

After we saved our work in the decided-upon protocol, we headed upstairs, each grabbing an extra backpack on the way.

"How about we put a change of clothes and important stuff like passports and wallets in the backpacks," Morgan said when we were in our room. "The rest of the clothes can go in the suitcases."

I was already pulling out the suitcases from the closet. "That's what I was thinking, too."

CHAPTER 46

Last night we'd made the decision to skip meditation and Krav Maga this morning. We'd resume our schedule at the new place. Morgan and I still woke up before sunrise.

Morgan showered first, so I took the time to meditate on my own. Deep breaths in and out. Going to my inner sanctuary … it's covered in blood. What was I doing? I was making it up. *Stop it.* I was just anxious because someone had come near the cabin yesterday.

There were hurried steps in the hallway. Someone was talking.

Before I could get up to see what was happening, there was a hard knock on our door and then it opened.

Lee looked determined. "We have to leave NOW! There are multiple armed men outside. Grab what's most important and meet in the kitchen in one minute."

"Fuck!" I scrambled from the bed. "Morgan."

"I heard him." Morgan came out of the bathroom in a panic, naked, and hair wet. "I knew this was going to happen."

Within seconds we were dressed. We grabbed the backpacks we thankfully filled last night and raced out of the bedroom.

"The outward lasers have been tripped in four places, and Tanner saw six men on camera," Jack was telling Ivan as we entered the kitchen. "There are probably more of them, and they're armed with AR-18 rifles."

"Do we have to leave?" Ivan asked. "Can we not hold them off from inside until you have Sam, Lorraine, and any other reinforcements box them in from behind?"

"We don't want a shootout," Jack said. "We've planned for this possibility and have an escape route to Woodlands. We can make it out of here."

The room went dark.

"They've cut the power," Jack said. "Morgan, Nick, Sue, and Ivan, come with Lee and me. Tanner and Jorge, you take Dr. Roth, Mike, and Rose out thirty seconds after we leave."

There was enough light coming in through the kitchen window from the approaching dawn to see people's silhouettes.

I felt a push from behind, and then we were moving through the hallway toward the back door. I was reluctant to go outside, but I trusted Jack's plan.

At the door we each put on green rain jackets. Lee, Jack, and Ivan picked up assault rifles.

"Just in case." With his free hand, Jack passed black handguns to Sue, Morgan, and me. "You flick this, then point and pull the trigger."

We placed the guns in the pockets of our jackets.

Cool wet air rushed in when the door was opened. It was blustery outside.

Lee led the way as we ran low and as quiet as we could into the forest.

We were going up and away from the direction of Woodlands. The thin path was steep and slick, but no one faltered. We came around a rock outcrop and small bluff. At the top was a lookout. We paused there. There was a boat approaching. It was still a distance away, but its trajectory was directly toward our dock. Big drops of water from the trees above were hitting our parkas, making a splattering sound. Below we could see the green metal roof of the cabin. Our second group had just come out the back door.

Just south there was slow movement in the forest. From that angle, the men in the trees wouldn't be able to see our people.

"Let's go," Jack whispered.

We were now heading south toward where the vehicles were parked. We'd gone up and around the intruders. The narrow trail was rolling and steep on either side against the mountain.

After about ten minutes, we met up with the path we'd walked the other day. That's when we heard five successive bursts of weapon fire a short distance from us.

Lee and Jack looked at each other, faces heavy with concern.

"Was that them shooting at us or us shooting at them?" Jack whispered.

"Both," Lee said. "I heard two different types of guns, one ours."

Two more short bursts of fire erupted.

"Let's head back and help," Jack said.

Lee shook his head. "No, we stick with the plan and keep moving forward."

Jack gave a reluctant nod and motioned for us to continue along the wider path.

Morgan, Sue, and I looked at one another, trying to stay calm.

I felt conflicted about whether to go back and see if the others needed help or if that just made it easier for the Naintosa security to kill us all. I felt for the gun in my pocket to make sure it was still there.

"Let us go." Ivan was bringing up the rear.

We moved at a jog, with Lee and Jack in the lead, then Sue and Morgan just to my right.

I sensed movement below to the left of us. As I looked, my left foot slipped on an exposed root. As I went down on my knee, there was a crack of a gunshot and heat seared my hairline. I lost my balance and went over the edge of the path.

Twenty feet below in the thick brush stood Peter Bail holding a gun in his hand and a rifle slung over his shoulder. I was falling right at him. My leg clipped a branch, flipping my body over. I looked up to see Morgan crumbling to the ground. It was all happening so fast but in slow motion.

Hitting Bail cushioned my fall. We slid and rolled together down another twenty feet. A tree trunk finally stopped us, with Bail taking the full impact. He was slow to move, but I wasn't. I rolled off him to my knees.

He shot Morgan!

Bail was on his back with his head pointing downhill. He twisted his body, raising the gun in his right hand up toward me.

I didn't hesitate or think about the Krav Maga moves Lee had taught us. I just acted. I jumped on him and reached for the gun before it was pointed right at me. I grabbed the barrel with my left hand and pushed it down with all my weight.

Bail was looking up at me with surprise on his face as he tried to pull the gun away.

I kept my elbow locked straight.

His arm was across his chest and the gun pointed to the ground. It went off, sending a bullet into the dirt. The barrel became warm from the explosion inside of it.

I felt a pain in my back as he buried his knee into it.

Bail twisted and bucked in an attempt to roll me off.

I hit him with my free right hand. I used the heel of my palm to land blow after blow.

He tried to shield my strikes with his left hand, but I just kept hitting.

I moved up, straddling him just below the chest, left arm still locked and holding the gun and elbowed him hard in the face with my right. I don't know how many times I struck Bail, but he stopped resisting.

There was blood coming from his mouth, lip, now crooked nose, and from a gash on his cheek. His eyes were closed.

The gun came free and I picked it up. When I'd hit him with the last elbow, I felt bone crack. Had I killed him?

There was a hand on my shoulder. I spun, lifting my arm that held the gun, but the grip became so hard it immobilized me.

It was Lee. He let go of my shoulder and let my arm fall.

I asked the only question that mattered. "How is Morgan?"

He appeared concerned. "Can you climb up to the path?"

I looked up and could only see Sue above. There was shock on her face.

Lee felt Bail's neck.

There was a swishing sound of a windbreaker rubbing up against branches.

I turned and raised the gun in the direction of the noise.

In one fluid motion, Lee had dropped to one knee as he spun his assault rifle from around his back to pointing at the target.

It was Brad. He was forty feet away, lower down the bank.

Looking at him looking at us, I was certain he was the one who'd killed Summer. No doubt.

Brad had a rifle in his hand, pointing downward. His eyes were wide and he looked scared. He turned and started pushing through the wet underbrush away from us.

Lee took one shot and Brad collapsed, disappearing from sight. Lee stood up. "I didn't kill him, just took out his leg. Now he can't change his mind and come after us." He pointed back at Bail. "This one's still alive, barely. You paid real good attention when I was teaching you."

What do I do? I didn't want killing someone on my conscience forever, but I didn't want Bail coming after us again. I decided to just leave him lying there.

"Fuck, you assholes!" Brad's shout was muffled. "I need help."

Lee raised his eyebrows, gesturing that it was my decision.

"We leave both losers here." I stepped on something hard. Looking down I saw it was the gun Jack had given me. As I reached for it I realized my backpack had stayed on the whole time. I placed one pistol in each jacket pocket. I scrambled up to the path as fast as I could; barely noticing I had Bail's blood all over my right wrist and elbow.

Lee was right behind me.

Ivan and Jack were crouched around Morgan. Ivan was holding the shirt Morgan had packed for herself on the inside of her left thigh just below her groin. Blood blotches covered the shirt.

"Oh, God, is she going to be okay?" I knelt down and held her hand.

Morgan was moaning and every other breath was a gasp.

"Her femoral artery was hit," Ivan said. "That is not good."

I began to panic. "We need to get her to a hospital."

Sue was beside me and I felt a sear of pain as she touched my head. "I saw bits of hair fly off when you tripped. The bullet must've grazed you before it hit Morgan."

"Fuck. Why couldn't it have been me? Why wasn't I watching where I was going? Why didn't I see Bail a second sooner? Fuck!"

"Let's get going," Jack said. "Morgan needs help right away and we've made a lot of noise."

Ivan stood, reached for his belt, and pulled it off. It was braided leather, so when he pulled it tight there was a hole for the buckle to go through. He used it as a tourniquet above Morgan's wound and to hold the shirt in place. "Lee, if you carry Morgan over your shoulder, her head facing forward, she should be okay."

Lee handed his rifle to me and picked Morgan up as Ivan instructed.

Morgan cringed in pain and then went limp. She'd passed out.

"Nick, you put pressure on the wound." Ivan placed his hand on the shirt acting as a bandage to show me.

I passed Lee's rifle to Sue, who'd just picked up Morgan's backpack.

Jack went to the front of the line, Lee carried Morgan easily, and I applied pressure as instructed. Ivan was next to me and Sue brought up the rear.

Why had it gotten to this point? It had gone too far. There were likely more casualties behind us as well. I held back my emotions.

Morgan moaned. I hoped she wasn't in too much pain.

Jack raised his left hand, indicating for us to stop.

The first of the cabins were just ahead and we could see where the road began.

We moved to the edge trying to blend in with the bushes.

There was a crunch under Jack's boot. He bent down and picked up a cell phone that had a big crack down the middle of it. "This is Lorraine's."

The foliage around where Jack stood was matted down.

"There's blood spatter that the rain hasn't washed away," Lee said.

"Someone was dragged over here." Jack pointed to the underbrush and followed where it had been disturbed. After about ten steps he stopped. He bent over, almost disappearing from sight.

After a moment he came back to us. "It's one of theirs. Throat's slit. Lorraine must've done it."

We all looked around, but there was no sign of Lorraine.

Ivan said to Sue, "Turn and point the gun in the direction of the path in case someone comes up behind us."

Sue looked awkward holding the big rifle. "I hate guns, but at this point I'll shoot any Naintosa thugs I see."

"Just be careful not to shoot any of our second group if they have caught up to us," Ivan said.

Ivan went up to Jack and we cautiously moved forward.

There was a gray van and SUV parked in the turnaround area on the opposite side to our Chevy Tahoes. Someone was standing in front of our vehicles in a similar dark green rain suit as Bail and Brad had been wearing.

Jack jumped forward, rifle butt against his shoulder, eyes aligned with the sight. "Freeze."

The person, not very big, hadn't been expecting us and jumped back against the front grille. They dropped the gun in their hand and raised their arms. Blonde hair tumbled out from under the fallen back hood. The pink fingernails gave her away.

"Angelica?" She *was* one of Bail's thugs?

She glanced my way and looked scared.

Ivan hurried to check the other two vehicles.

Lee carried Morgan to the back of the first Tahoe and I followed, still holding her thigh.

Angelica's eyes moved from Morgan to me as we passed.

"You know her?" Jack kept his gun leveled on Angelica.

I looked back. "She was my neighbor in San Francisco. Angelica played me, was probably the one who shot up my place and broke in three times. Bitch." Why had I been so gullible?

"That wasn't me." Angelica pleaded. "It was Brad. He was also instructed to kill Summer Perkins." She gave that up pretty easy. Naintosa sure had become lax on hiring for their security force.

"By whom?" Jack now pointed the gun at her head.

Angelica closed her eyes tight, pushed against the front of the vehicle, and went silent.

I opened the back hatch of the Tahoe. Lee gently placed Morgan inside. She grimaced.

Ivan jogged across the road to us. "Nick, go help Jack. I will take care of Morgan."

I was reluctant to leave Morgan's side, but did what he instructed.

Jack took a step toward Angelica. "Where's Lorraine, the lady watching the vehicles?"

Angelica shook her head, still cowering. "I didn't see anyone."

Sue stepped forward, dropping the rifle and backpacks. "I got this." She reached over Angelica's shoulder and grabbed the back of her jacket. Sue's forearm pushed against Angelica's neck. Sue then pulled Angelica's right arm down with her left hand, locking the elbow. It was exactly as Lee taught us.

Angelica squirmed to resist.

Sue pulled Angelica's right arm harder and her upper body bent forward. Sue delivered four hard knee blows to Angelica's abdomen, grunting with force on each one.

I could hear Angelica's breath leave her as she squeaked in pain.

Neither Jack nor I made any attempt to stop Sue.

Sue elbowed Angelica between her nose and cheek, just as she let go of her.

Angelica pitched over and fell into the shallow ditch lining the road that had a few inches of water in it. Blood began to trickle from her nose. She was out cold.

I looked at Sue standing there with fists and teeth clenched and I nodded. "Wow."

Jack went over, knelt down, and felt for a pulse. "She's alive." He turned Angelica's neck and opened her mouth so she could breath, but didn't bother pulling her out of the ditch.

I heard a door close. Looking toward where the sound had come from, I saw a partially hidden cabin across the road. A light went on inside.

Jack and Sue were watching as well.

"They could be calling the police," I said.

"We have to get out of here," Jack said. "There's too much explainin' and we'd get detained."

"But we were just defending ourselves." I realized Jack was right. Even if none of us got charged, we'd be in custody for a while. "This has gotten way out of hand."

"I know, it shouldn't have to be like this," Jack said. "But this is the way they do things, to intimidate people from exposing them. If we'd stayed in the cabin, we'd all be dead."

I hurried to the back of the SUV. Ivan and Lee were finishing bandaging Morgan's wound. There must've been a first aid kit in the vehicle. I hoped with all my heart that Morgan was going to survive.

Jack had followed me. "Is she going to be okay?"

"She has lost a lot of blood," Ivan said.

Sue came over. "There's movement back along the path."

A distant gunshot rang out.

"Let's go," Jack said.

Ivan was already in the back, so I closed the hatch. Then we all raced to get in the vehicle.

Lee was the driver and Jack the front passenger.

I pulled half of the backseat down so there was room for me to be next to Morgan. I applied pressure to the bandaged area.

Ivan adjusted the tourniquet.

Morgan tensed in pain and tears ran from her clenched eyelids. The bandage was already damp with blood.

"I saw someone in green raingear cross the path." Sue sat in the portion of the backseat that was still up.

Lee got the Tahoe turned around and we took off.

Feeling helpless, I asked, "Ivan, is there something in the kit to help her with the pain?"

"No." He was fighting back tears as he looked at Morgan. "Try to keep her from moving around as we drive."

"Where's the nearest hospital?" I asked no one in particular.

"That's where we're heading," Jack said.

I looked out the back window and through my tears saw two men in green raingear running to the gray SUV. "They're coming after us."

"I saw." Lee accelerated the vehicle.

We went up and around a bend. The paved road was bumpy, curvy, and only one lane for the most part. The road began to climb and we went around a switchback that the long wheelbase of the Tahoe was barely able to maneuver. A Range Rover was approaching as we came to a one-lane bridge and we had to stop and let it pass.

Sue looked down over the steep edge of the road. "I see them coming."

I held on tight to Morgan. She stared straight at me and I didn't want to lose eye contact. Her sharp blue eyes seemed to be turning dull.

We drove around another steep, sharp switchback. Then the road became two lanes.

Lee opened it up.

Ivan's head and mine hit the ceiling as the Tahoe became airborne over a rise and then we were pushed to the side around a corner. That didn't faze us as we hung onto Morgan to keep her as still as possible.

There was a long, rolling straight stretch ahead of us with forest on either side. At the other end was a police cruiser with its lights flashing coming toward us. It disappeared for a few seconds as it went through one of the dips in the road.

Lee hit the brakes hard, turned into a driveway, and cut the engine. The trees and underbrush were wild and thick, so we were hidden.

We all looked out the back window. In a few seconds the police drove by at speed. Just after it passed the car's siren went on.

Lee started the engine and backed out.

We could hear tires squealing and saw the cruiser move to the middle, forcing the gray SUV off the road and to a stop.

Lee accelerated and got us out of there. "That'll slow them down."

Jack pulled a cell phone from his pocket and selected a contact number. "Sam, what time did Lorraine relieve you?"

We were entering a residential area, so Lee had no choice but to slow down.

"Meet us at … what's the name of that hospital?"

Lee stared straight ahead. "Lions Gate."

"That's it," Jack said, into the phone. "Meet us on the street outside the emergency entrance of Lions Gate Hospital in fifteen minutes."

Jack made another call. "Can you have the plane ready to go within the hour? We need to leave as soon as we get there. Same destination."

Morgan's breathing had become more labored.

I brushed back the hair that had fallen over her cheek. "We're almost at the hospital."

CHAPTER 47

Jack took a small pad of paper and a pen from the glove compartment and began writing something.

We drove alongside a strip mall and Lee pulled into the right turning lane. The street sign next to the red light read *Mount Seymour Parkway*. He turned us west and weaved through Thursday morning traffic.

Morgan's breath was getting faint.

"Let me see," Ivan said.

I pulled my damp hand back.

Ivan surveyed the blood soaked bandage. He took whatever was left in the kit that had absorbing power and compressed it over Morgan's wound.

I noticed there was blood on the carpet. "Please hold on, Morgan."

Lee merged the vehicle onto the freeway and we climbed a hill.

Morgan focused on Ivan and touched his hand that was on her leg.

He gave her a sad, caring look back.

I'd taken her other hand and she gave it a gentle squeeze.

"Nick …" Her voice was weak, eyes half open.

I had to lean closer to hear her.

It took effort for her to speak. "I love you."

LAWRENCE VERIGIN

I leaned in and gave her a soft kiss. "I love you too."

"I'm sorry … I never intended …" She let out a lingering breath and the pressure from her hand went away.

Ivan jolted forward, placing his hand on her neck and then his cheek next to her mouth. His face grave, Ivan locked his fingers together, right hand over left and arms straight. He began pumping her chest over and over. After about ten times, he bent down and checked for breathing again. Then he resumed trying to resuscitate her heart.

How could this be happening? I heard myself say, "Do you want me to do mouth to mouth?" *She can't die.*

"That would not help in this situation." Ivan's voice was strained.

I never released Morgan's hand. Tears had erupted from my eyes. I couldn't imagine my life without her.

I barely noticed Sue's hand on my shoulder.

Tears ran down Ivan's cheeks. "There is nothing more I can do. She has lost too much blood." Ivan pointed at her thigh. "Most is internal."

Morgan's left thigh had swollen considerably.

I kept gripping her hand, staring at her lifeless body. *She can't die.* This had gotten too out of control.

"Keep going, Nick. Don't give up. Keep fighting. I'm okay. I'll be with you." It was Morgan's voice in my head.

The rear hatch opened and there were people outside.

"Nick, you have to let go of Morgan's hand so they can get her out," Ivan said.

No, I don't want to. I can't let her go. This isn't fair. She can't die.

Someone had their arm around me as I watched them take Morgan's body out of the SUV and place her on a gurney.

Ivan was talking to someone in a white coat.

Jack was trying to hand another man in a white coat some papers and a set of keys. The man was shaking his head in protest.

It was Lee who had his arm around me and Sue was at my side.

"We have to go," Lee said.

Sue took my hand.

"Why couldn't it have been me? The bullet was meant for me."

Sam was holding an open door of another white Tahoe parked on the street. He helped me get inside. This one had three rows of seats.

Sue went around to the other side and held the door for Jack and Ivan to get to the third row. Lee was in the front passenger seat and Sam drove.

"Wait a second," Jack said.

The gray SUV of the Naintosa security thugs pulled into the emergency lane, right behind our abandoned Tahoe. An ambulance pulled in right behind them. The SUV was blocking the ambulance's ability to pull into the bay in front of the hospital doors. A horn honked. The Naintosa vehicle was boxed in.

"Pull out slow," Jack said. "Hopefully they won't notice us leaving. We need a head start."

Sam did as Jack requested.

I closed my eyes and felt inconsolable anguish.

CHAPTER 48

I didn't know whether I'd passed out or was so grief-stricken about Morgan I'd retreated from reality, but when I opened my eyes, we were at the airport.

We pulled into an empty hangar and everyone got out.

I noticed Sue was limping when she came around to my side.

"Are you okay?" I asked.

"When I kneed that bitch she had something hard in her pocket." Sue took my hand. "It's you I'm worried about. You're all scraped up from the fall, and we need to bandage where the bullet nicked you."

I felt where it still stung and there was dry blood in my hair. Looking down, my clothes were all muddy and I realized my back was sore. I couldn't have cared less.

It was still raining as we left the hangar to the jet on the tarmac. It was bigger than all the ones Jack had us on before. The inside was like a lounge, with many caramel-colored swivel leather chairs and lacquered black tables. But none of that mattered to me as I slumped into the first seat.

Sue sat across from me.

Ivan sat down next to her. He looked like he'd been crying. He must've felt like he'd lost a daughter.

"Take this, son." Jack handed me a glass of amber liquid with one ice cube and a pill.

The Scotch warmed my insides and reminded me that none of us had eaten that morning. I wasn't hungry anyway. Within a minute, I felt lightheaded.

I awoke with a dull headache as the plane was landing. The chair I'd been on had folded out into a bed. There was a blanket over me and a seatbelt around my waist.

Sue and Ivan were seated in the same spots as before. They wore matching gray cotton sweat suits.

I saw that I was in the same outfit. There must've been a supply of them on the plane. Who dressed me? I didn't really care.

The plane touched down.

"Where are we?" I asked.

"Halifax," Ivan said. "We need fuel."

"Then where are we going?" My head really hurt.

Jack was seated on the other side of the aisle. "Paris."

I put my hand where the source of pain was coming from. There was a bandage there now. Someone had cleaned me up after I'd passed out.

"How do you feel?" Sue asked.

"Like shit."

Ivan said, "Try to get more sleep."

"I feel bad that we left Morgan at the hospital," I said.

"Me too," Jack said. "But you understand that we had no choice?"

"I know."

"Morgan mentioned at her father's funeral that she wanted to be cremated when her time came," Ivan said, facing Jack. "Can we arrange for that?"

"I'll look after it when we land," Jack said.

I closed my eyes and turned away, unable to hold back tears.

INTERLOGUE 5

endrick wasn't sure why Carlo had asked him back to Luxembourg only three days after their last meeting. Carlo had been calling him at least once a day with trivial questions. It was as if Carlo had been worried about his attitude and performance. Here they were, chitchatting again. Hendrick had more important matters to deal with.

And why was Malcolm Carter there? Malcolm could be trusted, unlike his treasonous brother, but Hendrick still felt awkward talking to him about their business in the last few years. Malcolm's specialty was finance, so he was an integral member of the group, but what was the point of him being there today?

Hendrick had brought his eldest son, Hendrick V, with him. He was seated to Hendrick's left. The twenty-eight-year-old would be ready to take over his companies by 2020.

Hendrick IV couldn't resist another piece of bread that Carlo's chef had baked, and dipped the slice in truffle oil and aged balsamic vinegar.

Carlo took a sip of his family estate wine while he waited for Hendrick's answer to his question.

Hendrick swallowed the bread, feeling satisfied by the taste. "My marketing geniuses have come up with the idea of calling the foods *natural.* Everything that grows can be called *natural* and it sounds healthy. You could even charge a premium."

"Brilliant." Carlo raised his glass.

"Yes, ingenious." Malcolm's Texan drawl was stiffer than his brother Jack's, in part due to him working with fellow bankers his whole career.

The cell phone in Hendrick's gray suit pocket began to buzz and ring. He pulled it out and flipped it open to look at the number. "I must take this call. It's the security team leader with news from Vancouver." He rose and walked toward the large window overlooking the river at the bottom of the cliff.

"Dr. Schmidt, it didn't turn out quite like we'd planned," said the voice on the phone.

"Tell me what happened." Hendrick leaned against Carlo's desk. He didn't like the sound of what he heard.

"They knew we were coming. They had sensors in the woods."

"So?"

"Most escaped and none were captured alive."

"Who was killed?"

"We managed to take out Dr. Timothy Roth, Morgan Elles, and Tanner Reed. I lost three of my men."

Morgan Elles—that was the end of the Elles family. Dr. Roth was supposed to have died in the fire at his lab. What other damage had he done in the short time longer he'd lived? *Ficke.* "And the rest of them got away?"

"Yes, sir."

"Seriously?" Hendrick held onto the desk with his free hand, his inner temperature rising. "The mission was a failure. You didn't eliminate Jack, Barnes, or Dr. Popov. Do you know where they are?"

"They flew out of Vancouver, sir. I will have a destination for you shortly."

Hendrick was finding it hard to breathe, he was so angry. "And

Peter Bail?"

"We haven't seen Bail since he flanked the targets once we knew they were out of the cabin. We heard shots fired in the proximity of his position and blood spatter when we investigated, but no trace of him. Also, Caulder and Seymour had held security positions, but none have checked in or have been located."

"Find them and finish your job."

"Yes, sir," said the Naintosa private security team leader. "Sir, I found a blackboard in the cabin outlining deductions of a population-control plan. I took a picture of it and will e-mail it to you. We've obtained several laptop computers. I will have their contents retrieved and forwarded to you as well."

Could they have figured out the plan? "After you send me the e-mail, delete the picture from your camera, and wipe the blackboard clean."

"That will be a problem, sir. The police are all over the forest and cabin. I wasn't even able to dispose of the bodies."

What a disaster. The bastards may have figured out the plan and the police would be nosing around Naintosa again. "Is that all?"

"Yes, sir."

"Keep me posted on further developments." Hendrick flipped the phone closed.

"It didn't go well?" Carlo asked.

Hendrick walked back to the round table and drained the remainder of wine in his glass. He looked at Malcolm. "You'd think at seventy, your older brother would slow down."

"Unfortunately he's very resourceful and thinks he's twenty," Malcolm said.

"What about Nick Barnes?" Hendrick V asked.

"Escaped."

"For an ex-journalist amateur, he's become quite an adversary," Carlo said. "Like I told you before, Hendrick, it's better for you that

Barnes and Jack weren't killed."

"Some of their group were killed, so it's still going to point back to Naintosa," Hendrick said. "Peter has to be found and implicated as the mastermind. Someone needs to speak with Jacques at Interpol."

CHAPTER 49

It was Friday, March 15, 2002, 7:00 a.m. local time when we landed in Paris. That meant it was Thursday, March 14, 10:00 p.m. back on the west coast of North America.

I was awake for the last two hours of the flight. Whatever pill I'd been given had knocked me out pretty good. I still had a headache and thought I'd puke if I ate anything, but Ivan insisted and the food stayed down.

Everyone looked haggard. And we didn't know what had happened to Mike, Dr. Roth, Jorge, Tanner, Rose, and Lorraine.

There was a white Mercedes-Benz van beside the hangar where our jet had come to rest. A tall, slim man with slicked-back dark hair stood next to it. The temperature was mild and the sky was filled with puffy clouds.

My heart felt like it weighed a thousand pounds.

This time we had to show our passports, but to a customs agent who came to us. It didn't take long for us to depart the Aeroport de Paris Orly, heading north to the center of the city.

I'd never been to France but wasn't interested in sightseeing. My shoulder hit the window as we sped through a roundabout, bringing me out of my self-absorbed thoughts.

"I can see the top of the Eiffel Tower." Sue pointed to the right. I knew she was trying to distract me from my grieving.

The van we were in had an extra two feet of height over the regular vans in the United States, so the front window was taller and we could see more from the second row.

"Yeah, I can see it too." I made an effort to sound interested for a second.

We had entered the most historic part of Paris. It was packed with tourists mingling about in the morning sun. We passed the Arc de Triomphe, which was impressive and larger than pictures indicated. Traffic became heavier, slowing our progress.

I had to admire the beauty of the tree-lined streets and the architecture of the buildings.

The street became parallel to the La Seine river and we could see the full Eiffel Tower on the opposite side. It was massive and inspiring with its steel girding. At the next light we turned right, crossed the Seine, took the first left, and followed the river on the other side.

A long flat boat with a glass top slid by below, filled with onlookers.

On an island with bridges on either side stood the Cathedrale Notre-Dame. That caught my attention. It was bigger than I'd imagined, and the gothic details looked amazing. I stared at the gargoyles lining it until we passed.

We turned right onto a street full of restaurants and shops. After a few more blocks through the trees on our right there was a park. We turned left into a narrow alley. A large black iron patterned gate two stories tall opened. The van proceeded past a security booth and into a rectangular courtyard.

"We've arrived at our temporary refuge," Jack said from the seat behind me.

The building took up a whole block. It had a flat yellow cut-stone façade and rows of large windows lining its five stories. Three guards welcomed us. One ushered us through a double glass door.

Inside, our footsteps echoed on the off-white tiled floor. Six small tables holding white busts were positioned around the foyer. At the center was an open staircase with round, polished-concrete spindles holding the railings. Through the middle was a glass-encased elevator; the six of us and our escort filled it.

Jack pressed the button that had a five on it.

When the cylindrical encasement opened there was only one door in front of us. That's where the staircase ended as well.

Our escort unlocked the door and passed Jack the key.

The apartment was spacious with white walls under a high ceiling framed by a gold-patterned crown molding. Touches of gold were spread throughout the furniture on table legs, edges, and in the bright floral patterns of the upholstery. The thick mauve curtains framing the picture windows even had gold sashes around them. The scent of orchids permeated the air, coming from four vases.

"Everyone gets their own room." Jack pointed to the hallway on the right. "Go take your pick."

We all still had our backpacks. I had Morgan's as well.

"You'll feel better once you've had a shower." Sue touched my elbow and led me toward the bedrooms.

The room Sue chose for me had a floral bedspread, curtains, and two upholstered chairs. I didn't care what it looked like.

I went straight to the en suite and turned on the water. Alone for the first time since Morgan's death, I didn't hold back my emotion. I wailed for the loss of Morgan inside the shower until I collapsed to the floor. Then I lay on the wet tile and cried some more.

Finally, I dragged myself out of the bathroom and climbed into the bed, drained, pulling the duvet over my head.

CHAPTER 50

I'd slept for a while and then just lay there. I kept rehashing what happened. Was this all worth the loss of lives, the loss of Morgan? It was late afternoon when I pulled myself out of the bed and put on the one clean pair of jeans and sweatshirt I'd brought with me.

Jack and Sue were standing in the living room next to one of the two large windows. Sue gave me a tender hug.

Jack put his hand on my shoulder. "Did you get any rest?"

"Some."

Sue turned my body toward the window. We looked across the street to a large park. It must've been the one we noticed coming in.

"That's Luxembourg Gardens," Jack said. "It'll be nice to have that as our view while we're here."

"We can go for walks," Sue said.

"Uh, I think we should all stay inside for a while," Jack said. "For security."

"You're right." Sue sounded reluctant.

Jack's cell phone rang. "Let me take this." He walked from the room as he placed the phone to his ear.

I looked back out the window. Our view was just over the broad trees that surrounded the perimeter of the park. There was a large estate-like building on one end with a sizable circular pond in front of it. A tree-lined boulevard with a tall hedge in the center of two gravel paths led away from the structure. Colorful flowers were blooming in a variety of areas. Rows of metal chairs were placed in what seemed to be the prettiest vantage points. It was a sunny day and many people were wandering about.

Sue and I stood motionless, just looking.

Jack came back through the door he'd departed from. "Jorge and Lorraine were able to get Mike and Rose out."

"Tanner and Dr. Roth?" Sue asked.

Jack shook his head. "Not so lucky."

"Fuck, two more?" I felt another wave of guilt for being fortunate enough to survive and for my part of involving others in such a dangerous project.

Jack gestured with his arm toward the sitting area. "I'd like to have a word with you."

I could only imagine how Jack felt. The security for the group had failed. We'd waited too long to leave the cabin.

Sue and I went over to the flower-patterned sofa. It was stiff and not as comfortable as it appeared to be.

Jack sat down in a matching chair to our right. "I know this has been difficult. God knows we didn't want to lose anybody."

Sue reached over and held my hand.

I tried to keep control of my emotions.

"Three people died," Sue said.

"Words cannot express how bad I feel. They were all good people." Jack sounded bereaved and took a few breaths, his clasped hands placed on his knees. "Their deaths weren't for nothing. They all knew there was risk involved, and what we're doing was important enough to take that risk. They were honorable, putting their own lives in jeopardy, having the chance to save many more."

Sue nodded and squeezed my hand harder.

"Nick." Jack leaned forward. "Morgan and her parents died exposing what Dr. Schmidt through Naintosa and Pharmalin—and now we know others—are purposely doing to the world. The whole Elles family was wiped out for this cause."

I took a deep breath to fight back a wave of tears.

"The worst thing we could do is give up now," Jack continued. "Their work would be wasted, and their goal would be lost. Not just the Elleses, but also Bill, Summer Perkins, and Dr. Roth. Tanner, too, played a vital role in trying to protect us and believed in what we were doing."

The three other men had entered the room. Ivan sat down in a chair on the opposite side of the coffee table from us; Sam and Lee stood back against the wall.

I experienced a moment of clarity. Jack was right, and I felt the need to add to what he'd just said. "Even though we'll mourn the people who gave their lives for the cause, there's no need to further ponder how the result could've turned out differently."

Jack's eyes focused on mine and I could see tears form. He gave me a nod of gratitude.

I made a point of looking at each person in the room. "When this all started, I knew it would be dangerous, but I never imagined it would end up like this. It just proves how much we need to unveil these unscrupulous peoples' plan. We have to fight for *everyone* who's died and *everyone* they plan on killing. This is by far the most important work of our lives and we need to do it together. So let's get started at finishing."

Sue gave my hand a quick squeeze. I glanced over at her and she mouthed, "Fuck, yeah."

Jack motioned to Lee. "We'll need a couple of laptops."

"I was able to bring one with us," Lee said. "I'll get three more."

CHAPTER 51

I t had been a hard night. I missed Morgan's warm, beautiful body next to me, her soft breathing lulling me to rest. In the morning, I decided on a mantra, "Do it for Morgan." I repeated it to myself over and over. It would keep me moving forward.

Everyone looked solemn and jetlagged, but we were all showered and ready for the day by 7:00 a.m.

Jack had arranged for a plane to fetch Mike, Rose, Lorraine, and Jorge.

The dining room was formal with a gold chandelier hanging at the center. A long dark varnished hardwood table that sat sixteen took the majority of the space. It was big enough for us to work on one end and eat at the other. The owner of the flat really had a thing for flowers; even the chair cushions in the dining room had a floral pattern. Sue deduced that the place had a Victorian-era look.

Sam made us waffles. "You can't get thick cut hickory-smoked bacon here." His voice was such a deep baritone that it was as if the room shook a little the rare time he spoke.

"At least you know the food is safe." I sat down. "There are strict agriculture practices in France, and they haven't allowed any genetically engineered food in."

"I am not sure about the glyphosate use," Ivan said, sitting across from me.

"Maybe the French will best survive this mess." Jack was at the head of the table.

"Most European countries are against genetic engineering." Sue sat next to Ivan. "Maybe Europe is the part of the world they want least affected? The seed bank *is* in Norway."

"Well, I guess we should hang out in Europe then," Jack said. "It's a shame that the United States would take the brunt of the population control."

"I still can't figure out why they would focus so much on the United States and even Canada," I said. "Not to sound prejudiced, but why wouldn't they target areas that are already overpopulated, like China and India?"

Jack shrugged. "No idea."

"Let us just stop this plan from continuing anywhere," Ivan said.

No matter how many people read our report, I wasn't sure it would make enough difference to stop what was already in motion. I didn't want to say that out loud.

Sam came from the kitchen with eight more Belgian waffles.

Jack spoke while he was chewing. "These are great, Sam."

Everyone nodded their approval.

Sam took a seat next to me.

"Jack?" Sue said. "Will the police be coming to talk to us about what happened in Vancouver?"

"Most likely," Jack said. "I wrote a note explaining what had happened and left it at the hospital, and I have one of my lawyer friends talkin' to the authorities. He's also working on getting Morgan's body cremated and her ashes sent to us."

I thought for a moment. "They should be sent to her aunt in South Africa. She would've wanted that."

Jack nodded. "I'll have Morgan's aunt located and make the

arrangements."

Knowing we hadn't just abandoned Morgan helped relieve some of my guilt. I realized that I should call Detective Cortes. "Can I call the United States from here?"

"Sure," Jack said. "Who're you wantin' to call?"

"The detective who was working on Summer's case."

"Use the phone in the living room or your bedroom."

I'd kept detective Cortes' card in my wallet and went to retrieve it in my bedroom.

He didn't pick up, and after six rings it went to voicemail. "Hi, Detective, it's Nick Barnes. I just wanted to let you know that Brad …" What was his last name? Oh yeah … "Caulder was the one who killed Summer Perkins. I last saw him in Vancouver, Canada, two days ago. He'd been shot in the leg. I hope you can catch him. I'm out of the country." He could figure out the rest.

I went back to the dining room to finish my waffle and coffee.

"Who owns this place?" Sue asked Jack.

"A friend. He's a major contributor to the Council for Ethical Farming."

Lee walked in. "Jorge, Lorraine, and Rose will arrive tonight."

"What about Mike?" I asked.

Lee shook his head. "They couldn't convince him to come. He went off on his own."

CHAPTER 52

Jorge and Rose both had leg sprains sustained while running through the wet forest, but neither complained and both went to work. Lorraine was unscathed.

Jorge told us that the Naintosa security men had shot and killed Tanner and Dr. Roth as they had scrambled to reach the others at an outcropping. Mike, Rose, and Jorge were pinned down behind the rocks until Lorraine saved them. She'd distracted the pursuers by shooting one of them. The confusion of the attackers trying to locate Lorraine allowed them to escape.

Lorraine explained that Mike had been stubborn and wanted nothing to do with the continuing danger we were all in. We could use the seed bank information, but he was going to hide someplace on his own.

"He was scared and overreacted," Jorge said. "We couldn't talk him out of it."

I shook my head. "I hope he makes it."

"The dumb fuck," Sue said.

Jack, Sue, and I set up the new laptops Lee had purchased and made sure the Internet connection was working.

Ivan had chosen to work on the one brought from the cabin. "This is Dr. Roth's computer."

"I just grabbed the closest one as we were leaving," Lee said.

"Do you have the password?" Ivan asked.

"I cleaned out the safe." Lee was standing next to the dining room door and opened it. "The password list should be there. Let me go look."

Jack had e-mailed Sue and me the backup files, and we saved them onto the new computers.

"All but one," Lee said, coming back into the room.

"What?" Ivan asked.

"The password—alpha, lima, lima, bravo, uniform, tango, numeral one."

Ivan shrugged and keyed it in. "It is correct."

"I wonder what the significance of that is?" Sue said.

"Dr. Roth's mind worked in mysterious ways," Jack said. "Ivan, I've sent you the files."

"Let's take a quick look to make sure we have everything, then see what needs to be completed," I said.

"I need a little more time to finish my part," Jack said.

Heavily accented talking came from Ivan's computer. It sounded like Dr. Schmidt.

"Hmm, I think Dr. Roth was not sharing everything he knew with us," Ivan said. "I was locating his files and found this. All of you come and watch this with me."

We gathered around the laptop—Sue and I sitting on either side of Ivan, Jack and Lee standing behind us.

Ivan started the video from the beginning. It was filmed on a handheld camera through a narrowly opened door. The picture was shaky. Dr. Schmidt was wearing tan shorts and a white polo shirt. He had very hairy stubby legs and had gained weight since the last photos I saw of him, all in his gut. Sweat beads glistened on his nose and above his upper lip.

"That's the Bolivia lab," Jack said. "My team had taken a shot of the room from the same angle."

I remembered seeing that picture.

Another man was in a lab coat, tall, slim, and wearing glasses. "We've had a breakthrough."

"That is Dr. Daniel Smith, Pharmalin's head scientist," Ivan said. "I met him when I was still at Naintosa."

"The date stamp shows that this was taken six months ago." Sue pointed to the red numbers at the bottom of the screen.

"We'll be able to actually *cure* colon cancer," Dr. Smith continued. "Here, let me show you."

"No, no, no!" Dr. Schmidt's face turned red. "We absolutely cannot have that. We want the drug to extend lives, three, maybe five years maximum. It can only appear to cure the cancer."

"But Dr. Schmidt, what I'm saying is that we *can* actually cure it."

"*Nein.*" Dr. Schmidt banged his fist on the table he stood next to. "That defeats the purpose all together."

The camera operator touched the door loud enough to make a sound. Dr. Schmidt and Dr. Smith both turned in the direction of the camera. That was the end of the video.

"Dang," Jack said.

"Holy fuck," Sue said.

"*Hospadi,*" Ivan said in Russian.

"I wonder who shot that and how Dr. Roth got ahold of it?" I said. "And why he never showed it to us?"

"We have Hendrick on tape admitting that he explicitly doesn't want the drug to cure cancer." Jack went to sit next to Sue. "We have the smoking gun."

"But why did Dr. Roth not show this to us?" Ivan asked.

"No idea," Jack said. "Maybe that was Roth's insurance policy."

CHAPTER 53

March 19, 2002

J ack, Sue, Ivan, and I were having a final read-through of the report that had taken us three days to complete. There were three stacks of CDs sitting in the middle of the dining room table. Lee had Dr. Schmidt's confessional video burned onto them.

"It has too much opinion and theory, and not enough unbiased research," Ivan said. "Naintosa is going to easily point out the flaws and discredit the report."

"I think there are enough facts," Sue said. "The video is going to really sway people."

"It's the best we have now," Jack said. "It'll get people thinking and talking. Like I said earlier, this report is the next step after the Elles exposé. There are more steps to follow."

I agreed with all three of them.

Ivan looked stern. "Then I will spend the rest of my life proving the validity of our findings."

"And I'll be right with you." Jack reached over the edge of the table and patted Ivan's shoulder.

CHAPTER 54

Sue had saved the list of 1,115 people, companies, organizations, universities, and independent media she'd compiled over a year ago to send the exposé to. Jack added thirty-one more people to it. We had e-mail addresses for 906 and mailing addresses for the rest. Everyone would get the report and video.

Jack personally met with four key people that could circulate the report and video to the widest audience. He followed up with phone calls to the rest whom he knew on the list. Jack said everyone he spoke with seemed interested in the information.

Ivan e-mailed the report to the Council for Ethical Farming with a detailed letter asking for help to further research and investigate the findings and theories. He heard back from them within a day, agreeing that they would sponsor his studies and that he should return to Oslo right away.

The website containing the report and video was ready. We included Dr. Elles' exposé and would keep it on until we were ordered to remove it. Further information would be added as we obtained it.

Sue and I called as many of the people we'd sent the report to as we could. We told them that if the world didn't learn about what was going on right under people's noses and react, living would be like a lottery. Not getting sick and dying would be like a crapshoot.

INTERLOGUE 6

April 18, 2003

H endrick put the phone down after his conference call with Davis and Carlo. He was facing the window of his study but was too angry to notice the Chris Craft idle by on Lake Como.

Those *fickt* with their stupid report were spreading all sorts of propaganda that was beginning to hurt sales and the plan. If he could just have those little flea bastards killed, like drop a bomb on the estate in Burford, some of his problems would go away. But Davis and Carlo were too cautious and said it would create a whole new set of issues.

He hadn't been able to find out who had taken the video of Dr. Smith and himself. That along with the never-ending setbacks on the life-extending drugs would be the death of him. He was continuing the work of his father and grandfather. He was steering the direction of mankind and only taking a profit as reward. His work was needed for the world to survive. Did anyone appreciate that? What thanks was he getting from the stupid population that kept banging out more and more babies? He was their steward. They'd still be living in the fucking dark ages if it weren't for his family.

Hendrick felt a sudden sharp prick at the back of his neck. He began to turn, but only managed a fraction before paralysis took over his body and he collapsed to the tiled floor. His chest constricted and his lungs couldn't take in air.

He saw familiar black rubber-soled loafers in front of his face. "Junior, help me."

"I am, father." Hendrick V knelt down. "I'm helping the *family*."

It took what little strength he had to say the words, "Why would you do this to me?"

"You've fucked everything up. Grandfather and Great-Grandfather would be so ashamed at what you've done. Now I'm going to finish what they started and do what you were not able to accomplish. Father, I'm taking control."

Hendrick V stared down at the dead body of the man who'd groomed him to take over the family businesses. He had an urge to kick him in the head but didn't. Instead, he stepped over the corpse and went to the computer screen on top of the desk. He checked to make sure the fabricated threatening e-mail had arrived in the Inbox. He opened it and made note of the timestamp in the top right corner. "Good."

Hendrick V reached into his pocket and withdrew the incriminating evidence. Placing it underneath the corner of the desk, near his father's head, it was sure to be found by investigators.

Satisfied with his work, he left the study, leaving the door slightly ajar, before removing the thin black gloves he wore.

CHAPTER 55

April 19, 2003

"Is this the bread Rose wanted?" Sue held up a loaf of French bread, trying not to break through the crust with her fingers.

"I think so." I looked at the list Rose had given us for the extra ingredients she needed to prepare Easter dinner. "We can get the cheese and pâté next door."

Jorge was standing watch, as usual, when we exited the bakery. Sue handed him the bag containing the bread.

"I'm here to protect you, not be your *burro*," he protested with a smile.

It would be hard to imagine anything bad ever happening here. We were in the village of Burford, near Oxford, in England. The one strip of shops along High Street was situated on the side of a hill. The town dated back to the thirteenth century, and all the stores were old and quaint. The modern vehicles driving up and down the street looked out of place, as one expected horses and carts.

It was a beautiful, sunny morning, with only a hint of spring chill. Lilac mingled with the scent of baking bread. After our shopping was complete, the three of us walked the two blocks to the estate we were living in.

Sam was at the two-story wrought iron gate to let us in. "Looks like you got everything Rose needed."

Sue smiled. "And then some."

"Jack and Lee are back." I pointed at the black Range Rover with tinted windows in the driveway.

"Just arrived," Sam's voice rumbled.

"Is Ivan here yet?" Sue asked.

"I'm going to pick him up at the train station in an hour," Sam said.

We walked up the driveway. On either side was grass and newly planted flowerbeds at the edges of gnarled shade trees. We saw Lorraine walking the perimeter and waved.

The stone house was a twenty-thousand-square-foot monster that had two stories above ground and one below. We only used five thousand square feet of it. It had originally been built in the sixteenth century as a hospital or monastery, but of course was fully modernized now. Everything in it was large, including the double doors we had to go through to get inside. There were crystal chandeliers in every room that could accommodate one, and marble floors with radiant heat. The owner had a liking for big white furniture and polished teak tables. Every five days there was a flower delivery, even in winter, so the house looked and smelled like spring year round.

We had left Paris two months after we sent out what was now called *The 2020 Report*. Another financier of the Council for Ethical Farming owned the home and allowed us to use it for as long as we needed. That was good, because we'd already lived there for the past eleven months and had no reason to want to leave.

The kitchen was large yet ergonomic to use. Oversize stainless steel appliances were surrounded by granite countertops and white cabinets. A rack hung down from the middle of the ceiling and held all sorts of pots, pans, and cooking utensils.

"What are you talking about?" Rose said to Jack as we came in.

"This is my dream kitchen."

"I just thought it might be too big." Jack turned to see us enter. "Howdy, y'all."

"Great to see you, Jack." I put the grocery bags on the island.

Jack hadn't been around that much in the last nine months. He'd spent his time fighting lawsuits from companies that protected the interests of Dr. Hendrick Schmidt, Davis Lovemark, and Carlo Da Silva. They'd been drawn out as the main players in the population control scandal but still tried to keep their anonymity behind faceless organizations. Jack also had to spend time on Moile R & D, the water-quality testing company he'd been developing. Lee was always by his side.

Through his representatives, Dr. Schmidt denied that the new colon cancer drug Pharmalin was about to release was only meant to prolong patients' lives for a few years. He was adamant that the formula people would receive actually cured the disease. All of GM Comm's media outlets were touting the drug as the biggest ever breakthrough in the fight against cancer. Time would tell. No one could locate Dr. Smith, the other scientist in the video, for comment.

Jack looked every one of his seventy-one years, tired but in good spirits. "I see you've been helping Rose out."

"They're a pleasure to have around." Rose winked.

"Uh-huh." Jack patted my shoulder. "How's the book coming? Can I read it yet?"

"Soon. I just need to finish the last draft, and then it goes to the editor I've found. I was in London on Thursday and Friday talking to editors and I think I met the right one." I had plenty of free time as of late, so was able to work on my novel. When I'd finally decided to base it on our experiences of the last three years it flowed out of me with more ease. It had turned out to be an ecological thriller delving into the unscrupulous practices of genetic food engineering. Even though it was labeled fiction, it was based on fact.

"Can't wait." Jack turned his attention to Sue. "I read your latest article, Miss Sue. Brilliant."

A worldwide environmental group had picked up on our report and was running hard with it. They'd approached Sue and me to write follow-up articles for their monthly magazine. I had written a few, and Sue was now a regular contributor.

"Let me go freshen up and we'll catch up at lunch," Jack said.

"Lunch will be served as soon as Dr. Popov arrives," Rose said.

"That gives us time to get some work done," Sue said. "Come on, Nick."

The desk in the study was so big that we were both able to work from it. Sue was kind enough to give me the side that looked out the window into the garden and pond. The room held two shelved walls filled with rare and vintage books, many of them collector's items. There were original works by Jane Austen, William Wordsworth, and George Eliot, to name a few, as well as more contemporary authors. We'd spent much time admiring them.

Sue looked thoughtful. "It's going to be nice to have everyone here for a few days."

I tried to smile. "Yeah." I still missed Morgan a lot. Sue comforted me and was helping me get through it. I didn't like talking about it much, but my grief underlay my thoughts and she knew it. Sue had always been there for me. I picked up the photograph I'd had framed and kept beside me when I wrote. Morgan's aunt had sent it to me. It was a picture of a plaque on a bench in a park Morgan had played in as a child. It commemorated her life.

"I know you wish Morgan were here," Sue said.

"Not just Morgan." I didn't want her to think I didn't care about the others who'd been killed.

"When we get together, I think of everyone who lost their lives in this ordeal as well," she said.

I sat back in my chair. "We still don't know what happened to

Mike. He's probably dead too."

"I hope not."

I looked at the computer screen in front of me with no inspiration. "I don't think I'm going to do any more today. The updates can wait until next week." I was in charge of the content on the website.

When I got up, Sue came around the desk and gave me a warm hug and kiss on the cheek. She had never been like that before, but ever since we arrived in Europe she'd become all touchy-feely with me. Sometimes I protested, but really I didn't mind … I kind of liked it.

Sue kept her hand on my arm. "You know what you need to get back into?"

"I know. I just don't feel like it these days." I hadn't meditated much since we were in Europe. The couple times I'd tried, I couldn't clear my mind and relived scenes of our escape from the cabin to Woodlands.

"Let's go see if Ivan's arrived," she said.

Even though we were as safe as we could be, I sometimes thought that Bail would jump out from around a corner and attack us. We never heard what happened to Bail, but he could resurface at any time. Lee had feelers out, but no sign of him in the last year.

I'd spoken by phone with Detective Cortes three times and he told me that they'd arrested Brad Caulder. Caulder had admitted to working for Lovemark and shortly afterward was found stabbed to death in his jail cell. I'd asked Cortes to look into Angelica as well. He'd checked the report on the incident in Vancouver and her name wasn't mentioned. When he went to her apartment, she'd moved out. She was alive, but there was no record of her whereabouts. His suspicion was that Angelica Seymour wasn't her real name.

We walked under the dual spiral staircase and around the marble statue of the naked woman, into the foyer, just as Ivan came through the door.

"Hello, hello." He approached, his arms outstretched.

We spoke with Ivan on the phone and communicated by e-mail, but we hadn't seen him since Christmas. The Council for Ethical Farming had given him everything he needed to perform his studies. Now he had a bodyguard with him wherever he went.

Ivan's "assistant," Eugene, was Sam's cousin but looked and sounded like his twin. The giant African-American baritone-voiced man followed Ivan into the manor carrying two suitcases.

Sue gave Ivan a warm hug. "So good to see you."

"Dr. Popov. Eugene." Rose had entered the room. "Go wash up and then join us in the dining room for lunch. Nick and Sue, please come and help me bring the food out."

Rose had become a surrogate mother to everyone. She had even talked several times to my and Sue's mothers, who were back in Washington State and worried about us.

Once the food was on the table, Jack, Ivan, Sue, Lee, Jorge, Eugene, and I sat down for lunch. After much encouragement, Rose had begun to eat her meals with us as well. Sam and Lorraine were on guard duty. Rose made sure Jorge had taken full plates out to them first.

"You're spoiling us, Rose." Jack picked up a bowl heaped with mashed potatoes. "Roast beef for lunch today and a turkey feast for Easter Sunday tomorrow."

"I plan to gain ten pounds this weekend," said Ivan.

"It's my pleasure." Rose had a proud look in her eyes.

Bowls and plates of food were being passed around the rectangular teak table.

"Any updates, Ivan?" Jack asked.

"The neonics study is coming along. The further we delve into it, the more havoc we see it creating in people with potential cancers and the environment, especially bees."

"It's proving Dr. Roth's theories correct?" I said.

"Yes," Ivan said. "Unfortunately in the time it will take to complete the study and then Naintosa trying to revoke it, there will be tons of it sprayed in the world."

"And the impending lawsuits. My life has become lawsuit after lawsuit." Jack raised his hand and looked at everyone around the table. "But that's the way it works, and it's worth every minute and every dollar to fight these bastards."

I couldn't help but admire Jack's tenacity—actually, everyone's tenacity.

"Have you had any progress finding anyone who has the resources and ability to conduct the cancer drug study?" Ivan asked.

Jack shook his head. "Not yet. The labs that have the means don't have the desire to go up against Pharmalin."

"Be patient," Ivan said. "Something will happen."

Jack turned to Sue and me. "That reminds me, Chief Inspector Plante asked to meet with y'all again next Thursday in London."

"Again?" Sue said. "What now?"

Chief Inspector Jacques Plante of Interpol had interrogated all of us at least once. This would be the third time for Sue and me. He was really good at his job. When he looked at you, it was as if his eyes bored into your brain and extracted the truth.

"I'm not sure what it's about this time," Jack said. "We have no choice but to put up with his questioning. I'll have a lawyer there for you. Just be honest as usual."

"Still no idea who's on Dr. Schmidt's or Lovemark's payroll?" Sue asked.

"No." Jack was cutting into his roast beef. "Not being in the inner loop makes it darn near impossible to get that kind of information these days."

Jack had told us that someone was always looking out for the best interests of Schmidt and Lovemark at Interpol, but we didn't know who. The last one Jack knew of had died two years ago. Whoever it was now had to be feeding Inspector Plante information somehow.

"Have you obtained any more proof about the seed bank?" Ivan asked.

"We have aerial photos, so we know where it is," Jack said.

"Sue and I are going to see if we can get close to it the week after next," I said.

Ivan looked up. "Are you sure that is safe?"

"We've kept up with our Krav Maga training, workouts, and shooting practice," I said. "We can defend ourselves and are in good shape."

"But still," Ivan said. "You are so important to all of this. Can we not send trained spies?"

"Don't worry about us," Sue said.

"We're tired of sitting here and writing." I pointed out the window. "We need to do some work out there."

"Jorge, Lorraine, and two men who know the area in Norway are going with them," Jack said. "They'll be okay."

I understood Ivan's concern, but I was tired of being treated like I was delicate. I yearned to get out into the field.

"What's the latest on the Plycite gene?" Jack asked.

"Naintosa had to admit they have it," Ivan said. "They are denying they would ever use it."

"I heard that Germany and France are in the process of adopting even stricter testing for making sure genetically engineered food doesn't get into their countries," Sue said. "And the exposé and report factored into their reasoning."

"The Scandinavian countries are following suit and Russia," Ivan said.

"Well done," said Jack. "I wish there was progress in the States. Everything in the news is full of GM Comm spin. They're saying anyone who's against genetic engineering is anti-science, uneducated, fear-mongering, fanatical, and a conspiracy theorist."

"Unfortunately that's kind of what we expected," I said.

"There's more and more truth about it on the Internet," Sue said.

"However, everyone's distracted by the US invasion of Iraq," I said. "Which is understandable."

"So much of the world is a mess," Ivan said. "Are your old friends a part of the reason for the wars in Afghanistan and Iraq, Jack?"

Ivan knew Jack was keeping in touch with some of his past powerful allies for information purposes, but there were still some allegiances there that could hurt our cause. They'd had a number of discussions about it, and Jack always assured Ivan that he had it under control.

"My brother has something to do with the funding," Jack said. "But he's not talking to me. I'm still a traitor in his eyes."

I decided to redirect the conversation. "Do we know more about the Pharmalin and Naintosa lab in Colombia?"

"That may be our next trip after the seed bank," Jack said. "I just heard it's up and running. We need to get proof of what they're doing with the human testing and get it shut down."

"I think that's where we'll find the most proof of the population control plan," I said.

"That part is what most people are having trouble believing," Sue said.

There was still much work to do and it was going to take a long time, but we were making progress. A growing number of people, organizations, and governments were seeing the dangers and reacting.

As each day inched closer to 2020, we had to make sure that our proof reached critical mass before the population control plan did.

INTERLOGUE 7

April 19, 2003

Carlo sat in a wrought iron chair gazing out at the Mediterranean, waiting for his guest and pondering. A quartet of crickets performed in the dry grass nearby. The grapevine-intertwined trellises above only provided partial shelter from the afternoon sun. As he reached for the sangria, his visitor walked out onto the veranda.

"Thank you for stopping by." Carlo motioned to the chair on the other side of the table. "Would you like some refreshment?"

"Don't mind if I do." Davis always looked awkward in shorts; his legs never tanned and his knees were knobby.

"I didn't know you were staying so close by," Carlo said.

"My wife, youngest daughter, and I thought we'd spend Easter in Spain." Davis reached for the glass filled with burgundy liquid, fruit, and ice. "So, I thought it best to discuss this in person."

"Yes," Carlo said. "I anticipated it happening, but not so soon."

"Do you think Nick Barnes did it?" Davis took a sip of the sangria. "Oh, this is tasty."

"Everything in the glass was grown on the estate. And no, I don't think he killed Hendrick. I don't see how he could have."

"I agree," Davis said. "Yet having Barnes incarcerated for any length of time would be good."

"It discredits the whole group of them."

"Especially after we tell the world." Davis sneered. "He won't need to be convicted."

Carlo pondered for a second. "Okay, I'll make the call."

Davis took another sip of his drink. "We need to meet with young Hendrick, after of course giving him ample time to grieve."

"He contacted me an hour ago." Carlo leaned in, looking concerned. "He wants to meet with us right after his father's funeral."

"Hmm. Hendrick the Fourth only died yesterday." Davis' eyes narrowed. "So much for grieving."

"Indeed."

CHAPTER 56

April 20, 2003

The delicious smells of Easter cooking already permeated the first floor that morning.

As I entered the living room from the foyer, Jack, Sue, and Ivan were standing next to the long couch, talking. They all held newspapers in their hands and turned to me as I approached.

"We've just read that something's happened," Sue said.

"Dr. Schmidt is dead," Jack said.

"Really?" That was unexpected. I felt like I needed to sit, so I went to the closest chair. "Wow."

The three sat down on the couch across from me.

"How and where did it happen?" I asked.

"At his villa on Lake Como in Italy." Ivan held out the newspaper for me to take. "It happened the day before yesterday, Friday. Cause of death is uncertain at this time, and foul play has not been ruled out."

"I'm sure there were many people who wanted him dead," Sue said.

"But he would've been hard to get to," Jack said.

What did this mean? How would that affect us? "This is a good thing for us, right? The evil bastard is gone." I wasn't sure.

"His eldest son would be the one to take over the companies," Jack said. "We don't know what he's going to be like."

"Maybe as ruthless as his father," Ivan said. "Or worse."

Jack's cell phone rang. He pulled it out of his black slacks front pocket. "Yes, Sam."

"I feel like there's something that could make things worse by Dr. Schmidt dying," Sue said. "I don't have the sense of relief we should."

"Me neither." I had a foreboding ache in my stomach.

"Let 'em in." Jack motioned with his free hand. "Inspector Plante is here."

"Why?" Ivan asked.

"Don't know." Jack stood. "Let's go find out."

We all walked to the foyer.

Jack opened one of the large main doors and we watched four men approach. Each had on a black suit covered by a charcoal knee-length raincoat. Chief Inspector Plante was one step ahead of the others. When they reached the entrance there were no polite greetings.

"You couldn't wait until Thursday?" Jack asked.

Plante didn't acknowledge Jack's question.

One of the men produced a pair of handcuffs from the inside of his coat.

Plante looked determined. His steel eyes bore past his hook-shaped nose right at me. "Nick Barnes, you are under arrest for the murder of Dr. Hendrick Schmidt."

ACKNOWLEDGEMENTS

I would like to thank the following people for their assistance, guidance, and encouragement:

Diana, my fantastic wife, for her support, patience, and putting up with my long hours of writing;

Authors Scotty Schrier and Eve Gruschow for their input and detailed discussion about the story—there were late Wednesday nights and a lot of fun;

Author James Ullrich for contributing to the first half of the story;

Editors Karen Brown and Amy O'Hara for taking what I wrote to the next level ... or two;

Virginia Herrick and Richard Coles for their proofreading expertise;

Bennett Coles and everyone at Promontory Press for their hard work at publishing the book;

Marla Thompson for the cover design, typesetting, and interior design;

Cindy Goodman for the photography;

Dr. Maria Bautista, for all medical terminology, and for her reactions and advice;

Lance Connelly of Krav Maga BC for teaching me the martial arts techniques;

Kathryn Brown for her sage advice on editing, cover design, and book promotion;

Neetu Shokar for coming up with the title;

Alisha Stewart, who I can't say works for peanuts, because of her fake nut allergy;

And most of all, I would like to thank the readers who have enjoyed my books and spread the word to others about them.

ABOUT THE AUTHOR

Lawrence Verigin is also the author of acclaimed novel *DARK SEED*. His goal is to entertain readers while delving into socially relevant subjects. Lawrence and his wife, Diana, live in Vancouver, Canada.

Contact
Website: www.lawrenceverigin.com
E-mail: lawrenceverigin@gmail.com
Facebook: Lawrence Verigin
Twitter: @lawrenceverigin